SOLBAKKEN

A TALE OF GENERATIONS

Other Books by Wendy Jo Cerna

The Baby-Catcher Gate (2017)

The Agreements (2020)

SOLBAKKEN

A TALE OF GENERATIONS

A Novel

By

Wendy Jo Cerna

Solbakken: A Tale of Generations

SQUAREFREE PUBLISHING
www.squaretreepublishing.com

Solkbakken: A Tale of Generations is a work of fiction. Any similarities to persons, living or dead, are not intended by the author. The places, incidents, and circumstances portrayed are the product of the author's imagination, apart from real historical figures such as Francis of Assisi, Yeshua, the Emperor Trajan, the 34th Division of the 5th Army known as the Red Bull Division, as well as biblical instances such as the crucifixion and resurrection of Christ. While artistic license has been applied, all effort has been made to remain true to historical context and facts.

For more information about bulk purchases, please contact Square Tree Publishing at info@squaretreepublishing.com.

Cover Design by Sharon Marta

ISBN 978-1-957293-16-5
LCCN 2023906139

For Tante Tuppe (a.k.a. Aunt Eva)

& Great-Tante Maria

Women who never gave birth

yet mothered generations of children

including me

He remembers His covenant forever, the promise He made, for a thousand generations.

Psalm 105:8 (NIV)

Like a devoted gardener, I will pour sweet water on parched land,
streams on hard-packed ground;
I will pour My spirit on your children and grandchildren—
and let My blessing flow to your descendants.

Isaiah 44:3 (The Voice)

PROLOGUE

I AM A SOLDIER. I carry out orders and fulfill assignments because I have been trained to do so. Because that is my job. My profession. My life.

Or at least it has been.

Today I am not so sure.

Today I want to find another life. Or, at the very least, another assignment.

I have rarely questioned the chain of command under which I have lived. Even under strange circumstances and difficult mandates.

"You are a man under authority."

That is the message my father drilled into me.

He was a soldier too.

A man under authority goes where he has been told to go, and does what he has been told to do. Why? Because he believes in the justness of his cause. Because he trusts in the higher perspective of his higher-ups. Because he knows he is only a small cog of a much bigger wheel.

But my father also told me, as he lay on his death bed, "Son, there are some duties that will haunt you. Some commissions that will sift your soul. Fulfill your role but guard your heart for from it flows your true life." While he and I were never particularly close, I still miss him and the advice he gave which seemed to come at just the right time with just the right message.

The rain that has been unceasing for days finds it way under my cloak and down my neck, soaking my tunic. I let it run. The sensation returns my mind to the present and I am gutted afresh by the realization that Mila is truly gone.

"How do I endure this yet again?" I whisper to the air, hoping for some random tidbit of fatherly wisdom to spring forth from my memory. But nothing emerges.

I step back under the large oak tree where the hole has been dug and her body lowered into the ground. It is a peaceful spot. Mila would like it here. The rain on the leaves. The plops dripping onto her face. The smell of fresh grass and wildflowers.

The earth I hold clenched in one fist has turned to mud. The gold coin from her necklace, which I grip in my other fist, digs into my palm until I am sure the visage of the emperor Trajan will leave its imprint in my skin.

"Not meaning to rush you, sir," says the young soldier standing a respectful distance behind me away from the hole in the ground. "But the day is nigh gone."

I have forgotten he is there. No one else has come to grieve with me. Arabella and Damon moved to the south coast years ago with their children. I will, of course, inform them of her passing for they deserve to know. But all else are gone who would have or should have come to mourn. And while there are many who respect me in this place, there are none who are close to me or to her. I do not allow it.

"Right," I say, finally recognizing that the cloudy gloom of the day has dimmed to murky dusk. I let the damp dirt fall with a thud into the hole and onto the shroud in which she is wrapped.

The sound echoes in my mind to other times. Other burials. Other faces. Other lives… ended.

"Too many," I whisper. "Too many."

"What's that, sir?"

"Nothing," I say, taking a deep breath and turning away. "Carry on."

I tuck her necklace into the small pouch that hangs from my neck.

"If I may, sir," the young man says as I step back and he steps forward. "Most folks wouldn't have done all you did for your granddaughter. Mila lived a good… a good… life. Thanks to you, sir."

I know he means to say, "A good, long life," but he refrains. They all refrain from those types of comments. But I know they say them. The men under my command. The villagers. The powers that be.

And I refrain from correcting his assumption that she was my granddaughter. What good would it do to add 'great' or 'great-great' or whatever the more accurate title? It would only add to the fuel that fires the speculations about my life. I would not be in this far-flung outpost of the empire if I lived like others live. But I do not question this posting. I understand that to leave me in Judea or even Rome caused too many problems. There is no simple explanation for me.

Well, there is. But they don't like it. Don't want to admit that it is even a possibility.

But the longer this goes on, the harder I am to hide.

Lord knows, they have tried to pay me off or get rid of me. Honorably, at first. And then, less honorably. But to no avail. In the end, they have chosen to shuffle me off to obscure places and utilize my knowledge, strength, and loyalty.

Some days, I think I have come to terms with this assignment—this unexpected, unasked for, unprecedented assignment. Afterall, I am a man under authority. Asking, "Why me?" has done me no good. And so, I have settled into a sort of resignation that for whatever reason, Heaven's Great Commander has chosen this for me. Not Caesar or Herod or any emperor, king, or governor, but God Himself. My ultimate Superior.

But on days like today, I am exhausted by this call.

Mila was twenty-five years old—far outliving any expectations anyone had for her. This edge-of-the-world spot she was thrust into because no one else would take her, was actually the perfect place for her. And though I had sworn off interaction with family many years prior to her arrival, she thawed my conviction to never again allow my heart to love so deeply.

Now, I remember why.

"Is there no way out?" I ask The Commander for the millionth time as I trudge back to my stone home along the ramparts. "This 'blessing' has become more than I can bear."

The heavens are silent, save for the constant drips upon my head. Upon my shoulders. Upon the earth. Drips that seem to say, "Enough. Enough. Enough."

Resolution arises amidst the shattered pieces of my heart. I must do what I have thought of doing many times before. It is time for me to slip away like others have done. To leave the Roman army that has been my life. Not just find another territory within the empire in which to exist, but to wander far outside its realms. Hadrian's wall can no longer hold me here in Britain.

I must disappear somewhere no one knows my past or has even heard the whispers of it. But let's say I succeed. Let's say Rome, too, has had enough of me, and lets me abandon my post. Let's say I find a new assignment or a new place or a new people. What happens when they, too, discover my unusual qualities? What then? Disappear again?

Maybe so.

Maybe so.

"Excuse me."

I look up, surprised to find a silver-haired gentleman standing on the path in front of me. It is dark, but it is not so dark that I should have missed his advancing presence. I suddenly regret not having brought my faithful companion Maximus with me. He would have sensed a strange presence long before I did. He would have sent out his low rumble of a growl that has caused men in many places and circumstances to think twice before approaching me. But I left my dog at home wanting to spare him, and perhaps me, the pathetic whimpers I know would have accompanied the things I have just accomplished. His canine heart was as attached to Mila as any human heart, and maybe more. He was her eyes. Her ears. Her protector. Her friend.

I pull to an immediate square halt, assessing the countenance of the man on the path in front of me.

He stands like an officer, but he is not one I have ever met. And I have met them all. At least, all who call this frontier home. And he is not a local for no one dresses in such resplendent garments here. No one has the means to do so. Or the audacity. Certainly not a Caledonian allowed across the wall for trade. I am familiar with each of them.

Why, then, do I feel as if I know him?

"Pardon me. I did not mean to startle you," the man says, the green of his eyes glowing over the six feet that separate us, as if an interior light is about to burst through their surface.

"No need to apologize," I respond, wiping my sleeve across my damp eyes. "I am the one who should apologize to you for my inattentiveness. I was far away in my thoughts. How can I help you? Are you searching for someone?"

"I am," he replies.

I wait for him to say who he seeks, but he only smiles.

"Have you been sent from Bath?" I ask, assuming by his dress that he is among the Roman elite who take extended visits at the hot-springs spa in the south.

"No. I have come much farther than that."

"From Rome then?"

He smiles and it is perhaps the most radiant smile I have ever seen in my lengthy existence.

“Well, you must be tired from whatever journey you have taken,” I say. “We are not an easy destination from most anywhere. Are you in need of an inn? There is one not far removed from here. I can show you the way, if you’d like?”

He steps forward. I feel my hand drifting upward under my cloak to my belt where my dagger abides sheathed in its leather holster. But I cannot grasp it. My arm suddenly has no strength. I am frozen under his gaze.

He places a hand on my shoulder.

“You offer me a way to rest that quickly flees,” he says. “I have come to lead you into a rest that remains.”

Just then, the young soldier arrives along the path fresh from his grave filling duties.

“Everything alright here, sir?” he asks, coming up behind my left shoulder.

The stranger drops his hand but remains in place.

I am not sure how to reply. For some reason, my heart is pounding in my chest. Not from fear. But from something else. Something I cannot yet identify.

I turn my head slightly to address my conscript while keeping my eyes locked on the other man.

“All is well,” I say, and the words ring true. “Return to your duties.”

The young man eyes the situation one more time, but does as I command.

When he is well past ear shot, I say, “Show me the way you offer, good sir. For I am weary to my very bones.”

The stranger smiles.

“He knows, Felix,” he says as a dense cloud envelops us.

TORA

"**HAPPY BIRTHDAY TO YOU**. Happy birthday to you. Happy birthday, dear Mom, Grammy, Tora, Auntie." The names and titles garble in layers atop one another over the computer airwaves. "Happy birthday to you!"

The people that fill my screen—each in their own little box—smile, cheer, and clap. I blow them kisses and say, "Thanks one and all. I love you!"

"Love you too!" or some such version bounces back to me, and my heart accepts their intentions.

"Before everyone leaves, Hazel has a special salutation for her Grammy," our son-in-law Isaac says, waving his arms wildly to get everyone's attention.

"Simmer down, everybody," my husband Peter says. "We are about to hear from our brilliant, shining granddaughter!"

I am almost embarrassed at how much we love this child. She is currently our only grandchild, and maybe that's what makes our affections so intense. But, from what I've heard from all my friends who have about a dozen grandkids each, this is quite a common phenomenon.

In her sparkly princess dress she has chosen for this occasion, Hazel stands and folds her hands primly in front of her. The fake jewels on her tiara shimmer over her auburn tresses as she sets her chin just so.

"I would like to wish my Grammy happy birthday in four different languages," she announces.

I see smiles of appreciation pass over the faces that surround her on the screen.

"Spanish—*Feliz cumpleaños, Abuela*. French—*Joyeux anniversaire, Grand-mère*. Italian—*Buon compleanno, Nonna*. And Norwegian—*Gratu...gratul...*"

Her face scrunches in a concentrated scowl.

"Gratu..." she tries again.

Isaac swoops in and whispers in her ear. He is a developer of linguistic software for children, and I can see his fingerprints all over this gift.

Hazel nods, and then pushes her father away.

"Gratulerer med dagen, Mormor!" she shouts, lifting her arms overhead, and then plunging them down to her toes in a dramatic bow.

The crowd erupts in applause. I can see the pride on Isaac's face. But no one is more pleased or proud than me.

"Bravo! Bravo!" I say, wishing beyond wishes that I could seal this gift with real hugs and kisses. *"Mange tusen takk."*

"What does that mean, Grammy?" Hazel says.

"It means 'many thousand thanks' in Norwegian," I say. It's one of the few phrases I know from my grandparents' native tongue.

"Oh, it sounds funny," she says.

"Yes, well, unlike you and your father, I am not a linguist."

"What's that?" she asks.

Her mother, our daughter Mariah, pulls her back to herself. "Daddy will explain," she says, knowing as I know that the questions with this child can be endless. Interesting and entertaining, but endless.

"I appreciate you all taking the time to celebrate with me," I say once Hazel has been mollified.

"It's not every day you turn sixty-five, Mom," says Brian, our youngest lounging on his sun-filled patio, nineteen-hundred miles away.

"Yes, I know," I reply with a wince. "I am trying to accept it as the blessing it is. But attaching myself and that age together still seems a bit surreal."

"You look great," my cousin Katie chimes in. "I can only hope to be as lively and healthy as you when I reach your age."

I place my hands on my heart and nod.

"You are not too far behind me," I say.

"Totally aware," she replies with a laugh. "Sorry my sister couldn't be part of this, but my mom said to send her love. She needs help to get on her computer even though we've written down step-by-step instructions for her. But you know, at a hundred and one, that she can even use a computer is quite remarkable. I've got to hop off and go pick up my dog from the groomers. Lovely to see you all. And happy birthday." She waves and her square disappears.

Several other friends and family do the same until there are only three squares left filled with my immediate family.

"You are healthy, aren't you, Mother?" Mariah asks.

"Yes, I am feeling much better. What about you? You look a little peaked."

"Oh, I'm just tired. That's all," she replies, brushing off my concern.

"Did you get tested?" Isaac asks me.

"She did," my husband Peter replies.

"And?" Mariah says.

"And it was not COVID," I reply. "Just some other type of influenza."

"Well, that's good, at least," Isaac says.

I see Hazel whispering into her mother's ear. Suddenly Mariah is laughing and shaking her head.

"No, honey, she's not," Mariah says.

"Is so," Hazel insists. "She just said."

"What's going on?" I ask.

Hazel leans forward until her face fills the entire section of her family's place on the screen. Her eyes, which are the color of her name, stare right into the camera.

"You are, too, an influencer, aren't you, Grammy? That's what you said, right?"

Peter and I look at one another and chuckle.

"How does she know what an influencer is?" Brian pipes up.

"Cuz, I know stuff," Hazel says. "And she is too."

"I think Hazel's right," my husband says, grabbing hold of my hand and giving it a squeeze. "Grammy has influenced all of us, right?"

"That's not exactly what an influencer is, Dad," Brian scoffs.

"Well, you have your definition and I'll have mine," he replies in my defense.

"I'm gonna be an influenza when I grow up," Hazel says, plopping back down on her mother's lap.

"Not an 'influenza', sweetie," Isaac corrects. "An 'influencer'."

"Same dif," Hazel says.

Brian lets out a guffaw. "I don't know about the flu, but COVID sure has influenced the heck out of the whole stinking world. Maybe she's got a point."

"Yeah, see?" Hazel says. "Uncle Bly gots my back, bro."

"Gots your back, bro?" I say. "What are you letting this kid watch, Mariah?"

"Oh, Mother, she spends so much time in front of a screen these days, I honestly don't always know," Mariah says.

"But we are seriously monitoring as much as we can," Isaac adds. "It's just hard when we're all working from home, and trying to do our job, and be her constant companion and overseer all at the same time. Things are not what they were in your day of raising kids."

"We know," Peter says. "Not accusing you of anything. It is a tough go for everyone these days. We know you're doing your best, and we appreciate it. Just wish we could help out."

A silence suddenly settles.

A sigh escapes my lips.

"Well…" Isaac starts.

Mariah puts a hand on his arm and shakes her head. "Don't," she says quietly.

"Way to go, Dad," Brian adds. "Let's ruin the whole party with a vax argument."

Peter raises his hands into the air. "My bad," he says. "Sorry. You're right. Didn't mean to stir that all up. Let's not go there. Let's keep this about Mom."

Tears fill my eyes despite everyone's best efforts to keep the peace. I am so tired of this strange time we live in. So tired of having to navigate even the seemingly simple things, like having a family birthday party. Peter puts his arm around my shoulder.

"The numbers are coming down from this latest wave of the omicron variant," Mariah says. "Maybe things will be better soon."

"Let's hope so," Peter says.

I shake off my melancholy, trying to recapture the spirit of conviviality we had just moments before.

"I love you all, and I truly am thankful for this party you organized, and the beautiful flowers that showed up at my door this morning, and the lovely set of paints I received, and the gorgeous scarf, and the hand painted card I got in the mail," I say.

"That's from me, Grammy," Hazel shouts.

"I know and it is amazing. Just like you."

Hazel claps her hands, and a black bundle of fur leaps up onto the couch beside her. She grabs the puppy and waves one of its paws with her hand.

"ShoSho says happy birthday, too. Right, ShoSho?"

The dog looks up at her adoringly and licks her face. She giggles.

"ShoSho thinks I'm amazing too, Grammy!"

My heart squeezes. Fresh tears spring up.

"Everybody knows that, Haze-amaze," Brian says. "That's my new name for you. Haze-Amaze. Like it?"

Hazel stops for a second, and ShoSho curls up in her arms.

"I think I can go with that," she says with four-year-old seriousness.

We all smile.

"Okay, guys, good to see ya. Time for me to take a run before the sun goes down," Brian says. "Happy birthday, Mom."

"We will talk soon, Mother," Mariah adds. "Enjoy the paints. Hope to see some new pics on your Instagram feed soon."

"Shalom, shalom," Peter and I say in unison, using the standard family farewell passed along from my Grandmother Arnhild. She was Norwegian and not Jewish. At least, not that I know of. So, why she adopted this Hebrew saying, I do not know. It was just what she always said when we were parting and, to my eternal regret, I never thought to ask her why or where it came from.

"Shalom, shalom," they all reply.

We wave until only Peter and I remain staring back at ourselves from my laptop. He reaches forward and hits the 'leave meeting' button.

TORA

LATER THAT EVENING, I am standing out on our back deck, bundled up against the night's dipping temperatures. It is the end of an unseasonably warm day in what has been an un-usually snowy February, even for Minnesota. Peter has tried to keep the deck cleared throughout the winter but eventually resigned himself to just keeping a path shoveled down the middle to the far rail. We like to stand out here in the evening and enjoy the view to the lake regardless of the time of year. Several inches of the snowpack around me have either melted or condensed in the past twenty-four hours. But tonight, we are dipping back into the teens with a forecast for more snow by tomorrow night.

Ah, Minnesota weather. Rarely a dull moment. At least we never run out of something to talk about with the cashier or the postman or the neighbor or whoever else crosses our path.

But tonight, tonight is lovely. The clear skies have lured me out onto the deck. I shelter my cup of tea up against my chest, relishing the wafting peppermint steam. The sun set long ago over Lake Minnetonka and the stars have filled the indigo expanse. In the summertime, this view is interrupted by the upper branches of our aged oak trees and their leafy canopy. Not that I'm complaining. I love the rustle of the wind through their midst and the shelter of shade they give us. But in the winter months, I appreciate the broader view I am afforded by the shed foliage.

I take a sip from my cup, and allow my mind to wander back to savor the virtual moments with family and friends that my children organized for me today.

The patio door slides open behind me, and I turn to find my husband of forty-two years approaching with his own cup of tea. Peter is still the most attractive man I know despite his receding hairline and thickening waistline. He sidles up beside me and places his cup on the deck railing, stuffing his hands into his down vest pockets. We consider the heavens together in silence for a moment.

"A penny for your thoughts," he says after a bit.

"Oh, just relishing all the greetings and people. The kids did a great job of gathering up folks from all different chapters of my life."

"They sure did. Course, I may have lent a hand with some of those contacts too."

"I had no doubt you did," I say, slipping my hand through the crook of his arm. "I'm sure they've hardly ever met some of our college friends like Amy or Rick. And getting David to send in a recorded greeting from Iceland…holy mackerel. Just so fun."

"Daphne and Judah were a hoot."

"Oh my gosh, those two should start their own comedy club."

"Agreed," he says, lifting his cup to his lips.

"It was good to see Andy and Vera. She sounded better than the last time we talked. And Clay looks quite content in jolly old England. Must've been the middle of the night over there."

"Yup. Something like that. Said he didn't want to miss watching his kid sister turn 'old'."

I turn to him with a scowl.

"His words, not mine," he says. "I told him with your family DNA, you've hardly reached middle-age."

"Well, there is that," I agree.

Again, we settle into quiet admiration of our view.

I lean my head onto his shoulder. It is just the right height for me. I am a fairly tall woman of a fairly sturdy build. But he is taller. And sturdier. I am always glad for this. As a teenager, I despaired of ever finding a man that I wouldn't have to perpetually live in flat shoes just to keep from towering over. Not that I adore high heels, but occasionally, a nice two- or three-inch heel on a good pair of boots is fun. Of course, since March of 2020, when the onset of the pandemic locked us all behind doors, I've worn mainly slippers or my stable walking shoes with their pricey orthotics. There's been nowhere to go that requires a good set of heels.

"You doing alright?" Peter asks. "Sorry to have stuck my foot in the jab, no-jab muck with the kids tonight."

I don't reply.

What is there to say that we haven't already said? I agree with my husband and our stance on this whole subject. But I can also see the other side of the issue. And, I also feel intensely the price we pay to have our own opinion.

"I miss her, too, ya know," my husband says, tracking my silent response. "I miss all of them."

I pat his arm and exhale. "I know."

A stiff breeze blows across the lake and up the shoreline. I stand upright and pull my hood over my ears.

"Too cold? Want to go in?" Peter asks.

"No, I'm fine. Think I just need a few minutes out here by myself. Is that okay?"

He turns and gives me a kiss on the cheek. "Sure, birthday girl. You get whatever you want. At least for about..." he says, pulling his phone out of his pocket and checking the time, "thirty more minutes."

"Is it really that late?"

"Yes, indeed. Way past my bedtime," he says, scooping up his mug and retreating back into the house.

The sound of our neighbor splitting wood echoes over the ice. Honestly. That man has an obsession with his wood stove. But I can't complain. I enjoy the smell of the fire he perpetually stokes all winter.

My nose begins to drip from the chill, and I pull a tissue from my pocket.

Maybe it's not just the chill. Maybe the touch of melancholy I have been trying to tamp down all day has finally caught up with me.

What do I have to be sad about after such a wonderful celebration?

The state of the world? For sure. The tension in my family? Uh, yeah. But all in all, my life is good. I have a supportive and productive husband. He has been able to keep his law practice humming without a hitch through all the shutdowns. Our home is paid for. Our cars run. Our children still speak to us... about most things... most of the time. Our neighbors are kind, by and large. We are healthy, thank God. We have a bevy of good friends and extended family ties. We have a ridiculously cute granddaughter. I enjoy my volunteer opportunities. I have time to pursue my hobbies—painting, reading, gardening, and hiking. I may be profoundly average at all those things, but they do bring me joy.

“Why are you downcast within me, O my soul?” I ask myself with the words of the psalmist rattling round my heart. The answer is not new. It is the same jumble of thoughts that haunt me at night when my head is on my pillow and my eyes stare out into the darkness. It is this almost suffocating sense of panic I get in quiet moments like these when I think of time and years and age and my complete inability to slow down the inexorable march of it all. It is a sense of angst over all that has already flown by, and what little I have accomplished.

I have never had a career. We decided that if we were going to have children, I was going to be a stay-at-home mom and raise them. And I was, and I did, and I enjoyed it. I helped out Peter with his practice when he was first getting started. But we hired much more efficient and qualified staff long ago. My husband is well respected amongst his peers and in the community. We love spending time with our extended family and church family. I love volunteering with the after-school art program at our local elementary school, and being a baby-cuddler in the NICU at Southdale Hospital. Although, the pandemic has put the kibosh on both those activities. I miss them dearly, having realized that the “therapy” I provide has been as therapeutic for me as for those I serve.

In recent years, I had the ability to spend oodles of time and energy on my parents in their final days. My mother, Louisa, passed away two years ago, just shy of her hundredth birthday, and my father, Sigard, left us last summer at the ripe old age of one-hundred and five. My older brothers helped me in all of that, too, though neither one lives close by, and neither one is exactly a spring chicken themselves. Andrew is twelve years older than me and lives in Arizona. Clayton is eight years older and makes his home in London. I am now, and have always been, their much younger baby sister. But that is—quite literally—relative.

I am getting old.

Why am I so surprised?

It happens to everyone. Everyone who is fortunate enough for it to happen to.

But what have I done?

Am I an influencer to anyone, anywhere, for any good reason?

"My children, Lord," I whisper toward the sky. "Have I even influenced my children? These people who have consumed my heart and my days. You have promised to keep them in the way we raised them up. You have promised to pour your Spirit upon them, and let your blessings flow to our children and our children's children."

My prayer drifts out onto the night air on the clouds of my breath.

The steam has ceased to rise from my mug. I pivot and head toward the door just as I see Peter in his pajamas sliding it open with my phone in his hand.

"Looks like it's your cousin Billy," he says, giving it to me. "Probably one more salutation of good cheer."

I exchange my mug for the phone and step into the house. My husband shuts the door behind me.

"Hello, Billy," I say. "What are you still doing up? You almost missed the chance to wish me a happy birthday."

"Is it your birthday?" he replies. "Sorry… I, uh, totally forgot about that. Not why I called."

His tone is serious. His words clipped.

"What's going on? Everyone okay in your family?" I ask.

"Yes, we're fine but… well, I was just driving by your Uncle Einar's place an hour ago or so, and noticed the porch light was out, and no smoke coming out of the chimney. I know you guys keep it pretty cool in there over the winter but there's usually a telltale trail up over the roof to show the heats still on."

"What's going on?" Peter mouths.

I put the call on speaker.

"Bill, I'm gonna let Peter listen in on this. That okay?"

"Sure, you bet. So, I was saying I noticed something wasn't right over at Einar's, so I swung on in. And, I hate to tell you this, but somebody broke in."

"What? Are you kidding? Who would do that up there?" I spout.

These days, my Uncle Einar's home stands empty for much of the year, save for my occasional retreat up into the north woods and the autumn weekends when my husband and his compatriots use it as their hunting shack. It is old, but it is not a shack. It is the original family homestead that my grandparents built in the early 1900s after immigrating from Norway. Until recently, it has been continuously occupied by someone in the family. My dad's brother, Einar, was the most recent owner and resident. He had left the family farm as a young man. Got an engineering degree from the University of Minnesota. Served in the military during World War II. Never married. Worked all over the country. Travelled the world. And then, when his parents both passed away, showed up to say he'd like to live in the house. No one argued. No one else really wanted the place. Everyone was happy to give him the responsibility. He died three years ago at one-hundred and six in his rocking chair beside his bed.

"Well, now, I don't know who might have done it," Billy replies. "But I got the sheriff coming out in the morning. It's quite a mess in there. Can't say as I know if anything was taken, but there's belongings all over the floors. Looks like every drawer and cupboard was emptied out. No windows broken as far as I could tell. I turned the heat back on. Good thing it wasn't too cold last night. Can't imagine why they'd turn off the heat of all things."

Billy is the grandson of my dad's Tante Tora—the auntie I'm named after. He lives on the property next door to my grandparents' farm where his grandparents built their homestead. Their original house is long gone, but Billy has built a lovely home on the family land, and has managed to not only live off the land but thrive as few can in the challenging environs of northern Minnesota.

"Did you check in the garage?" Peter asks. "Think there were still a bunch of Einar's tools and such out there. And a new lawnmower we used around hunting time."

"Didn't go in there. Sorry. Just locked up as good as I could. Seems they busted the frame along the kitchen door to get in. The porch door must've been unlocked."

"Darn, maybe we forgot to lock up when we left in November," Peter says.

"Did you let my brothers know?" I ask. "Or Tante Tilda?"

"I tried calling Andy but just went to voicemail. I couldn't figure out what time a day it might be for Clay, so I didn't even try him. Figured I'd wait to let Tilda know. Nothing she can do about it, and will probably only get her upset. Glad I got a hold of you so late."

"You need us to come up there?" Peter asks. "I've got a pretty busy week ahead but I can see what I can shuffle around."

"Got nothing pressing on my plate," I say. "I'll come up. Is the house habitable?"

"Well, now," Bill resumes. "You will have to do a little work to clear off the junk strewn all over a bed before you can lay down, and clear a path on the floor into the bathroom. I didn't want to pick anything up or throw anything away before one of you guys have a chance to see what's missing or not. Do you think Auntie Tilda's girls will want to know what's happened?"

"You know them. They only ever go up that way to see their mom. They rarely ever come out to the farm anymore, but I will let Katie know. Just saw her this evening on my Zoom birthday call," I reply.

"Oh, yeah…" Bill says. "Carin mentioned something about that earlier in the week. Just don't got much good internet up here still. Have to go into town for that fancy online stuff all you city folk are doing."

I laugh at his remarks. "Oh, now, William Arthur Hallstrom, if anyone can figure out how to get internet service up and running and efficient in the north woods, it would be you. It hasn't happened because you haven't wanted it to happen. Admit it."

No response.

"Thanks for giving us a call," Peter says. "I've gotta hit the hay. We will call you in the morning and let you know when we'll be coming up. Sure appreciate you looking out for the place."

"What's family for? Good-night," Billy says. "Oh, and happy birthday, Tor."

TORA

THE SNOW STARTS TO FLY right before I get to Hackensack. I am a good two and a half hours into my trip, but still have about that same amount left to drive. I set my windshield wipers on low and make sure I know where the four-wheel-drive mechanism is on my new Toyota 4Runner. Just in case. The roads can get quite dicey up here in a big-time hurry. Not for the first time, I wish Peter had been able to come with me. But shuffling his schedule was not as easy as he had hoped, especially given the absolute need for reliable internet service.

I assured him I could handle things myself, and that Billy and Carin were just down the road if I needed anything. He made sure my rig was packed with all the usual emergency gear, and that I had my phone charger and winter boots. It is not my first rodeo, but I allowed him to hover and feel useful. It is, however, my vehicle's first rodeo. Part of a big surprise from my husband for my birthday. The exact rig I have been wanting, and the first brand new vehicle I have ever owned. I think I'm old enough. So, though I am missing his company, I am tickled to get to test out my present on its maiden voyage to the north country.

My brothers have been notified via email of what has happened. I placed a call to Cousin Katie, but have not heard back from her yet. Told them they could tell their kids what was happening or not. I haven't even told my own kids yet. Figured I would assess the damage first before dishing out anything more to be stressed out about. Both Brian and Mariah have real affection for the old farm at Solbakken.

Back in the early days, my Grandpa Axel had a barn full of dairy cows and several fields cleared for hay. Later on, he sold all but one of the cows, and turned the fields into either wild rice paddies or groves of fast-growing timber. When those harvests got to be too much for him, he sold a bunch of those acres to Billy, keeping just twenty acres of the original place surrounding the house. Most of that has all grown back into thick forest, except the few clover fields my husband has cultivated to keep the deer fed and happy until he can shoot them. We tore down the barn in the mid-nineties since it was imploding upon itself and becoming not only an eye-sore but a hazard. So, we use the term *farm* loosely these days.

It is located up past Bemidji in a small township east of Lower Red Lake. When my forefathers first came to America, they were part of a group of families hailing from the same region of southeastern Norway, who were looking for land and opportunities. They were mostly farmers. And in the era when they arrived, the state of Minnesota and the federal government were negotiating agreements with the Ojibwe tribe that occupied the land around Upper and Lower Red Lake. While most of the land immediately adjacent to the lakes remained in the tribe's possession, large swaths beyond that were slowly being sold to incoming immigrants.

The homesteaders who got the land west of the lakes toward the Dakotas got some of the best farmland in the world with rich black topsoil that was three feet deep in some places. But my grandfather and his peers bought land on the south and east side of the lakes. Maybe they didn't know until they arrived, but one has to wonder if someone might have at least scouted out the area, because this land is not rich farmland. It is mainly forest and bogs.

The Ojibwe might have laughed at the foolish white men who travelled so far to try and farm those sections of land. But the tribe still lamented other territory lost, and fought to maintain what they had been promised regarding fishing rights and total autonomy of the area surrounding the two large, connected bodies of water. I am chagrined to say I know more about their struggles now than I ever did as a child with grandparents living only a mile or so from the embattled grounds. Having a husband who is involved in real estate law, with occasional detours into environmental law, has exposed me to some of the ongoing issues between the native tribes and commercial development in our state.

My phone begins to ring, and I search for the button on my steering wheel that allows me to answer. It rings several times before I find it.

"Hello," I say.

"Hey, Mother," Mariah says. "Where are you? I hear you're headed up to Solbakken."

"News travels fast," I reply.

"I had to call Dad for some advice about our insurance claim, and he told me about what happened. I can't believe it. Who would do that? And why? There's not much of value in that house, is there?"

"Well, I just passed through Hackensack. And I have no idea who ransacked the house or why. And, no, there isn't much of anything worth anything to anyone except us."

"I'm just so shocked. It's weird to think of crime happening out in the middle of nowhere. Did you hear from the sheriff yet? What about the people living in Janet's old house? Didn't Billy say they were sort of a rough bunch?"

"I did ask Billy about that this morning before I left home, and he said Janet's house has been empty since before Christmas. But, interestingly enough, Janet just asked him a few days ago if he would be available to help a new renter get situated. Think that might be happening this week sometime. And he said he's meeting the sheriff around noon."

"Shh, sweetie, I'm on the phone with Grammy," Mariah says, and I hear Hazel chirping away with questions.

"What's she asking?"

"Oh, I have you on speaker and she heard you say Hackensack. She wants to know if Paul Bunyan's girlfriend is still there."

I smile, marveling at the memory of this brilliant grandchild of ours. She was two the last time we passed this way together. "She sure is. I saw her standing by the lake same as always."

"Did you wave, Grammy? Did she wave back?"

"I did wave, but I think her arms might still be too cold from the winter to lift up for a wave yet. Maybe in the summer you can drive up with me and we will stop by on our way north. What do you think?"

"Yea! Can I, Mommy? Can I?"

"We'll see, sweetie. Now go take ShoSho outside before he has an accident."

"Bye, Grammy!"

"Bye, sweetheart. Have a nice day," I say.

"Oh, she's already gone," Mariah says. "This new puppy has about the same amount of boundless energy as she does. They are a good pair. Keeps her occupied, for a little while, anyway."

"Looks like a cute little guy. What breed did you say he was?"

"We're not exactly sure. The mom is a black lab, but the dad is an anonymous donor. That's what the neighbor we bought him from says. Hopefully nothing too big. The hair looks kind of curly so we're hoping for a poodle or something like that. But whatever it is, it is. Hazel is in love and there's no going back."

"I remember how that goes," I say, thinking of Mariah's own obsession with her pets as a young child. "Where did you come up with the name?"

There is no answer.

"Mariah, you still there?"

Again, no answer. I check to make sure the call is still connected. It is. Maybe I'm going through a bad reception area.

"Mariah? Can you hear me now?"

"Yeah, sorry, I uh… I've just had a bit of a headache all day and it has me a little nauseous."

"A migraine, you think?" I so hate that she suffers from those from time to time.

"Something like that… So, yeah, you were asking about the dog's name," she says, moving right along.

"I was but I'm more concerned about you," I say. "Do you have your meds available? You know you have to get in front of that thing or…"

"Yes, Mother, I have everything I need. Don't worry."

"Okay, okay. Just want to make sure you're alright."

"I will be fine."

I inhale and try to let go of my worry. She is thirty-four years old with two undergrad degrees and a master's in business administration. She is the Chief Operating Officer of an IT recruitment firm based in St. Paul. She can take care of herself. Not to mention she has an intelligent husband who works from home and loves her fiercely.

"So, the dog's name," I say, moving right along as well.

"All Hazel's doing. She told us in no uncertain terms the day we got him, 'His name is ShoSho. 'When I asked her about it, she said, it's just like what Grammy and Papa say instead of 'bye-bye'."

"Oh, that's so cute! I love it. And Grandma Arnhild would be so pleased to know her send-off blessing is being used by the next generation. Even if it is with a dog."

"Yeah, I felt that way too. Sort of a kiss from heaven even though Hazel never got to meet her."

We fall silent for a moment, and I feel the warmth of my grandma's love from somewhere distant and sweet echoing in my family.

"Well, hey, I've got to get on a call soon but I just wanted to check in," Mariah says. "Are you getting snow up there?"

"It just started a little while ago. Nothing too heavy yet. But there is a fair amount on the ground up here. Is it coming down in The Cities?"

"No, not yet. Maybe tonight sometime. Be careful. And keep us informed."

"Will do."

"Oh, wait. I almost forgot again. I was going to ask last night. Did you and Dad send in those DNA kits we got you for Christmas?"

"We did send them in last month, but they say it can be up to six weeks before we hear back."

"Okay. Cool. Just wondering. Sort of curious to see where we all come from."

"Yes. I'm curious too. Although I don't expect any deep dark family secrets will be revealed."

"Well, that is why they call them deep and dark secrets, cuz nobody knows about them," she replies.

"I guess. Who knows? Maybe we will find out we're related to the Queen of England or something."

"That sort of secret would be fun. Gotta run. Shalom," she says, and the call ends.

"Shalom, shalom," I reply to the empty car.

As I turn onto the two-lane highway that we call the cut-across, I enter one of our many state forest lands. I breathe in the cool shadows from the tall pines that line the road as far as the eye can see. Only an occasional driveway juts off from either side and back into the trees. The snowflakes begin to increase in size and number, but the wind is minimal in this hallway of green.

I am thankful for the chat with my daughter. The past few years have left us looking from opposite sides over a chasm of politics and paradigms that neither one of us truly knew existed until the pressures of the pandemic forced them all to the surface. We have argued, disagreed, and knocked heads on a variety of subjects. Brian is mostly in agreement with his sister and brother-in-law, but surprises us every now and then with his moderate stances. He has always been more of a peacekeeper than his ambitious elder sibling.

We have reached a truce, or at least an understanding with one another over our different perspectives. Mainly, we just don't talk about those things anymore, and we try to respectfully appreciate each other's ability to see the world from different angles. But the issue about access to our granddaughter based upon our vaccination status—that has been the real kicker.

The road and the trees blur behind my latest wave of tears. I seem to have cried a lifetime full of them over the past months. I am not a crier by nature… At least, that is how I've always thought of myself. But now? Now I cry almost every day. When I'm praying. When I'm gardening. When I'm painting. When I'm lying in bed at night. When I'm driving.

A deer leaps out of the ditch and bounds across the road in front of me. I am jolted out of my reverie. It is not close enough to do any harm to me, or me to it. But it has made me aware of how unaware I have been. Time to refocus. Time to think of what's ahead.

A house.

A mess.

A mystery.

"Shalom, shalom," I whisper once again, and once again my heart receives Grandma Arnie's blessing. And I am thankful, for I am in need of it.

FELiX

GRAVEL ROADS. Feels good to be rumbling over them again. I've always liked them better than the modern ribbons of concrete, though I do admire the feats of engineering involved with freeways and interstates. But a good gravel road? Brings back memories.

As I pass through the woods and farmlands, I admire the dressing of snow mounting up on the pine boughs and golden reeds in the ditches. Black cows scattered in the field to my right break up the blanket of white that stretches hundreds of yards before another row of trees fills the horizon. Their bovine heads lift up languidly as I pass in my Chevy pickup, a cape of snow flowing out behind me.

My destination is just up ahead. I feel the familiar flutter of excitement for a fresh assignment. Who will I meet this time? Why am I here? What does my Commander have in mind? It will unfold as usual. One step at a time. One obedience at a time. One revelation at a time.

The year? 2022. The place? Northern Minnesota, USA. Solbakken, to be exact. A town that has almost disappeared from the map. The nearest real town is St. Gerard about twenty-five miles to the east. It is all new territory for me.

Maximus sits in the passenger seat, his nose pressed up against the window, eyeing the herd of cattle. Slobber and steam from his small woofs and rumbles make the view from that side increasingly foggy.

"It's okay, boy," I say, reaching over to stroke his smooth brindle coat. "They may be big but you're faster."

He turns and licks my hand. Then he focuses his attention straight ahead and sits at alert. Upright. Ready. He knows too. We are about to embark on a new adventure together.

Up ahead I see two driveways branch off opposite one another. One to the north and one to the south. Snowbanks indicate that someone has recently plowed. I turn my blinker on to turn north. Then I smile to myself.

"Who cares what direction I'm turning? There's not another vehicle in sight."

But I have been told that turn signals are a common curtesy when driving a car or truck or SUV or whatever else one might call these machines. I try to obey the law of the land whenever I arrive anywhere. Keeps the attention upon me to a minimum.

Just then a large white truck with the words 'Beltrami County Sheriff' painted on the side comes to a screeching halt at the end of the opposing driveway. The truck slides a bit before coming to a complete stop only a foot or two from my front bumper. The driver, in full sheriff regalia, offers an apologetic wave. I wave back, thankful my law-abiding blinker was on.

I turn into the long driveway, and the sheriff vehicle takes his leave down the road I have just travelled. I keep an eye in the rearview mirror on the place the sheriff exited. I see two other vehicles parked next to a farmhouse tucked between two clumps of birches and pines. The tired white of the house's vinyl siding blends into the snow-covered yard, save for the deep green shutters lining the windows. A garage is attached on one side of the house and a shed stands separate on the far side of the driveway. Lights are on in the house, but I don't see anyone about.

My truck sways and jerks over the uneven surface. Up ahead, another farmhouse hides behind a row of overgrown shrubs. If I had arrived in the summer months, I'm sure the leaves would have made it nearly impossible to see any structure behind them. But the empty branches allow me a peek.

It is easy to see that this house is not nearly as well-maintained as the one on the other side of the road. Several shutters hang at odd angles from the windows, and the blue wood siding is in desperate need of a fresh coat of paint. But I am not surprised. I knew this part of what lay ahead. I am coming ostensibly to help the homeowner make some much needed repairs. She believes me to be an out of work handyman happy to have a place to live for a short stint in exchange for services rendered and a nominal rental fee. Janet Bjorklund is her name. I have only ever met her over a computer call.

I am supposed to meet someone named Billy here today.

Even as I think this, a truck pulls up behind me and stops. The driver gets out and walks over to my window. He is a good-sized fellow. Tall and thick with strands of dull blonde hair sticking out from under his baseball cap. He wears no jacket over his tan coveralls. They are dirty. Well worn. Much used. But the hand he reaches out to me as I roll down my window is clean and well-groomed.

"You must be Felix," the man says. His large, calloused hand engulfs my own in a firm handshake. "I'm Billy. Janet's cousin."

"Nice to meet you, Billy," I reply.

Maximus quickly leans over my body to make his own greetings.

Billy pulls back.

"No need to fear," I say. "This is Max. I know he looks ferocious, but as long as he's with me, he won't do you any harm. And, once he gets to know you, the only thing that might cause you concern is him trying to lick you to death."

Billy ducks down to get a closer look.

"What kind of dog is that?" Billy says, still quite wary of my companion.

"He is a Cane Corso. Comes from an Italian breed of dogs from clear back in Roman times. Not too many of them around anymore."

"Can't say as I've ever seen one like it. That's for sure. They bred for security or hunting or what?"

"They were originally bred for the army. Military dogs. So, security and protection run strong in them. But also, quite good hunters. I've had this guy for ages and he's been a fantastic family dog too."

"Oh, you got family?" Billy asks. "I thought Janet said you were going to live here by yourself."

I smile and nod.

"Yes, that's right."

I unbuckle my seatbelt and command Max to get back to his side of the truck. He whines and stands on the seat, his frame filling much of the cab. "Just sit down and relax. I will be right back," I say to him.

I roll up the window, leaving it cracked for air and get out, my boots crunching on the hardpacked snow where I land. "Been by myself for a while now," I reply to Billy. "Just me and my dog."

Billy lifts up a hand like a stop sign. "No need to explain. Just want to make sure I've got the right guy," he says.

"Yes, I'm the right guy," I assure him. "You want to show me around?"

Billy nods and we head through a narrow opening in the shrubs to the house.

"Sorry. Didn't have time to cut back these branches," Billy says. "Barely got the driveway plowed. Been busy handling a few things across the way for another cousin."

We go up the three steps to the front door. The side iron rails that line the small porch wobble precariously when I touch them.

"Looks like there's plenty of projects around here," I say.

"You betcha," Billy says, sliding a key into the door and shoving it open. The bottom rubs harshly against the wood floor inside. Ruts and scrapes show evidence of many such openings. "Glad to have someone here who will do something about it. The last bunch Janet had in here certainly didn't help the cause at all."

"I hope to do better," I say. "Everything okay with things next door? Saw the sheriff coming out on my way in."

Billy runs a hand over his scruffy chin and shakes his head.

"Had a break in," he says. "Roughed the place up pretty good. Never seen anything like that up here before. Usually quite a peaceful place."

"Sorry to hear that. Is your cousin okay?"

"Oh, yeah, no one was hurt. No one was there at the time it happened. The place belonged to Uncle Einar Anderson. He's more of a cousin than an uncle, but that's what everyone up here called him. Passed away a few years ago. The nieces and nephews keep the place going, but no one lives there full time anymore."

"I see. Well, if he needs any help, let me know. Happy to pitch in and prove to be a good neighbor."

"She… my cousin is a she. Tora is her name. That was my grandmother's name."

"Ah, I see. And is she Janet's sister?"

"Well, no. They are both my cousins, but Tora is my Grandmother Tora's great-niece and Janet is my Grandfather

John's great-niece. So, while they are both my cousins, they are not each other's cousins. You will find out soon enough. Everyone up here is related one way or another."

I smile.

"Perfect," I say. "Love to connect with family… with families."

TORA

I WANT TO WEEP… again. What a mess! Every square inch of the floor is littered with stuff. Paper. Silverware. Books. Coats. Blankets. Plates. Napkins. And God only knows what lying underneath all of that. Billy and I cleared off a corner of the long table in the dining area so that I can fill out the paperwork provided by the sheriff. He wants me to make a list of things missing. We have carefully waded through the entire house and garage. The only glaring absences are the old television, a small carved table, and the new lawnmower. Beyond that, I have no idea.

All the knickknacks and treasures displayed from various trips abroad still sit undisturbed on shelves, desks, and little nooks. Grandma's foot-treadle sewing machine remains solidly in its place. Probably too heavy to move. Or simply undesirable. Crystal goblets, depression era glass, and an entire set of Fiestaware, are still visible behind the glass doors of the built-in hutch. Clearly the thief, or thieves, were not in the market for antiques.

But Uncle's desk is completely torn apart. The drawers have been pulled out and emptied. The files have been turned upside down with paper scattered everywhere. Old bills. Cancelled checks. Letters. Cards. Receipts. Note pads. Address labels. All over the floor.

Grandpa Axel's bookshelves are empty. All his preciously collected books strewn willy nilly on the sofa and chairs; each looking as if it had been leafed through and shaken out before being tossed aside. The cupboards at the bottom of the stairs have been thrashed through as well, with photo albums dumped in piles on the floor. Plastic containers I know once held old letters from boys at war, relatives in the old country, and children gone to college, are hollowed out of all content. The scrapbooks containing family history and genealogical trees carefully researched by Uncle in his later years, are also victims of the abuse that has been perpetrated on the house.

I stand in the middle of the living room, close my eyes, and take a deep breath.

"Sweet Jesus," I whisper. "Where to begin?"

The house is silent.

Billy has left to greet the new tenant in Janet's house across the way. Sheriff Reggie Dumfrey has also returned to his office in Bemidji, with assurances that he and his department will do all they can to track down who did this.

"I'd say get that front door fixed as fast as you can, and maybe invest in a surveillance camera of some sort," Sheriff Dumfrey had advised. "I don't think you have to worry about them coming back. Seems if there was something to take here, they already took it. But it might give you folks some peace of mind, seeing as you're not up here too often."

It is something we have talked about, but just have never done. Perhaps it's time. I will put it on my list of things to discuss with Peter tonight.

I open my eyes and look down at my feet. A colorful corner of paper sticking out from the detritus catches my eye. The edges are worn and fragile, so I tug with care as I reach down to pull it out. Easter lilies illustrated in warm, glowing colors line the borders of the page. On the bottom, two interlocked rings are painted in gold and silver. The middle of the page is pre-printed in flowing script with blank slots filled in by a fountain pen in beautiful handwriting. Ah, the age of good penmanship, where a steady hand and a flowing pen were valued.

My grandparents' names fill the empty slots. Axel Johan Anderson and Arnhild Isabel Pederson. Married this twenty-first day of June, in the year of our Lord 1912, at Bethlehem Lutheran Church, Solbakken, Minnesota.

I carefully smooth the dog-eared edges. This is part of my problem. Amidst all of the garbage strewn everywhere, lie things like this. The vast majority are probably things that should have been gone through and thrown away after Uncle died, but none of us took the time or saw the necessity. Now, our hand has been forced. Time for a thorough and deep cleaning of the old homestead.

"I will do the best I can to get this place cleaned up and back to being the lovely home you two built," I vow, lightly touching my grandparents' names.

As I swivel to find a spot to begin stacking and separating the invaluable from the unvaluable, my foot stumbles on some unseen object at the bottom of the pile. I fall onto the couch, holding the marriage certificate aloft to save it from harm. My butt lands uncomfortably on an upended book. I yelp and pull it out from under me quickly.

"Digging Deep—How to Uncover the Roots of your Family Tree."

I have to laugh. Oh, Uncle. I'm sure this is not what you had in mind, but I will certainly be digging deep, and who knows what I might uncover? It is one of those privileges one has when a family house gets passed on from generation to generation. The nooks, crannies, and crevices never really get fully cleaned out. Not the way one would if one knew fresh, strange eyes would be assessing it all for possible purchase.

"Tor, we're coming in. That okay?" I hear Billy's voice at the kitchen door.

"Yes, come on in," I say, pulling myself up from the plaid cushions of the sofa. "Just trying to figure out where to begin."

I set the certificate atop a bare spot on one of the short bookshelves, and slog my way to the kitchen. I am surprised to find another man with my cousin. He is youngish but not too young. Maybe early-40s. He pulls a stocking cap off his head, revealing dark wavy hair which tops his smooth, olive toned face.

"Tor, this is your new neighbor Felix… uh, sorry, didn't catch your last name," Billy says, turning to the man.

"Felix Benedizione. At your service, madame," the stranger says.

"Oh, well, how kind," I say, and he reaches out to shake my hand. "And what an interesting last name. Sounds like an Italian benediction."

"That's exactly what it means," Felix replies.

"That is lovely. Welcome to the neighborhood. Sorry you have to see the place like this. I will just tell you; this is not the norm up here. If you've come to escape the crazy of the city, you actually have come to the right spot."

"Good to hear it," Felix says. He turns and runs his hands along the frame of the kitchen door. "Your cousin tells me the same. He also says you might need a hand getting this door repaired. I just happen to be pretty handy with things like this. Mind if I take a look?"

I look at Billy for assurance that he hasn't placed me into the hands of a serial killer.

"Don't worry, Tor. Janet did a full background check this time. Right, Felix?"

Felix nods and smiles. “True.”

“Learned her lesson with some of Mikey’s crew that she let live in there,” Billy says. “I’d stay and help but I have a meeting with my lumber guy in town in half an hour. Call me if you need me to pick up something on my way back. Should be home around seven or so.”

“Okay,” I say, a note of hesitancy creeping into my voice.

“If you are not comfortable with me being here without someone else, I can wait and come back when your cousin is back,” Felix says.

The kindness in his warm brown eyes is undeniable.

But didn’t they say Ted Bundy was a charming fellow?

“Um, no offense, Felix, but I think I would actually prefer that,” I say. “Plus, it will give me some time to clear a space for you to work. I truly appreciate your willingness to jump right in and help.”

He nods graciously. “No offense taken. I understand.” He replaces his cap on his head and begins to leave. “You can let me know when a good time might be. I don’t have a phone but just come and knock on the door. I’ll come right over. Probably better get back and see that Max is behaving himself.”

“Who is Max?” I ask before he can get out the front door.

“Just my dog,” he replies. “Well, not ‘just ’my dog. He’s a lot more than that to me. Good-bye for now, Tora. Nice to make your acquaintance.”

Billy and I watch out the kitchen window as Felix strides down the driveway and over the road to his new-to-him abode.

“Seems like a nice guy,” Billy comments.

“Yes, but you never know,” I say.

Billy sighs. “I guess you’re right. I’ll check with you when I get back from my meeting. It would be a good idea to get this door sealed up and locked tonight. Don’t want the boogey man coming in in the middle of the night,” he says, putting spooky hands up by my face and laughing.

“Ha, ha. Easy for you to say,” I respond as tears inexplicably surface.

"Hey, Tor. I'm only teasing," Billy says, putting an arm around my shoulder. "I know this is unsettling. Sort of has everyone up here a little on edge. But don't you worry. We've got your back, cousin."

I nod and shake off my silly tears.

"I know," I reply. "Can you help me get my things in from the 4Runner? I've got a big box full of contractor garbage bags. Might as well get started tossing and sorting. I have a feeling I'm going to be making several trips to the county landfill before this is cleaned up."

"No doubt," Billy says. "I'll help you out as much as I can. But you might want to call in some reinforcements like Andy or Katie or someone. This shouldn't all have to land on your lap."

I pull my boots back on and slip my arms into my down parka. We head outside together. My rig is in the garage, which normally we would access via a short hallway beyond the kitchen. But given that this hallway is under a foot of yet-to-be-identified substances, it's easier to take the long way around via the front door.

The snow, which had let up for a while, has begun to fall again in earnest, and the wind has kicked up a few notches. I flip my hood up over my head, wishing I had tugged on my gloves as well. Billy still wears no coat—only his overalls and a sweater. He seems immune to the deteriorating conditions.

"Yes, I've been thinking about that," I say with a shiver. "But Katie is running pretty wild with her design company, and Andy is trying to be more intentional about caring for Vera."

"How is she doing these days anyways?" Billy says as we walk toward my rig.

"Okay. But lots of adjustments as things progress. Parkinson's is an ugly disease."

He nods, and dips inside the rear end of the SUV I have opened remotely. He comes back out with the box of garbage bags and my suitcase. I grab my cooler and bags of groceries before following him back up the steps, through the covered porch, and into the house.

"Honestly, Billy, this might sound weird, but as bad as this mess is, I'm okay with tackling it by myself. It gives me something purposeful to do. You know what I mean?"

Billy sets his load down on the counter, scooching aside various mounds of debris to make a spot. Then he scratches his chin and shakes his head. "Can't say as I do. I've never been lacking for something purposeful to do."

I laugh. I know that's true.

He pats me on the arm. "Like I said, just holler if you need help. I'll try to get back early so Felix and I can get your door set straight tonight. And don't worry about the driveway, I'll come back in the morning and give it a good plow."

He turns and tramps his way back outside. I realize as he goes that I already am truly not tackling this by myself, and I am grateful.

I search for a space to set down my burden, finally settling on the somewhat empty sink. As I open the refrigerator to place my cheese, lunch meats, and veggies inside, I see the lone picture still displayed on the freezer door. It is stuck in place by two large magnets—one a loon painted on a birch round, and the other a long rectangle filled with the 2015 Minnesota Twin's schedule. I stare at the faces in the picture lined up in row upon row, looking upward toward the photographer who was far above them on the Solbakken community school roof. It is my family—large and extended, all decked out in red t-shirts displaying the family crest designed by my cousin Katie.

The year was 2011. The eldest cousins, aunties, and uncles sit in chairs on the front row; my dad and mom, Auntie Tilda and Uncle Richard, along with the cousins from their generation. I count twelve of them. Much reduced from the original forty-six first cousins, but still a good representation considering the youngest sitting there is Tilda, and she was probably ninety at the time. Uncle Einar is not amongst them, though. He stands in the far back row next to the second and third cousins, once or twice removed. I wonder, as usual, what it was that kept him always at a distance from his peers. He was not an unfriendly man. But neither was he terribly amiable. I always thought of him as being a bit afraid to get too close to anyone.

Maybe Mariah is right.

Maybe there are family secrets.

TORA

THE KITCHEN FLOOR HAS BEGUN to emerge, and the bathroom is accessible by the time I see the headlights from Billy's truck sweep up the driveway. His tires leave good size impressions behind him in the four or five inches of white flakes that have fallen in the hours he has been in town. I hear two truck doors slam before boots stomp up the steps. He must have picked up our new neighbor on his way.

I brush a layer of dust and lint from my sweatshirt as I peek at my reflection in the window above the sink. Strands of my silver hair have escaped the quick ponytail I swept them into hours before. I tuck them behind my ears and sigh. It is still a bit shocking to see myself so gray. I have colored my hair for years, allowing myself the illusion that I didn't really have that many ‘pigment challenged’ follicles. But in a concession to the pandemic, I decided to use the months of semi-solitude to let it go natural. The result is what my dear husband calls his new platinum blonde wife.

He is generous.

It is gray.

“Hey, ho,” Billy says, with a simultaneous knock and opening of the porch door. “Your repairmen have arrived.”

“Would you like us to dispatch with our boots on the porch?” Felix says from behind him.

“Yes, that would be great,” I reply, shoving the pile of filled garbage bags up against the cupboards as much as possible.

“And would you mind terribly if Maximus stays out here too?” he asks. “I will leave him at home should I come again. He just needs a chance to acclimate to the new environs.”

“He sure put up a fuss when we tried to leave him alone. Never seen such a big dog look quite so pathetic,” Billy says with a laugh.

“Yes, I’m afraid he is quite attached to me,” Felix says, and I see the large furry head of Maximus pressed up against his master’s side.

“Sure, that’s fine,” I reply. “I can appreciate a good dog. We always had them when the kids were growing up. Now my granddaughter has one, and they seem to be fully enamored with one another.”

“Appreciate that,” Felix says, commanding his canine companion to sit and stay on the welcome mat. With the kitchen door left open to make the repairs, the dog is able to keep an eye on things and make sure I’m not the one who may be an axe murderer.

Maybe I should get another dog.

“You’ve made some progress, Tor,” Billy says, shaking snow off his ball cap.

“Yes, one inch at a time,” I reply. “How did your meeting go?”

"Oh, real good," he says. "Got another new sawmill out north of St. Gerard a ways. They do some things I'm not geared up to do yet. Think we'll be able to do business together."

"Good to hear there's some new industries up here," I say.

"Yup, there seems to always be a few of us crazy enough to make a go of it."

Felix enters the room in his stocking feet.

"Okay if I hang my hat and coat here?" he says, gesturing toward the row of hooks behind the door.

"Yes, perfect," I reply.

He does as requested and then turns his attention to the fractured door frame. Running his hands all along the top, sides, and bottom, Billy watches him assess the situation.

"What do ya think?" he asks.

The two men launch into a discussion about the repair strategy.

"Think there's some tea around here somewhere and maybe some instant coffee," I say when there is a lull in their conversation. "And I have some cookies I just baked a few days ago… if I can find what stack I buried them under."

"Just coffee for me," Billy says, patting his generous mid-section. "Carin has me under a strict one sweet per day policy. Might have exceeded that already today, truth be told. I will grab my tools from the truck and be right back, Felix."

"Oh, I brought my own kit," Felix says, reaching back out onto the porch.

"Yup, yup. Saw you toting that case. Shoulda known it was your tools. Just a different looking sort of chest than I'm used to seeing," Billy says. "I always prefer to work with my own tools. Just feels right in the hand, eh?"

Felix nods and undoes the leather flap that secures the top of his kit with a bronze looking buckle. It is an aged wooden box with leather handles. The wood is a warm golden color. It is worn smooth, but looks sturdy with finely crafted corners.

"That reminds me," I say. "I should check in the garage for Uncle's tool box. Hoping it didn't walk away too."

"Was he a carpenter?" Felix asks as he begins to pry away a particularly shattered board from the door frame.

"Einar could fix just about anything, if he put his mind to it. Engineer by training," Billy says. "But in his later years, I'd say he was more of an artist. Liked to create things more than fix things."

"Really?" Felix says, continuing with his work. "What sort of things did he make?"

"The bookshelves out in the front room," I say. "The shed across the lawn, but that was quite some time ago. His latest interest, before he died, was bowls made from burls off the trees around here. I'm sure there's some around here somewhere. They are quite lovely."

"Would love to see his work whenever you find one. No rush," Felix says.

I fill two mugs with water and turn to set them in the microwave.

"Oh, my gosh," I say. "I didn't realize until just this moment. They took the microwave too."

"Well, that's a shame," Billy says.

"Honestly, now that I think about it… I believe Peter said it wasn't working anymore. It's on his list of things to replace before next hunting season. So, I guess the thieves did us a favor. Will have to do this the old-fashioned way."

I retrieve the tea-kettle from the shelf above the stove, give it a good rinse, fill it with fresh water, and place it on a burner. Locating my Tupperware container of cookies, I pull a wooden plate from the cupboard beside the sink, and stack a few oatmeal raisin cookies on its decoratively painted surface. It is the plate Grandma Arnie always used for her coffee and cookie breaks. *Fika*, she called those times—which means a stopping of everything to sit down for coffee and treats. It's really more a Swedish word than Norwegian, but Grandma remembered hearing it used when she was a child, and she liked it. If she had Swedish relatives on her side, she never admitted it.

Memories of family and friends gathered in these rooms on warm summer afternoons, crisp fall mornings, and frigid Christmas vacations, flash through my mind. Someone was always stopping by, dropping something off, returning a dish, checking on family news, or just needing a good cup of coffee with one of Grandma's famous raisin-filled cookies. Solbakken used to be a humming community. Never frantic or hectic. Just a steady hum.

Setting the plate on the small round table that sits in the middle of the kitchen, I leave the men to their work and head toward the garage. I think I know where Uncle stashed his tools. The box he kept them in is nowhere near as neat or nice as Felix's, but that may be an advantage. Might have kept the thieves from thinking it was anything of value.

I carefully navigate down the hallway between the kitchen and the back bedroom, shoving things aside as I go. As I open the door leading into the garage, a blast of cold air greets me along with the musty smell of cardboard, leaves, wood shavings, and mice droppings. It is still strange not to see one of Uncle's rigs here. He always took such care with them. I remember as a kid he drove up to the farm one summer in a brand-new Chevy pickup. It was a deep navy blue with white wall tires. Grandpa had admired it but wondered aloud how he could have afforded it. I don't think Grandpa ever owned a new vehicle in his entire life.

"General Electric must have some deep pockets," he had remarked.

Uncle had not commented. He drove that truck for years until a log truck somewhere out in Maine lost its load on the road next to him. Uncle had survived, but his truck had not. Next time we saw him, he was driving a brand-new Chevy 2500 with a crew cab. Cherry red.

Grandpa's only remark about that rig, as I recall, was, "Glad you're a Chevy man." Grandpa was over a hundred years old at the time. But he'd never forgiven Henry Ford for what he saw as his part in stirring up Hitler to unprecedented heights of antisemitism back in the 1930s and '40s.

It was the last truck Uncle ever bought. The family took his keys away when he turned 102. His eyesight was still sharp, but his reaction time had slowed significantly. After Billy repaired the bumper, and pounded out the dents from about the tenth deer that had the misfortune of feeling the effects of those slow reflexes, we decided it was probably safest for man and beast to keep Einar off the roads.

He protested. We won.

I flick on the overhead light in the garage, and see his lathe and skill saw in the far corner shrouded under a canvas tarp. They both have some monetary value, but were probably too heavy and cumbersome for the intruders to grab. My furry slippers crunch over leaves that drifted in last fall or the fall before that as I shuffle across the floor. The deer hunters usually leave the place pretty tidy, but sometimes the garage door gets left open while they are here, allowing in nature's autumnal offerings. The low row of cupboards along the back wall all stand open, and boxes of various sizes and vintages lay scattered on the concrete slab. A square of barren cement with splashes of gasoline on it indicate the spot where the lawnmower once stood.

I remove a stepladder from a hook on the wall and open it up, careful to clear any junk from under the feet. I test it. It feels stable. Ascending the stepladder, I peer over the shelf that runs parallel to the cupboards three feet up from the countertop. It is about five feet deep with a barely visible window in the center on the back wall smudged to near opacity from dust, dirt, and time. Uncle's cross-country skis lay on one side next to the kick sled he used to slide out to the end of the driveway to gather his mail during the winter months. Old paint cans and several sheets of plywood sit cattywampus next to the sled. Newspaper shredded into cozy mouse abodes sit tucked between the cans, with a variety of seeds scattered all around them. Trails of droppings lace the scene, making me hesitant to reach out and move anything.

The last place I saw the tool kit was on this shelf. Tugging the edge of my sweatshirt over my hand, I gingerly lift the raised side of the plywood, sending cans and mouse habitations skittering sideways. The tool kit lays tucked under the plywood, and I reach out to tug on the metal handle. It is heavier than I imagined and does not come easily in my direction. I wedge my shoulder under the plywood so I can pull with both hands.

Metal scrapes on metal and I realize it must be rubbing over a screw or nail. I lift upward. It slides more easily but it is cumbersome. I ponder calling Billy into the garage to help. I'm not sure hefting it over my head and down the stepladder is the world's greatest idea. But I hear the two men laughing in the kitchen, and decide not to interrupt whatever they are engaged in.

Stabilizing myself as much as possible, I ease the long metal case over the edge of the shelf, and down toward my chest. Then I back carefully down the steps. Once on terra firma, I decide to keep the kit close to my body.

"What on earth does he have in this thing?" I mutter as I head back into the house.

The kettle begins to whistle.

Maximus begins to howl.

MAXIMUS

I DO NOT LIKE SOME WHISTLES.

Not only do they hurt my ears, they remind me of things.

Trains and ships. Factories and machinery. Cruel men. Short tempers. Battlefields. Dead friends.

Other whistles are okay.

They take me to other places. To birds and workers. Songs and dances. Kind faces. Soft hands. Warm fires.

I loved Mila's whistle.

Hers was melodic and pure like a flute.

Hers was soothing like a calm stream.

Hers could be funny or sad, quick or long, bubbly or slow.

Hers was unlike any other I have known.

Master has a good whistle too. It tells me where he is. Where I need to be. When I need to be there. It is firm but not harsh. Commanding but not demanding.

I understand his whistle and I obey it.

But Mila's whistle… that was different.

I followed her whistle and longed for her whistle and soaked in her whistle. She did not even know she was doing it most of the time. She whistled better than she talked. But I always knew what she was saying.

Sometimes I howled along with her song and she giggled with delight.

That was the best of times. My times with Mila.

Master and I have had many times.

Some good. Some not so good.

We have eaten strange food.

Some good. Some not so good.

We have met many people.

Some good. Some not so good.

I can never forget the one time.

The time that changed all time.

The man that changed all men.

It was long, long ago, but he is fresh in my memories always.

He had a good whistle too. It was a lot like Mila's.

Maybe a little louder. A little stronger. A little more mysterious.

We did not get to hear his whistle very long. But I will never forget it.

When I hear it again, I obey it without hesitation.

Sometimes, when we come and go, I hear it. But Master says, no, I am only imagining things.

But I don't know about that. I hear things he does not. I know things he does not.

But I do not always know what a whistle means. Especially a new whistle. In a new place. With new people.

And so, I howl.

I howl until the only thing I can hear is my own voice in my own head.

Until Master speaks. And then I know. His words, his demeanor, will tell me.

Is this friend or foe?

FELIX

"**IT'S OKAY, MAX**. It's okay," I say, stepping over to where he sits, his head thrown back in a howl. "It's just a tea kettle. Calm down."

I pull a biscuit from my pants pocket. Maximus snarfs it from my hand. His howling grinds to a halt and he settles back onto the mat.

"By golly," Billy says, going to the stove and removing the kettle from the burner. "That's a hefty howl. Bound to stir up the wolves around here if he's not careful."

"Wolves, you say?"

"Oh, ya. Got a whole pack of 'em around here right now. Been battling to keep them away from my cows. Ole Skarsgaard lost one of his sheep last week. His place is just south of the store. Right on the outskirts of town… such as it is these days. They've gotten quite brazen. Talking to the DNR about thinning their ranks a bit."

"Hunting them?" I ask.

"Not legal right now in the state of Minnesota. Had a few years when it was. But that changed again recently. Now if they're threatening your livestock, the DNR will come and remove them," Billy says. "The Red Lake Tribe keeps pretty good tabs on the numbers and the comings and goings too."

I nod and get back to replacing the damaged door frame.

"Say, just wondering, what language was that you were speaking to your dog? Not one I've heard around here," Billy says, holding a new piece of wood in place as I set the nails.

"Oh, that," I say, a bit chagrined that I didn't even realize I was not speaking English.

It is part of the challenge of my many comings and goings—keeping my language current with the environment and time in which I have arrived. I appreciate that I don't have to study it or acclimate to it even. I just seem to know it. One of the prerequisite giftings for my assignment. But Max… well, he seems to still like my native tongue the best. That or Hebrew.

"Aramaic," I reply. "He understands me best when I speak Aramaic."

"Can't say as I know where you'd even speak Aramaic," Billy says.

Tora reenters the kitchen toting a long metal tool box. She sets it onto the floor with a big exhale and straightens up, stretching from side to side.

"Sorry about that," she says, opening a cupboard and taking out some mugs. "Didn't mean to upset your dog."

"Not to worry," I say. "New place. New whistle. He will get used to it."

"Hey, Tor," Billy says, going to where she stands pulling tea bags and instant coffee together onto the counter. "Felix's dog speaks Aramaic."

Her eyebrows go up.

"Well, he doesn't speak it," I say. "But he does understand it."

"That's what I meant," Billy says, untwisting the cover from the coffee jar.

"Aramaic? Isn't that a Middle Eastern language?" Tora says.

"Yes. My mother was Jewish," I say. "That was her first language. She was also fluent in Hebrew and conversant in Greek and Italian. But Aramaic is what we spoke at home as I was growing up."

"Whoa, that's a lot of languages," Billy says. "You speak that many too?"

"Uh, yeah. I can get by with most of those. Comes pretty easily for me," I say. "Like my mother."

"And your father?" Tora asks.

"Roman… Uh, Italian. He was a military man, stationed in the Middle East. So, he picked up a smattering of languages, too. They're both gone now," I say, trying to nip the background check in the bud.

"Sorry to hear that. They must've died fairly young," she says.

"Relatively, yes," I say.

"Coffee or tea?"

"Tea will be fine," I say.

"I've only got Lipton," Tora offers. "Nothing herbal. Will the caffeine bother you?"

I shake my head. "No. Not at all. I don't require a great deal of sleep anyway."

"Hmm," Tora says, handing us our drinks without taking any herself but grabbing a cookie from the plate. "Wish it didn't bother me. But, alas, any little thing seems to upset my sleep these days. Probably even this bit of sugary goodness," she says, raising the cookie. "Not part of aging that I particularly enjoy."

"What part do ya enjoy?" Billy says. He sips his coffee, eyeing the treats, but managing not to indulge.

I keep my focus on the job in front of me.

"See ya found Einar's tool box," Billy says to his cousin. "Everything still in there?"

"I haven't opened it up yet," Tora replies. "But judging by the weight of it, I'd say it's quite full."

She bends down and tries to open the lid. The metal box is dented and rusted in places. It might have been green at some point, but most of the paint has chipped away. Tora is having trouble opening it. Billy sets his mug down and lifts the kit onto the counter as if it weighs nothing at all.

"Looks like you're gonna need a key," he says.

"A key? You think I can find a key in the midst of all this?" she says, spreading her hands out to include the jumble all around us.

"Yup, now, you have got a point there, then," he says.

I stand up and set my hammer on the table. Opening my tool chest, I reach in and pull out a thin pointed set of pliers.

"I might be able to get it open," I say, showing them my small tool. "If you don't mind the risk of maybe damaging the lock a bit."

Tora and Billy look at one another and shrug.

"It's already damaged," Tora says. "Can't see as it will devalue it much by picking the lock."

"Heck no," Billy adds. "If there's any good tools in there, I can find ya a new carrier anyways."

The two of them step back at my approach. I lean down to get a clear view of the lock apparatus which sits above a well-worn red and black decal. Lettering around the sticker's edges is nearly gone, but the number thirty-four is still visible below what appears to be the head of a red bull. I slide the pointed end of my pliers into the lock and jostle it from side to side. No movement.

"Hmm, it's a tough one," I say, repositioning the pliers and trying again. After a few maneuverings and a quick prayer, the locked flap springs open.

"Well, will ya look at that?" Billy says. "You got all kind of interesting skills, Felix."

"I have gathered a few along the way. Would you like the honors?" I say, stepping back and gesturing to Tora.

She gives me a quick smile. I see a hint of excitement in her clear blue eyes. It is the first time in my brief acquaintance with her that she has not seemed overwhelmed. Or maybe melancholy is a better word. Or maybe some of both.

The lid lifts with a creak, revealing a handled metal shelf full of tools. Wrenches, screwdrivers, a couple of hammers, some pliers, an awl, and a container of sockets. Most look to be in pretty good shape, although a few have clearly put in time doing their part to make projects, repairs, and maybe even art.

"That is a relief," Tora says. "Everything looks to be present and accounted for."

Billy reaches out to the handle. "Mind if I see what's underneath?" he asks Tora.

She shakes her head. "Go for it."

Billy removes the shelf with a tug, sending a flathead screwdriver flipping out onto the floor. It narrowly misses Tora's foot. But she is not paying attention. She is leaning over the tool kit with eyes agog and jaw dropped.

Billy grabs an oatmeal cookie from the plate on the counter, and lets out a whistle before cramming it into his mouth.

Max comes to full alert. The hair on his back is raised but he does not howl.

"Well," Tora says. "I surely did not see that coming."

TORA

"**WHAT DID YOU DO WITH THEM?"** Peter asks me.

"I gave them to Billy to put in his safe," I reply, turning the heater up a notch on my 4Runner. "Didn't want to keep them laying around tempting somebody else to break in."

I am sitting in my rig on the road a mile west of the farm. There is a slight elevation here that somehow attracts the best cell signal in the area. It is the only place I have found that I can rely on to have an uninterrupted phone call in this neck of the woods. Texts generally go through without a problem. But this is not a texting type of conversation.

"Probably a good idea," my husband says. "Did you talk to Sheriff Dumfrey yet?"

"No," I say. "Billy said maybe we should just wait until the morning. It's not an emergency so no need to drag him all the way out here."

"Well, that is his job, Tor. My guess is he is used to answering all kinds of calls at all kinds of hours of the day and night."

I sigh and tug my gloves tighter onto my fingers.

"I know. I just… I don't know. I just need to process it a little before bringing the authorities in. I mean, what if Uncle Einar is the thief?"

"What did Billy think about that possibility?"

"He didn't rule it out," I say. "We know Uncle travelled a lot, but we did not recall him doing any treasure hunting. Where would he have come up with bags of gold coins?"

"Who knows," Peter says. "But it would explain a few things, don't ya think?"

"Yeah, we kinda thought the same thing."

Uncle was known for both his frugality and his generosity. The only grand expenditures he ever made on himself were his trucks and his travel. At least, as far as any of us knew. But whenever there was a family need or financial crisis, Einar always loosened his purse strings to help out. He had given each of his nieces and nephews generous assistance with our college funds. Said a good education was invaluable, and he wanted to do something for us that would last. We did not argue but we did wonder. When I asked him about it once, he just shrugged and said, "I'm a bachelor. GE pays pretty good."

I knew of other occasions too. Like when Aunt Tora came down with cancer. For some reason, she had always been his confidant. Even when he was a kid. So, when she needed medical attention, Einar footed the bill. That's what Billy told me only a few years ago. At Uncle's homegoing service, several other of the extended family came up to us and told of similar grand gestures. A mortgage paid. A car payment made. A debt erased. And many smaller but just as significant gestures. Savings bonds purchased for new babies. Birthday cards with hundred-dollar bills. Wedding expenses underwritten.

He never wanted any credit. Most of us never even knew the extent of his giving until after he was gone.

It was strange how he knew what to give to who. He was not that close to any of us. At least not emotionally. Kept his distance there. But somehow, he seemed to keep track of all of us. Me, my brothers, our children, our cousins, our other uncles and aunties. No one knew how he did it. He just did it. And we accepted his gifts.

I stare out the window of my SUV over the snow-covered field leading to a dark line of trees and up into the night sky. Stars are much more abundant up here. Well, I know that's not true. The stars are always there. We just can't see them with all of our manmade city lights. Sort of like Uncle. He was always there in the background, doing his thing. We just did not always see him.

"Yes, Billy and I discussed all of that," I say. "We waited for Felix and Max to go home. Didn't want to pull out all the family laundry in front of him."

"How did Felix react to the bags of gold?"

I shake my head.

"He, uh, wasn't as surprised as we were."

The phone is quiet.

"Peter, did you hear what I said?"

"Yes, I heard you. Just, you know, wondering about your new neighbor. What if he knew they were there? What if he came looking for them already? What if he's your burglar?"

From where I am situated on the road, I can see the lights on in Janet's house, and a swirl of smoke drifting up into the night sky.

"We discussed that possibility too," I admit. "But the break-in was before he arrived. And Janet did a full background check on him. And..."

"And what, hon?"

"And, well... he does not seem like the type of guy who would do something like that."

I brace myself for the lecture coming from my attorney husband about the types of guys he's seen commit all types of underhanded things over the course of his career. But no lecture comes.

"Do you need me to come up there?" is his only reply.

I stop to consider that offer. It was, in fact, my first impulse when we discovered Uncle's hidden loot, to call my husband and ask him to come up and help me. But I know how busy he is—how needed he is on other fronts. And maybe it's just my pride, but in this weird situation I see an opportunity. A chance to accomplish something by myself for once. Not exactly by myself, but without him.

"You know, I think with Billy's help and Sheriff Dumfrey and maybe Felix, too, I think I will be okay."

The line is quiet again.

"I will keep you up to date on anything that develops," I promise. "But that may take a while, and I still have a boat load of junk to clean up. So, don't worry. Honestly, it is the most interesting thing that has happened to me in quite some time."

"Yes, it's been a while since you've had a good adventure," he says. "Let's just hope it stays good and doesn't turn into… well, into something not so good."

I nod and stare at Janet's place, remembering something her new tenant said when we took the coins out of the tool chest. He had taken some into his hands and held them up into the light. I can see the look on his face. He was smiling, and I swear I heard him mutter under his breath, "Good man. Good man."

"Tor, you there?"

"Yup. I'm here. You're there and…"

"And God is still on the throne," he finishes the sentiment we used to use often when he had to be gone for long stretches working on different cases.

He sticks closer to home these days. Modern technology has facilitated some of that. But some of it is because he's no longer a young attorney accepting any and every case that comes his way. He is well-established and well-regarded. I am proud of him. Sometimes, though, I wish I wasn't mainly known as Peter Dahlgard's wife. Sometimes I wish…

"Good night, Tor," my husband says. "Talk with you tomorrow. Love you."

"Love you too," I say. "Shalom."

"Shalom, shalom."

Our call ends.

As I shift the SUV into drive and head back to the house, a star shoots across the sky.

"I wish I could be known for who I am. I wish… I wish I could know who I am," I send out my thoughts to the night sky.

Maybe that's two wishes.

Maybe I'm too old to make wishes upon a star.

Maybe God doesn't care how old I am.

"And while I'm wishing or praying or asking," I speak out my addendum, "I wish I knew where Uncle came up with all that gold."

FELIX

"Go ahead, Max," I say, leaning down and whispering into his ear. "Go find her."

He takes one quick look up at me and then bounds off over the meadow, the grass and wildflowers parting wildly in his wake. It is always his first desire when we come back. She is always his first desire.

I don't blame him.

I hope to see her too.

But I don't always know who I'll get to see during my off hours. When I'm not on assignment somewhere, I come and go as I wish. Such is not the case when I am on a mission, as I am now. Then even my 'down-time' or 'up-time,' depending on how you want to look at it, is purposeful and strategic.

I follow after Max through the lush meadow though he is long gone. Won't probably see him again until we return to

Solbakken. But he will be fine. More than fine. He will be ecstatic. I smile to myself, thinking of how the two of them will bask in each other's presence, and run and skip and play in ways Mila never could while on the planet.

The flowers exude their fragrance all around me. I breathe deeply, closing my eyes, and letting the song of the realm envelop me. I am transported back to the first time I returned when Enoch showed me the way.

What a relief it was. What a joy. What a refreshing.

My Commander truly had seen me. How exhausted I was. How desperate for change I didn't even know was possible, yet longed for nonetheless. Living suddenly became bearable again when I learned how to travel between the realms. How to ride the clouds. In fact, it became more than bearable. It became a joy.

"Hello, Felix," a familiar voice says beside me.

I open my eyes and stare into the face of my father, Magnus.

"Hello, Father," I respond, throwing my arms around him.

He wraps me tight. I relish his strength. His wisdom. His love. It flows from him freely in ways it never did before. It is one of the joys of this place—we know without speaking, and we express without fear.

"You are content," he says, pulling back and peering at my face. "Must be a good assignment."

"Oh, it's an interesting one alright," I reply. "But they're all interesting."

"Yes, I suppose that's so. I just know at times it has been more difficult or stressful than others. True?"

"True."

"I want to hear all about it. Shall we walk?"

I nod and we begin to stroll. Side by side. Father and son. No hurry. He is exactly who I was hoping to talk with over the goings on with Tora. I have reached the point in the story where she walks into the kitchen with Einar's tool kit, when Father and I enter a beautiful village.

"Hold that thought, Son," my father says. "I want my friend to hear the rest."

The road we walk on is gravel. Smooth. No ruts or washboard like those in northern Minnesota. But still gravel. Neat houses made from white stones rise up around us. Some are small. Some large. All are situated perfectly in their surroundings as if one with them. Trees, shrubs, grasses, rocks, and earth all merge with the structures in true harmony.

Father turns down the path leading to one of the smaller looking buildings.

"Whose home is this?" I ask. "I don't recall us ever coming here before."

He doesn't respond but only smiles.

A tidy wooden door opens of its own accord as we approach, and we step inside.

"Anybody home?" Father calls into the cool dimness.

"In here, Magnus," a man responds, his voice echoing down a long hallway.

It is always surprising here how expansive the interiors of buildings are compared to what appears on the exterior. We follow the voice, the clop of our sandals reverberating off the marble floor. Portraits hang all along the length and height of the passageway. Men, women, children, babies, groups, couples, families. Not a single inch of the wall can be seen behind them. I admire them as we pass by, but Father has his face set straight ahead toward the light that fills the opening at the end of the hall, as if he's seen it all before. Maybe he has. Probably so.

"Magnus! Magnus Benedizione, how good to see you, my friend," a man with rich brown skin and regal clothing says, coming to greet us as we enter a cozy but fine dining area.

He and Father exchange a hug and a kiss on each cheek before Father turns to introduce me.

"Jaspar, this is my son, Felix," he says. "Felix, this is my much-revered friend, Jaspar Ambani."

I greet him with the respect I can feel is due him. He smiles warmly while assessing me from head to toe.

"Ah, so good to see you again. You were only a very small child last I laid eyes on you. And now? Now I hear you have been given special status," he says. "You are one of the cloud-riders, yes?"

"Yes," Father says with both pride and humility in his voice. "Quite a privilege he has been given."

Yes, I am one who comes and goes on the clouds.

Not anything I asked for. Didn't even know I could.

For me, it simply came due to time and circumstance.

I was in the right place at the right time.

Though for many years, I argued with that fate. Now I accept it. Now I relish it.

"Come, my friends," Jaspar says, leading us to his well-appointed table. "Come and refresh yourselves with eat and drink. And then tell me how I may be of service to you."

We chat easily over the luscious meal of exotic vegetables, dried fruits, and warm flat bread. The wine is exquisite. Heavenly. I savor it as I listen to the two old friends catch up with one another. It becomes apparent to me that the portraits lining the hallway depict the ever-expanding legacy of Jaspar's family line.

"Yes, yes," Jaspar laughs. "It is getting harder and harder to keep up with all of them. Such a blessing! Oh, I love them all. You should see the new set of twins that just arrived. Cute as can be and so full of promise."

Magnus nods knowingly. He understands.

"But you have not come only to gloat with me over my family blessings, have you?" Jaspar asks.

"Not exactly," Father says. "Son, why don't you fill Jaspar in on your latest mission? It will be good for him to hear what you are in the middle of. And he may have some insights for you as well."

I don't argue for I have learned this is how these types of meetings go. I rehearse earthly events that are unfolding, and I gain a heavenly perspective in order to be more fully equipped for the needs of the hour.

"I have landed in a place called Solbakken, America, in the family of Anders of Norway," I begin.

Father and Jaspar nod while sipping their wine, fully engaged in the narrative that unwinds as I speak.

TORA

HAVING CLEARED THE JUNK from the queen-sized bed in the bedroom just off the kitchen, I hop in and pull the covers up to my chin. A cold north wind finds its way through the cracks and crevices of this old house, and it is chilly despite me having cranked the thermostat up several notches. I check my phone. It is 2 a.m. The ibuprofen I have taken to help alleviate the throbbing that has commenced all over my body, thanks to the exertions of the day, is beginning to take effect. But my mind is buzzing. Sleep may be wishful thinking.

After Billy and Felix left, I spent hours sorting and tossing, clearing off counters and forging pathways. One quick tour of the upstairs left me in despair, so I decided to leave that for another day. Plenty to do on the ground floor. All the while the contents of Uncle's tool kit hovered and swirled through my brain.

Gold coins.

Bags of gold coins.

What the heck?

Are they real?

Are they valuable?

Where did they come from?

Who should we tell?

What should we tell them?

Clayton.

I sit straight up in bed and switch on the bedside lamp.

Of course. Why didn't I think of him before?

2 a.m.… Must be mid-morning in London.

I think about getting geared up and taking the SUV out to the 'phone booth' on the road, but quickly reject that idea. Too cold. Too snowy. Not going to risk getting stuck out there in the middle of the night. Billy is helpful, but even he can reach his limit for one day. Plus, there's no guarantee Clayton will answer his phone.

"You busy?" I text my brother, who is a curator for Roman antiquities at The British Museum in London. Now that he is in his seventies, he no longer works the long hours he used to but pretty much sets his own schedule. Retirement for him is anathema. I imagine he will continue working until he is as old as some of his exhibits. Or close.

My fingers tap on my iPhone as I await his response.

Clayton lives by himself in a large flat not far from the museum where he works. Divorced after a disastrous short marriage to a French film star many years ago, he never remarried. Yet he never seems to lack for female companionship. From what I can tell at my distant observation post, these relationships always seem to be more about companionship than love for him. Whenever a woman gets too serious, Clayton makes himself scarce, settles into a season of solitude, and then reemerges with a different companion. It makes me feel sorry for him on some level, but he appears to be content.

Though our father, Sigard, was nothing like this in terms of relating to women, he and Clayton are very alike in other ways. They are both men with many interests but especially intrigued, no, enraptured by history. Clayton obtained his undergraduate degree in history from Concordia College in Moorhead, his master's in European History from Yale, and his PhD in Roman Antiquities from Oxford. Yes, he is the scholar in our family. Our dad couldn't have been prouder.

Dad's own love for the subject led him to be a high-school history teacher for many years. American history. World history. The history of Central Asia or Central America or Central Europe or central wherever. He taught some of all of it over the course of his career in education, which took him to several mid-sized towns around the state of Minnesota. The boys grew up in Alexandria where I was born. But by the time I was three, we moved to Little Falls where Dad taught until he retired.

Though he worked odd contracting jobs during the summer months, we always took a two-week vacation sometime in July. It was always a road trip and always somewhere around North America. Between Dad and Clay, our travel was well mapped out with every possible historical landmark, battle ground, birthplace, or museum within an hour's drive of our route circled in red. We visited as many as my mother could stand—which was quite a few—but never as many as my dad or brother would have liked.

Our mother, Louisa, preferred a good hike up a trail or a day at the beach or a bike ride through a town. She had been a physical education teacher when my parents first met. A career she put on hold until after I was in elementary school. But even when she was at home raising us kids, she taught tennis lessons, swim lessons, and ski lessons throughout the year. Physical activity was her joy and her passion her entire life. She jumped out of a perfectly good airplane on her ninetieth birthday. In tandem, of course, with an instructor. But nonetheless, still impressive.

My oldest brother, Andrew, took after our mom. His love of sports began in the cradle, I think. At one time or another in his life, he participated in baseball, football, golf, tennis, skiing, basketball, track, and even some serious competitive badminton. Good at everything, he was never great at anything. But he enjoyed it all. So, owning a sporting goods store in Arizona for forty-plus years, suited him to perfection. Just sold it to his daughter and son-in-law a few years ago so he could get more time on the golf course.

And me? I have always felt like I am a mixture of both my parents except without the element of passion. A fact which was quite perplexing to them and to my brothers who never did anything halfway. I'm not sure why I am the way I am either. My passion seems to have been spread so thin over so many different areas that it lacks the necessary depth to propel me into expertise in any one area. I'm an okay singer. An average painter. A so-so athlete. A mediocre gardener. And an ordinary mom. About the only unusual thing I've accomplished in comparison to the rest of today's culture, is to stay married to the same man for over forty years. And, I certainly can't take all the credit for that.

Many times, when I stop to assess my life, I am saddened to think that instead of living an extraordinary life, I have led an extra ordinary life.

"Hey, Sis. You up at the farm?"

Clay's text lights up my phone.

"Yes. Making headway on clean up. Am I catching you at a bad time?"

"All good. Got a few minutes. Sorry I can't be there to help."

"Maybe you can…"

"How so?"

I pull up the pictures I took of the coins Billy and I spread out on the table. Felix commented right away that he thought they looked quite old and might be of some significant value. Evidently besides carpentry, languages, and lock-picking, he also has some knowledge of coins. From the hours we have spent together, I have concluded that he is probably not a serial killer, but a world-renowned cat burglar? That I have not completely ruled out.

"Gonna send you some pics of what we uncovered in Uncle's tool box. Tell me what you think," I text, attaching the photos.

The pictures are not great, I know, but I think they're clear enough to give him some idea of what we found.

My phone is maddeningly silent for several minutes.

"Did you get the pics?" I ask, knowing the cell reception issues of my current environment. A few more seconds tick by before I receive his reply.

"WTF?!"

I have to laugh. "Any inkling as to what they are? How old? Where from?" I ask.

"Oh, I've got some ideas," he texts back. "But let me do some discreet digging before I make any wild speculations."

"Clayton!!! At least give me a clue."

"Too many possibilities. Just be patient. How many are there?"

"We counted fifty in one bag and sixty-two in the other. Only a few look to be the same vintage, or whatever you call it."

"I can see that. Get me pics of every different type in groups if you can."

"Will do. But will have to wait til tomorrow. Treasure is locked up in Billy's safe for the night."

"Good idea. I've gotta go. But I promise to follow up ASAP."

"Thx. Love ya."

"Cheerio."

Now my mind is not only buzzing, my heart is pumping. Clay did not outright dismiss the coins as party favors or fakes. He is surprised. He is intrigued. That does not happen unless he gets the scent of a possible historical find. I've seen it in him before. Like the time when we were kids when we found a glass beer bottle underneath a bunch of debris behind the ball field where Andy was playing a baseball tournament. Clayton and I had been dragged to enough of our elder brother's games that we often found amusement doing other things while Mom and/or Dad played the faithful fan. Though I was eight years his junior, he was good at including me in his wanderings and turning them into adventures.

A tiny little reflection caught his eye that day, and he carefully sifted through what looked to me to be a pile of garbage. He had pulled out the bottle and brushed it off as if it were the lost treasure of Queen Nefertiti or something. We took it home, though Mom insisted it reside in the trunk of the car for the journey because of the odor that clung to it. Clayton swaddled that bottle like it was the baby Jesus himself before nesting it into a box in the trunk. As I recall, he picked his fingernails all the way home he was so nervous something might happen to it. After much research, he found out it was an antique Schell's beer bottle from the oldest brewery in Minnesota. I don't even know what he did with it, but I will never forget the excitement I saw in him as he hunted down the origins.

An eerie howl echoes through a field outside my window bringing my focus back to my present environs. Another howl answers back from a different direction. Before long, it feels as if I am surrounded by a chorus of wolves with a few coyotes thrown in yipping descant. Eventually, they all settle back into whatever cave or den they came out of, and the night is completely quiet save for an occasional gust of wind that rattles the windowpane above my head.

I have forgotten the sounds of the country or the lack thereof; the quiet, interrupted only by birds or beast or weather. Peter and I don't exactly live in the midst of the city, but I am used to more man-made noise, even if it's just a jet flying overhead. Nature by itself can be quite unnerving. I remember coming to the farm as a kid. Sometimes I came all by myself for a week or two during the summer. My brothers were at language camp or baseball camp or geology camp or some such educational activity. I was deemed too young for such extended time away from family. Mom had a side gig as a lifeguard at the YMCA day camp outside of Little Falls. I went with her most of the time. But at least once or twice per summer, I was sent to the farm.

And I loved it.

Grandpa and Grandma all to myself.

Good times.

But I do recall that I usually struggled to fall asleep for the first night or two I was here. Too many unidentifiable noises. Even the sound of a fly buzzing on a windowsill seemed amplified by the all-encompassing stillness of the countryside. So, Grandpa would come up the stairs with a book under his arm to the bedroom Tante Tilda used as a child. He would tug on the string for the small lamp that hung on the wall over my bed and climb up next to me. And he would read. *The Circus McGurkus, Thidwick the Big-Hearted Moose, Mary Poppins, Madeline,* and countless others came alive with his baritone voice that still carried the hints of Norway in its lilt. I would snuggle up against his soft flannel pajamas and listened until sleep inevitably won out. Very rarely did I ever last through more than one story.

Even now, just thinking about it, I feel the gentle tug of slumber pulling me into its arms.

A MOOSE WITH AN UMBRELLA followed by a poodle walking on two feet prance across my vision. Music from a calliope accompanies them. I feel the desire to follow, so I step in line behind the pup who twirls and leaps in welcome. I leap and twirl, free from any aches or pains. Free from age. I am young and happy.

Someone takes my hand. Someone older. Someone bigger. Someone I know.

I look up. It is Grandpa Axel. He smiles at me and I smile back. Contentment settles into my heart all the way down to my toes. It is the safest I have felt in a very long time. He walks. I skip to keep up with his long strides.

The moose and the poodle dance off down a narrow path. We wave, and they bow slightly in acknowledgement before disappearing.

"Where are we going, Grandpa?" I ask.

"To the tree," he says.

A thrill runs up my spine.

"Our tree?" I ask.

He nods.A field of tall grass stretches out before us, and in the middle rises a beautiful tall oak tree. It is in full leaf and shimmers as if recently drenched by rain. The trunk is so thick it would take a ring of ten or more people to surround it with arms stretched wide.

"Why are we here?" I ask.

"You will see," he replies.

The tree seems to grow as we approach. Underneath its canopy, I can no longer see the sky above.

"Come and sit," Grandpa says, leading me to a small bench carved into the base of the oak.

We sit for some time, listening. I lean into his side.

"Tell me a story, Grandpa," I say.

He nods and looks up into the leaves overhead as if picking one out for special consideration. Finally, he reaches up and plucks one from a branch not far from his head. The leaf becomes a book in his hands. He sets it on his lap and tenderly lifts back the cover.

"What's the name of the story?" I ask.

"*The Day of the Big Wind.*"

I reach up to his face and touch the crooked bump in his nose. He has read this story to me before, but I have always fallen asleep before the ending.

"Does it hurt when you tell the story?" I ask.
"Not anymore," he replies.
"I'm glad. I don't like that part of the story."
"I know, Tora-bird. Neither do I. But without that part…"
"Without that part, what?"
"Listen. Stay alert. And you will know."

AXEL

It was a June afternoon in 1903, sunny and warm with only a small breeze coming from the south. Ole and I had secured the large family trunk and the small family trunk onto the boat with straps and ropes. Pa's chest of books was stowed between them. He had given us specific instructions about where and how to secure this treasured item. And we had followed his instructions to a tee down to the types and numbers of knots he prescribed. Two wooden chairs Ma's father had carved for her as a wedding gift were also carefully stacked and tied down near the front of the vessel, away from the churning paddle wheel in the back.

The rest of the space was dominated by the dining table Pa had made last year to match the two chairs. We were still six chairs short of having a seat for everyone in our family to be able to sit at said table. Besides Ole and me, there were four younger sisters—Tora, Petrina, Hanna, and Marta. And from the way Ma had been showing up looking green around the edges every morning while making breakfast, my guess was we might be needing a highchair in the not-too-distant future.

Not a fancy boat by any means, the Dan Patch was Pa's invention based on the large steamboats he had once travelled upon on the Mississippi River as a young man. Though born and raised in Norway, Pa had gone back and forth to America more times than anyone else I knew. "Got restless," was all he could give in way of explanation when I asked him about it once. My siblings and I were born back in the old country during one of his more extended returns to the family farm north of Kristiania.

Besides being a bit of a wanderer, Pa was a tinkerer - an idea man. He had an uncanny way of re-inventing things with what he saw as improvements. Sometimes they were. Sometimes they were not. This boat was one of his better re-inventions.

Man-powered by two cranks on each side of the boat which turned the paddlewheel in the back, it moved quite efficiently up and down the Red Lake River to the Lower Red Lake's far eastern shore and back. He'd mainly used it in the last year since our arrival from Norway, to transport timber to the sawmills in Crookston and Thief River. It was sturdy and flat without any side rails, making loading and unloading an easier task but also making the deck a fairly hazardous environment for families with small children like ours.

Thus, only Ole and myself had the privilege of making the sojourn to the new homestead via the lake, while the rest of the family and the livestock had to traverse the bumpy road around the lake's south end with Pa. Tora had argued with Pa's decision. She wanted to help the big boys on the boat. But Pa said Ma needed her help more with the little kids and that was that. Tora had not even said good-bye to me when they left, she was so mad I hadn't tried to convince Pa of her capabilities. I knew when Pa had made up his mind there was no use arguing, but I was a bit ashamed of my lack of courage to stick up for my sister.

Even though Tora was a year younger than me, she was just about as strong and a fair amount smarter. She'd already read every book in Pa's library. She was at least my equal for the boat crossing endeavor, but the Dan Patch was a two-man operation. And no matter how much she argued with our pa, I was deemed more a man than she for this particular mission.

Pa and Ma and the kids had departed two days prior so that Pa would be able to get them settled at the new house, and meet us on the other side when we docked. We had remained behind in Thief River with Ma's folks, who were sad to see us all go, but also a bit relieved, I'm sure, to have their house back to themselves.

It was only the second time Ole and I had manned the boat by ourselves. The first time was a few weeks prior on what Pa called a 'trial run.' We had done well. Over and back in one day with a load and without a hitch.

"Let's get going, Axel," Ole yelled in Norwegian from the back of the boat where he already stood beside one of the wheeled cranks. When we were by ourselves, we always reverted to our native tongue, but not in front of Pa. He always chastised us, saying we were now in America and we should talk like Americans. "Pa will be looking for us. Don't want him getting anxious."

I tugged a knot around one of the vessel's cleats one last time and stepped back to my place across from my brother. The waves were not large this close to the shore, but I still felt a bit wobbly. Ole laughed as I slid sideways in a puddle of water and lunged for the handle of the crank to keep myself from going overboard. I could swim, if I had to, but I preferred not to. Especially not fully clothed. Especially not since we'd lost Gudrun.

"Get your sea legs," my brother said. "We've got to set sail."

Lower Red Lake lies within the boundaries of the Chippewa Reservation, which is a closed reservation, meaning all the land is owned in common by the tribe. So, any and all travel or commerce takes place under their laws and purview. Pa had made arrangements for us to meet him at Jerome's Landing, which lies within the reservation but is connected to Jerome's Trading Post, which lies just beyond that line. Not sure how all that was worked out. Not mine to figure out, I figured as I set my feet and began to crank the wheel on my side of the Dan Patch in unison with my brother on the other side.

We worked hard to get up our speed, but once we did, the boat skimmed along pretty good. I appreciated the fresh wind in my hair. Kept the sweat from trickling down my neck and the black flies from landing and delivering their particularly stinging bite. Ole and I kept our eyes on the far horizon, though the lake was so large, it would be some time before we would actually see land. He checked a small compass Pa had given him to make sure we kept our course due east.

At sixteen, Ole was three years older than I and about three times stronger. His growth spurt last summer had launched him well over the six-foot mark, and his work with Pa in the lumber yard had begun to fill out every inch of that frame with ropy muscles. More than once I had to yell at him to ease up a bit so we didn't wind up going around in circles.

I guessed we were more than halfway across the lake when the first big thunderhead began to mount up behind us. A crack of thunder caught our attention. We both wheeled around at once to see what was going on. Lightning lit the western horizon, which had darkened considerably since we left shore. Ole's brows knit together as he hollered at me.

"Give her all you've got."

I widened my stance and leaned into my work. My arms already ached from the distance we had crossed but the storm behind us had boosted my system with a load of adrenaline. Our speed picked up. But so did the wind.

Coming from our back, it pushed us eastward and soon we were going at a pace I'd never before encountered on any trip with Pa. It was exhilarating and terrifying at the same time. I peeked over at my big brother. His face was set like flint forward. I tried to mimic his focus, but the ever-increasing waves all around us made that quite a challenge.

"Keep pushing," Ole yelled.

"What?" I yelled back.

He thrust one arm firmly forward and pointed before pumping his fist.

I got the message.

Just before the first big plops of rain landed on my head, I could have sworn I had gotten a glimpse of the shiny white sand dunes of the lake's south-eastern shore. We were getting close to Jerome's Landing, but we were too far south. Ole noticed, too, and signaled me to correct our course. The shore by the dunes was unpredictable. Deep in some places and then a foot deep in others. If we hit one of those sand bars too far from shore in this weather… I did not want to think about it.

Was that the landing up ahead?

I took my hand off the handle to wipe the rain from my eyes.

It was only for a second.

But it was the exact second that the big wind came.

AXEL

THE WAVES ENGULFED ME and sucked me under. I flailed my arms and struggled to find the surface. The water was cold. My legs cramped. I reached down to extract my feet from the weight of my boots. I hated to lose them because they were the only boots I had, but needs must. Once rid of them, I shot upward and found daylight. Ole's face emerged through the choppy waves. He was reaching for me, extended far out over the edge of the boat. Farther than was safe.

"Swim, Axel! I can't reach you," he bellowed over the wind.

I was doing all I could, but the boat and my brother just kept drifting further away. My head was doused by a wave. I had to fight to keep my mouth from sucking in water. Up I bobbed once again. Ole was standing now and gesturing wildly.

What was he saying?

I could barely hear him.

I could barely see him over the white caps all around me.

"Go that way!"

He was pointing toward the dunes.

Of course.

The dunes.

The shore was many yards away, but the sand bars under the water must be close. Pa had warned us to steer clear of those waters because of the many high ridges, but now they just might be my salvation. I waved at Ole to let him know I understood. Then I turned from the boat and began to battle my way in the opposite direction toward the dunes.

Thoughts of our older sister Gudrun played across my mind. The picture of Pa carrying her limp body up out of the frigid water of the pond, her skates still dangling on her feet. Ma screaming. The girls crying. Ole and I mute with shock.

Ma had told us the ice was getting thin. To stay by the shore. But in our little game, we had forgotten. Gudrun went after the stone we were sliding over the ice with branches. When Ole yelled at her to forget about it. To come back. She had turned. And then… the crack of the ice. The terror on her face.

I yanked my mind back from that awful day.

I had to swim. To kick. To fight.

But my arms were so tired.

If I hadn't been paddling the Dan Patch for almost an hour already, it would have been easier. I did not want to die like my older sister. I did not want to break Ma's heart like she had. But I was getting exhausted. I was losing hope.

And then, miraculously, my toes felt sand. I extended my legs downward and under my feet was earth. Soft and sandy but solid earth. I struggled to stand against the buffeting waves, but when I did, both my head and shoulders were above the water level. I turned around to see where Ole might be. He was jumping up and down on the boat and waving. He had seen me.

The rain was still falling in sheets, and another flash of lightening sobered any sense of elation I felt. I hunkered down until only my head was over the water not wanting to become a human lightening rod. I hoped Ole thought to keep low too.

Suddenly I wondered, how was he going to get to the landing without me?

But an immersing wave brought me back to my own reality. I might be on a sand bar, but I was still about a hundred yards from shore with no idea how far away the next ridge might be. And, I was still in the middle of a humdinger of a thunderstorm. I caught my breath, rested my arms, and then launched forward.

Three more times I swam and found a welcomed sand bar. Each one taking me closer to safety. Each one a little higher than the last. I was becoming hopeful I might actually survive. Maybe this hope allowed me to relax my guard. Maybe I got a little over-confident. I don't know exactly what happened, but I didn't see it coming—a rogue piece of lumber appeared on the top of the waves and caught me square in the nose.

I slipped under the water.

The world went dark.

AND THEN I FELT ARMS BENEATH MY ARMS.

Were they Pa's arms?

Was he pulling me out of the water the way he pulled Gudrun out of the water?

Was I dead?

I didn't know.

How does one know?

The darkness remained.

And then, I awoke, sitting up with my back against a birch tree, my shoulders shrouded in a soft woven blanket. Raindrops plopped on an animal pelt that stretched overhead. My clothes were cold and sopping wet but, in this shelter, I was safe from further dousing. It was hard to open my eyes. The lids were heavy, and my nose ached something fierce. I reached up to feel it, but someone's hand stopped my efforts.

"No," a voice beside me said. "Leave it."

I turned my head, and there, seated on the grasses sticking up from the white sand, was a boy. About my age. About my size. But as brown as I was white, with thick black hair plaited in a braid that ran down the side of his neck and onto his bare chest. His trousers were much like mine and just as soaking wet. Draped over a branch under the canopy was a plaid button up shirt. It, too, dripped from the edges.

"English?" he asked. "Do you speak English?"

I nodded, careful not to move my head too much or too quickly.

"I am Thomas," the boy said, with an accent that told me English was probably not his first language either. "Thomas Everwind. What is your name?"

"Axel Anderson," I replied.

"Are you hungry, Axel Anderson?"

"Yes, I am," I said. "But first, are you the one who pulled me out of the water?"

Thomas's face was somber and fixed.

"Yes," he said.

He dug into a beaded leather satchel, and pulled out a stick of smoked meat.

"Deer," he said. "It will strengthen you."

I took the piece of jerky from his hand, and began to chew. It was filled with flavors I did not know, but immediately liked.

"Deilig… uh, delicious," I said between mouthfuls.

"My mother's recipe. I will tell her it is… how did you say? Dei…?

"Deilig."

"Yes, deilig," Thomas said, and crossed his arms and watched me.

"Will you eat too?" I asked.

He shook his head.

"My time to eat has not yet come."

He retrieved a canteen and offered it to me.

"Water from our well, not the lake," he said with a faint teasing lift to the edge of his mouth.

"Thank you," I said, and drank deeply of the fresh cool water. "Do you live near here?"

"Not far," Thomas replied.

We sat in silence as I finished the deer jerky.

The wind began to die down, and the sun peeked through the clouds. I searched the lake for any sign of my brother, but did not find him.

"How far is Jerome's Landing from here?" I asked.

"A good walk. A quick drive. A long swim. Come," he said, standing up and reaching down a hand to pull me up. "The sun will dry us."

I stood and folded the blanket that had been around my shoulders. Setting it down near Thomas's satchel, I followed him out onto the rolling sands of the dunes. Driftwood was piled on the beach beside one large length of lumber.

"This is what hit your face," he said, pointing to the board. "Not me."

"I did not think it was you," I sputtered. "I… you… it happened so fast."

A hint of a smile entered Thomas's eyes.

"Did you see the log hit me?" I asked.

Thomas nodded. "From my vision, yes."

"Your vision?"

Thomas sat on the soft sand that was already beginning to dry and warm under the ever-increasing sunshine. He stretched his long lean legs out in front of him, and leaned back on his elbows.

"Three nights ago, I searched the land," he said, his eyes suddenly focused on a place far distant. "The bear came and the moose came and the wolf came. But they did not speak to me. Two nights ago, I searched the air. The eagle flew by and the heron and the sparrow too. But they did not speak to me. Last night, I searched the water. A fish swam to me. His fins were white and his eyes blue. I did not know what type of fish this was. But the fish began to speak. From his mouth coins of gold dropped into my hands. I asked the fish, 'Why do you share your wealth with me?' but before he could answer, a tree began to fall in the water. It was about to fall on him and crush him. I dropped the coins, and pulled the fish from the water."

He spoke with such certainty, such sincerity, I believed every word he said, though I did not understand how it could be so. Then I remembered something else Pa had told us about the sand dunes. He had told us the sand dunes were sacred to the tribe that lived around the lake. They had a name for this place that Pa had told me repeatedly, but I could never quite remember or pronounce.

"Am I… what is the word? Illegal here?" I asked.

Thomas looked at me quizzically.

"You know," I said. "On your sacred ground. Trespassing. That is the word. Am I trespassing on Chi-waasada…?"

He sat up straight beside me. "Chi-waasadaawangideg. You know this name?"

"A little. Not very well. My Pa told me about it."

"Your father must be a man who listens carefully."

I searched his face for any sign of anger or offense at my words or my presence.

"Do you want me to leave?" I asked, starting to get up.

Thomas grabbed my forearm. "Not yet, my fish," he said. "Perhaps you have gold coins to give me."

I froze.

"I am only joking," Thomas said, releasing my hand. "Sit. Your people will find you."

I sat back down casting glances at my rescuer. He was the first Indian my age I had ever spoken to, and I did not know what to make of him.

"My vision is not yet complete," he said, staring out over the vast expanse of water toward the west. The clouds were at our back and the sun was on our faces. "I will spend one more night and wait on the Spirit. But I believe, Axel Anderson, that you and I are fated to walk through life along a common path."

TORA

SUNLIGHT STREAMS THROUGH THE bedroom window and reflects off the blue glass bird I had returned to its perch on the windowsill before bed last night. I don't know where the bird came from, or who it even belonged to, but I know it has always resided in that spot on the windowsill in the back bedroom. I allow myself moments to watch the blue reflective rays bounce around the room, as shadows from the tree branches dance in the breeze outside. The movement almost looks like water… like waves of clear blue.

My dream from the night before bobs up and down on the waves in my mind. Surfacing and then going away. Resurfacing in a different place. I try to piece the images together. Waves. Wind. Lightning. Uneasiness rustles around in my chest. But then I see the sand. The big white sand dunes.

Ah, this is Grandpa Axel's story. I have heard it before, but now I see it in ways I have never seen it before, and I know things. Things I had never known before.

I refocus on the blue glass bird. A little whisper says, "That's it, Tora-bird."

It's almost as if Grandpa is in the room.

Almost like I can hear his voice.

I give my head a little shake.

"Back to reality," I say aloud to myself.

Yet something about that dream… It feels as real as that bird. I haven't had a dream that vivid in many years. As a child, I used to dream like that. Wake up knowing things. Seeing things. But when I told my parents, they chalked it up to too much time in front of the television, or too vivid of a bedtime story. They apparently didn't even want to entertain the possibility that I might, at best, be hearing from God or, at worst, be psychologically unstable. I did not like having what seemed to me to be very important, brushed aside and ignored. Eventually, I stopped telling them about my dreams.

And then, eventually, I stopped dreaming.

I grab my phone. It feels solid, tangible, real. I turn it over and check for messages. No word yet from Clayton. It's only been five hours since I contacted him. He's probably busy. But I am anxious to hear from him.

I fling the covers back and swing my legs over the side of the bed, sliding my feet into my slippers and emptying my mind of the dream… just like I used to.

As I do, I see the corner of a book peeking out from under the dust ruffle. I hesitate to retrieve it, realizing I have not even checked under the bed for what may be crammed under there.

But there is something familiar about the faded blue cover. I bend to pull it up. I am immediately cheered by the sight of what I find. *Madeline's Rescue* by Ludwig Bemelmans. What it is doing under Uncle's bed, I have no idea but, in the current state of disarray in this house, it is feasible that most anything could be anywhere. I check the clock on the nightstand, and allow myself the luxury of just a few more minutes under Grandma Arnie's thick quilt. I kick off my slippers and slide back into bed. As I open the book and read aloud, I attempt to mimic the French accent Grandpa always used with these books. It was heavily flavored with Nordic spices, but still quite good. I'm not sure I can even come close to the lilting charm of it. But I try.

"In an old house in Paris
That was covered in vines
Lived twelve little girls
In two straight lines."

The illustrations bring back so many memories of Grandpa, soon they are swimming in front of my eyes beyond a vale of tears. Then they are replaced with snippets of images. A tree. A bench. A book. A story.

I let the book fall flat on my chest.

The dream from last night floods my mind again.

It is as real to me as the book in my hands.

I allow Grandpa's words to sit and simmer on my heart. I can picture the Dan Patch and the infamous crossing of Red Lake. And when I think of Thomas Everwind, now I can see his face. And now I know, he was at the sand dunes to receive his vision. Grandpa had never told me that before. He had only told me that Thomas happened to be in just the perfect spot to rescue him. And he was, but that wasn't the only reason he was there. Maybe Grandpa felt about Thomas's vision the same way my parents felt about my dreams. They did not know quite what to do with them.

I had heard the story of the big wind before. But there was never any mention of a vision, let alone of gold coins.

Coins from the mouth of a fish.

Sounds almost biblical.

My phone pings. I quickly grab it, hoping it might be my brother. It is my husband.

"Good morning," Peter's text says. "Get any sleep?"

"Some. Guess who I got a hold of last night?" I text back.

"Clayton?"

"Did he call you?" I say, a bit disappointed that he has guessed quite so easily.

"No, after we talked last night, I lay awake wracking my brain for some kind of clue as to where those coins might have come from. And about 2 a.m., a light bulb went on, and I thought of Clay."

I smile. This is what being married for forty-plus years does to people.

I fill him in on the details of my exchange with Clay.

"Excellent," Peter replies. "Glad to have him on the trail. What's your plan for the day? Gonna bring the Sheriff in yet? Gotta do it some time, Tor."

"I am aware," I say, feeling more of an edge than I would have liked. "I am planning on doing that sometime today. After I take some more pictures for Clay and after I've talked with Billy and Carin, if she's around. She is always so level-headed. I'm sure she will have some good suggestions about how to proceed."

"Alright, my love. Do what you think is best. I will be praying. My day is packed with meetings. And I have to run all the way down to Owatonna to retrieve some documents, so won't be too reachable until this evening."

"Okay. Good to know," I say. "Thanks for the wake-up call."

"Shalom."

"Shalom, shalom."

I think about telling him about my dream with Grandpa Axel, but I can tell that he is already ramping up for a busy day. And it's not a story that I want to rush through. I will wait and give it the space it deserves for a well-thought-out and well-listened-to conversation. I guess there is something in me that does not want to risk having a dream dismissed again by someone I love. Not that Peter would do that… I don't think. But I don't know. He is a man of faith. A man who prays and believes in a big, powerful, wonderful God. But so did my parents. And, so did my grandparents.

It's time to get up and get dressed. I put on a pair of comfortable jeans and a turtleneck. My hair gets twisted and clipped up off my neck. I brush my teeth, splash my face, and rub on some deodorant. Once I have brewed myself a cup of instant coffee, and eaten a slice of toast, I am armed for the day ahead.

The morning zips by as I continue to wade through the mess in the bedroom. I have determined to take one room at a time and, since this is where I'm sleeping, it has taken first priority. By eleven o'clock, I am dusting the tops of dressers and vacuuming the rug. I step back and take in the order I have created. Everything looks pretty much the same as it always has. But I know that under that bed, and in that closet, and in every drawer, the clutter of the ages has been sorted and de-cluttered. If a room could breathe more easily due to sudden weight loss, this bedroom would be doing it.

When I turn into the kitchen, I sigh. So much still to do here. But first, I need to haul some big black garbage bags outside and into the back of my SUV. It will clear some floor space and give me operating room. I go to the sink and check the thermometer that resides outside the kitchen window. The sunny skies have pushed the temp up into the mid-thirties. Water has begun to drip from the roof forming icicles that sparkle in the sun.

Outside, I can see that Billy has already cleared the snow from the driveway. Don't even know what time of the morning that man begins his day, but it's a lot earlier than me. I am thankful that he has done as he promised last night because I know things can get very slushy with this variable weather. The driveway can become quite the obstacle course to navigate if ice becomes the overriding element.

I don my boots and parka and head into the garage. I have decided that the shortest route for toting the garbage outside with the least number of obstacles is through the front door. So, I back my vehicle out of the garage, through a sizable puddle and swing the rear end of my SUV toward the steps. Setting the rig into park, I pop the back door open and head back into the house. I grab two bags by the neck. They are ridiculously heavy, so I settle for dragging one at a time out the door, over the porch and down the front stairs. As I wrestle the first bag into the back of the 4Runner, I am startled by a wet muzzle nuzzling my hand.

Maximus stands beside me, his head up to my waist sniffing the contents of my vehicle.

"Well, good morning," I say, with a final shove of the bag and a quick rub of his head. "Guess you've decided I am friend and not foe."

"Max," I hear Felix yelling from his place across the road. "Here, Max."

The dog's ears perk up. He tilts his head as if deciding whether he should obey or not.

"Better scoot along there, fella," I say, scratching behind his ear. "Don't want to get you in trouble. Besides, I've got places to go and people to see today. You can come back later though, if you'd like."

The look in Max's eyes is so understanding, it feels as if he truly comprehends what I'm saying. His head does a little bob and then he bounds off down the driveway toward home, splashing through every puddle available to be splashed in. I hope Felix doesn't mind.

Just then my phone buzzes in my coat pocket.

It is Clayton.

I hope our call doesn't drop.

"Hello," I say.

"Sis," he says. "Get those coins some place safer than Billy's house."

FELIX

MAX FLIES UP THE STEPS of Janet's house and through the front door, tracking wet paw prints over the floor boards. He spins around three times before coming to heel by my side. I am not thrilled by the mess he has made, but I am happy to see him so happy. Some of our earthside adventures bring out more of his protective side than his playful side. But not this one. Haven't seen him this puppy-like since… well, since Mila.

I wave at Tora as she stands in the driveway across the road. But she doesn't see me. She is on a phone call. Although our time together thus far has been brief, I am already fond of her. She is likable. Not something I can necessarily say about all of the people I am assigned to on my various missions. I am thankful that my Commander always graces me with love for them all. But liking them? That He seems to leave up to me. And this person, this Tora Dahlgard, I not only love but I like.

Clearly Max has reached the same conclusion.

"Okay, buddy, you've greeted the neighbor and had a good romp, but now we need to get down to work," I say, giving his head a good rub. "Our landlord is expecting us to hold up our end of the bargain."

He trots over to the corner of the kitchen and grabs the handle of my tool kit between his teeth. His neck muscles ripple under the effort of carrying it to me.

"Good boy," I say as he carefully sets it at my feet. "Now, where to start?"

I turn in a circle, surveying the multiple places I could begin my work. A list on the refrigerator door catches my attention. I walk over to read it. In neat hand printed letters, twenty-two tasks are enumerated. Number one on the list, the front door. Number two, the ceiling leak.

"Let's get this door set straight and planed so we can come and go without further destroying the floor. Then let's get that ceiling fixed so we can stop listening to that bucket fill up with drips and drops. What do you think?"

Max gives a quiet harrumph in approval, and we begin our day.

Over the course of my long existence, I have picked up many skills. It is satisfying to put some of them to the test again. I can already see a few things that may require some larger implements than what I have, and I wonder if perhaps Billy or Tora's Uncle Einar might have some that I can borrow. I enjoy getting to play with new technology as it unfolds and I have opportunity. I hum old hymns and melodies as I work, and Max curls up contentedly on a sun-filled spot on the kitchen rug.

My mind slips back to my time with my father and his friend Jaspar. I shake my head and smile at the continual unfolding of revelation I receive as I ride the clouds between the realms. Just when I think I know the whole story, there is more to know.

Father knew it was time for me to hear this chapter of the family legacy. He knew it was time for me to meet this man who quite literally saved my life in ways I never understood. My mother, Lydia, had told me of our flight from Judea to Egypt when I was a young child. She told of the night my father came to her and pleaded with her to go.

We lived on the outskirts of Bethlehem at the time. Just my mother and me. She had been banished from her family when she became pregnant with me, the child of a non-Jew—a Roman soldier. Her parents served in the household of my father's father who was a Roman prefect. They were loyal and hard-working servants, but they lived with strict boundaries between their way of life dictated by their faith and that of their employers—my paternal grandparents. When those boundaries could not inhibit the growing attraction between my father Magnus and my mother Lydia, both sets of parents threw up all kinds of obstacles to keep them apart. But love has a powerful way of overcoming most any obstacle, and one day I was conceived.

Forbidden to marry by both sets of parents, Lydia was sent away and Magnus was heartbroken. Determined to care for her still, he tracked her down and gave her as much money and resources as he could scrounge from his pay as a royal guard in the service of King Herod. They both counted it fortunate that the small apartment she found to live in was right next door to a young couple with a young child of their own. A couple who was not only non-judgmental about her circumstances, but downright helpful and kind.

For several years, this arrangement worked as well as such arrangements can work. My mother made money as a laundress and my father visited as often as was safe for him to do so. And then came the night of the great distress. The night Father ripped open the door and begged her to flee.

"Where, Magnus? Where can we go? Will you come with us?" Mother had pleaded.

"I cannot come. I have my duties. But you must go, my love. Trust me. You and Felix must flee."

"But for how long? How will we live?"

I was but a child of two at the time, but I remember the moment as I stared at them from my bed only a few feet from where they stood. I remember her weeping and maybe, although this is less clear, maybe I remember the tears of my father as well. Certainly, I remember the feeling of utter distress.

"You must go, Lydia. You cannot stay here! I cannot tell you the details lest I lose my head as well, but trust me when I say it is very, very dangerous for you to remain here. You must leave Bethlehem. You and the child."

"Magnus, I don't understand. You are asking the impossible. I have no extra money. You know I live day to day. Meal to meal. We cannot just flee."

Then Father had reached inside his tunic and drawn out a leather pouch.

"Do not worry about the money," my father had said. "Take this."

He set the pouch into my mother's hands. She opened it and her other hand flew to her mouth.

"Magnus! Where did you…? How did you…? Did you steal this?"

"No, I did not steal it. It is a gift," he said.

"From who?" she asked, her eyes swimming with tears and questions.

"From the man who confirmed to me that which I have suspected may be coming. Herod is angry beyond anything I have ever seen before. What he is about to do… I only wish I could save more. That is all I can tell you," he said. "Just take it. Take it and go and live."

"But, how will I carry Felix? And our things? And I am just a woman by myself. You want me to walk these roads alone? You of all people know that is not safe."

Then a knock came at our door. Mother was frightened but Father assured her.

"You will not be alone," he had said, opening the door.

"Are they ready to go? Mary and I and the child are all set. We must leave soon."

I recognized the voice of our neighbor.

"Just a few minutes, Joseph. Let Lydia pack a bag and some supplies. I promise we will be quick."

THIS PART OF THE STORY I KNEW and the part that followed in Bethlehem. The horrific slaughtering of all boys aged two and under in the city of David and its vicinity. King Herod had heard from some visiting dignitaries from the east that a new king had been born in that area during that time. One they called The King of the Jews—the very title Herod himself carried. He was determined that no one would threaten his reign.

I only learned of the part my father played in this tragedy hours before his death when he could bear to keep it from me no longer. This was the duty that haunted him. This was the commission that sifted his soul. It had changed him irrevocably on an internal level, though he remained in the service of Rome for the rest of his natural days.

But until my visit with Jaspar, I did not know the rest of the story.

It was he who had given the gift.

Jaspar was a man also in service to a king—a foreign king in a foreign land. Learned in the ways of mathematics, alchemy, astrology, and medicine, Jaspar was an advisor to his king. He was a trusted man. A wise man sent on a mission to find the one the stars foretold was to be born the King of the Jews. And so, he went. He and a company of wise men journeyed from their home in a royal city in a far-off land, to the royal city of David in the land of Judea.

There they found the child, and they worshipped him, offering gifts of costly frankincense, myrrh, and gold. And then, being warned of Herod's true motivations, who they had consulted on their approach to Bethlehem, they left Judea without consulting him further.

But as they were leaving, they passed a royal check point in the road just beyond Herod's palace. It was there that the paths of Jaspar and my father passed ever so briefly, yet with such lasting impact.

"Are you not the men sent from the east?" my father had asked Jaspar, the one who rode at the head of the delegation on a marvelous Arabian steed.

"We are," Jaspar had replied.

"And do you seek to leave without permission from the King?"

"We have permission from The King."

My father had smiled in the replaying of this scene. For at that time, he had not known which king Jaspar was referring to. It was the truth. But a truth from a higher authority than the one under which my father abided back then.

"Then you may pass," Father had replied.

Jaspar and his horse had not moved even after his colleagues behind him were well past him and out of sight of the check point.

"Will you not follow them?" Father had said.

"I recognize you," Jaspar had replied. "You are the one who has a child with mother next to the home of the carpenter and his family, yes?"

My father had stepped back and stared at the foreign dignitary.

"How do you know me?"

"I saw you when we came to see the carpenter's son. The one who plays with your son. Is his name Felix?"

"What do you want from me?"

Even in the re-telling in the place outside of time, both my father and Jaspar's eyes had filled with memories. The horrific scene that had played out due to the evil in one man's heart, still reverberated in their souls.

"I can never forget the look in your eyes as you warned me of what was to come, my friend," Father had said in our recent visit. "You were so sad and so angry and so kind all at the same time. If I had not seen your eyes, I might never have accepted your gift."

Jaspar had placed his hand on Father's arm and nodded.

"I know. It was perhaps more than what I was supposed to do and less than what I was supposed to do but I had to do something. When Joseph told me of his dream of the angel telling him to take Mary and Yeshua away from Judea to Egypt, I asked if he would be willing to take one more. Two, actually. Just the neighbor and her son."

"Joseph was a generous and courageous man," I had commented to the two older men. "I will never forget the years I spent in Egypt with him and his family. With Yeshua. Though I knew him not for who he was at the time. He was simply my friend."

"Ah, but what a friend, eh?" Jaspar had commented.

And we three had smiled, relieved to know the fullness of the redemption story. Relieved to be in a realm where our only duty was to fulfill the commissions given by the One who so loved the world, He gave His only son.

"We would not be here if you had not given this family such a blessing," Father had said. "And Felix would not be seeing what he is seeing in Solbakken. True?"

Then the two of them had sat back and looked at me with beautiful love and complete satisfaction.

"Yes, as a man much wiser than myself once said, when we choose life, the blessing continues for a thousand generations," Jaspar had concluded.

"And, if my counting is correct," Father had added, "that blessing still has many generations to go."

TORA

THE 4RUNNER'S REAR END is packed to capacity with garbage bags to the point that I cannot see out the back. Thank goodness for cameras and mirrors. I've even filled the passenger seat with smaller boxes and grocery bags packed with detritus. I am headed to the county landfill down by Bemidji, and I need to get a move on because, after that errand, I have an appointment with Sheriff Dumfrey.

After my conversation with Clayton, I had hastily loaded my rig and headed down the road to Billy's place. He and Carin listened intently to all I'd learned from Clay. Words like grading, authentication, attribution, and encapsulation followed by something called slabbing, were all part of the long string of sentences that flew from my brother's mouth so quickly, I struggled to assimilate them. But what I knew beyond a shadow of a doubt was my brother was beside himself with excitement. Even with only the pictures I'd sent him last night, he was quite sure we had uncovered something important. Far more important than an old beer bottle.

When I'd asked him to speculate about possible value, he had hesitated to give me solid figures but did say if even one of the coins was what he thought it might be, we were talking about tens of thousands of dollars and possibly more. The look on Billy's face when I told him that was priceless. He'd gone to his safe and grabbed the two bags handing them to me like they were contraband narcotics.

"Glad I didn't know any of this last night," he had said. "Might not have slept a wink."

The treasure is now stowed safely in the glove box wrapped tightly in plastic grocery bags to conceal and protect. I am quite sure I won't be stopped along the way by highway robbers and, even if I am, they'd probably take one look at the mountain of junk in my trunk and run the other direction long before they got around to digging in the glove compartment. It's funny what one worries about when one is carrying hidden treasure. Makes me almost empathetic to drug runners. Almost.

I have just passed through Blackduck when my phone rings. My son Brian's name pops up on the screen.

"Hello, son," I say, pleased with how easily I am able to answer the call.

"Hey, Mom," Brian replies. "How's it going? I hear you are on a mission up at the farm."

"Yes, indeed, I am."

"What a trip. Can't imagine why anyone would want to rip through that old place."

I don't say anything.

"Mom? You still there?"

"Yup, still here. On my way to the landfill to dump a bunch of junk, and then headed to the sheriff's office for a little meeting."

"They got a suspect or a lead or something?"

"Not that I know of. I will ask though."

"Then why you going?"

"I, uh, have some evidence to give him," I say.

"Cool. Just like on TV," he says.

"Something like that alright. Everything okay with you? How's the job going?"

"Yeah, it's all good. Starting to go into the office a couple of times a week now. Glad to have some human interaction again even if it is with a bunch of tech geeks."

I laugh, knowing how difficult it has been at times for my gregarious son to fit in with the less gregarious nature of some of his colleagues. Many of them had told Brian that one of the biggest benefits of the pandemic for them was being able to work from home and not have to see another person for days on end if they did not want to.

"So, you just calling to check up on me?" I ask.

"Sort of," he says. "Sort of not."

"Well, that's mysterious. Pray tell, what's going on? I have enough mystery on my hands right now without getting more from you."

There is a long pause.

"Brian?"

"It's about Mariah," he says at last.

My mother senses begin to tingle.

"What about Mariah?"

"I think she could use your help. But she's afraid to ask."

"What kind of help?"

"The kind a mom is especially good at. But that's all I'm gonna say. You've got to call her yourself, and she has to tell you herself. She will kill me if she finds out I am making this call."

"Okay…" I say as all types of scenarios run through my mind as to what might be up with my daughter—none of them good. "Is it something that can wait or is it something I need to do right away?"

"I'd say the sooner the better. And then I'm pleading the fifth."

"Okay, okay. I will stop prying," I say. "Thanks for the heads up. Appreciate it."

"Just doing my duty," he says. "Sorry I can't be there to give you a hand with the clean-up. Probably pretty interesting to go through some of those things now that you have to."

"Oh, that is for darn sure," I say before I can stop myself.

"Wait. Did you find something totally lit?"

"What do you mean 'lit'?"

"You know, dope, sick, rad, awesome."

I don't respond.

"Mother? What are you keeping from me?"

My fingertips fidget on the steering wheel.

"I will let you know when I have more information. I promise. But for now, let's just say we found something unexpected."

I need to get him off the call so I can call his sister. It has been a long time since Mariah has needed me for anything. Not since she was pregnant with Hazel and was so sick….

"Mom! What? Come on," my son says, interrupting my revelatory train of thought.

"Nope, I'm pleading the fifth too. Listen, I'd better go if I'm going to call Mariah before I get to Bemidji."

"Alright, alright. But promise you will give me the whole scoop. And, promise not to let her know I snitched on her."

"I promise. Love you. Shalom, shalom, my son."

"Shalom, Mom."

BEFORE DIALING MY DAUGHTER, I PRAY.

"If the issue she is having is the issue I hope she is having, please let her be willing to let me help. Amen."

I take a deep breath.

"Call Mariah," I command my vehicle.

The phone begins to ring.

Once, twice, three times.

Maybe I will just have to leave a message. But what message?

"Hi, I hear you are having problems… Hi, this is Mom, are you pregnant?"

If she doesn't answer, I will hang up and let her call me back.

"Hello, Tora? It's Isaac."

"Oh, hello, son," I say. For years, I have told him he can call me Mom or Mother but he has landed on Tora. At least it's better than Mrs. Dahlgard. "Is your wife around?"

"Uh, she's, uh… indisposed at the moment. Anything I can help you with or can I have her call you back?"

"Have her give me a call when she has a chance. Tell her it's not an emergency or anything. Just checking in."

"Okay. I will let her know."

Just then I hear Mariah's voice in the background.

"Who is it?" she says.

"It's your mom," Isaac replies, his hand obviously muffling the microphone.

"Hey, Mother. How's it going?" Mariah says when she gets on the call.

"Oh, good. On my way to Bemidji to drop a load of garbage at the landfill. Then I have a meeting with the sheriff."

"Okay. How long are you going to be up north?"

"Don't know for sure. Still lots to do. So, I imagine it will be at least a week."

We have a moment of silence.

"Is there a reason you called?" she asks.

"Not really. Just … you know. Seeing how you are…"

I hear a deep sigh on the other end of the line.

"Did Brian call you?"

"He may have," I confess. "Are you okay?"

The quiet simmers.

"Well, that is the last time I ask him to keep a secret," she mutters.

"He didn't want to tell me anything. And honestly, I don't really know anything except that you are hurting in some way and that he thought I might possibly be the one best suited to help you out. That's all."

I turn onto the road that leads to the landfill. Only five more miles to go. Probably not long enough to have this conversation. I search for a wide area on the shoulder of the road and pull over.

She has not spoken but, she has not hung up.

"Mariah, sweetie, I'm just gonna ask. Are you pregnant?"

Two semi-trucks with trailers full of refuse rumble by. Chunks of Styrofoam blow out from the opening of one and distribute themselves onto the road, the ditch, and a few tree branches.

"Yes," she says in a strangled voice.

"That's wonderful. It's really, really wonderful," I say, trying to control my excitement. "How far along are you? Do you know?"

"About eighteen weeks," she says, blowing her nose.

"Hey, wow, that's so much further… I mean, that's… that's great. How are you feeling?"

"I am feeling scared and sick and tired and I don't even know… Haven't managed to get too excited or hopeful yet. Maybe once we get past the twenty weeks mark. Maybe then…"

"That's understandable. And that's okay. One day at a time. That's all you can do," I say. "What about physically? How's that going?"

"Some days, well, actually, some hours of some days I'm fine. And then other times… I can't even keep water down." I hear her tears flowing, if such a thing is possible.

I inhale deeply before venturing my next question.

"How can I help?"

She does not answer.

“Whatever you need, honey,” I add. “I know how sick you got when you were pregnant with Hazel. And I know having her to care for now only makes things even more challenging.”

“Isaac is caring for her just fine, Mother.”

“I did not mean to imply that he wasn’t. But he has a full-time job, too, and I know he said it has not been easy to keep her… you know… occupied.”

“Gee, Mom, maybe just get vaccinated and we can have this conversation again. Maybe that’s what you can do to help me.”

Here we go again. My chest begins to burn and my eyes sting. “Sweetie, I will get tested if that would help but you know how Dad and I feel about the vaccination.”

“Really? Your stupid misinformed opinions about this are going to keep you from helping your daughter, and your granddaughter, and maybe your next grandchild? Really, Mother? You know what… just forget it. I can’t handle one more thing right now. Certainly not this. Thanks for the call… I guess. Goodbye.”

The call ends. My tears begin to flow.

TORA

"MRS. DAHLGARD, NICE TO SEE YOU AGAIN," Sheriff Reggie Dumfrey says, shaking my hand as I enter his office. "Did my deputy offer you some coffee or water?"

"She did. Thank you. I'm good," I reply.

"Take a seat," he says, indicating the chair opposite his large oak desk.

The lawman's uniform is crisp and laden with various stripes and patches. His arms and chest stretch the fabric to its fullest capacity, making me think what most folks intent on messing with him must think—not a good idea.

"How is the clean-up going at Uncle Einar's place?"

"Well, I just dropped an SUV full of garbage at the landfill, and I can now see the floor in a couple of rooms. So, it's going."

"Glad to hear it. Get that door fixed then?"

"Yes, Billy, and my new neighbor, Felix, got it all squared away that very night. So, I am snug as a bug in a rug. A very messy rug but nonetheless…"

He smiles.

"Yeah, heard about your new neighbor. Seem like a good guy, ya think?"

"As far as I can tell, yes. He's been very helpful and I like his dog."

"You can tell a lot about a fellow by his dog, I always say."

I nod.

"So, how can I help you? Like I told you on the phone, we don't have any leads yet on the stolen goods. Have feelers out to all the pawn shops in the area, but nothing has come up so far. Not sure it will, but we can hope," he says, eyeing his computer screen and then returning his full attention to me.

I open the tote bag on my lap and draw out the plastic wrapped package bearing the gold coins.

"We wanted you to be aware of something we discovered while digging through my uncle's tool chest," I say, unwrapping the outer camouflage from the bags of gold. "Just to be clear, we have no idea where these came from or how he got them. We are wondering if you might be able to help us find out if they were stolen or not. And, we are guessing that they might be the motivation behind the break-in."

Carefully, I place one bag on the sheriff's desk and pull out a handful of coins for him to see. He sits back in his office chair, swiveling from side to side, and lets out a long, low whistle.

"Well, I'll be jiggered," he says before scooting forward to pick up a few coins.

He bounces them in his hand, weighing them.

"Solid," he says, holding one after the other up to the light. "Are they real gold you think?"

"My brother Clayton happens to be quite the scholar in antiquities. Works as a curator for a large museum in London. I sent him pictures of the coins last night. He is speculating that they may be quite valuable. So much so that he urged me to get them someplace safer than my cousin Billy's home safe."

"How many of these did you find?"

I pull out the other bag and set it next to the one already on the desk. His eyes pop wide open.

"There's over a hundred coins total," I say. "Clayton thinks they are mainly from the time of the Roman empire with some from various periods before and after. We sent him some more pictures this morning. He is making some discreet inquiries."

Sheriff Dumfrey hands the coins back to me and turns back to his computer.

"I can make some of those kinds of inquiries too," he says, typing quickly on his keyboard. "See if there's been any reports of big antiquities robberies—though I'm sure your brother probably has more of an ear to the ground in this area than I do. How long do you suppose he's had them? Any idea?"

"Not really," I reply. "Probably quite some time. We—Billy, his wife, my husband, my brother and myself—have been sort of reconstructing our memories of Uncle Einar's life. He never lived extravagantly. But he was always very generous with the family. And I mean generous. I can tell you some stories some time when you have a minute. We wondered about that at times, but none of us ever truly knew the extent to which he had subsidized so many of our lives until after he was gone and we compared notes. We all just thought he'd made some good investments or something. He had a good career as an engineer with GE without ever getting married or having any kids. My dad always said Einar was not lucky in love but he was lucky with money."

"Hmm," the sheriff says, scrolling up and down on his computer screen. "Well, I can do some research for you and get back to you." He sits back into his chair and looks me full in the eye. "You think your uncle could have stolen these from somewhere in his travels?"

I shrug.

"Let me give my friend Jerry Nelson over at First National Bank a call," he says. "He's the president. Totally trustworthy guy. Think we'd all be more comfortable having this treasure stashed away someplace real secure. Would that be okay?"

"Yes, of course," I say, feeling a pressure lift from my chest.

His phone begins to buzz in its place on his desk. He flips it over to check it but doesn't answer.

"If you need to take that, go ahead," I say. "I should be getting back to my excavation anyway."

"Oh, no," he replies. "Just my daughter. I'm sure she's reminding me about my grandson's birthday party tonight."

Inexplicably, I burst into tears.

"Mrs. Dahlgard, what's going on? Did I say something wrong?"

I shake my head and choke out, "No… I'm just… I'm okay."

A silly thing to say when it is clearly not the truth. I am mortified at my outburst.

"Listen, you don't have to be embarrassed. I hear all kinds of sticky situations in my line of work. Not much you can say that might shock me. Guaranteed," he says. "Why don't you tell me what's going on?"

He hands me a tissue. I rein in my tears before explaining the conversation I have just had with my daughter. He listens and nods all the way to the end.

"Well, tell ya what," he says. "You're not the first parent I've had this sort of conversation with over the past months. Lots of strain on families nowadays. I'm sure your daughter is feeling it too. Everybody is pretty much doing the best they can but not everybody agrees on what that best should look like."

"Yes, that is true. Sorry to be so dramatic," I say, blowing my nose. "Sometimes I am at the end of my rope and I don't know how to go forward. I have been so used to being able to fix things for my kids all their lives… And I don't know how to fix this."

He takes a pen and writes something on a sticky note.

"Here. This is the number of my friend Pastor Mel Strickland up at River of Life Fellowship in St. Gerard. I've known her most of my life. She's got some of the best listening ears I know. Plus, she's a lot wiser about relationship issues than I am. Give her a call. Have a cup of coffee. I think it might help."

I accept the note and tuck it into the zipper pocket of my tote bag.

"Right now," he continues, "let's get Jerry on the horn and see if we can't get these coins into a safety deposit box over at the bank still this afternoon. Sound good?"

I nod.

It does sound good to have something in my life secured.

FELIX

EINAR'S SKILL SAW SLICES THROUGH the 2 x 4's like butter. I enjoy the sheer power of the device and cut a few more boards than I actually need just for the pleasure of the experience. I am thankful Tora has let me borrow it.

The garage is chilly but sheltered from the February wind that has begun to blow this morning. Mud puddles are everywhere on the roads, lawns, and driveways. The snow we received a few nights ago will soon be gone along with much of what was underneath it if these temperatures keep up. But I am guessing they won't. From what I have read and heard, Minnesota spring times can make an appearance anywhere from March until May.

Max is inside with Tora. She has placed a thick rug by the kitchen door for him, and repurposed a metal bowl for a water dish on his behalf. He has made himself at home. Between my cutting in the garage, I can hear her whistling to herself as she works. I'm sure Max is loving that as well.

I take my boards out to the truck that I have backed up to the garage door, and stack them into the pickup's long bed. Wiping the sawdust from my hands, vest, and pants, I return to the saw, unplug it, and set the canvas tarp back over it. Then I sit on the short flight of stairs leading up to the back door inside the garage and remove my wet boots. Time to go retrieve my dog and get back to the house across the road.

"Tora," I call through the door. "Okay if I come in?"

"Yes, yes," she hollers from the front room. "I will be right there."

Max lifts his eyelids to look at me when I enter the kitchen, but doesn't make a move from his sprawled position on his back.

"You are going to have to come home with me at some point, you know," I say to my faithful companion who seems to have switched his loyalties quite quickly.

Tora laughs as she comes through the door.

"This guy sure knows how to relax," she says.

"Sorry about that," I say. "He's not exactly a small presence."

"Oh, not to worry. I quite like having his company," she says, bending down to scratch his belly. My dog's eyes roll back in his head.

"How did it go out there?" Tora asks.

"Got everything done I needed to get done plus a little bit more."

"Excellent. Uncle would be pleased to know his tools are being used again. Can I get you a cup of coffee before you head back? I bought the real deal yesterday when I was in Bemidji and brewed up a big pot this morning. And I still have a few of those cookies left."

She is already moving toward the mugs that hang on a rack beside the stove before I can answer. I am glad to stay for I know my real work is here with this gentle, searching soul.

"Sure. Sounds great. A little warm up will do me good. Besides, my dog does not seem in much of a hurry to leave."

"Milk or sugar?" Tora offers.

"Just black, thanks."

We take our coffee and sweets and sit at the round table in the kitchen. I can see that the dining room floor has begun to emerge from its blanket of detritus, but the table and chairs are still stacked with papers.

"Are you making some sense of all the emptied files and drawers?" I ask.

"Yes, I am slowly picking through and organizing what needs to stay and what needs to go."

"I will be making a run to the landfill over by Blackduck tomorrow if you have some more bags that need to go by then."

"Oh, gosh. I don't want to bother you."

"Not a bother," I reply, taking a sip from the steaming mug. Her home brew is as stout as any I have tasted in quite some time. Just the way I like it. "Happy to do it."

"Okay then. I will stack some things on the front porch to-night before I go to bed. And you can come in and take what you can whenever you're ready to go. I can give you some cash today, or you can let me know how much it costs when you get back, and I will reimburse you. I took a big load to Bemidji yesterday before meeting with the sheriff, and it was only about twenty dollars."

"Good deal. I'll let you know when I get back."

We sip in silence, the whir of the air pushing up through the floor vents the only sound in the room save for Max's snores and sputters.

I am curious to hear about her conversation with the sheriff, but I don't want to appear too eager to hear about the coins. They are not my main focus. It is not the first time I have seen them appear. In fact, it's about the tenth or eleventh time I've run across them in my travels, though each time the number and variety varies depending upon the one who has held them for a time. About the only surprising thing to me this time is how many Einar has managed to keep and multiply. Without knowing him at all, I know him simply by this one aspect of his life.

"So, tell me a little bit about yourself, Felix," Tora says. "Do you have any family around here?"

"Some distant relatives," I reply. "But no one I've ever spent any time with before."

"Interesting. Where did you grow up? I know your dad was in the military so maybe you've been all over."

"I have spent time in a lot of different places. That's for sure."

"No wife or kids though?"

I look down into the dark liquid in my cup and sigh. I always hate this question.

"Not currently, no," I reply.

"Oh, sorry, don't mean to pry," she says. "You just seem like such a nice young man and I just thought… well, it's really none of my business."

I smile at her discomfort and try to put her at ease.

"It's just a very long story," I say. "Maybe I'll tell you one day when we have more time."

"Okay. Yes, I'd like that."

"You have a couple of kids, don't you?" I ask, turning the spotlight in her direction.

"Yes, my husband Peter and I have a son, Brian, who is thirty-years-old and lives in California, and a daughter, Mariah, who is thirty-four who lives down by The Cities with her husband Isaac and their daughter Hazel, who is four-and-a-half."

"That half year is important at that age."

She smiles.

"Oh, yes. And if you get a chance to meet her, you will find that she is four-and-a-half going on sixteen-and-a-half."

"I hope I do get that chance."

I see the sheen that develops on Tora's eyes before she can hide her emotions from me, so I steer the conversation elsewhere.

"What do you do for work or fun?" I ask.

She explains to me about Peter's law practice and her various volunteer projects along with her hobbies, but nothing seems to ignite the same sort of passion I saw in her eyes when she described her family.

"Do you have any dreams?" I ask.

She sits back in her chair with one eyebrow raised. I hope I haven't offended her.

"Well, that's interesting you should ask," she says. "I had the most vivid dream just last night. More real than any I have had since I was a child."

"Really?" I say, not wanting to deter her from telling me about it, though I wasn't exactly asking about a nighttime type of dream. "Anything you want to share? I find dreams fascinating."

Her eyes drift off to a place of memories. She begins to tell me about her Grandpa Axel and the story of the big wind. I sit back in my chair and absorb her tale. She is articulate and engaging beyond what I think she gives herself credit for.

"So, did your grandpa and Thomas remain friends? Do you know?" I ask when her story winds down.

"They did, I believe, though I never met Mr. Everwind. He died sometime before I was born. But I remember my dad talking about his son Joseph who served in the army with my Uncle Einar. They were in Italy together near the end of the Second World War."

"Interesting. Did you ever meet him?"

"No, sadly. He was killed in action near the end of the war. Uncle never really talked about his time over there. But my dad told us a story or two that he managed to extract from his brother. And when we were on our long summer road trips, he'd pull one out to keep us from squabbling with one another… mainly me, squabbling with Clay. Andy was too mature to even be bothered by me."

"Did your father serve in the war too?"

"He did very briefly near the end of the war in the Pacific. Mother said he was going to be a part of the big push on Tokyo but then, well, Truman dropped the bombs… And you know how all that ended. So, he came home without having seen any real action. But he had enough creditability with Uncle to at least get him to talk about his experiences in Italy. I wish I knew more, ya know. Einar was such a private man."

She sips from her mug and then sighs.

"It is strange how little we know one another, isn't it?" she says. "My Tante Tilda has sometimes mentioned to me how different Einar was when he came home from the war. They were quite close as kids. And she was so excited to have him home but… well, it was as if part of him never fully came home. He didn't hang around here very long. Think Grandpa tried to keep him busy on the farm for a while. But that didn't really work and then he just disappeared. Got work as an engineer in various places all over the country. He didn't come back here for a long time. He was always sort of our mystery uncle. My brothers were convinced he worked for the CIA," she concludes with a laugh.

I run my hands through my sawdust filled hair, sending flakes of it onto the floor. "Oops, I'll clean that up," I say, standing to my feet. "Got a broom around here?"

"Oh, goodness. Don't worry about it. It only adds to the décor," she says, spreading her arms out and smiling.

"Okay, well, thanks for the coffee and cookies. Sure appreciate the use of the saw, too, not to mention the dog watching," I say. "Max, buddy. Time to go."

He stands and stretches his paws out front, his rear end up in the air.

"You can come back any time," Tora says as Max walks to her and places his big old head in her lap.

I can see the comfort he brings her. Once again, I am thankful for his partnership in my mission.

“Say, Tora,” I add. “Have you asked Tilda about the coins? If she and Einar were close like you say, maybe she knows things you don’t. Might be worth a conversation.”

“You know, I was thinking about that on my way home yesterday. Her memory is a bit suspect these days but it’s usually pretty accurate the further back you go. Maybe I will.”

Max and I walk to the garage door with Tora trailing behind us. Before we head out, I turn and say, “For what it’s worth, it’s been my experience that asking the older generation about their lives is always enlightening. Never know what you might find out.”

MAXIMUS

THE RUG IS KINDNESS.
The water dish is sweetness.
Her home—her grandparents' home —is full.
But her whistle is sad.

I like the smell of coffee, family, and gatherings that rise from the floors and echo from the walls.

She talks of mess, garbage, chaos.

But I feel the order, the love, the commitment beneath it.

I have seen chaos before. I have marched through madness. I have smelled despair.

This is not that.

What she wrestles with is something else.

Maybe not as dangerous but just as deadly.

It is the thing I see humans suffer so often.

No other animal seems so confused.

We know who we are, why we are, who we serve.

But these humans…

I hope this is why we have come.

It probably is.

To help her see, to know, to discover.

The coins are not the treasure.

She is the treasure.

TORA

THE WOLVES AND COYOTES are quiet tonight. As is my phone. Haven't heard back from London yet, and not a peep from Mariah or Brian. Not that I really expect any communication from them. I talked with my husband earlier and told him all about the chats with our children. He was equal parts angry, sad, and excited. But he has gone to bed hours ago, and I am left with my ponderings and wonderings in this quiet, empty house in the woods.

Maybe Cousin Katie is still up. She's a bit of a night owl. Maybe I should fill her in on everything before she hears about it through the family grapevine. Maybe I should check with her before I go and visit her mom. Maybe I should ask how her sister Debbie is doing. Maybe I don't want to know. Maybe she's in rehab again. Maybe she's not.

"You awake?" I text my younger cousin.

I leave my phone on the nightstand and make one last trip to the bathroom.

"Yes, I'm up. What's up?" I see her reply as soon as I get back to the bedroom.

"Well, much to tell. Probably better done with a phone call but I'm up at the farm and you know how that goes."

Laughing emojis fill my screen and explode.

She knows.

"Give me the outline," she says.

And I do.

As briefly and concisely as possible, I tell her the story.

Her responses are one perfect emoji after another.

She is clearly more versed in this language than I.

"Um, wow!" she texts when I have finished. "Do you need me to come up? Can't do it this week but maybe next. Need to see my mom soon anyway. Let me know."

"Okay. Will probably be done with the clean up by then but would love to see you," I reply. I hesitate and then add, "How's Deb?"

No quick response. No emoji.

Not good.

"Not sure. Haven't heard from her in a few months," her next text reads.

"Sorry. Will keep praying."

"Thanks."

"Of course. Always have you guys in my heart. Are you okay if I visit your mom tomorrow?"

I haven't seen my auntie in person in over two years due to the pandemic. Katie has tried to keep visitors to a minimum to protect her mother. So, we have abided by those boundaries up until now, and I am prepared to honor them still if she says no.

"Yes, go ahead," her reply comes quickly. "She's been complaining so much about all this isolation and since the CDC numbers are so much better, we have decided to loosen the protocols. Have to weigh which is worse—the virus or being bored to death. Just be prepared to hear the same story about five or six times and answer the same questions at least that many times. She will love it."

"Okay. Appreciate that. Love ya. Will chat soon."

Hearts fill my screen and then all is quiet. Again.

I plug my phone into the charger and lay it face down on the bedside table. Just as I am about to turn out the lights, it pings. Thinking it is Katie with one more caveat about visiting her mother, I flip it back over.

It is not Katie.

It is Mariah.

My stomach clenches as I open the text.

"Hey, sorry about today. Very hormonal right now," her text reads.

I let out the breath I did not know I was holding.

"Understandable. Sorry for prying."

"You'd know soon enough anyways."

"Love you and yours. Shalom, sweetheart."

"Shalom, shalom," comes her immediate response.

The ball in my gut unwinds. I return the phone to its previous position and turn out the lights. This is something my daughter and I have learned to practice over the past tumultuous months more than any other time in our lives – apologies.

The wind has stopped blowing outside and I close my eyes and settle into the silence. Images of the people I love scroll through my mind's eye, and I pray for them one by one. My children and grandchildren. My husband and brothers. My nieces and nephews. My auntie and cousins. My new neighbor… and his dog. My heart is full of the goodness, the pain, and the complexities of love.

My breathing slows and sleep welcomes me.

ONCE AGAIN, I FIND MYSELF SEATED next to Grandpa under the big tree. A dog is curled up on the ground with his head laying on my feet and his eyes searching my face.

"Hello, Max," I say, reaching down to pet his head.

His short stub of a tail wriggles wildly.

"Who's this, my Tora-bird? A new friend?" Grandpa asks.

"Oh, don't you know Max? He lives across the road. He is our neighbor."

Grandpa Axel extends his hand to Max's great, boxy head. The dog sniffs, and then begins to lick it.

"I think he likes you," I say.

"Good. Probably not a good thing to not be liked by this guy."

I laugh.

"Oh, Grandpa, don't be silly. Max would never hurt a fly," I say, continuing to pet the burly, muscled beast.

"Hmm, I wouldn't be so sure of that," Grandpa says.

Just then a leaf from far, far above us flutters out into the sky.

Max sits up, his head scanning back and forth following the path of the descending foliage. As it comes ever closer, he leaps from his place and jumps up to grab it in his mouth. Then he circles around and delivers the leaf gently onto my lap.

"Good boy," I say, patting his head and lifting his gift up by its stem.

"Now, that's an old one," Grandpa says, bending down to take a look at the leaf. "Don't think I have ever seen this one before."

"Really?" I say. "I thought you'd seen them all by now."

He laughs. "Oh, Tora-bird. I may have sat beneath this tree for time and eternity, but there is much I do not know. How about we discover what this leaf holds together? Would you like that?"

I nod vigorously and Max seems to do the same.

Carefully, Grandpa takes the leaf from my hand and as he does, it transforms into a book. The cover is fine leather with golden words etched onto the spine.

"What's this one called, Grandpa?"

He turns the book onto its side and reads, "*Becoming a Soldier.*"

I nestle into his side as he opens the cover and flattens the first pages.

Max resumes his place by my feet and rests his head in my lap.

He is ready to listen too.

FELIX

"**YOU CLUMSY OAF!** Look what you've done."

The back of his hand met the back of my head.

"Take them back to the water and rinse them off," he commanded.

I bent down to pick up the basket and the fish that I had dropped onto the powdery sand on the road. My puppy, Maximus, already had one of them in his mouth and was prancing proudly about.

"Max, here," I hissed. "Bring it here."

I scrambled for him on my hands and knees.

But I was too late.

My step-father's foot landed in the ribs of my new dog, and sent him catapulting sideways. Max yelped and his fishy trophy flew at my head. I grabbed its slippery body and threw it into the basket as I jumped to my feet.

"Leave him be!" I yelled. "He has done nothing to harm you."

"He has caused you to trip and send part of our catch into the dirt! Why your mother ever allowed you to bring this beast into our home, I will never know."

Max scrambled to his feet. He shook his head as if clearing the cobwebs. Then he turned his sights onto the man who stood before me. All six feet and two-hundred pounds of him. Solid. Chiseled. Hard-working. Hard-headed. My step-father, Jonas.

"Maximus," I warned. "Max, no."

I could see in his eyes that the dog was intent upon protecting me. And though he was only six months old, he was sturdy and strong, and I had no doubt he would risk his own harm to keep me from harm.

Jonas turned to look at the source of the low rumble that was building in Max's chest.

"If that dog so much as pees on my foot, it will be the last thing he does. Do you hear me?"

"Papa, he is only a puppy," my younger brother Nathan piped up as he reached down and hefted Maximus up by the nape of his neck, lifting him clear up to shoulder level to keep his dangling feet from hitting the ground. The dog struggled for a moment but then calmed under Nathan's soothing voice. "He meant no harm. I will stay and help Felix clean up. We will be quick as a whistle."

He dropped Max onto the road and the puppy sprinted away from us back toward town as if fully aware of the threat that had been made against him.

"Max will beat us all home," Nathan said with a laugh.

He was the only one amused.

My step-father shook his head in disgust and stared at me. "You can't even give him a good Jewish name. No. You have to give him a Roman name. As if this family doesn't have enough problems with you in our midst."

He turned with the two large baskets of fish hanging off the end of the pole that draped over his shoulders. We had had a good day on the sea. The baskets were laden with fish, but he carried them as if they weighed nothing at all.

I had always admired his strength.

His heart? Not so much.

"Be quick about it. The sun will be down soon," he yelled back at us.

As if we needed reminding.

Mother and the girls would be preparing our Shabbat dinner. Jonas had pushed the very limits of how long we should have stayed on the water. So, Nathan and I would truly have to scramble to get home in time.

"Thank you," I said to my brother as we rinsed the fish in the sea.

"Two are better than one, yes?" he said with his usual equanimity.

"Yes, I am thankful for your help. But I am also thankful for your intervention with Max. Father is not fond of him."

"What else is new? Who do you know that he is fond of?"

A second ticked by.

"Agnes," we said in unison.

We shared a sardonic smile as we thought of the way our youngest sibling had somehow made her way into the impenetrable heart of her dad. We finished our task and hit the path to home.

Halfway back to town Nathan said to me, "You should leave, Felix. You hate fishing. You hate Father. You're a grown man. Why do you stay?"

This was not the first time my brother had challenged me with this line of thinking. He knew my answer. He knew why I stayed.

"I am old enough to protect mother," he said, as if reading my thoughts. "I may not be as big or strong as you, but I have a voice with Father that you do not. True?"

I did not answer.

"Of course, this is true," he answered his own question. "You are meant for bigger things, I think. For things beyond this little fishing village. And you know that Father will not leave this business to you… you know that, yes?"

I nodded. I knew that though he treated me like a son in front of the neighbors, behind closed doors he had made it abundantly clear that I would never, could never, be truly his son.

When he had first met my mother and me after our return from Egypt when I was five, he treated me with great kindness. And I was over-joyed to have a man in our lives. In fact, I was the one who talked Mother into marrying him. She had reservations. She could not name what they were, but she felt them. Yet, the prospect of having a husband, a home, a family, and a sense of respectability, outweighed the niggling of her gut.

They had married and we were happy. We were a family. I was his son.

Until Nathan was born.

Then I became only the step-son.

Jonas had an heir. Bone of his bone and flesh of his flesh.

I was extraneous. A spare.

From that point on it seems I could do nothing right. The back of his hand that I had felt that day was so familiar I could tell you where the blood vessels popped and each knuckle lay.

Not that I blamed Nathan. He was a good and kind brother. When he was born, I loved him immediately and that love had only grown as he had grown.

As I walked beside him on the road, I could see that what he said was true. He was no longer a gangly, skinny child. His fourteen-year-old frame was filling out nicely, and he was already as tall as his father.

If I left, it would not only be Mother that I would miss.

"Besides," Nathan continued with his lecture. "Ever since Yeshua and his family moved away, you don't even have any friends left around here. Again, I will ask. Why do you stay and put up with his constant demeaning, my brother?"

Our home on the edge of the village came into sight and standing by the front gate with her hands shielding the descending sun from her eyes, was our mother.

"Felix, Nathan! Come quickly!" she yelled. "You must wash and get ready. All is prepared."

Nathan reached out a hand and placed it on my shoulder as we picked up our pace.

"Yes, she would miss you," he said, a mischievous grin beginning to erupt. "But, look at me. I am everything a mother could dream of in a son."

He punched my shoulder and began to jog.

"Coming, Mother!" we both yelled.

IT WAS FIVE DAYS LATER. Early in the morning. Before work. The sun had not yet risen over the horizon. I don't even remember what started it, but Jonas and I had another row. And once again my head had felt the blow of his hand. But this time, his head had felt mine as well.

His enraged face told me everything I needed to know.

It was time for me to leave.

To Jonas's credit, he did not yell. He did not return my jab. He simply stared at me and walked out the door, grabbing the fishing baskets.

"Nathan, let's go, son," he said.

Mother was in tears. The girls cowered behind her.

Nathan, too, had tears in his eyes, but I also saw a look that said, "I told you so," playing just beneath the surface. He risked his father's wrath by stepping to me and embracing me. I returned his hug.

"Go, my brother. Be who you were meant to be. I will always love you," he whispered for my ears only. "And I will protect them."

"Nathan!" Jonas bellowed.

Mother tugged on his coat.

"You must go," she said, anguish and resignation written on her face. "I will not take the chance of losing two sons in one day."

She put her hand on my brother's cheek. "Go."

Nathan waited for me to nod that I had heard him. That I had understood. And then he sprinted out the door to catch up with Jonas and the rest of the fishermen making their way to their boats.

"Girls, clear the dishes and go fetch the water," Mother said to my two sisters, Agnes and Martha.

They obeyed but kept their eyes on me.

When Nathan was gone and Jonas far from ear shot, Martha said, "Where will you go, Felix?"

"Will you take Maximus?" Agnes added.

I hung my head, ashamed that my sisters should have been exposed to the violence between me and their father. They were only nine and eleven. Too young for such business and too old to forget it.

"Girls, do as I say," Mother ordered as she wrapped two loaves of bread and dried fish into a cloth.

"Please don't go," Agnes pleaded, running to wrap her arms around my waist.

My heart twisted.

Martha came and gently pulled her away.

"Our brother is a man now," she said with wisdom beyond her years. "We cannot ask him to stay."

Her lovely blue eyes met mine. Her full lips were tight, her cheeks flushed. She would be a beauty one day. I was sorry I wouldn't be there to see it.

Agnes let go of me, and Martha lead her out the door by the hand. But as they left, I heard Agnes ask, "Can we ask him to leave the puppy?"

I wondered where the puppy had gone. Hadn't seen him since the night before. Maybe I would just have to leave him behind. Maybe he would like that better anyway.

I went into the room I shared with Nathan and gathered my few belongings, shoving them into a rucksack. With one last look around the small space, I vowed to remember the goodness that resided there and not just the ugliness.

Mother entered, holding out the food she had gathered.

"Take this with you," she said. "Do you have a jug for water?"

I nodded.

"And here," she added, reaching into the folds of her apron and taking out a piece of parchment. "Here is where your father lives. He is a centurion in Capernaum now."

"How do you know this?" I asked, taking hold of the paper and staring at the address.

She put her finger under my chin and lifted my head until our eyes meet.

"Magnus loves you. He has always loved you. And he has always made a way for me to know where he is stationed because he has known this day would come," she said with a sad, aching smile. "The day when you would be better served to live as a Roman than as a Jew."

"But, how can I… will he… what will I do? I can't just stop being a Jew."

"No, this is true, but, that is not what is required of you. It will not be an easy road—to guard your heart while serving Caesar—but it can be done with the help of the Eternal."

I hung my head and sighed.

"You must go to your father in secret," she continued, "until he can outfit you with the things you will need. He will not be able to recognize you as his son in public… He and his wife have several others from what I have heard. But he will be able to give you a place, a station, a life. He can give you what I cannot. What Jonas will not."

I sank onto the bed with the address still in my hands. Was I simply going from one fire into another?

Mother sat beside me. Max ran into the room and leapt onto the bed where he knew he should not be. But neither of us shooed him off.

"Where have you been?" Mother said, stroking his soft coat. "You almost missed the boat."

"How can I take him with me?"

"He will be a good companion, my son. You will need one. And I think one day it will be more a matter of him taking care of you than vice versa."

She was wise and generous in her words even as I knew her heart must be breaking.

"One more thing you must take," she said, stuffing her hand back into her pocket. "I no longer need these, but you will."

She dropped a sack of coins onto my lap.

Max sniffed them. His tail wagged despite the solemnity of the moment.

"You still have these?" I said in amazement. "I thought they were spent long ago when we lived in Egypt."

She reached up and tucked a stray hair back behind my ear. Her hand lingered near my cheek.

"My son, this is a mystery that I do not understand. This is all I know. This gift, given on the night we fled Bethlehem, has sustained us, fed us, and clothed us for many years. And not just us, but our neighbors and strangers who have come to our door. Every time I have given some away, others take their place. I do not know how it can be so, and I have prayed that the Eternal, bless His name, would show me if this is sorcery or if this is His hand. With all my heart I believe the coins come from above. For only in generosity and courage do they multiply. If I hold unto them out of fear or lack, they diminish. So, I have learned to hold them lightly. To bless others whenever I can as quietly as I can."

"Then you must keep them," I insisted, handing the bag back to her. "I do not have as good a heart as you. I am not courageous or generous or even kind. Surely, they will disappear altogether in my hands."

She shook her head and placed them back onto my lap.

"You will learn to be all those things and more. I have seen this in you since you were a child. This treasure is yours to steward. Just don't forget the One who gives you power to produce wealth. The One who sustains you. He has said by the great prophet Isaiah that He will give you the treasures in darkness, the riches stored in secret places that you may know that He is the Eternal One who calls you by name."

I reluctantly accepted the sack of coins and wedged them deep into the recesses of my bag. Max leapt to the floor and spun around twice before looking up at me with eager anticipation.

"He is ready to go," Mother said as we stood together.

I looked into her lovely face, wondering when I would see it again. There were no more tears in her eyes. In fact, all I saw was hope and love.

"But you know I will become a soldier, don't you? That is all he can help me to become. A Roman soldier," I protested. "An enemy of our people. How can you possibly send me to do this?"

"Felix, the son of my youth and my heart, I am not the one sending you," she said. "Shalom, shalom."

TORA

MY FOCUS FOR THE MORNING is the living room. It has taken me some time to get to this chore for I laid in bed for a few minutes pondering another dream. Just as vivid as the last, this one is not a story I have ever heard before. Yet I know the main characters—my neighbor and his dog. Maybe my imagination is working overtime after our chat yesterday. Felix told me things about himself without really telling me anything. Maybe my curiosity is simply filling in the blanks. Besides, the dream couldn't be about Felix and Max because the setting was someplace like the Israel of the Bible. Maybe my current reality and my biblical knowledge base are doing a mash-up of some sort. Maybe I am so intent upon figuring out the origins of the coins that I am making up fantasies to satisfy my curiosity.

Truly, I don't know, but instead of dismissing this dream, I took out the journal I brought with me, and wrote down everything I could remember. Only then did I shed my bedclothes and get myself ready for the day ahead.

The cup of coffee in my hands is tugged close to my chest as I stand at the edge of the front room and scan the scene before me. Grandpa's books are still strewn everywhere. They will get replaced to their proper spot on the bookshelves. The record albums, some in their jackets and some not, I will return to the stereo console in the corner. Grandma Arnhild had quite a collection. She loved Andy Williams and Mitch Miller singalongs but she also had a healthy dose of classical symphony recordings as well as choir albums from various countries.

But, funnily enough, her favorite collection was her assemblage of Beatles albums. I will never forget the Christmas my brother Andrew came home from a tour in Vietnam and gave her *Sgt. Pepper's Lonely Hearts Club Band.* She was in her mid-seventies at the time, and I didn't know at first if he had given it to her as a prank, or if he thought she might truly like it. The look on her face after she unwrapped it was equal parts perplexed and intrigued.

Grandpa scoffed, saying, "That's not the music an old lady should be listening to."

That was all it took for Grandma to unseal that packaging, put the album on the HiFi stereo, and turn up the volume. My mother and I danced that night through, song after song while my brothers sang along, helping Grandma learn the lyrics. I don't recall what my dad or his dad did. Think they may have left the room.

Much to my grandfather's dismay, that was just the beginning of Grandma's love affair with the British group. Eventually she owned *A Hard Day's Night*, *Help!*, *Abbey Road, The White Album,* and *Yellow Submarine.* She enjoyed them all, although she admitted that last one sort of lost her. They were always the first music I played when I was here by myself in the summers of my youth. I would put one on and Grandma would sing as she baked or washed dishes. Grandpa would go find something to do out in the barn or the shed or the field. Anywhere he didn't have to listen to that 'carn-sarn' music. He was not fond of cussing, so he made up his own expletives.

I set my coffee on a shelf and kneel amidst the disheveled stack of music. Right on the top I see John, Paul, Ringo, and George, surrounded by the Lonely-Hearts Club, looking just as intriguing and other-worldly as I remember when I first laid eyes on the album cover all those years ago. I pull the vinyl from its jacket and go to the stereo, lift the lid, and flip the switch. The 'on' light turns green and I set the album onto the turntable. Some of the stereo's automatic functions have ceased to function, but it still works great if you do things manually. So, I push the arm into place and carefully set the needle onto the first set of grooves.

The familiar chords and lyrics fill the room and lift my mood. Grandma's expansive heart and childlike joy seem present once again as I begin the not so joyful tasks of the day. Sometimes I wish I knew more of how she arrived at being the person I knew her to be. She had lived through so much—immigration, two world wars, the depression, the Spanish flu, the loss of family members, cultural revolutions, assassinations, Vietnam, the Cold War, and more. And yet somehow, she still chose to embrace life and find joy in the midst of it all.

Oh, to have *fika* with her again and hear her gentle yet strong voice.

Today I will have to settle for her music.

I am mid-way through *The White Album* and my second cup of coffee when I turn my sights onto the mess in the far corner of the room at the base of the stairway. This is the nook where Uncle Einar placed his genealogical research along with all the family photo albums, letters, and documents. The marriage certificate I found the first day I was here has come from this family library, I am sure.

I bend down and pick up a plastic bin with a few old letters in it. There should be a whole stack of letters stored in here, I know. I see some poking up from various places at my feet. This is going to take some serious effort to set right.

Do I want to do this now or later?

My stomach growls, and I realize I haven't eaten anything all day.

Maybe I'll go into town, pick up some lunch and take it over to Tante Tilda's.

"That sounds like the best idea you've had all day," I say to myself as I roll my neck from shoulder to shoulder, trying to ease out the kinks that have developed.

Right before I place the plastic bin onto the sofa to come back to later in the day, I see the back of a photograph laying atop the few letters still contained in the box. The writing on the back catches my attention. *Gin and Buck, Con Amore, Isabel. 1944.*

Hmm, the names don't sound like any I know of in our family line. Maybe they are friends or something.

I turn the small black and white picture over. On the front are two young men standing straight and tall in their army battle fatigues. Behind them is a small stone house, and beside them on either side are two donkeys laden with cargo of sorts.

One of these men I recognize. It is a young Uncle Einar. But the other? He has a shock of dark hair swept to one side over his wide forehead. His high cheek bones and dark complexion make me think he may be Indian. Could this be his friend from Redby? The Everwind boy Father told us about? I have never seen a picture of him before, but it would make sense.

And Isabel?

Con amore, Isabel.

This is curious. Is this perhaps a war-time love? Someone left behind in Italy?

I dig through the few envelopes still in the container. Two are in Norwegian with postmarks from the early 1900's. One bears my father's handwriting with a foreign stamp on it and a date of September 1945. I want to stop and read it, but set it aside for later as I continue my search. And there, on the bottom of the stack, I find it. A letter from Italy also postmarked from the Fall of 1945. I carefully extract it from the fragile air-letter envelope and unfold it.

I sigh. It's all in Italian.

The only thing I can read is the name at the bottom.

Isabel Ricci.

"Maybe Tante knows something about this too," I say, tucking the photo into the letter envelope before rising to turn off the stereo.

"Ob-la-di, ob-la-da
Life goes on, brah…"

TORA

IF YOU ASK TANTE TILDA where her house is in St. Gerard, she will tell you, “It’s on the corner of Oak and 10th two blocks down from the old folk’s home.”

Katie has tried to get her to say retirement home or assisted-living facility or memory-care unit, but to no avail. It will always and only be the ‘old folks’ home’ to her even though she is older than ninety-nine percent of every one currently living there. If you happen to mention that, she will tell you that while she may have aged, she is not old.

In all my previous visits with her, I have walked away thinking the same thing.

I wonder if that may have changed since I last saw her. From what Katie says, I'm afraid it may have. What did Solomon say in Ecclesiastes? Time and chance happen to us all? Some just a little slower than others, I guess.

After parking my car along Oak Street, I sling my tote bag onto my shoulder where the photo of Uncle Einar and his buddy, along with the letter resides tucked inside my journal. The smell of greasy burgers, French fries, and fried mushrooms has already permeated my car in the short few minutes it has taken me to drive from the Tastee Freeze to Auntie's house. She requested her usual when I made the call this morning to see if she was available for lunch and offered to bring whatever she wanted.

If she was seventy-five and battling heart disease or something, I probably would not have complied with her wishes. But the woman is over a hundred years old.

"Let her eat what she wants," I say to myself as I ease out of my door and bump it shut with my rear end. I have donned a mask as per Katie's text earlier. Not something I have seen many folks doing up north as compared to down in The Cities. But happy to comply if it gets me in the door.

The two steps up from the street level, as well as the walkway leading up to her porch, are running with rivulets of melting snow and ice. It is a balmy thirty-three degrees today.

As I am mounting the stairs onto her porch, the front door swings open, nearly knocking me backwards.

"Thanks for the coffee, Tilda," a middle-aged woman in a plaid parka says loudly back into the house. "I will come by again next week. Make sure you're behaving yourself."

I hear Tante's laughter from inside.

"Why should I start doing that at my age?" she hollers back.

The woman chuckles before she turns and notices me standing there with my hands full of Tastee Freeze bags.

"Oh, golly," she says through her mask. "Didn't see you there. Do you need a hand?"

"Just keep the door open. That would be helpful," I say. "I'm Tilda's niece, Tora Dahlgard."

"Yup, she told me she was expecting you. Can't wait to get her hands on those fried mushrooms," she says as I pass her and step into the house. "I'm Mel Strickland. Your auntie's pastor from River of Life."

I stop.

"Oh, say. I was thinking of giving you a call. Got your name and number from Sheriff Dumfrey. He's been helping us with the break-in we had out at the farm."

"Yes, I was sorry to hear about that. Reggie… uh, Sheriff Dumfrey is the right guy to have on your team. He and I go way back."

"That's what he told me. He seems to think you might be the right person to help me with some other things… more personal things. But I understand if you only see people by appointment or only people who are in your congregation."

Her green eyes sparkle in striking contrast to the deer-hunter-orange mask covering her nose and mouth.

"Hey, if you're part of Tilda's family, you are part of mine," she says. "When would you like to meet? I've got some free time later this afternoon."

"Really?"

"Tora? You gonna stand out there all day and let my mushrooms get cold?" Tante Tilda hollers from the kitchen.

Pastor Mel and I share a look.

"Told ya she's been waiting," she says. "Just give me a call when you're done here. I will be in my office all afternoon."

The pastor exits and closes the front door behind her. I trek across the living room into the kitchen. Auntie is seated by the table, a napkin already tucked under her chin. I set the bags down and bend over to give her a hug.

"Hello, Tora-bird," she greets me just like she always has.

“Hello, Tante, it’s so good to see you in person,” I say, feeling the sharpness of her shoulder blades under her cardigan. She is thinner than I remember.

When I pull back to look into her face, she peers up at me with watery eyes.

“I’m so done with this pandemic,” she says. “Take off that damn mask so I can see your face.”

“Uh, Katie requested I wear it while visiting with you,” I reply.

“How the heck are you going to eat?”

I laugh and comply. She is the boss.

Then without any further ado, she grabs the bags and digs out her mushrooms.

“There’s ketchup in the fridge,” she says, plopping the first tasty morsel into her mouth. “And I’ve got some Fresca in there. Get me one of those, too, while you’re at it.”

I do as requested before even taking off my coat.

Our lunch is quiet. Auntie is focused on her food. I take the time to soak in the place. It has not changed in many years. The plates on the wall over the sink commemorating the Lutheran church’s centennial and the town’s sesquicentennial and the country’s bicentennial are still there. The cherry covered curtains on the window. The hunter green canisters with various sized roosters painted under Flour, Sugar, Coffee, Tea. The cookie jar shaped like a clown that half enticed and half terrified me as a child. The two-toned cupboards with cream background and sage green doors. All exactly as I remember.

It's like stepping back in time. I am so swept up in my memories that I am almost shocked when I look back at Tilda. For she is no longer the tall, vivacious auntie of my youth with her thick brown braids wrapped neatly around her head, and her garden gloves flopping perpetually out of a pocket somewhere. No, she is a stooped over, silver haired shadow of herself—her hands sprinkled with age spots and her face lined with an intricate network of wrinkles.

She tugs the napkin from under her chin and neatly cleans up the drips on the side of her mouth.

"As good as usual," she says, crumpling up the bag and wrappers from her food. "How was yours?"

I nod and give her a thumbs up as my mouth is still full of one of the best burgers north of the Twin Cities.

"So, Katie tells me someone roughed up the farmhouse," she says as I swallow down a gulp of Fresca. "What's the latest? Any news?"

I fill her in on all I know thus far but don't yet mention the gold coins. She putters around the kitchen in her slippers, wiping down the table and putting the kettle on the stove.

"You want some cocoa or tea?" she asks. "Don't seem to have any coffee."

"Cocoa sounds good," I reply.

"Okay. Now, tell me about that new fella living over at Janet's place," she says, tugging open the Tea canister and withdrawing two pouches of instant hot-chocolate.

I tell her all I know of Felix and his faithful companion, though I don't go into my dream about them. She may be more understanding of it than I am, but I think I will wait and pass it by Pastor Mel first. I know her church is, by reputation, accepting of gifts of the Spirit in ways some other churches up here are not. In fact, I remember Auntie telling me about some pretty interesting tales of 'moves of the Spirit' that have happened at River of Life over the years. I have never personally experienced anything like what she has described, but she is not the exaggerating type, so I tend to believe her.

"Auntie, there's something I found at the farm this morning that I want you to look at," I say, drawing my tote onto my lap and extracting my journal with the letter and photo.

"Katie tells me the place got ransacked. Got any news on who may have done it?"

I repeat the story I just told her, and she nods and takes it all in as if for the first time. Then I hold out the small black and white photo.

"Do you have any idea who this man is with Uncle Einar?"

She pulls a set of reading glasses out of her sweater pocket and places them on the end of her nose before taking it from my hand.

A sad sort of smile washes over her face. She nods and nods, taking her time with the photo as if interacting with the subjects in some way.

"Sure," she says. "I'd know those two anywhere."

The kettle whistles. She sets the photo on the table before pouring water into our mugs.

"That's Einar and his buddy Joseph Everwind," she says, turning the picture over. "Gin and Buck were their nicknames they got during the war. Did you find this among the mess?"

"I did," I reply. "And I think it came in this letter."

I retrieve the air-mail correspondence from my purse.

"It's all in Italian. So, I don't have a clue what it says. But it's signed by someone named Isabel Ricci. Did Uncle Einar ever talk about her? Maybe a hot Italian lover or something?"

Tilda returns the picture to me and then sets the tea kettle back on the stove before attempting to rip open her packet of cocoa. I watch for a few seconds, hoping she will succeed. She tosses the unopened packet at me.

"Carn-sarn things," she says. "Makes me feel like an old lady."

I restrain from comment and tear off the end of the pouch before handing it back.

"Well, any clue about Isabel?" I ask.

"Oh, sure," she laughs. "But she wasn't his girlfriend. Don't think he ever had eyes for anyone except Grace."

"Um, okay. Who's Grace?"

"Thought you wanted to know about Isabel."

"Well, yes, I do," I say. "But you brought up this other woman. So, you tell me—who is Isabel and who is Grace?"

Tante sets her mug down and then eases herself back down into her chair.

"Wouldn't you like to know?" she teases, her eyes suddenly sharp and full of mischief.

Oh, my goodness. Are centenarians supposed to act like this?

"Yes, actually, I would like to know. If you'd like to tell me," I say, taking a sip from my warm drink.

"Isabel was an old woman he met… actually they met… he and Joseph in Italy during the war," she says, "They took care of her for a while when she was sick. I think she may be the one who gave them the coins."

I spurt out the cocoa in my mouth.

"Here, dear," Tilda says, handing me a paper napkin from the holder in the middle of the table.

"So, you know about the coins?" I say, cleaning up my splatter.

"Oh, sure. Suppose it's alright to talk about 'em now that Einar's gone. He made us promise to keep it all very hush, hush. Didn't want anyone treating him any different or come begging for this, that or the other thing."

"So, who all knew about the coins?"

"Just me, Richard, Sigard, and Louisa, far as I know."

"My mom and dad knew? Why didn't you tell any of us about all this?"

"Didn't even know they were still around. None of my business. Einar was in charge. They were his to do with or not do with as he pleased."

"But why do you think this woman gave him all those coins?"

"Not sure. Can't remember," she says, and her head begins to nod over her cup.

"Auntie, are you okay?"

Her head bobs back up.

"Oh, just time for a nap, I think," she says, pushing her drink aside. "Come and help this old woman up, will ya?"

I go to her and tug on her outstretched hands. She rises, and I tuck her arm into mine. "Where to, your majesty?" I ask.

"I like the couch in the front room in the afternoon," she replies. "Only old people sleep in their beds in the middle of the day."

I smile and assist her to her desired place in the living room where I stretch the crocheted afghan over her.

"So, you gonna tell me about what happened out at the farm? Heard it got ransacked," she says, relaxing into the velour pillow.

I crouch down by her side and repeat the story once more. Her eyes droop and flutter but she fights off the beckoning nap long enough to hear me out once again.

"You told me that once already, didn't ya?" she says and I nod. "My forgetter seems to be stronger than my rememberer these days. Sorry about that."

"That's okay, Tante, I don't mind," I say.

She pats my hand and nods.

"Tante, just one more thing," I say, hoping to catch her before she slips into la la land. "Who is Grace?"

Her eyelids droop shut but she smiles. "Grace," she whispers with a soft sigh. "Grace was the love of his life."

FELIX

TORA'S SUV HAS JUST TURNED EAST out of her driveway when Max begins to bark. He is standing at the base of the stairs that lead up to the second story of the house. There is one bedroom up there with a long cubby hole on one side stretching the length of the house under the eaves. I have not spent much time up there yet. I inspected for any leaks in the roof that may have needed immediate attention but did not find any.

"What's going on, buddy?" I ask, coming up beside him.

His hair is not raised along his back, but he is intensely staring upward.

"Is something up there?"

Before I even finish the sentence, he takes off, leaping two stairs at a time until he reaches the top and spins to look down on me.

"Alright, alright," I say with a laugh. "I'm coming."

When I get to the top, the window that graces the small landing area opens, and the stairway suddenly extends through it up into the heavens.

My dog launches himself upward into the brilliant light and is quickly out of sight. Now I understand. I have been so concentrated on my earthly 'to-do' list that I missed the summons upward. But my canine companion did not.

The light draws me up the spiraling stairway. I pass many other beings coming and going, some only a blur and others not. I shed the cares of the earthly realm one by one as I ascend. By the time I get to the top, I feel the usual buoyancy that accompanies my entry into eternity.

The top of the stairs is broad and busy. Max sits there panting and waiting for me. I stroke his head, looking around for who we might be meeting. A soft hand rests on my shoulder, and I turn around.

"Mother," I say. "How lovely to see you."

She embraces me.

"Come, my son. I have things to show you. You, too, Max."

She slips her arm through mine, and we glide through space to a small stone house tucked into a hillside with my dog at our heels. Flowers overflow the window boxes under the two front windows. The shrubs and trees around the house are lush and full of fruits and berries. Birds are abundant in their branches and in the air overhead. It is a charming spot.

"I want you to meet someone," Mother says, knocking on the sturdy wooden door.

A petite dark-haired woman opens it.

"Ah, Lydia, you've come," she says. "And this must be your son I've heard so much about. Felix, isn't it? And who is this?" She holds out a hand for Max to sniff.

"This is Maximus," Mother says.

"And I am Isabel," the woman replies, giving Max's chin a good scratch. "Come through. I will lead the way."

We enter the snug kitchen area with its table for three and shelves lined with plates, tins, and bowls. Isabel continues through the room to a short hallway that leads us out the back of the house. We cross over a cobbled stone patio surrounded by banks of blooming shrubs. Isabel leads us to a path that extends into the hills behind the house. It is steep and winding but lovely.

"I hear you are at Solbakken," Mother says as we hike up the path behind Isabel, who is surprisingly swift for her size. Max has left us behind and is traipsing right beside our leader.

"Yes, having an interesting time, as usual. Encountered the coins again," I reply.

"Yes, I know," she says.

"Have you been observing again?" I ask, knowing that she often keeps tabs on my comings as goings, as mothers want to do.

"Only a bit," she laughs. "Enough to see Tora and the coins. That's why I have requested your presence here. I think this may be helpful."

We continue to climb. Along the way, sheep and goats, rabbits and foxes, deer and mountain lions, step out to greet our leader. She calls them each by name, and they linger near her as she introduces them to Max. Then they step into line behind her like a parade of adoring fans. By the time we reach the peak of the mountain, Isabel has acquired quite a following.

She stops and waits for us. Her animal parade gathers round her even as we do with Max contentedly in the middle of it all.

"He is waiting," she says, pointing to a figure below us standing in a lush mountain meadow. He is surrounded by wildflowers, and a circle of birds fly right above his face. He laughs as the birds roll and twist, spiraling upward as if in tandem with his laughter.

The animals around us seem to want to participate in whatever is going on around this man and they run, leap, bound, and skip down the hillside toward him. Max is no exception. The man hears their approach and turns with outstretched arms to embrace them one at a time.

"Follow me," Isabel says. "When we arrive, he will have room for us too."

"Do you know this man?" I ask Mother.

"We have spoken," she replies. "He is of the lineage of your son Daniel."

She speaks of my son – the middle of five children with my wife Priscilla. Three boys and two girls. My heart fills with a mixture of emotions as I think of them and the time we spent together in the earthly realm. The love and laughter. The pain and worry. The highs and the lows of family.

Daniel was a charming child. A boy that everyone loved. For him, the goal in life was to have adventures and fun. He threw himself headlong into the pursuit of both through his teen years all the way into his thirties. Until the day came when the hedonistic tendencies he embraced in the process took their toll on his body and soul. I will not soon forget the day his wife dropped his emaciated body on our doorstep and said, "Take him or I will let him die."

We never saw his wife or his children again. At least, on that side of eternity.

Priscilla and I nursed Daniel back to health over the course of many months. His body began to grow strong again, but his soul remained in a dark, agonized place. The turning point for him came, as I recall, the day his sister brought him a puppy. He had grown up with Maximus always being a part of the household but, Max was my dog. This puppy, who he named Vita, which means life, was fully Daniel's from the first day she lay in his lap. She was the best medicine anyone could prescribe. She was indeed life for him.

"Son, are you coming?" Mother says, gently tugging on my hand as we descend behind Isabel to the meadow.

The animals that joined us as we trekked over the mountain have all laid down in the meadow near the feet of the man. He is dressed in a plain linen tunic with a simple rope tied at the waist. Max, however, runs back and forth between us as if he is eager for Mother and I to meet him.

"Easy there, buddy," I say. "We're coming."

My dog falls into place by my side as we approach the man. He is shorter than what he appeared from up above and slight in build. His beard is trimmed and tidy. His hair cut short with a completely bald area on top. Several of the birds have settled on his shoulders, and one atop the shiny crown of his head. If it didn't look so perfectly natural, it may have been comical.

"Lydia, Felix, and Max," Isabel says to us as we approach. "This is Francis."

"So, you are of those who ride on the clouds?" Francis says, gripping my hand by way of greeting and placing the other hand under Max's head.

"Yes, we have that privilege," I reply, trying not to stare at the little brown bird who stares at me from atop Francis's head.

"Lydia told me all about you and your canine companion when last we met," he says. "What a life you lead! My time on the planet was so short—merely two score and five. Half of that I lived in reckless disregard for man and beast. Yet I am thankful and amazed at what the Eternal One formed in me and through me in only a few short years. Come. Sit. Let us talk. You have not come all this way only to gaze at my feathered friend." He reaches up his finger to coax the sparrow onto a different perch.

Isabel sits on a smooth gray stone where two sheep curl up by her feet. Max trots over to join them as if he belongs to their flock. My mother has chosen to seat herself directly on the lush grass. Francis and I join her, and we four humans form a circle in the center of the meadow. A rabbit leaps onto Francis's lap, claiming it before any other can as the mountain lion snuggles up against his back.

"You have quite the menagerie here," I say, watching the birds perch deftly on flowers and shrubs all around us. "Do they live with you in your home as well?"

"Ah, but this is my home," the gentle friar replies. "I neither want nor need any other. But let us turn to the matter at hand. Isabel and I have conversed many times about the blessings of our lineage, haven't we?"

"Yes, we have. Many times, and with many of our various family lines. It is one of the true joys of this sphere, that we can connect the dots and follow the bouncing ball, as it were, of the blessings. How delighted I was to learn of my connection to you through my grandmother many times over and your cousin many times removed, Marie-Claire," she says to Francis.

"Marie-Claire," he replies wistfully. "What a day. What a time. What a woman."

"Can you tell Felix the story of Marie-Claire and the coins?" Mother asks.

Francis closes his eyes and breathes deeply. I find myself leaning forward onto my crossed legs, eager as a young child at bedtime to hear this tale.

FRANCIS

"FRANCIS!" MY FATHER YELLED for me over the noise of the crowd. "Francis, come and help Pierre load this wagon."

I was only about ten feet from him on the other side of our booth, but the frenzy of buyers and sellers hawking their wares at the fair was tumultuous. The markets in our hometown of Assisi in Italy could be raucous but, it was nothing like this. Father had tried to tell me on our journey here what it would be like.

"You must keep your wits about you, son," he had said. "Paris is full of wonders and women and wine that will please your senses beyond anything Italy has to offer. At least, in my humble opinion. Look at your mother. Is she not a woman above all women?"

How could I argue with that? My French-born mother was indeed lovely and refined. Born from wealth of her own with generations of aristocracy behind her, my father was still smitten with her charms and her 'French-ness'.

"But the city also is full of beggars and thieves, paupers and opportunists. Stay alert. Do not wander far," he had warned.

It was my first business trip with Father. My older brothers went with him often and had become skilled salesmen, experienced with bargaining and maneuvering with all sorts of buyers of my father's fabrics in his mercery business. He sold silks, linens, and fine cottons from all over Europe and parts of Asia. Now it was my turn to learn, to become invested in the business of producing wealth instead of just spending it. Something I was already quite good at.

"Coming, Father!" I yelled back as I shoved my way through the wholesalers that surrounded our wares. Their loud haggling and bartering were amplified by the stone buildings behind us and the waters of the Seine River in front of us. Languages of every variety filled my ears. Mostly we communicated in French, which, thankfully, I was quite conversant in due to my mother. But my father could also speak some English, German, and Turkish thanks to his many interactions with international merchants over the years.

The buyer Father was dealing with at that moment must have been from the Germanic states. I did not understand what he was saying, but recognized the crisp guttural sounds of that tongue. The bundles of linens the wholesaler had purchased were heavy and took all my teen-aged strength, as well as that of our French worker Pierre, to muscle onto the cart bed that awaited the load. My shirt was nearly soaked through from the efforts of the day in the warm August heat. I would surely have to change before the night's festivities.

As I bent to gather another bundle of the fine fabric, I noticed a pair of eyes peering at me from behind a trunk of silks. The young lad they belonged to froze when I spotted him, his face covered in grime and his tattered clothing a sharp contrast to the beautiful fabrics all around him.

"What are you doing?" I hissed in French as I lifted my load. "You must go before my father sees you."

The boy did not move.

"Go!" I swung my boot at him, and he scrambled away.

A pang of regret filled me immediately. He was just a boy. A hungry boy, from the looks of him. Pierre and I had chased away at least a dozen like him already that day. Yet the more we scattered, the more that showed up.

"Francis, this is my friend Wilhelm Gutterman," Father said as Pierre and I secured a tarp over the merchandise in the cart. "Wilhelm, this is my youngest son, Francis."

"Another son? You are a man most blessed," Wilhelm said in heavily accented French.

"That is what my wife tells me," Father agrees. "You are staying in the city tonight? Come and dine with us. We are staying at the usual inn."

The two men continued in their conversation, slipping back into the Germanic language neither Pierre nor I could follow. So, we went back to our respective sides of the booth, keeping our eyes and ears open for other possible buyers. The sun was beginning its descent, casting an orange glow over the river. My stomach began to growl despite the many not so appetizing aromas drifting up from the waterway and the gutters. We had been so busy all day that we had stopped only to eat a baguette with sausage purchased from an old woman selling them on the street corner sometime around noon. The clock on the tower at the end of the block said it was well past 8 p.m.

People began to filter away, wrapping up last minute purchases as the merchants all around us began to close up their booths and secure their remaining inventory. I was busily doing the same at one end of our booth, and Father and Pierre at the other end, when I looked up into the face of a young woman. An infant wrapped in a sling over her chest and a toddler holding her hand, she could not have been more than seventeen or eighteen years old herself. Though she and the child bore the same hungry look as the many other beggars I had seen that day, their threadbare clothing was clean, and they had shoes on their feet.

She reached out a hand but did not say a word.

The baby did not cry.

The toddler did not speak.

It was as if they wanted to remove themselves from the very act they were committing—to gain what they needed without losing what they possessed.

I could not tear my eyes away from them.

"What is your name?" I said, keeping my voice down lest Father notice.

"Marie-Claire," she said, her voice a hesitant whisper that pierced my soul.

Though I was a spoiled youth, I was not a craven one. In fact, my father sometimes scolded me for being too emotional—too feeling.

The little boy by her side stared up at me with dark brown eyes that seemed about two sizes too big for his little head.

"Jean-Marc," he said, pointing a finger toward his own chest. "Antoinette." He pointed to the swaddled infant.

"I am Francis," I said with a nod. "Francis of Assisi."

At that moment, I do not know what overcame me, but I set down the fabric I had been loading into a trunk, and reached down into my pocket. I pulled out the pouch of money I had been saving to spend on frivolities and food that night, and opened the purse strings. My first instinct was to give her a few coins but then I simply handed her the entire pouch.

"Here," I said to Marie-Claire. "Take this. Take all of this."

She received the pouch like a gift from heaven. Tears filled her eyes and rolled down her cheeks.

"Merci," she whispered over and over in a stunned monotone.

Just then another poor beggar jumped up behind Marie-Claire and tried to snatch the bag from her hand.

"Hey!" I yelled. "Stop!"

The beggar had his hands firmly gripping the top of the pouch while Marie-Claire clung to the bottom with hers. They began to wrestle. Little Antoinette awoke and began to cry.

"What have you done, mon Ami?" Pierre came up behind me.

"I am just trying to help this mother and these children," I said, tugging at the surprisingly strong hands of the boy.

"Soon you will have an angry beehive," Pierre scolded as yet another boy joined the fray.

Insistent on helping Marie-Claire and her children, I gripped the first beggar boy by the neck and flung him to the ground even as Pierre shooed off several more.

"What is going on here?" Father yelled, coming to my side and assessing the situation. "You foolish, foolish boy. Don't you know whatever you give them will only disappear into their wasted lives? These gutter snipes have no idea what to do with money. How do you think they got to the gutter in the first place?" He pointed directly at Marie-Claire, who seemed frozen in her place by his condemnation.

Pierre continued to shoo away the riffraff before rousing Marie-Claire into action and ushering her down a narrow alley. I prayed she would escape. I prayed she would live. More than anything I had ever wanted in the world before; I wanted her and her children to live.

The ruckus finally calmed. Father stood staring at me, unable to disguise his disappointment.

"You have just wasted your money," he said. "The money I worked for you to have. What do you think that girl will do with it? How long do you think it will last? A day? Maybe two?"

I had no answer for my father about what she might do with the money or how long it might last. I did not really even care. For in that moment, I had experienced something I had never experienced before. In emptying my pockets for the sake of another, I had filled my own soul.

Aren't the workings of God a wonder? He never runs out of ways to display His goodness toward us.

Look! Even now, He opens a window for us to see what unfolded for dear Marie-Claire after she left me that day.

A PORTAL APPEARS ABOVE FRANCIS. The small audience, both man and beast, swivel to observe the projected story.

Creeping vines served as mortar holding together the façade of the old brick building that Marie-Claire hustled little Jean-Marc toward. She furtively looked over her shoulder to see if any still followed her home from the fair, or from her stop at the bakery. Satisfied that they were alone, she yanked the rusted iron gate open that led into the decrepit entryway, and guided her son in ahead of her.

"Jean-Marc, go quickly. Take this up to Grand-Mère," she said, thrusting the package of food into his arms. "Tell her to go ahead and eat. We will be home shortly."

The little boy darted from her side into a dim hallway and up a spiral stairway to their third-floor flat. Marie-Claire's heart thumped wildly under the sweating cheeks of her swaddled infant daughter. The running had either calmed the baby or startled her into silence, though she was awake and staring up at her mother.

"Ah, mon coeur, what a day," Marie-Claire whispered to Antoinette, stroking her pink cheeks. "We are not yet done."

Thick black eyelashes fluttered over the infant's chocolate-colored eyes as if she was trying to comprehend her mother's words. Marie-Claire bent her neck to kiss the soft black curls that lay matted against her daughter's head like a fancy knitted cap.

"We will be home soon, ma chère. We must do one more thing before we rest," she said, looking up to the window of their flat. She snugged the sling once more around her ribs, feeling the pouch of coins tucked safely between their two warm bodies.

After they had escaped from the market with the merchant's helper, she had thanked him and bid him adieu before winding her way through different alleyways and streets to make sure to lose any with aims at stealing what she had so recently been given. She could not forget the kind eyes of the young man who had placed the pouch so gently, so certainly in her hands. Nor could she shake the words his father had yelled at him. Words directed at his son but clearly meant for her as well.

Was he right? Was she a person who did not know how to handle money? How could she know? She had never had any money to handle. For her, money only came and went. In her hand one day and into the hand of another on the same day. Since her father had died the year before, and her husband had been crippled on the job, she had learned to stretch any money they had beyond any reasonable measure of stretching. She had worked as a parlor maid until the week before, when she had been fired for appropriating a half-eaten apple and a discarded heel of bread from the kitchen garbage pile.

Then the day had come, this day that she dreaded, when there simply was no money, no job, and no hope. The day she left her mother to tend her sick and dying husband, and took her children with her onto the streets to beg.

Marie-Claire walked briskly in the increasing evening darkness, a lone stray cat her only fellow traveler. The chapel was three blocks away. She needed to hurry to catch the end of the evening mass.

Light spilled from the simple stained glass over the chapel's doors as she approached the stone structure that jutted out from the side of the larger cathedral. She pulled on the bulky iron handles and eased the dark wood panel open. Incense wafted toward her and candle flames flickered at the breeze that pushed in behind her. Père René preferred to do the evening prayers here since so few came in the summer months and in the winter, it was easier to keep warm for those who needed refuge from the cold. His eyebrows rose ever so slightly when he spotted Marie-Claire's arrival. She genuflected and slipped into a pew beside an elderly couple she did not recognize. It had been some time since she had been able to attend mass. Only a scattering of a dozen or so other worshippers were present.

With head bowed over her now sleeping daughter, Marie-Claire breathed deeply and tried to calm her racing heart and mind. The Latin words the priest chanted were familiar and soothing. The cadence calming.

She began her own stream of silent prayers, starting with thanksgiving for the unexpected windfall of the day, with the generosity of the merchant's son, with the food on their table, with the health of her children, and with the care of her mother. As always, she asked for healing for her dear Albert. His crushed feet were now filled with gangrene that suffused their flat with the most horrific smell. Yet his spirit was still as kind as the day they met. His heart not embittered by his lot in life. His faith still present and real. She marveled at him. And she prayed for him.

They had no funds for a doctor. At least not until today.

Is that where the money should go?

Her mind and spirit were so engaged in the conversation with God, she did not notice the mass had ended or the other attendants were all gone until Père René slid into the pew beside her.

"Marie-Claire, ma fille, so good to see you," he said. "Antoinette sleeps?"

She nodded.

"And how is our Albert? Any improvements?"

Her head dropped as she shook it back and forth.

"Ah, je suis désolé. We will continue to pray though, oui?" the kind priest said, patting her hand. "Is that why you have come? To say prayers for Albert?"

Marie-Claire lifted her head and looked into the eyes of the man who had walked with her and her family through the very difficult past months. He had been a great comfort and assistance to the family, bringing not only his sacraments and prayers, but food and other small tokens of care whenever he could. She loved and appreciated this humble servant of God. She trusted him.

Digging into the space just below Antoinette's little chin, she deftly eased the pouch of coins out into the open without waking her.

"I have been given a gift, Père," she said, handing the pouch over to the priest and watching him tug open the drawstring.

His eyes popped open. He quickly pulled the string tight, and handed the treasure back to the girl.

"Where did this come from?" he asked.

She explained the desperate situation at her home that had taken her into the market to beg that day. And the hours of no one taking mercy on them and the sudden generosity of the young Italian man named Francis of Assisi.

"Why didn't you come to me? We would have given you food and drink," the man of God said after she finished.

"Oui, I know. But you have already done so much and…" she struggled to go on.

He reached over and squeezed her hand.

"Pride is not a good reason to not ask," he said gently. "It is more blessed to give than to receive, but sometimes we are all in need of receiving."

"Forgive me. I know. I am just so weary and, well… If I had come to you, I would not been given this gift. Is this not receiving too?"

The middle-aged man nodded his head of thick gray hair and smiled.

"Our God does work in surprising ways. I will give you that," he said. "What will you do with this gift?"

"That is why I have come, Père." She reached into the pouch and drew out some of the coins, measuring until she felt she had half. "These I want to give to you. To God. To the work of this house, to the people of this place."

Père René sat back in surprise.

"Surely not so much, ma fille," he said, waving off her offer. "A coin or two, perhaps, if God has touched your heart to do so, but no more. You have a family to care for now. Perhaps for a long time to come."

Marie-Claire grabbed the priest's hands and poured the coins into them, closing his fingers over them when the last one dropped.

"No. I have been praying ever since I left the market today. I am certain that I have heard to give half back to God. To entrust to Him what was not even mine this morning. To care for the sick, feed the hungry, clothe the naked, and shelter the homeless. All the things you do here with so little resources of your own. And I still have half to care for my family until I can find another job. Which, I pray will be soon."

"And Albert? Will you now finally call the doctor?"

She nodded.

Antoinette began to stir.

"I must go home now," Marie-Claire said, standing to her feet.

The priest joined her with tears in his eyes.

"I have never heard of this man, Francis of Assisi, but I bless him and hope that one day in eternity, he will see the ripples of blessing that his generosity perpetuated in this place."

"Oui, Père. I hope so too."

I HAVE BEEN SO ENTHRALLED WITH THE showing of Marie-Claire's life that I am startled when Isabel speaks up.

"We have seen them. Haven't we, Francis? The ongoing effects of that one moment in the market," she says to the friar as her fingers dance tip to tip in barely controlled excitement.

His face is awash with contentment as he nods. "Yes, indeed, we have."

"What happened to Albert?" I ask. "Did he get the care he needed?"

Isabel and Francis share a quick look.

"He did not require it," Francis says. "By the time she returned home, he had returned home as well."

"Oh, I see," I say.

"It was his choice," Isabel adds, stroking Max's head. He seems to be following the entire story with interest. "He heard of the coins from Jean-Marc as he lay on his bed struggling to focus on his little son. He knew his wife's heart would be to spend every dime on his care. And he knew that the time for a doctor had long since come and gone. When his mother-in-law took her grandson away to make sure he ate, Albert turned to the wall and surrendered his spirit to the Eternal One."

I sigh at the ways of the world. A chickadee flits onto my knee. A young deer totters over and flops by my side, his head on my other knee.

"Your friends are good at comfort," I say to Francis.

"Oh, they are the best, although I'd say you've got a good comforter by your side as well," he replies, looking at Max. "You know I am still so astonished by the goodness of the Eternal in my encounter with Marie-Claire. From that day onward, she never lacked. She worked and gave with great wisdom all the days of her life. Those few coins never did run out like my father predicted. And my life began to take a completely different course from that day forward."

"So marvelous," Mother remarks. "I love how the Eternal One works everything together for good."

Francis claps his hands in delight. The rabbit's ears perk straight up, and the mountain lion that has slumbered by his back throughout the storytelling, lifts his head and peers around Francis' side. The friar rubs the cat's tawny head. "Yes, that is exactly true! The very thing that held me captive—the very thing the Eternal required of me to surrender—is the very thing that set Marie-Claire and her family free!"

TORA

"MEL!" THE OLDER WOMAN BY MY SIDE lowers her mask and yells from the doorway of the gymnasium to the pastor who is at the top of a ladder reaching precariously sideways with the end of a banner. "What are you doing? Get down from there before you break your neck!"

Mel only reaches further still until the end of the banner is looped onto a hook and securely in place. "We Are One Family" it reads atop a wide-angled photo of what looks like the entire school community grouped together in the shape of a heart.

"I've got it, Mom. Take a chill pill," Pastor Mel yells back as she descends the ladder, folds it up, and totes it to a utility closet.

"She never has done as I have asked," Ellen Strong says to me. "Ever since she was a little girl, if she had it in her head to do it, it was going to get done."

I smile watching Pastor Mel lock up the closet and head our way.

"I have a daughter much like that," I reply. She is now the COO of a tech corporation."

"Sounds about right," Ellen says. "I always believed that if Melissa hadn't become a pastor, she might have become the President of the United States."

"Mother, are you telling stories on me?" Pastor Mel says as she approaches, reaching out a hand to shake mine. "Nice to see you, Tora." Her green eyes sparkle over her face mask that sports the same phrase as the large banner.

"Only speaking the truth," Mel's mother remarks, slipping her mask back up over her nose. "I'll let you two visit. Gonna head back to the office for a bit. Almost done with the monthly balance sheet and then I will be heading home. Nice to meet you, Mrs. Dahlgard."

"A pleasure to meet you as well," I respond.

Mrs. Strong turns and strides off down the carpeted hallway lined with classrooms. She is compact, slim, and brimming with an energy that is remarkably similar to her daughter's. The apple has not fallen far.

"Do you need me to mask up?" I ask, tugging my mask out of my coat pocket.

"Probably a good idea. I've got folks that yell at me for still wearing one and for making the kids wear one. And I've got folks who yell at me for not wearing one when I'm out in public. Hard to win these days. Walk with me," Pastor Mel says. "I have to check in on a third-grader who has made her way to the principal's office today."

We walk in the opposite direction of where Mel's mother has disappeared back across the gym to a double set of doors on the far side. I have to hustle to keep up with the pastor's pace even though she is several inches shorter than me.

"Quite a setup you have here," I say. "Is the school K-12?"

"Yes. Just added high-school grades about three years ago. And then the pandemic hit and, well, we're muddling through like everyone else. So, we shall see how it all pans out over the next months. As the Lord leads, that's how we roll."

"And your mother? She's the bookkeeper?"

"Just on the church side of things. She used to own her own CPA business when I was growing up. She likes to keep her hand in the pot. Not literally… just, you know, likes to keep busy."

"Does your father help out too?"

"Well, he does but only from his place in glory now. He passed away a couple of years ago," Mel says.

"Oh, I'm so sorry," I say.

"No need," she says, tucking her brown bobbed hair behind her ear. "The cancer was so aggressive we barely had time to pray, and he was gone. Hard on Mom and me, but for him, blessedly short." We turn the corner at the end of a short hallway, and I see the double-doored entry for the school at the end with offices on either side. "How was your time with your Auntie Tilda?"

"Yeah, um, good. She's remarkable at her age, but definitely slowing down since the last time I saw her face to face over two years ago. Thanks so much for keeping tabs on her through this difficult time."

"Oh, my pleasure. I make it a point to keep in contact with all my seniors. Especially those at home by themselves. Think Tilda's girls have done a good job of hiring in a housekeeper and a gal who cooks up some meals for Tilda a couple of times per week. She used to gripe to me about all this 'unnecessary help' but not anymore. Now I think she's finally recognizing that the help is necessary."

"I'm sure that's mostly Katie's doing. Debbie seems to have her plate full with her, uh, her own needs," I say.

"Yes, I am aware. Breaks her mom's heart but Tilda's not giving up on her. If Deb only knew the love her mom has for her, and the prayers she's prayed for her," Pastor Mel says, reaching for the door handles under the sign that reads Front Office. "Come on in. I will only be a minute."

We step into the office where a young woman sits behind a front desk, and two short couches run along each side wall under miniature versions of the We Are One Family banner.

"Pastor Mel." The young woman stands to greet us. "They're waiting for you."

"Thanks, Chelsea. Has she simmered down?"

"Well, I haven't heard any yelling for a few minutes, so I'd say, yes," the front desk attendant replies.

"She is a live wire, this one," Pastor Mel says. "Reminds me of myself. Could you get Mrs. Dahlgard a glass of water or coffee or whatever she needs? I won't be long."

"Sure thing," Chelsea says as Mel enters the principal's office. "What can I get you?"

"Just water would be fine," I reply, taking a seat on a couch. I tug my phone out of its pocket on the side of my bag and check for any messages.

"Here ya go," Chelsea says, returning with a cup of cool water. "Make yourself at home."

The phone on her desk chirps. She trots around the counter that runs along three sides of her large desk and swoops up the phone, yanking her mask down as she answers.

"River of Life School, Chelsea speaking. How can I help you?"

Her head bobs up and down or back and forth as she adds a few "Yups" and "Nopes" to the questions coming from the person on the other end of the line.

I return my focus to my phone, scrolling through various social media, checking to see if my children have posted anything interesting. It's one of the few ways I know what they're up to these days. Pictures from my virtual birthday party fill Brian's page, bringing a smile to my face. Guess that was only a few days ago.

"No, Dr. Everwind, I don't think that will be necessary," Chelsea says.

My ears perk up.

Dr. Everwind?

"No, nobody was hurt. Just some amplified conversation about family tree branches," Chelsea adds. "I was passing by the library when it happened. Got the privilege of escorting her down to the office so Miss Granger did not have to leave the other kids."

Just then Pastor Mel comes out of the principal's office along with a girl and a young woman who I assume to be the principal.

"Hold on, Dr. Everwind, they're just coming out right now," Chelsea says into the phone. "Would you like to speak to Principal Smischney? Uh-huh. Okay… You bet. Just hold on a minute and I will get you transferred." Chelsea puts a hand over the phone and says to the principal, "It's Sophia's mom. She'd like to talk to you."

"Send it through," the principal says, shaking Pastor Mel's hand. "Thanks for coming over. You mind getting this one back to her class? They should be done with their media break by now. So, best bet is Miss Granger's classroom." She places a hand on Sophia's shoulder. "Remember, your words are powerful. Let's use them for good. Right?"

Sophia gives a barely perceptible nod.

"No problem," Pastor Mel says. "Sophia and I can find our way. Can't we?"

The young girl shrugs. "I guess," she says, her dark eyebrows bunched over her intense brown eyes. "I can find my way back on my own, you know. It's not that far."

Pastor Mel laughs. "Oh, I have no doubt about that, Miss Sophia Everwind. I think you could find your way through a blizzard walking sideways with a pack of monkeys on your back."

The comment elicits a begrudging smile from the young student.

"But I'd sure like your company cuz I'm walking that way anyway," the pastor says, steering Sophia toward the exit with one hand on her back. "And you can meet my new friend Mrs. Dahlgard. But first…" She mimics pulling her mask up on her chin.

Sophia sighs and tugs the We Are One Family mask, which she wears like a sling around her chin, only slightly higher.

I stand to join them, tucking my phone back into place. The pastor makes the introductions.

"What do you say to my friend?" Pastor Mel prompts as we three make our way out into the hallway.

"Nice to meet you," Sophia says, lifting her eyes up to mine without moving her head.

I am struck at that moment that I have seen those eyes somewhere before. As we march back across the gym to the hallway of classrooms, the picture of Gin and Buck flashes across my mind.

"Okay, Miss Sophia," Pastor Mel says before opening the door to Miss Granger's classroom. "I understand your desire to defend your family tree, but I would like to remind you that we are all connected in the body of Christ. And everyone's heritage is valuable and unique just like a foot or a finger or an ear are all equally valuable and unique in your body. True?"

Sophia nods begrudgingly.

"That's what Miss Granger said," she says.

"Well, good. So, let's not let comparisons make us angry with one another," Pastor Mel says, placing a hand on the girl's shoulder.

Sophia's chin lifts up.

"Tell Kenny Ogelsby that," she says. "He's the one who said my family should have stayed on the rez where we belong."

Pastor Mel's lips tighten and her enviably full eyebrows raise to disappear under the fringe of her wispy bangs.

"Really?" she says. "Tora, I will be with you in a just a minute."

The two of them disappear into the third-grade classroom and I lean up against the wall and wait. I admire the opposite wall filled with paintings of trees each adorned with names and dates of generations on various leaves and branches.

Pastor Mel steps back into the hall.

"Let's get to my office," she says. "Need to pencil in some time in my calendar for a chit chat with Kenny Ogelsby and his mother."

TORA

"I'M NOT QUITE SURE WHERE TO START," I say, sitting in one of the comfortable arm chairs in Pastor Mel's office. She sits in front of me in the matching chair, a coffee table spread with beautiful artistic books between us.

"Wherever you'd like," the pastor says, her hands clasped in her lap and her feet crossed at the ankles over her lime-green Nike's. She is relaxed but engaged. It's easy to see she's been here before many times but, I am suddenly anxious. This is not my norm.

"Would you feel more comfortable if we unmasked?" she asks. "I'm totally okay either way here in the privacy of my office. We are the requisite six feet apart."

"Yes, I would appreciate that," I say with relief, removing the cloth from my face. "So, do you often help the principal out with troubled students?"

"Sometimes," she replies. "Sort of a good cop, bad cop thing."

"And which are you?"

She smiles.

"Depends on the kid."

"And with Sophia which were you?"

She doesn't answer.

"Sorry, none of my business," I say. "It's just… well, it's so odd. The name Everwind keeps popping up all around me today."

I lean down and dig into my purse, retrieving the letter and photo from Isabel.

"This is not what I had intended to talk with you about. But… well, I just showed Auntie these things. Found them today amidst the clutter out at the farm," I say, handing the items over to Pastor Mel. "I have learned that the letter is from an old woman that Uncle Einar met while serving in Italy during the war. The photo is also from her."

Pastor Mel examines the photo and flips it over.

"I recognize Einar. But the other fellow… Is he an Everwind? Sure looks like one," she says, glancing at me and then back at the photo.

"Yes. His name is Joseph Everwind. Buck and Gin were the nicknames they got in the army. They were good buddies. I'm not sure if they were friends prior to the war, but I know my Grandpa Axel was friends with Joseph's father Thomas Everwind who lived over by Redby, I believe."

"Yup, yup, that's where most of them still live. Sophia's grandfather, who, if I'm not, mistaken is also called Thomas, was, and maybe still is, one of the managers at the Red Lake Nation Fishery," Pastor Mel replies, opening up the letter. "They come over to see the grandkids play ball or act in plays or whatever they're up to around here. Quite an active group. You able to read this? Looks like Italian."

"It is, and no, I can't," I say. "But I think I know someone who might be able to help me."

Pastor Mel tucks the letter and photo back together and hands them to me.

"Interesting," she says. "What ever happened to Joseph? The one in the picture."

"Sadly, he was killed at the end of the war. That's all I know."

"Hmm, well, I'm sure the family would love to see that pic. I can let Sophia's parents know, if you'd like? Can't give you their contact info, I'm afraid, unless they consent."

"Totally get that. Sure would appreciate it," I say, setting the packet back into my bag, my mind swirling into places beyond the room I am in. Back to Italy. Over to Redby. Out onto a boat. Up on a sand dune.

"Anything else on your mind?" the pastor asks.

"Well, yes. The real reason I'm here... actually, there are several reasons, now that I think about it. I'm up at Solbakken by myself, and normally I would be processing all of this with my husband, who is very good at helping me sort through my concerns... but... I guess I just need an objective perspective on some things."

"I will do my best. Fire away," she says, her open manner inviting me to go deeper. I admire her. She seems to be a compassionate, passionate soul well placed in her profession and community. Truth is, maybe I envy her just a bit.

I take a deep breath and begin to unfold to her the story of our family's journey through the past few years of pandemic and upheaval. She nods and listens, occasionally interjecting a question for clarification. My eyes and nose begin to drip as I relive the heated exchange between my daughter and myself on the phone yesterday. She sets a box of tissues on the coffee table where I can easily reach them.

"I'm at such a loss," I say, wiping away the drips. "My kids have been my life. And my granddaughter… I can't even begin to tell you what she means…"

"Oh, I've got three of my own. No need to explain," she remarks.

"Are they around here?" I ask.

"Two are in town here with my daughter and son-in-law, and one is down by Brainerd with my son and his wife. My husband and I stay as involved as we can."

"Have you had any of these types of difficulties?

"Sure. We have had some tough conversations over the past months, but I'll tell you what I believe is the most important thing. Keeping the lines of communication open whenever possible, and expressing value for one another," Pastor Mel says, reaching over to grab a Bible from the side table beside her.

"This is where I get my perspective," she says, holding up the thick book. "Mind if I read a verse that has helped me?"

"Go ahead. I'd love it."

She flips through the thin onion skin pages deftly, certain of her desired destination. When she reaches the page, she turns on a lamp next to her and leans the open book under the illumination it offers.

"Got this verse about half way through 2020, and it's been something I've held onto ever since. That and the direction I got from the Lord to not be too enamored with my own opinion," she says, chuckling. "He knows me so well. So, let's see. I am reading from the book of Amos, Chapter 3, verse 3. It says in the New King James Version, 'Can two walk together, unless they are agreed?' That's it. Just a short verse. Probably one you've heard before maybe when someone wants a good excuse to split up a church or a marriage or something. 'How can we walk together? We don't agree on anything.' But the Lord led me to this verse after I'd had a, let's just say, 'intense' conversation with my son-in-law over what was going on down in The Cities. Had to cool off for a day or so before I was even calm enough to accept a higher perspective. This verse, Amos 3:3, is what I read. Over and over I read it until I said to God, 'Okay. Nice verse, but I don't get why you've got me reading it right now.' So, I pulled out a few other versions and went back to the original language. What I found out is that the verse should more accurately be translated, 'Can two walk together unless they agree to walk together?' Then the lights went on. I don't walk with people through life because we agree about everything; I walk with them because we've agreed to walk together. Does that make sense?"

"Yes, yes it does. My husband and I have been married for over forty years, and I can attest to the veracity of that statement. I don't think anyone would be married longer than about a New York minute if we had to agree about everything."

"Exactly!" the pastor says, her eyes now fired with excitement. "Love is not really even love until it has been tested. And, I will just speak for myself here, but my love has been tested like never before during these past few years."

"Mine too," I agree.

She leans forward, her elbows on her open Bible. "But I can also tell you that I have found new depths of love, new heights of love, and new widths of love in the midst of all this craziness. I can more easily relate to the fact that we are called to not only rejoice in the resurrection life we share with Jesus, but also that we share in His sufferings. And that doesn't just mean His sufferings on the cross. It must also certainly mean the suffering of living amongst an unbelieving, unyielding, grumbling, complaining people just like us. When I pray, 'Lord, make me more like you,' that doesn't just mean make me a healer, or a teacher, or a leader, or a miracle-worker. It also means make me a humble servant with compassion and understanding for my fellow man. I don't have to set aside my convictions, or my world view, or my moral compass, or whatever you want to call it, in order to love people. But I do have to set aside my pride. Now, sometimes folks might choose to walk away or be upset or shut you out, and that choice is up to them. As for me, I choose to leave my heart open and look for opportunities to serve."

Pastor Mel settles back against the chair, adding, "I get that there are times when we do have to agree to not walk together any more. There are abusive relationships and toxic people and all that. But I don't think we're talking about that here today. Am I right?"

"Yes. That's true. I do understand that as well."

"Okay, good. I'm done preaching," she says, closing up the Scriptures. "Sometimes I can get carried away. Hope that was helpful."

"Yes, thank you. I will ponder that," I say.

My phone pings inside my purse.

"You need to check that?" Mel asks. "Go ahead."

I pull out my phone and check.

"Just my husband, Peter," I say. "He wants me to give him a call when I have a chance. Not the greatest reception out at Solbakken. So, I'll do that before I leave St. Gerard."

"Yup, I know how that goes. Is there something else you wanted to chat about? I've got a few more minutes before I need to go. Like to see all the students out the door on their way home at the end of the day. Give out a few hugs. Slap a few high fives. Let 'em know they're loved."

"Wonderful," I say, easing my thoughts to my next subject matter. "I, uh, don't know what your doctrine or theology is about dreams, but Auntie Tilda has mentioned that you are pretty open about sort of mystical kind of things. Is that true?"

Again, she leans forward.

"Ooh, I love all the mysteries of God," she says. "Dreams are everywhere in Scripture. Fascinating study if you ever have time. Have you been having dreams?"

"Well, yes, I have. I don't know if it's just being up in this house or what, but I haven't had dreams like this since I was a kid. I actually used to have very vivid dreams as a child. But these recent ones… they're so… so real. I wake up and it feels like I've been somewhere else all night."

"How many have you had?"

"Just two. I wrote the last one down," I say, retrieving my journal. "I'm gonna go back and write down the first one too. It was a story my Grandpa Axel used to tell me as a child about when he first came to Solbakken. Except in the dream, I saw things he'd never told me, and I knew things I'd never known. Then this second dream is so strange."

I hand Pastor Mel the journal, opened to the page describing my dream about Felix.

"The man in the dream looks just like the new neighbor out at the farm. Same name. Even the same dog. But it can't be him because it was all about a guy back in biblical times. I don't know what that means. I didn't want to tell Peter because I don't want him thinking I'm having dreams about other guys. I don't want to tell Felix either because… well, because that would be embarrassing."

She is skimming over the pages under the lamp's light. I let her read. When she finishes, she hands the book back to me.

"Very interesting. Very detailed," she says. "Let me think on this and pray on it, if you don't mind. Dream interpretation isn't something I do regularly, but I have done some. As Daniel said, 'Interpretation belongs to the Lord.' So, I try to wait on Holy Spirit before I throw out any thus saith the Lord's."

"Yup, I get that," I reply. "Appreciate anything you might hear or see. Hope I'm not asking anything too weird."

"Oh, golly, I'm telling you I have seen God do some pretty weird stuff." She laughs. "In fact, I have seen angels dancing and even danced with them once. So, no, it's not too weird. I've found that the God who set every star in place, has a vast storehouse of wonders, knowledge, and mysteries just waiting for us to tap into if we will ask and believe."

I nod and take a deep breath. I like this woman.

"Okay, now before you go, let me pray," she says. "Would that be okay?"

"Yes. Perfect," I say, bowing my head.

"Dearest Heavenly Father… "

FELIX

MAX'S SLOBBER HAS NEARLY obliterated the lower portion of the passenger side window on my truck by the time I stop to check on him after leaving St. Gerard Hardware and Bait Shop. I reach through the crack I have left to allow cool air into the cab and pet the top of his head.

"Okay, buddy," I say. "We're almost done. How about I see if the drugstore has any doggie treats? Think we're all out."

At the word treats, his ears perk up, and he lets out a big woof of approval.

"Be right back," I say.

I can feel his eyes following me as I cross the broad main street of St. Gerard headed for Thompson's Drugstore. Family owned and operated since 1972, the neon sign flashes under the name. It is situated between a woman's clothing store called

Francine's 2.0 and Northern Lights Pizza & Beer which looks like an establishment I may need to patronize later.

A white Toyota 4Runner with a very dirty undercarriage is parked right in front of the drugstore. It looks like Tora's. She did say she was going into town today.

As soon as I get past the tinkling bell over the store's front entry, I am greeted by a stocky middle-aged woman in a red apron. The black and white name tag at the top of the apron reads Gloria Thompson. It is surrounded by pins of the American flag, the Vikings, the Wild, and the St. Gerard Wolves.

"Welcome to Thompson's," she says. "The name's Gloria. Nice day out there, eh? How can I help ya?"

"I am wondering if you carry any dog food or treats?"

"Yup. Sure do. Aisle 22 back by the pharmacy," she says, pointing toward the back of the store.

"Thanks. And yes, it is a really nice day out there. Think it will hold on for a while?" I say, having learned that conversation about the weather is expected fare around here.

"Oh, now, I just heard we've probably got some snow coming over the weekend. But that's how it goes, dontcha know. Winter is far from over. We had a blizzard up here last year right around May Day," she says. "I say count your blessings today and let tomorrow worry about itself."

"Sound advice," I reply. "Say, is the pizza from the place next door any good?"

"Best in the county. Course, I may be a bit biased, seeing as my nephew owns the joint. But they got real good reviews online and such, so I'd say my opinion is shared by most folks up here then."

"Good to know."

The bell tinkles again and Gloria is on to her next customer, and I am off to search for the promised dog treats. I pass through women's cosmetics, seasonal greeting cards, and the cold and flu aisle before finding the animal food and toy section.

"Felix, is that you?"

Popping my head around the end cap that overflows with clearance hats, gloves, and mittens, I spy my across-the-road-neighbor.

"Hello, Tora," I say, stepping toward her. "Thought I saw your rig out front."

"Just came in to see if they have any PCR tests," she says with excitement glittering in her blue eyes.

"Oh, yeah? Have you been exposed?"

She flutters her hands in front of her face.

"Oh, no, no, no. Nothing like that. At least, I hope not," she says with a nervous giggle.

I'm a bit surprised by her apparent giddiness.

"I just spoke with Peter, my husband, and he told me I needed to get tested. Glad I talked with him before I left town. The little gal at the counter here went to find the pharmacist to see if they have any at-home tests. Said they don't always have them in stock. But she's checking, you know."

She is talking a mile a minute.

"Okay. Well, hope they have what you need," I reply.

"Oh, gosh. I didn't even ask how you are," she says. "You and Max doing alright?"

"Yup. He's waiting out in the truck. We just took a load out to the transfer station over by Blackduck. Got your bags off the porch too."

"Oh, wonderful. Good. I've got so much to do before they come and didn't even think about the big pile of garbage on the porch. Thanks so much for doing that."

"Are you expecting company?"

"Yes, yes, I am. That is if my test comes back negative. Didn't I tell you? Peter is going to bring Hazel up—she's our granddaughter. Haven't seen her in person since, well, gosh, May of 2020. But now my daughter Mariah, her mommy, is, well, she's not feeling too well right now. I tried to offer to help, but that got shot down because, well, the vaccine argument. And I was just over talking with Pastor Mel about all this, and we prayed over everything, and the next thing I know,

I'm calling Peter, and he says he's just had a call from Isaac, who is our son-in-law, and he asked if we would consider—can you believe that? Of course, we would consider. Not only consider but we would do it! He asked if we would consider getting tested because he is just swamped with work. Which, of course, they're doing all from home, and Mariah is barely doing her job let alone keeping Hazel out of, well, all the things Hazel can get into. And they have a new puppy on top of everything so…"

The torrent of information is interrupted by the arrival of the pharmacist behind the plexiglass plate at the counter.

"Excuse me. Mrs. Dahlgard?"

"Yes, yes, that's me," Tora says, flipping her full attention to the man in the white lab coat.

"I'm sorry to tell you that we are all out of the at-home tests. Looks like we may have more by Monday," he says. "Will that be too late?"

Tora's tizzy of elation deflates like a punctured balloon.

"Oh…" she says.

"Dr. Everwind," a young woman comes up behind the pharmacist. "Um, I just wanted to remind you that we still have a few of those government issued rapid tests. They're a little spendy but…"

"Hey, that's right. Thanks for the reminder, Sidney," the pharmacist says. "Would that be of interest to you, Mrs. Dahlgard?"

Much to my surprise, Tora doesn't answer right away. She seems to be frozen.

"Tora, I think he's saying they may have an option for you," I say, taking a step closer to make sure she's hearing me.

"Huh? Oh, yes. Yes, of course. I don't care what it costs. I will take it," she says.

"Alright. Let me go see where we've got those. Glad to say we have had very little use for these tests the past few weeks or so since omicron swept through. Thank God. I will get set up in the back. Have to administer this one myself," the pharmacist says, taking his leave.

Tora can't seem to take her eyes off him even after he vanishes from sight into a back office.

"Why don't you sit down while you wait?" I say, taking her by an elbow and guiding her to a row of chairs off to the side of the pharmacy window. "I'm not in a hurry. I can hang out for a minute."

She allows me to lead her like a woman suddenly caught up in a trance. We sit down between the blood pressure machine and a spinning rack of reading glasses.

"Seems like some positive things happening in your family," I say, hoping to draw her out.

She nods.

"It will be nice to have Hazel around at the farm. Grandchildren are such a blessing. And maybe the puppy too?" I ask.

"Oh, I don't know about the puppy," she says distractedly. "Say, is it just me, or did that assistant call the pharmacist Dr. Everwind? I seem to be hearing that name everywhere today, so maybe it's just my imagination playing games with me."

"No, I heard that too."

Just then Dr. Everwind reappears and opens a door next to the plexiglass window.

"Found what we needed, Mrs. Dahlgard," he says.

"Please, call me Tora," she says, rising to her feet.

"Okay, Tora. Why don't you follow me and we will get you tested. Takes about an hour or so to get the results back. Do you want me to call or text?"

Tora seems unable to respond. It's as if she's waiting for another option that hasn't yet been made available to her.

"If you want to wait for the results, we could pop over to the pizza place next door and grab a bite to eat," I offer. "I don't have to be anywhere soon."

She acknowledges me with a smile and a nod.

"Thanks, Felix. I think I'd like that," she says before leaving me alone in the hard plastic chairs as she goes through the door behind the pharmacist.

I stand and head outside to let Max out of the truck. We take a short walk. He sniffs every post, fire hydrant, and snowbank while marking his territory in yellow up and down main street. I tuck him back into the truck despite his whining protests before heading over to the Northern Lights Pizza & Beer. It takes some time before Tora joins me, so I take a stab at ordering for us.

"Canadian bacon and pineapple, please," I tell the teenaged waitress whose blond bangs slide over her eyes as she scribbles my order on her pad.

"Size?" she asks, flipping her chin to the side to clear her vision.

"How many slices in a large?" I ask.

"Eight," she says, glimpsing upward briefly.

"We'll take that."

"We?" she says, making a circle with her pen.

"Oh, yes. A friend will be joining me soon."

"Drinks?"

"Um, how about just water?"

"Fine," she replies, with one last flick of her long tresses before turning away.

I glance out the window and see Tora standing under the awning of the restaurant. She is on the phone. Her face is animated and her free hand waves around as if signing exclamation marks to her words.

Eventually, she scurries through the door with a shudder.

"Brr," she says. "Should have taken that call indoors, I guess."

"Who was it?" I ask. "If you don't mind me asking?"

"Oh, not at all," she says, wedging herself into the opposite bench of the booth and unzipping her coat. "It was my husband. Good thing he had a meeting to get into or I might still be out there chattering away. So much has happened today."

"Hoping to hear all about it," I reply. "I hope you don't mind. I ordered us a Canadian bacon and pineapple pizza."

"Well, I already ate," she says. "Sorry. Should have told you. I'll just get something to drink."

I hail the waitress. She sighs, and walks over to us, her hips swinging from side to side as she plops one foot down after the other.

"Yeah?" she says, when she reaches us.

"Could I get a Diet-Coke, please?" Tora asks.

The girl simply nods before repeating the performance on the way back across the room.

"Charming," Tora whispers with a smile.

"At least she has a job," I say with a shrug. "So, fill me in on all the happenings."

Tora begins to describe her visit with her auntie in such detail I feel as if I was in the room with them. I sit back and let her talk.

Our young server saunters back to us, slides our drinks across the table, and hands us paper-wrapped straws.

Tora unwraps her straw and shoves it into her soda without breaking from her monologue.

"So, then, just as Tante is about to fall asleep on the couch, she tells me that this Grace person was the love of Uncle Einar's life! Can you believe that?" she says, leaning closer over the table. "Never even knew he had a love-of-his-life."

I smile and nod with what I hope is appropriate enthusiasm. She sips from her drink and plows onward.

"And then, I'm over at the school this afternoon, and I meet a third-grader named Sophia Everwind who just so happens to be the daughter of the pharmacist, Dr. Patrick Everwind, who is married to the dentist, Dr. Robyn Everwind, who has an office over by Blackduck."

"Uh, huh," I say, trying to track the unfolding genealogy as I crumple the paper from my straw.

"So, I ask Patrick," Tora continues, "if he is related in any way to Joseph Everwind. And do you know what he tells me?"

I shake my head.

Tora swats the table and laughs.

"He tells me Joseph Everwind is his great-uncle! Doesn't that beat all?"

"Very interesting," I comment. "So, let me see if I have this straight. Patrick Everwind is the the great-nephew of Buck Everwind, a.k.a. Joseph Everwind, who is the son of Thomas Everwind, who was your grandfather's friend. Is that right?"

"Exactly right," she replies. "Patrick and Robyn moved back up here after they graduated from their various post-graduate studies down in The Cities. They wanted to be closer to home. Had some offers in Bemidji, too, I guess, but they felt like St. Gerard was more the size of town they wanted to raise their family. As if being a pharmacist and a dentist isn't enough, they have five children."

"My goodness," I say between sips of my tepid water. "How do they manage all of that?"

"I asked the same thing. Patrick says that his folks, as well as Robyn's, are nearby over in Redby and Red Lake. Her mom helps with the afterschool rides and dinner and such, and his dad takes the evening shift when both parents have to work late. Although now, with the older boys being in high-school, they have some different options."

The waitress approaches with a platter in her hands.

"Here's your pizza," she says. "I'll get your plates."

"Thanks," I say. "But we'll just need one plate. Guess she already ate."

"That's a lot of pizza for one guy," she remarks flatly.

"That's okay. I've got a big dog," I reply. "And, he loves pizza."

She peeks at me from under her curtain of hair.

"Mine too," she offers with a slight smile before leaving the table.

Tora checks her phone.

"Still another fifteen minutes," she says, setting it back down on the table.

"I'm sure it will all work out," I say, biting into a hot, gooey slice of pizza.

"Any good?" Tora asks.

I nod and swallow.

"Gloria next door was right," I say, swiping away a string of cheese from my chin. "It's five-star quality."

"Maybe Peter and I will bring Hazel here," she says, tears brightening her eyes. "I just can't believe I'm going to see her. Hold her. Sit with her. Read her a story."

She fiddles with her straw, the nervous energy she's entertaining needing somewhere to exert itself.

"Oh, say," she says. "As long as we have a few more minutes, would you mind looking at something? I think I remember you saying you could speak some Italian. Is that right?"

"Yes, I can get by," I affirm.

She digs into her purse and pulls out a letter.

I clean the red sauce and grease from my hands with a paper napkin.

"First let me show you this picture. It's my Uncle Einar and Joseph Everwind from their days in the army over in Italy during World War II," she says, handing me the photograph. "It was sent to them by a woman named Isabel Ricci."

My senses go on full alert.

Isabel Ricci.

"Ah, yes. I see," I say, both to her and to me. "Is this her home behind the two men?"

"I'm not really sure."

I am. It looks remarkably similar to the heavenly version I visited with my mother on my last foray into the other realm.

"This letter is from her. I'd love to know what it says," Tora says, sliding the correspondence over the thickly varnished pine tabletop. "Could you maybe translate it?"

Her fingers tap on the surface like someone fluent in morse code. I scan the sheet quickly, flipping it over to the back as well to get an overview. I am as eager as she to find out what it says.

"It appears to be written to more than one person because she begins with a greeting to her dear friends in the plural, saying she could only find the one address," I say. "She apologizes for writing in Italian and hopes they can find someone to translate. She knows their Italian is not very good. To which she adds, 'Ha-ha.'"

"Okay. Interesting. What else?"

"She expresses sincere gratitude for the care given to her when she was so ill… Uh, looks like perhaps in the prior winter. The way they went out of their way so many times to make sure she and Rico had food and fuel. She says she is feeling much better thanks to them, and was able to even take her goats back up into the hills behind the house over the summer."

I pause to re-read the following phrase a few times.

"Oh, okay. I think Rico must be a pet bird because she says, 'Rico flies beside me again. His feathers have healed. And he talks nicer.'"

"How nice," Tora comments before taking a sip of her drink.

"'It is so wonderful to have peace again in our land. If only my Giuseppe and Gianni had lived to see the day," I say, continuing to translate. "She asks some questions about how they are doing, hoping they have made it safely back to their families. Hopes they like the picture she is including of the two of them in front of her house the last time they visited. She has enjoyed it but thinks they should have it because she is an old lady whose days are winding down. And again a 'Ha-ha.' Then… hmm…"

Tora's tapping fingers stop.

"What is it?" she asks.

"She says she hopes the gifts she has given them have gone to good use."

"Gifts? Maybe Tante was right…"

I zip read to the end of the letter and then look up into Tora's expectant face.

"Well?" she prompts.

"Hold onto your seat. She says, 'I am so happy the coins have found a home with you both. If my Gianni had grown to be a man, I would have wanted him to be as noble and kind as both of you. Please use them however you see fit. I hope they will be a blessing to you as they have been to me."

My neighbor's hands are now both up in front of her mouth. "Oh my gosh," she whispers. "She *is* where the coins came from."

I nod, pleasantly surprised to hear of the continuing saga of the coins myself. The letter folds back easily into its well-worn grooves. I hand it to Tora, who holds it against her heart.

"This is so amazing," she says.

"Yup, pretty amazing," I concur. "But it would seem, from what I can extract from the letter, that Isabel was unaware at the time she wrote it that Joseph did not make it home from the war."

She leans back into the booth's red leather cushion.

"Oh, dear," she says after taking a few deep breaths. "Maybe… maybe half of the coins didn't make it to their destination. Maybe we're supposed to see that the Everwind family gets what she intended to give them."

"That well could be," I reply, lifting another pizza slice to my mouth. "Or, maybe, Einar gave them their share when he got back. Who knows."

Before I can even swallow, Tora's phone buzzes. She grabs it and flips it over.

"They've got my results!"

TORA

BY THE TIME I SINK INTO BED, I am exhausted and my body is screaming for rest. But my brain, oh my brain… Not to mention my heart, which is about to burst with excitement.

Hazel is coming!

Hazel is coming!

Hazel is coming!

Oh, and Peter too.

Even had a conversation with my daughter on the way back to the farm after receiving my negative test results. She was subdued but grateful. Setting parameters about where we can go with Hazel and would we please make sure she doesn't eat too many sweets and can we see to it that she flosses after brushing and on and on. As if we have never been parents of a four-year-old before. Although, admittedly, it has been a long time.

Then Isaac got on the phone and gave me an extensive instructional guide to caring for ShoSho. Thankfully, he says he has it all written down. I do appreciate the man's thoroughness and organizational abilities. Wish I had more of them.

My husband will drive down to Bloomington to pick Hazel and the dog up on Friday afternoon. They should be up here around ten o'clock or so depending upon traffic leaving The Cities. Which shouldn't be too bad since we have not yet reached either the fishing opener or the summer months. On those Friday afternoons, there is a mass exodus out of the metro area heading north for the lakes, cabins, resorts and golf courses, which can add hours to the drive. But it's still winter. Peter should be able to sail along. If the weather holds.

I lay on my back, staring up at the ceiling.

Deep breaths, Tora. Deep breaths.

I close my eyes.

All I can see is the detritus that still covers the floors in the two upstairs bedrooms. Tomorrow is Thursday. I will have all day Friday too.

Deep breaths, Tora. Deep breaths.

Count your blessings.

I do. I breathe.

I count.

I bless.

I sleep.

ON THE BENCH UNDER THE MAGNIFICENT OAK TREE, I am seated next to someone other than Grandpa Axle. Who is it? It is a woman. She is very familiar.

"Grandma Arnie! What are you doing here?" I ask.

"It's my tree, too, Tora-bird," she says with a pat on my arm. Never a one for effusive acts of affection, I remember that kind little love pat with fondness.

"Do you have a story to tell me too?"

“I do,” she says, reaching overhead and plucking a leaf from over her shoulder.

“What’s it called?” I say, scootching closer into her side. She smells of raisin-filled cookies and freshly baked bread.

She turns the leaf over as it morphs into a book.

“*The Lost is Found*,” she says.

“Ooh, that sounds like an adventure.”

“It is. Quite an adventure,” she says before launching into her narration. “In a land far away, in a time of war, two men have lost their way on a mountainous trail…”

"**GIN, YOU KNOW WHERE WE ARE?”** Joseph yelled over the gusting wind.

Einar shielded his eyes from the sleet and peered into the darkness. The donkey at his side stood still with his head dipped down against the weather. A minute ago, Einar thought he knew which way was north, but the trails through these hills were constantly twisting and turning. They seemed to be at another crossing point. He checked his compass again.

“This way, Buck,” Einar hollered over his shoulder, sure that the whipping wind would keep his voice from traveling much further than the few feet that separated them.

He yanked on the lead in his hand and the beast ladened with supplies begrudgingly began to move. Joseph and his donkey followed close behind. They knew the men on the frontlines were in desperate need of the things they were packing. They also know there were injured men up there who desperately needed to be evacuated. But the hills, the mud, the weather, and the enemy made both those missions complicated and fraught with danger.

Einar was glad Joseph, or Buck as everyone called him, was with him. Afterall, he didn’t have to do it. He had earned the right to turn down an assignment like this one, but he’d volunteered to come with Einar because they had become best pals.

Before the war, Joseph and Einar were not friends, even though they had grown up only a couple of miles apart. Joseph was eight years younger than Einar. They had only seen each other a handful of times when Einar, his dad, and his brother had gone over to Redby to buy fish from Joseph's dad, Thomas Everwind. But Joseph was just a little kid then. His older brother, George, and Einar's older brother, Sigard, had thrown a baseball around during those meetings as they waited for the fathers to conduct business. Einar had spent the time admiring Joseph's sister Grace - but only from afar.

Einar's dad and Joseph's dad called each other 'friend'—a status Einar knew went way back to the early days of their family's time in America. He had heard the story of their initial encounter so often, he could recite it in his sleep. But the two men were not intimate friends. In fact, Einar only ever saw them interact over fish. It was more than what the rest of his extended family did with their Chippewa neighbors. More than what most folks saw as acceptable on both sides of the reservation boundaries, at least in that era when the repercussions from the distribution of Chippewa lands under the Nelson Act were still felt acutely.

But all that had changed for Einar since he had arrived in Italy in 1944 as part of a wave of replacements for the decimated forces of the 5th Army. He was part of the 34th Division, also known as Red Bull Division. His regiment, the 135th, had a lot of boys from Minnesota in it, but he didn't know any of them. That was until he ran into Joseph. Once they had figured out their connections, Joseph had made it his business to teach Einar the ropes.

Einar still wasn't exactly sure why Joseph had become quite so committed to him so quickly. Maybe it was because of the fish business between their fathers. Maybe it was because Joseph saw how green and nervous Einar was. Or, maybe, it was simply about timing. Einar had arrived in Italy right when others had been shipped state-side due to wounds, illness, or death, and Joseph needed a new pal. Whatever the reasons,

Einar was distinctly aware that he owed the younger man. The eight years that separated them had become insignificant, particularly in light of the discrepancy in experience between the GI's.

Joseph had been part of the 34th right from the beginning when it was a National Guard Unit in Minnesota. They were the very first troops deployed from the United States after Pearl Harbor. He'd fought in Algiers and Tunisia where he earned his nickname Buck when he led the Allied forces up a treacherous goat trail on the sheer rock side of Hill 609 outside Djebel Tahent. In Italy, he'd already survived battles at Salerno, Anzio, and Rome. By the time Einar set foot in the Mediterranean country, Joseph was a battle-hardened veteran.

About the only thing Einar felt he had going for himself was his engineering degree, which earned him the nickname Gin. Though he had not officially been part of the Army Corp of Engineers, his skill set had become apparent in various situations, and the powers that be had put him to work. They kept him assigned to things like figuring out ways to cross flooded rivers, or finding ways to get supplies to the troops, or evacuating the injured. Of course, those tasks had their own set of dangers like landmines, snipers, and getting lost in the mountains.

Einar and Joseph trudged another half hour over the mud slick trails only to find themselves back in the very same spot where they had just been. They knew this because Joseph had wisely tied a small strip of cloth around the base of one of the trees at the crossing.

Joseph slogged up next to Einar, wiping crusted sleet from his eyes. "Grace would be laughing at us right now," he said. "My sister always said my tracking skills left something to be desired."

Einar sighed. Just the mention of her name made his heart skip a beat. He shook off the desire to pull her picture from his wallet and stare at her lovely face. That would have to wait.

"Let's find somewhere to rest for a few hours," he suggested. "We will only tire ourselves and these animals going in circles. Maybe this weather will let up and we can see where we're going. Get these supplies to the guys by morning."

Einar was doubtful about that and surprised, as always, by his friend's optimism. How he maintained that attitude after all he'd seen and all he'd lost over the past few years, Einar had no idea.

"You're a better man than I, that's for sure," Einar muttered under his breath. "That empty house we went past is just back a hundred yards or so. Looked like it at least had a roof. Wanna head that way?"

Joseph nodded, and they turned around.

The small stone house was tucked back into the hillside. Stone pathways went up behind it further into the hills. A wooden barn stood off to one side. When they tugged back the weathered doors of the outbuilding, they found three bleating goats in a small pen, and several hay bales stacked in a corner. They tied up their donkeys and loosened some hay from the bales to set before them as well as the goats, who gobbled down the fodder as if starving. A clay pot leaning up against the outside of the structure was full of rain water. Einar scooped out cups of it and filled the metal drinking trough that ran along one side of the structure while Joseph headed toward the house. Just as Einar closed the barn doors, he heard the three sharp chirps of his buddy's warning whistle.

A shiver ran down his spine that had nothing to do with the weather.

Joseph was pressed up alongside the house's rock exterior. He held a finger up against his lips. Einar proceeded with caution. When he came up next to his friend, Joseph pointed to the small window just above his right shoulder. Einar ducked underneath it until he could peer inside from the opposite side.

A flickering light was visible coming from underneath a wooden door on the far side of what looked to be a kitchen. Another door beside it was opened, leading to a darkened room.

The friends drew back from the window. Joseph gave hand signals that said, "Follow close behind, I'm going in."

They each armed themselves and crept to the front door. Joseph grasped the handle and pushed. The door wasn't locked. He eased it open slowly. In the dim interior, they saw that the kitchen held a small wooden table, three chairs, a cast iron wood stove, and a sink. It was not elaborate but it was not empty. It looked lived in with tins and bowls filling shelves alongside cups and plates.

Joseph gestured toward the first bedroom door that was open. Einar covered him as his comrade quickly dipped inside. He was back in a few seconds, the shake of his head indicating all was clear. Einar then positioned himself along one side of the closed door, his gun at the ready.

Suddenly, a string of Italian invectives burst from inside the bedroom in a high-pitched raspy voice. Buck and Gin stepped backwards and stared at one another. They recognized the cuss words as those that got hurled at them from angry Italian shopkeepers and old men. They had come to learn these were words that would make their mothers blush.

The soldiers exchanged silent communication agreeing to find out who was behind that door. Joseph held up his fingers—one, two, three—then kicked the door open, keeping to one side lest whoever it was inside decided to blast their heads off.

No shot was fired.

And the angry voice went silent.

They peeked around the side of the door into the room.

A narrow bed, piled with quilts, was pushed up along one wall with a chair and a short set of drawers next to it. Atop the dresser sat the source of the light; a small candle that was burned almost down to the nub. On a chair by the dresser sat a bird cage with a parrot in it who was nearly devoid of feathers. His head twitched back and forth taking in the intruders before letting loose another impressive volley of insults. Buck and Gin burst into laughter.

"It's just a dumb bird," Einar said.

But then another voice—thin and raspy—arose from under the pile of blankets. The GI's jumped back and hoisted their weapons.

"Rico, silencio," the voice growled.

A withered hand emerged from the covers and pushed them down revealing an equally withered face, flush with fever. Joseph and Einar exchanged a bewildered look. Joseph stepped forward and poked at the blankets with the end of his gun, making sure no other humans were hidden in their depths. He found no one besides the old woman, and they both lowered their weapons slowly.

The woman did not draw back but reached out for Joseph.

"Giuseppe," she said, barely above a whisper. A smile lit her face.

Joseph took her hand and said, "I'm not Giuseppe, ma'am. The name is Joseph. Joseph Everwind. My friends call me Buck. And this is my buddy, Einar Anderson. We call him Gin."

He pulled Einar around his side so the elderly lady could see him. She gasped, and her other gnarled hand stretched toward Einar.

"Gianni," she said as tears streamed down the deep lines around her eyes.

"Uh, the name is Einar Anderson, ma'am," Einar said. "We are Americans."

He spoke loudly, not sure if she could hear. Not sure if she understood English.

At the word Americans, Rico spewed a few well-chosen curses but with less vitriol than before. He seemed to have calmed some since his owner had spoken to the men.

"She's burning up," Joseph whispered, trying to extract his hand from the woman's. It was a surprisingly difficult task. "Not lacking for strength though." He shook his wrist.

She began to speak. A long string of Italian.

"What's she saying?" Einar asked.

Joseph shrugged. "How should I know? I speak Ojibwe not Italian."

"Yeah, I know. Just thought you might've picked up a word or two since you've been here. Besides the ones Rico here knows."

"I can ask where the bathroom is and how much a beer costs, but that's about it."

Joseph leaned over the bed and gently laid his hand on the woman's forehead. She sighed, relaxed, and fell asleep.

"Maybe we should see if there's any wood to start a fire," Einar said. "Think we'll be safe doing that?"

"I don't know, but we might have to risk it. This lady is pretty sick and we need to do something. Did you see any wood by the stove or in the barn?"

"Wasn't really looking. I'll go check."

Einar took off his pack and set it up against the wall. He started to do the same with his gun, but Joseph stopped him.

"Take it with," he said. "You never know."

Einar acknowledged his wisdom, picked it up, and stepped back into the kitchen. Behind the stove, an iron container held a few split logs and some kindling. He returned to the bedroom where Joseph was opening the drawers in the bedside dresser under Rico's watchful stare.

"Found some wood," Einar said, opening his pack to rustle up some matches. "You find anything?"

Joseph held up a small framed photograph next to the dwindling flame of the fire.

"Looks like a family photo," he replied. "Husband, wife, and a little kid. Taken quite a while ago, I'd guess."

He held it out for Einar to get a look. In the dim light, he could make out three figures standing in front of a stone house.

"Open it up and see if maybe there's anything written on the back like names or dates or something," Einar said as he dug out some matches from their waterproof packaging and returned to the stove.

The ashes inside were completely cold. There had not been a fire inside for at least a day. Maybe longer. He carefully erected a pyramid from the kindling and lit the ends, watching as the wood edges curlicued up with tongues of flame. Once he got the fire established, he went outside looking for more wood. What was in the house wouldn't last long. He checked the barn again. The goats were snuggled close to one another in a sleepy heap inside their pen. The donkeys looked up. One stamped a foot at his approach. The hay they had been given was gone. Einar rationed out some more, running his hand along the pack animals' haunches as they ate. "Nothing to worry about," he said. "Take a good rest. You're gonna need it." All the while, he surveyed the small space. There was nothing there in the way of fuel for a fire.

He went back out into the night, tucking his collar up around his ears against the heavy, cold rain that was still pounding down. Around the back of the house, between it and the rock hillside, he found what he was looking for. Wood. Split and stacked under the eaves. Einar piled some into his arms and went back into the house.

"Gin, come here," Joseph called from the bedroom.

Einar shook the damp off his head and shoulders, left the wood on the floor near the stove to dry, and entered the woman's bedroom. Joseph was kneeling on the floor next to the bed. The chest of drawers had been moved slightly to one side.

"What's going on?" Einar whisper, not wanting to wake the woman.

Joseph leaned back and handed the picture, which he had extracted from the frame to Einar. "Look on the back."

Einar turned it over.

"1890. Giuseppe, Isabel, and Gianni," he read aloud. "What's it say on the bottom? Rissu, Ricsis, Ricci… something like that."

"Must be their last name," Joseph said. "And the house looks like this house."

Einar flipped it back over. Joseph had found another candle somewhere and lit it. The room was brighter.

"Sure enough," Einar said. "Wow, pretty cool. I'm guessing she might be Isabel then. Way to go, buddy. You're quite the detective."

"Yeah, well, that ain't the most interesting thing I found," he said. "I dropped a nail from the frame when I was opening it up. So, I came down here to look for it, and I discovered a loose board. Get a gander at this."

He moved aside, and Einar peered into the box-like space under the floorboard where something was reflecting the rays from the candle up onto the plaster ceiling in small shimmering sparkles.

"Holy Moses!"

TORA

MOONLIGHT ILLUMINATES THE BEDROOM when my eyes fly open. I take a moment to remember where I am. The farm. Solbakken. Uncle Einar.

"Oh!" I say, sitting upright and flipping the bedside light on. "Grace is Joseph's sister! Grace Everwind."

I grab for my journal. It is not there. Must still be in my tote.

After a quick bathroom pitstop, I locate my bag on the dining room table. It sits atop a stack of genealogical records I am still trying to make sense of before reinserting them back into their binder. Digging into the depths of my bag, my fingers close over the familiar soft leather of my journal. I extract it and am about to turn back to the bedroom when a movement outside the dining room window catches my eye.

"Whoa," I whisper into the night.

Staring back at me in the snow outside about ten feet from the window is a wolf. It is covered in black fur from the tip of its snout to the pointed end of its drooping tail. The moonlight catches his eyes, and they glint at me across the space.

I am held breathless in his gaze.

Another wolf prances up from between the trees. Smaller and shorter, its coat is salt and pepper, blending more easily into the night shadows than its ebony counterpart. Making two circles around the first wolf, it lopes off toward the driveway. The black wolf remains for just a moment longer, its eyes still intent upon the window. I dare not move.

Logically, I know I am safe. But that doesn't stop my heart from pounding in my ears like a kettledrum. I have never been this close to a wild wolf.

He sniffs the air, lifts his head, and begins to howl.

Shivers run up and down my spine, over my arms, through my hair, and out my toes.

"Holy Moses!" I gasp.

An answering call echoes across the yard.

The black wolf ceases his howl, turns one last look in my direction, and calmly trots off out of sight.

My journal is clasped tightly against my pounding chest. I ease it down and return to the bedroom via the kitchen, making sure the front door is locked before getting back into bed. Like a wolf could open a door even if it wasn't locked. I think that only happens in fairy tales. But still…

It takes a moment for me to settle myself and clear my mind from this awesome, yet slightly creepy experience. In all my years of coming up here, I have only ever heard the wolves, never seen them.

What an extraordinary week. Maybe being sixty-five isn't going to be as boring as I thought. Never having had a career, I also never retired from anything. I have plenty of friends who have recently retired from decades of work who have all kinds of ideas and plans for their retirement years. But for me, turning sixty-five hasn't changed much of anything. My life looks pretty much the same as it has for the last few decades.

But this week… what is going on?

I open my journal, take a deep breath, close my eyes, and look for my dream behind my eyelids. For Gin and Buck. For a bird in a cage. For Isabel on her bed, in her stone home, in the mountains.

It all comes rushing back to me, and I write as quickly as I am able, intent upon capturing every detail before they recede into my subconscious.

Once finished, I reread what I have written. It is amazingly real, tangible, substantive. I draw a set of lines underneath the last paragraph of the description and write one word—Why?

Why do I dream like this?

Why now? After all these years. Why have they started up again? Why me? I don't know anyone else who dreams like this or, at least, anyone who admits to me that they dream like this.

"What is this all about, Lord?" I whisper, placing my pen inside the journal like a bookmark and setting the book onto the nightstand.

It is four-thirty in the morning.

The howls of the animals have ceased but the wind has picked up where they left off. I lay back down and try to sleep, but after twenty minutes of tossing and turning, I give up, switch the light back on, and get out of bed. Might as well do something useful. I can always take a nap later.

MY SECOND CUP OF COFFEE IS HALF EMPTY when I hear a truck pull into the driveway. Great. I'm still in my pajamas and slippers having immersed myself in re-constructing the family-tree binder on the dining room table over the past several hours. It is fascinating work seeing all that Uncle has researched and put together. Birth records and baptismal certificates. Marriage licenses. Passenger ship lists. Military service records. I am re-inserting each document under the sections Einar has labeled according to family lines, starting with my grandfather and his siblings in one half of the binder, and my grandmother and her siblings on the other half. It is easy to get lost in the flow of the generational history.

What time is it anyway?

A quick check on my phone says 6:47 a.m.

Good grief. Who would possibly come at this hour?

I run to the bedroom and grab my robe just as someone knocks on the outside porch door.

"You up, Tor?"

It's Billy.

"Yup, just a second," I yell, running a brush through my hair before unlocking the kitchen door and stepping onto the frigid porch to let him through the front door. Outside, the sun is just barely beginning to show an inkling of rising on the eastern horizon. "Good morning. What brings you around so early?"

"Is it early?" my cousin says, swiping his boots on the welcome mat and following me back into the kitchen. "Guess so. Sorry, been up for hours already checking on the herd. Had a pack of wolves prowling around last night. Wondering if you saw or heard anything."

"Actually, I did," I say. "Had two of them right outside the dining room about 4:30 or so. Scared the bejeebers out of me."

"Did one of them have all black fur?"

"Yup, the bigger one was all black. And there was another smaller one that looked to be more grayish. They started howling right in the yard. Creeped me out. Did they do any harm to your cows?"

"No, but they were trying. Carin woke me up around four. Said she'd heard them going right by the house. I've gotten so used to their racket, I sleep right through it. But she was concerned, so I went out on the ATV. Found the whole wolf pack, five of them, cornering a smaller heifer out in the back forty.

Fired a shot up into the air and scared 'em off. They've been around a lot this winter. Must be the heavy snowpack. They're looking for food."

"That is not great," I say. "Anything I can do?"

"Just give me a shout if you see them around again. I'm gonna get a call into the DNR and get somebody out here. Don't want to wait until I've got a dead animal before I do something."

"Have you told Felix about all this? Wouldn't want Max to get into a fight with those bad boys. I mean, he is a dog who looks like he could take care of himself, but five against one are not good odds."

"Yup, yup. Good idea. I will head on over there right now."

My phone pings inside my bathrobe pocket.

I pull it out.

"Oh, wait up," I say to my cousin who is halfway out the kitchen door. "I've got a message from Sheriff Dumfrey to give him a call as soon as possible. Want to be in on that?"

Billy turns around immediately and takes a seat at the kitchen table.

"I'm all ears, Cuz," he says.

"Uh, we'd better do this call either at your place or out on the road," I say.

He hauls himself back up.

"Get some clothes on, and we can go over to my place. I'll give Carin a heads up we're coming her way. Meet ya out at the truck," he says, stepping outside into the brisk dawn.

As I am yanking on a fairly clean pair of jeans and a sweatshirt, my phone pings again from its place on the dresser next to the picture of my grandparents on their wedding day.

I flip it over.

"Call me when you get a chance."

It's from my brother Clay.

Goodness sakes. A bunch of early risers today.

Well, in London it's not so early.

But for me…

Good thing I didn't go back to bed.

"I'VE GOT A DEPUTY DRIVING OVER TO THE BAIT and pawn shop in Cass Lake right now," Sheriff Dumfrey says to Carin, Billy, and I as we sit at their long dining table. My phone is on speaker propped up against a wooden bowl filled with fruit.

"Did they give you a description of who brought the lawnmower in?" Billy asks.

"Yeah, but nothing I'm ready to talk about just yet. My guy is gonna pull the store's security video and see if that gives us a fuller picture. I'll let you know if things heat up from there. Just thought I'd fill you in on where we're at right now," the sheriff says.

"I sure appreciate that, Sheriff," I say. "Can't imagine they got too much money for a lawnmower in March. Especially with the winter we've been having. They must've been in a hurry to get cash."

"Well, that's one thing I tell my young deputies all the time. We can be patient. The bad guys will screw up sooner or later," he replies.

"I'm glad this time it was sooner rather than later," Carin comments, her round cheeks flushed with the perpetual blush that comes from outdoor farm chores, healthy living, and Scandinavian roots.

"Thanks for the info, Reggie," Billy says.

"You bet. Oh, say, while I've got you all on the line, about the coins. I've done some searching and asking around, and I can't find any accounts of stolen coins around here. At least not of the volume and type you showed me," the sheriff reports.

"Well, actually, I think I'm getting some answers about that on this end," I say. "Looks like the coins were a gift to my uncle from an Italian widow right after the war."

Billy and Carin both say, "What the heck?" at the same time.

"Yeah, I will fill you in later," I say to them.

"Sounds like a story I'd like to hear too," Sheriff Dumfrey adds.

"I'd be happy to tell you when you have a free moment," I say.

"Okey dokey. I will make sure to circle back around to you on that. For now, I'd better get back to the grindstone. We'll talk soon."

The call ends.

"Um, you've been doing some detective work, it sounds like," Carin says. "Pray tell. What have you uncovered?"

I recount for them my conversation with Tante Tilda regarding the photo of Einar and Joseph. Then I tell them of Felix's translation of the letter from Isabel, though I stop short of the added details I saw in my dream.

"My, my, my," Carin says when I'm done. "How very interesting. What are you going to do now? Are you going to contact the Everwind family?"

"I'm not sure yet," I reply. "Did I tell you I met Patrick Everwind in town yesterday?"

"The pharmacist?" Billy asks.

"Yup, that's the one. Had a very interesting chat as he was giving me a COVID test."

"You got tested yesterday? Why?" he asks.

"Didn't I tell you Peter is bringing Hazel up tomorrow night?"

"Oh, that's wonderful," Carin says. "But why the testing?"

"A prerequisite for the visit as dictated by Mariah and Isaac," I reply.

"I get it," she replies.

"Well, holy mackerel, Tor! That's great," Billy adds. "Haven't seen your hubby… Well, I guess I saw him in November during hunting season. But Hazel… Golly, must be a couple of years since she's been up this way. It'll be great to see how she's grown."

"I know, I can hardly wait. I'm afraid my brain is a bit ditzy with all the excitement. So, back to the coins. I think I need to chat with Peter and maybe my brothers. Maybe Tante and Katie too. It sort of seems like a family legacy type of thing that I don't want to handle all by myself."

"How about we set up a Zoom call sometime soon?" Carin suggests. "Maybe this weekend?"

"Can you do that here at your house?" I ask.

"Sure," Carin replies. "We may live in the north woods but we do have internet."

I give Billy a look. "Well, I only ask because someone gave me the impression that Zoom calls were only for city folks."

"Oh, gosh, Bill," Carin chides. "Have you been playing the dumb lumberjack card again?"

"Only when I need it to get out of trouble," he replies. "Like when I forget somebody's birthday call. But you've got to admit, Tor, I had some big doings going on around here that may have distracted me."

I laugh. "Okay. I will let you off the hook this time."

"You hungry?" he asks, grabbing an orange out of the fruit bowl and beginning to peel it. "Help yourself. Carin keeps bugging me to eat more fruits and veggies. So, she's got them sitting all over the house, hoping I'll get the picture."

"Looks like it's working," I say, taking a hold of an orange for myself.

"I've got some banana bread, too, if you'd like, Tora," Carin says. "Just baked it last night."

"That sounds wonderful," I reply. "I haven't eaten a thing this morning. Might need some fortification before our next call to Clayton."

Billy hangs his head over his orange, intently tugging off one chunk of rind at a time.

"Everything okay, Billy?" I ask.

He looks up sheepishly, plopping a section of orange into his mouth.

"William Arthur Hallstrom!" Carin hollers from the kitchen. "What happened to the banana bread?"

She marches into the dining room and stands toe to toe before her hulking husband. Despite her diminutive five-foot-nothing frame, she appears to be the favored contestant in this match. She extends to her husband a quarter loaf of bread whose end has been not so much sliced off as hacked off. Billy remains mute, his jaw conveniently occupied with chewing.

"Fruits and veggies, my eye," she huffs, one hand on her hip, her slipper tapping the hardwood floor.

He shrugs.

"Nothing to say for yourself," Carin continues.

Billy swallows.

"It was delicious," he replies with a twinkle in his eye.

"Oh, honestly," his wife says with a half-disgusted, half-pleased smile. "I'll see if I can salvage a piece for you, Tora." She spins around and marches back to the kitchen.

I smile at their banter.

Suddenly I miss Peter. I'm glad he will be here tomorrow night.

"Is this one of Einar's bowls?" I ask, touching the smooth varnished surface of the bowl filled with apples, bananas, and oranges.

"Yup," Billy replies. "Gave it to us Christmas of 2012. I know cuz it's the same Christmas our grandson Lucas was born. Ten years already."

Carin returns with a luscious slice of buttered banana bread.

"Coffee?" Carin asks, handing me the treat.

I shake my head.

Billy says, "I'll take a cup."

"You know where they're at," his wife replies, sitting down to indulge in her own chunk of banana and butter bliss.

Billy rolls his eyes. "I guess I deserve that," he says, trudging to the kitchen.

Carin smiles at me and winks.

When Billy returns with his cup of java, I suggest we call Clayton.

“Once more unto the breach, dear friends, once more, or close the wall up with our English dead,” my cousin says, raising his mug up like a toast.

“Oh, and now he’s quoting Shakespeare’s Henry the V,” I say. “I’m never falling for the dumb lumberjack routine again.”

FELIX

MAX AND I HAVE HAD A VERY productive morning. The leaky roof no longer leaks. The crooked front door is no longer crooked. The broken windowpanes over the sink are no longer broken. And the mouse that has been leaving traces all over the countertops at night has been apprehended. I did remove it from my dog's mouth before he ate it whole. Never a joyful thing for me to see a dead animal. Especially after my visit with Francis. Has me looking at the animal kingdom with a whole new set of eyes.

But I'm sure Janet won't mourn the loss of one small rodent. She will probably be most grateful for Max's cat-like skills.

I go to the refrigerator where my landlord has stuck the list of wished for repairs under two pink lady slipper magnets. I have checked off the first three with the red marker that dangles from a string attached to the magnet.

"Number four… back door."

That's all it says. Back door.

"Alright, buddy," I say to the canine lounging on his back on the kitchen rug. "Time to see what's up with the back door. You need to go out?"

Max rolls over with a remarkably efficient movement and springs to his feet.

"I take that as a yes."

We walk past the stairs that lead to the second level and down the hallway to the back of the house. Just inside the back door, two bedrooms are positioned on either side of the hall. I have taken residence in the one on the east side of the house.

When we first arrived at the house and checked into the back bedroom, I noticed a long, snake-like tube pushed back against the wall by the back door. Max had sniffed it suspiciously and tugged it out into the open but, finding it had no life in it, he soon left it alone. I discovered that it was a most effective device for stopping cold air from drifting in under the bottom of the back entrance. I had crammed it back into place, and we had left it and the door alone since then.

Now I drag the draft stopper aside with my foot and turn the door's handle. It comes off in my hand.

"Well, here's the first problem," I say, sticking my finger into the hole where the handle should reside, and tugging on the wood-paneled door.

It swings open easily. Almost too easily. Seems as if the door stopper has stopped more than just drafts.

A screen door hangs askew on its hinges just beyond the wood door. It, too, seems to have no way of latching securely to the doorframe. Pushing it outward is only difficult because of the several inches of snow that have accumulated over the past few days. A much thicker blanket of the white seems to have been shoved aside fairly recently. Certainly, sometime this winter. Probably, in the past few weeks, as if someone has entered through this door.

Max bounds out beside me, nearly knocking me over.

"Excuse you," I say, catching myself against the stair railing. Good thing these are more securely fastened than the ones on the front steps.

As I watch him bound out toward the line of trees in the back yard, I notice indents in the snow going down the stairs and around the side of the house. Max's big old paws have obliterated the ones on the steps going down into the yard, but not the others. I carefully make my way to the trail and brush aside the recent snow. Underneath, slightly marred and melted, are boot prints. Two pairs of them.

"Hmm, someone's been around here recently," I say to myself.

Maybe just Billy checking on things. But Billy and who?

Out in the trees, Max suddenly begins to bark. I see him standing in what I call his war stance—his four legs slightly wider than usual, his chest barreled out, his ears on full alert.

"What is it, buddy?" I ask, following his path through the snow. Should have put my boots on first and a jacket. I tug the collar of my flannel shirt closer and button the top button.

I see sets of animal prints along the edge of the yard. Not Max's. Not the fine hoof prints of deer. These are made by paws. Some quite large. Some smaller. Several animals. Too big for coyotes.

"Must be those wolves Billy was talking about," I say, coming up alongside my dog who continues to bark. "Do you see something? Or just smelling the remnants of the wolf pack?"

His bark stops and lowers into a deep growl in his chest. He has not moved from his position. I scour the field beyond the trees. Some of Billy's cows are out in the middle around a feeding station. Their journey to and from that place is marked by a heavily trodden path. The wolf prints track right along the trees, but I don't see any leading out toward the cattle. It's mid-morning. I can't imagine any self-respecting wolf would be hunting cows at this time of day. Unless they are really hungry.

"Easy there, big guy," I say, stroking Max's head. He begins to relax but doesn't move. "I'll let Billy know what's going on. We will keep our eyes peeled though. Good job, buddy. Come on, let's get back to work."

I head back to the house, trying not to get any more snow inside my slippers than I already have. The icy crystals have somehow reached inside my socks and are rubbing up against my ankles. But before I reach the back door, I see that the human set of prints leads to the utility shed.

Against the complaints of my ankles, I redirect toward the shed, stooping underneath three drooping wires strung between two t-shaped poles. Must have been a functioning clothesline at one time. Probably on the repair list too.

As I approach the shed, I can see that its sliding metal door is also in need of some attention for it, too, is askew. Upon reaching it, I yank it upward and set it back into its grooves. Snow has drifted inside through the cracked opening, forming a long narrow shaft of white against the compact dirt floor.

It is dark inside. The windows on either side are covered by bins set on metal shelving. From the morning light that filters in, I can make out a string hanging down from a lightbulb in the ceiling. I tug on it, and it illuminates the small interior.

Max comes sniffing through the door, his nose busily exploring this new space.

On the back wall, a countertop runs the width of the shed. Above it is a wall with empty hooks and racks where tools must have once resided. All that's left is a rusty hand saw and a dented watering can. But under the defunct waterspout is something of interest.

"Well, will ya look at this, Maximus?" I say.

He lifts his snout over the ledge of the countertop, exploring the door of a small, white microwave oven. Unlike all the other items in the shed, it is dust free.

Max licks the handle where the remains of some long distant spaghetti dinner linger.

"Harrumph," he says, pulling back into a sit by my side.

"Yup, that's what I was thinking," I say. The appliance's cord is plugged into an outlet on the back wall. I press the Start button. Nothing happens.

The sound of a vehicle's tires crunching over the icy snow sends Max bolting out of the shed. He is greeting Tora and Billy by the time I make my way gingerly around the house. Tora is bundled up in a smart black parka with fur around the hood and boots that reach up almost to her knees. Billy is garbed in his usual plaid flannel shirt, coveralls, and baseball cap. Not sure if I have ever seen him in a coat of any kind.

"Good morning, Mr. Maximus," Tora says, her hands cupped on either side of his upturned face. She leans down and receives a sloppy, wet kiss on her cheek without any reservation.

"Hope we're not interrupting important work," Billy says.

"No, not at all," I reply, advancing toward them, careful to stay away from the set of footprints alongside the house. "In fact, you're right on time. I believe Max and I may have found something of interest to you. But can you hold on a second? It's out back in the shed and I really need to get some proper footwear on."

"Sounds intriguing," Tora says. "Do what you need to do. We'll wait."

I make my way into the house, quickly swapping out my wet slippers for boots and donning a down-filled vest before heading back outside. Billy is already on the far side of the yard, following the animal tracks near the tree line.

"Are those wolf prints?" I holler.

"Yup, sure are," he hollers back. "Did you see any of them this morning?"

"No. Can't say that I did. But Max was pretty edgy last night or rather early this morning. I'd say around four-thirty or so. He was pacing the hallway. I let him out thinking he had to go to the bathroom. Tore off across the yard and didn't come back for a while. Didn't make much of it at the time. Did you have some troubles last night?"

"They were looking to eat one of my heifers," Billy says, coming back our direction. "But I scared them off just in time."

"I saw two of them right outside the dining room window about the same time you let Max out. Made me a bit uneasy," Tora adds.

"I will certainly be more cognizant of their intentions with your cattle," I say. "Should have known Max was onto something. Will let you know next time he acts like that."

"Sure would appreciate that," Billy says. "So, what have you got to show us?"

I lead them around the house, pointing out the boot prints along the way.

"Not mine," Billy says. "Haven't been around the back of this house since… don't rightly recall how long it's been."

Max is already at the shed dipping in and out of the door as if eager to get us all inside as soon as possible. Billy and Tora follow me into the small space.

"Oh, my lanta," Tora says, striding to the back shelf. "Is that Uncle's microwave?"

"I was hoping you could tell me," I say.

Tora leans around the side of the appliance.

"Yup, this is it alright," she says. "There's a sticker for the deer hunter's association out of Bemidji on the side from 1998. Shows you how long he had the thing. I think it only stopped working this year."

"They don't make 'em like they used to," Billy says. "Wonder who brought it over here?"

"That's what I was wondering," I say. "Think you might want to look through Janet's house, too, because whoever left this here may also have been inside the house. Come. Let me show you."

I take them to the back steps and show them all the signs of someone having gone through the back door in recent weeks.

"We just had a phone call with the sheriff right before we came over here," Tora says. "Seems they may have a lead on the lawnmower being pawned over in Cass Lake."

"Dumfrey will want to hear all about this," Billy says, crouching down to get a good look at the boot prints. "These have been here too long to leave any real definition. But there's at least two sets of prints. Maybe even three."

"That's what I thought too," I say, going up the stairs. "Careful with this door. It's my next project. Didn't realize it was so broken or I might have gotten to it sooner."

Billy stops to assess the locks and handles on both doors.

"Hmm, I'd say these have been messed with," he says.

"Could it have been the last renters?" Tora asks.

"Well, could be," Billy replies. "But these footprints are pretty recent and that group has been gone since mid-December."

"They might have come back," I say. "Maybe knew the place was empty. Knew they could break in without too much trouble."

"Could be," Billy says, stuffing his hands into his coveralls. "One of the renters was Janet's grandson Mikey. Just graduated from St. Gerard last year. And when I say 'just', I mean just barely. He got pretty messed up after his dad David, Janet's son, got killed over in Afghanistan when Mikey was maybe a freshman or sophomore."

"So tragic. And hadn't his mother been out of the picture for some time?" Tora asks.

"Yup. Left David high and dry when Mikey was just a toddler. Janet's sister Mary, who still lives in St. Gerard, took Mikey in when his dad got deployed. And then, well, God bless her, she's been there for him ever since. When Mikey asked his grandma if he and two of his buddies could rent out this place, I think Janet knew Mary was about at the end of her rope with the kid. She was trying to give 'em both a break."

"Didn't work out so well?" I ask as the three of us move into the kitchen.

"Nope. After the fourth time I had to disturb Janet from her place by the pool in Tampa cuz Mikey had thrown another big kegger, she'd had enough. And ya know, I get it. He's a kid. He wants to have fun with his buddies. But those guys were tearing up the roads with their monster trucks and about lit my fields on fire with firecrackers. Then they decided one night that tipping cows might be fun."

"Is that a real thing?" I ask. "Does not sound like such a good idea."

"Well, after you've had a few too many brewskis, a lot of things that aren't good ideas seem like good ideas."

"What happened?" Tora asks, taking a seat by the table and unzipping her parka.

"My cows didn't take too kindly to it," Billy says. "Got them stirred up pretty good and then my bull decided he wasn't too pleased with them messing with his herd. Chased those yahoos across the field and into the ditch in a big-time hurry. One kid twisted his knee up pretty good jumping over the wire fence. Mikey got me out of bed at 2 a.m. to take him into the clinic cuz none of them were fit to get behind the wheel of anything."

"Good golly," Tora says. "Sounds crazy."

"What happened to Mikey and his crew after Janet evicted them?" I ask.

"Not sure," Billy says. "Mikey said something about looking for work in Bemidji, but I don't know if that ever happened. Confess I haven't kept up with him. Was just relieved to get him out of our neighborhood."

"Did the sheriff search this house after the break-in?" I ask.

"I don't believe he did," Billy says. "But I will ask. Maybe we should take a look upstairs first and see if we can find anything."

Tora suddenly stands to her feet.

"Would you gentlemen mind terribly if I let you do that on your own? As curious as I am, I really need to get back to the house and get the upstairs shoveled out before Peter and Hazel arrive. They may be bringing her little puppy with them too. So, I need to get the place ready for company of various kinds and half the morning is gone already."

"You go, Tor," Billy says. "We will give you a call if we find anything we need you to identify."

I agree with Billy and escort my neighbor to the door.

"Have you seen Max since we left the shed?" I ask, scanning the yard.

"No," Tora says, zipping up her coat. "He didn't follow us into the house. That much I know."

A wild barking echoes from somewhere behind the house followed by the bellowing of cows.

Billy marches out to meet me on the front stoop.

"Is that your dog?" he asks at the same time I ask, "Are those your cows?"

TORA

BILLY LEAPS DOWN THE STAIRS in two strides, dips through the opening in the line of scrubby lilac bushes, and runs to his rig. He flings open the back crew cab door and comes out with a rifle in hand.

"You coming, Felix?" he yells over his shoulder, already on the move toward the field behind the house.

"Might be a good idea for you to stay here," Felix says to me.

"Um, yes, well… I think I will get back to my place. Can't be much use to the two of you in whatever this is all about," I reply.

Felix nods and takes off after Billy.

Max is now half barking, half howling from somewhere inside the woods.

It is a serious, haunting sound.

I go down the steps and through the lilac bushes, watching the two men struggle through the snow until they reach the cattle path. At that point, they both break into a run. Felix pulls ahead of Billy about halfway to the tree line. The cows at the feeding trough have their heads cranked around to see what the fuss is all about. Others that have already retreated due to Max thundering past them trot further into the snowy field away from the onrushing men. They moo and shift from side to side restlessly, the whites of their bulging eyes visible even from my distant vantage point.

Felix and Billy disappear into the underbrush one after the other, slapping branches and bushes aside as they go. Max's bark becomes more insistent the closer they get.

"Over here!"

Felix's cry reaches me across the distance.

I am riveted to the spot halfway down the drive, looking back to where the action is occurring.

"Sweet Jesus," I whisper. "Keep them safe."

A gunshot rings out.

I flinch.

An animal yelps.

Is it Max?

I can no longer stay where I am.

Following in the men's path that they have plowed, I reach the cattle path and find myself jogging to the place I saw them enter the woods. The cows around the feeding area are fleeing en masse and forming a circle on the far side of the snowy meadow away from me. My heavy snow boots, my thick parka, and my sixty-five years all encumber my speed.

"Are you okay?" I yell into the woods as loudly as my winded lungs allow.

No answer.

I duck into the trees where snapped branches and boot prints mark their entry.

"Billy? Felix?" I yell as I go.

The snow is not as deep here under the trees, but the fallen logs and uneven terrain make the going slow.

"Tora," Billy finally yells back. "We're okay."

He is not far.

I see a flash of red between the branches. It looks like Felix's vest.

A few more strides and I can make out Billy's bulk kneeling in the snow beside Felix. There is something dark at his feet.

"What happened?" I ask, coming up behind them. "Where's Max?"

Felix turns to me.

"Tora, you might not want to see this," he says, putting a hand out. "Max is chasing after the wolves."

I stop in my tracks, huffing and puffing from the exertion.

"The wolves? Now? In the middle of the morning?"

I bend over with my hands on my thighs and take deep breaths.

"Did you shoot one?" I ask Billy, who has not moved at my arrival.

"He wounded one," Felix says.

"How many were there?"

"We saw three. But looks like there might have been more before Max got here," Felix replies.

I stand upright, wiping a trickle of sweat from my hairline.

"So, what's on the ground?" I ask.

Felix steps back to me.

"It's one of the cows," he says. "She's in rough shape."

"A cow? Out here in the woods? What was she doing out here?"

"Probably wandered off or got separated somehow… Not sure," Felix replies. "Billy says she's a yearling."

A tumult of snapping and bending branches comes at us from the opposite direction. Billy stands up abruptly with his gun drawn to his shoulder.

Felix leaps from my side to Billy and pushes the barrel to the ground." It's Max," he says. "It's just Max."

My cousin lets his weapon drop and his shoulders slouch. "Damn," he utters. "Sorry."

"It's alright," Felix says as Max bounds to his master's side and plants himself on full alert by his left leg. "Good boy. You did good, buddy."

Billy lets out a rush of air.

"Tora, can you go call Carin and let her know what's happened? I'm gonna have to put this cow down and we'll need help getting her out of the woods. And have her get the DNR out here right away, will ya?" he says without ever looking me full in the eye.

Even in profile, I can see the anguish and anger on his face.

"Sure, Bill. I'll go do that right now," I say.

"I will stay," Felix says, turning to me. "Can you take Max with you?"

"Will he come with me?"

Felix bends down and speaks directly to his canine companion." Call him," he says to me. "He'll follow you. He'll protect you."

I gulp. I hadn't even thought about the pack of wolves that still roams the woods." Max, come," I say, and he trots to my side and does not leave me even when the second gunshot rends the air.

MAXIMUS

THEY SAY WE DESCEND FROM THE SAME LINE.

The wolves and I.

Maybe so.

But I did not see it today.

Their eyes were vicious.

Hunting.

Hungry.

Maybe when the snow is less and the food is plentiful. When the weather is calm and bellies are full.

Maybe then they are dog-like.

But somehow, I doubt it.

Not that I have run with many wolves. At least not four-legged ones. Master and I have seen plenty of the two-legged kind.

Those make my hair stand up. Set my teeth on edge.

They cause more harm than anything this pack I saw today could ever do.

They steal from widows and abuse orphans.

They sit in seats of power and gulp down more than their fair share of everything.

They hunt in packs and alone. At night and in the day.

These wolves I would like to hunt myself.

Master keeps me in check.

Though from time to time…

Once or twice…

He has set me loose.

But that has been over the course of many decades, centuries even.

I will protect, as Master has bid me do today with Tora.

I will risk all to fulfill my duty.

But I will not hunt.

Not like the wolves.

Unless, of course, I am hunting wolves.

TORA

THE THIRD GARBAGE BAG of detritus from upstairs thumps and bumps down the stairs behind me as I drag it to join the other two in the dining room. Max turns his head in his spot on the rug by the kitchen door to acknowledge me then shifts back to staring off toward Janet's house. He has been like this for the past several hours, ever since we came back from the horrible scene in the woods.

Since talking with Carin, I have had no update from anyone, though I have seen two pickups and a DNR rig come down the road and turn into Janet's driveway from my view in the upstairs bedroom window. My sorting and tossing have kept me engaged in my own process, but I am aware of the sad drama playing out next door. I murmur prayers under my breath without even thinking about it.

The north bedroom is nearly set straight. There have been no big surprises, just books, photographs, and magazines scattered everywhere with random baseball score cards sprinkled throughout. Between taking care of cows and cutting hay, my dad and Einar played a lot of ball up here in the summers when they were young. 'Town Ball' they called it, where each little town would put together a team and play one another in a semi-organized league. Guess my dad was a good pitcher, but Einar was the star fielder and batter. Two leather mitts sit untouched atop the armoire in the corner of the bedroom under the eaves as if too hallowed to be disturbed. The doors stand wide open though, and all the clothing lies strewn over the bed.

Old cardigans, jackets, and trousers are jumbled together with a couple of baseball uniforms with Solbakken hand stitched on the back of each. I return most of the items to their place in the armoire except those too moth eaten or worn to be much good to anyone, even for dress-up. I remember doing just that with some of these very same items when I was a kid. Dad especially liked it when I'd don one of the uniforms and insist he play catch with me in the yard. I didn't often get his full attention. But I did when I was on the Solbakken team.

Max's bark jolts me out of my memories. I hustle down the stairs and into the kitchen to see what's gotten him agitated. I have learned in our short acquaintance that he is not a dog given to superfluous noise making.

"What's up, buddy?" I say as he greets me in the dining room and runs back to the kitchen door. "Is somebody here?"

I did not hear any rig pull into the yard.

"Tora?" Felix yells as he knocks on the outside door. "May I come in?"

"Yes, yes, of course," I say, sidling past my canine bodyguard to allow entry to his master.

Max is elated at his return and only sits after several commands.

"He's a bit wound up still," Felix says. "Always stays that way when he knows he's on duty."

"He has been a most comforting presence here. Thanks for loaning him to me," I reply. "How's everything going with Billy?"

"The cow has been properly removed. Billy's guys are taking care of that. Guess he has to make a claim with the state to get reimbursed for the loss of livestock. It's pretty clear based on the evidence that the cow was attacked by wolves and that the injuries were not treatable. Now they're discussing what needs to be done about the wolves."

"Will they shoot them or trap them or what?"

"Not sure. But I heard one guy say that just last week the wolves were returned to some federally protected species list. Which means you can only legally shoot one if you are defending an attack on a human."

"Did they say what you should do about Max? Can you let him roam around like he has?"

Felix scratches Max behind the ears. "We'll figure that out," he says as the dog leans into his side. "Did I hear you say that your granddaughter is bringing a puppy along with her?"

I plop down onto the stool beside the stove.

"Oh, golly," I say. "I did not think about that. Maybe I'd better discuss that with Peter and Mariah." I let my head sink into my hands. "It's just that a puppy is the last thing my daughter needs right now. She gets so sick when she's expecting…"

"Expecting? Congratulations," he remarks.

"Thanks, uh, probably wasn't supposed to let you know that," I say.

"Your secret is safe with me. And don't let me talk you out of having the puppy up here. You'll need to be aware and do things maybe a bit more defensively than you might normally. That's all," Felix says.

"You're right. But I am going to let them know what's going on so we are all informed in our decision."

"Okay. I need to get back to my to-do list. Want me to take these bags out to your SUV?" he says, pointing to my collection of black bags.

"That would be great," I reply, and we set to the task together.

The house seems a bit empty when I return inside. I am glad I have company coming tomorrow. Suddenly my stomach rumbles loudly. I check the clock on the oven. It is just past noon. Feels like it should be supper time, I've been up for so long. Fixing myself a sandwich with a side of chips, I go into the living room, setting my plate on a footstool. Makes me miss the table that is MIA. I go to the stereo and slide open the cabinet door that contains the albums, selecting Beethoven's Complete Symphonies by the Berlin Philharmonic. I place it on the turntable, keeping the volume on low. It is the perfect accompaniment to my meal.

As I munch, I draw the container of old letters I painstakingly refilled yesterday to my side. Skimming through, I withdraw a few and scan them. Scenes from foreign shores and foreign wars play out discretely in the words from my dad and Einar. I replace them and tug out a packet of letters that have been secured together by twine. Carefully extracting one, I see that it is postmarked from Norway with a date of 1906. The address simply reads Arnhild Isabel Pederson, Solbakken, Minnesota, USA.

Unfolding the letter, I see lovely handwriting all in Norwegian. Some of the ink is faded or blurred but most is legible to someone who understands the language. I flip it over to see who it is from. The words at the bottom stop my chewing.

It is signed Mormor Kari. From what I have gathered in my brief acquaintance with the family genealogy, I believe this is my grandmother's grandmother on her mother's side.

But what causes me to have to take a swig of water before I swallow are the words directly above her signature.

They are not Norwegian.

They are Hebrew.

"Shalom. Shalom."

Kicking off my slippers and brushing the last crumbs of my sandwich from my lips, I stretch out on the couch with the letter. Besides my great-great grandmother's name, which I read only hours ago on the family tree, I know next to nothing about the woman herself. I slowly pour over the letter, wishing I understood her native tongue.

A few words stand out. And a few names. But other than that, the content remains cloaked behind the mystery of language. I wonder if maybe my son-in-law's software might be able to help me translate.

I tug the Minnesota Vikings throw from off the back of the couch and toss it over my body. I am remembering the promise I made to myself that if I got out of bed at 5 a.m. and did something useful, I could always take a nap.

Now is the time to fulfill that promise.

With Symphony No. 1 in C major, Op. 21 playing in the background, I close my eyes.

"TORA-BIRD," SOMEONE CALLS MY NAME.

"Is that what you call her?" another voice asks somewhere over my head.

"Yes," the first voice replies. "Tora-bird. There's someone here who wants to read you a story."

I rub the sleep from my eyes and sit up.

"Oh, hi, Grandma," I say, squinting up into her familiar, kind face. I swivel to see the other woman seated on my other side. "Hello. Who are you?"

She smiles at me, and her deep blue eyes shine like crystals in the middle of her round face. Waves of glossy red hair tumble over her shoulders.

"My name is Kari Toresdatter. I am your *farmor's mormor."*

My eyebrows scrunch together and she laughs.

"That means I am your grandmother on your father's side, grandmother from her mother's side," Kari explains.

"Hmm, I think it sounds better the other way," I reply.

The two women smile and nod.

"We agree," they say in unison.

"Are you here to tell me a story?" I ask Kari.

She nods as a leaf comes floating down from the overhead branches and settles in the palm of her outstretched hand.

"What's this one called?" Grandma Arnie asks, though her voice is suddenly younger. Much younger. I turn to look and she, too, is now like me—a child. We are two small girls, dressed in flannel nightgowns, waiting eagerly for a grandmother's tale.

Kari Toresdatter turns the leaf on its side, and it becomes a green leather-bound book in her hands.

"It is called, *Never Forget*," she says, opening the book on her lap and glancing our direction. "It is the story of my Morfar and Mormor, Jacob and Berit."

In my mind I calculate that we are going back six generations before I was born.

Grandma Arnie and I clasp hands and lean into one another's presence. I like knowing her as a girl—as a friend.

Kari's eyes hold something profound in them and her voice sounds like the last echo of a church bell on a Sunday morning—pure, melodious, and beckoning.

"IT SHOULD NEVER HAVE COME TO THIS," my father said to me that Friday afternoon in the month of April, in the year 1792. "I should have stopped this long ago."

He sighed deeply, setting aside the quill pen he was using to record the day's sales and removing his spectacles. The bakery counter behind which he sat covered his thick girth but revealed his well-muscled neck and shoulders earned from decades of kneading dough.

Jacob and I stood side by side on the opposite side of the bakery counter from him, our fingers lightly touching between us. I still wore my work apron over my wool skirt and knit sweater. Jacob had removed his apron and it hung limply in the crook of his elbow. We had waited for my brother Peder to leave before daring to broach the subject with Pappa. For once, my brother had not seemed to want to run out to find his friends at the end of his shift, and I could barely keep myself from pushing him out the door. But Jacob had calmed me with his eyes and we had kept ourselves busy until we were finally alone in the shop. Just we three.

"Pappa," I said. "You have always told me to follow my heart. Yes?"

He nodded wearily, the grey strands of his beard scratching the front of his flour covered apron.

"Jacob is my heart," I added.

Pappa looked deeply into my eyes. I did not flinch from his stare. As his look passed to Jacob, I saw my love's chin start to tip downward in my peripheral vision, and I gave his little finger a squeeze.

"You must look him in the eyes," I had coached Jacob last night. "He must see that we are serious. He must see that you are a man whose mind is made up."

Jacob's head instantly bobbed back to a full, upright position inside the starched collar of his baker's tunic.

Moments stretched on. I reminded myself to breathe.

"I have raised you as my own son," Pappa said to Jacob. "I have trained you as a baker, as a tradesman, as a man. I have fulfilled every promise I made to your father; God rest his soul. My home, my family, my time, my skill has all been yours."

I felt that Jacob wanted to say something, to thank him. But I knew it was not the time to interrupt. Pappa was not done. I pinched Jacob's pinky again. The words died on his lips.

"And now you ask me for the one thing I cannot give you," Pappa said, folding his hands atop the ledger in front of him. I wanted to warn him the ink was not yet dry; it would stain his forearm. But I heeded my own warning. I stayed quiet.

Pappa pinched his nose where his glasses had left imprints along the bridge.

The door to the store suddenly opened, ushering in a gust of cool spring air along with a customer. It was Fru Sorenquist. Jacob and I spun around like two panels of a swinging door.

"Oh," Fru Sorenquist said. "The sign says you are still open. Am I interrupting?"

Pappa stood, forcing a smile onto his face.

"The sign should have been changed," he said, giving me direction with his eyes to flip the sign on the door like I should have done half an hour ago. I scurried to comply, leaving Jacob abandoned in the middle of the floor.

He recovered himself, turned to the unexpected customer, and quickly drew his apron back over his head before securing its ties around his waist.

"Fru Sorenquist. How nice to see you. We just happen to have two loaves of your favorite rye bread still on the shelf. They must have been saved just for you," he said, moving behind the counter, easing past Pappa to the two dark loaves on the display racks. "Would you like both or just one?"

"I will take them both." She reached into her shopping bag to retrieve her coin purse. "Please forgive me the late hour, my son Halvor is home from his schooling in Stockholm and I lost track of time. He was just asking if I had seen you, Berit," she said, turning to me.

"Tell him hello," I replied, busying myself with end of the day clean-up to keep her from seeing the flush of my cheeks. It was the bane of my red-haired existence—this inability to keep my face from revealing my inner agitations.

Halvor Sorenquist was once my friend. Once Jacob's friend.

But after what he attempted to do to me last summer after the village picnic, everything has changed. My anger and humiliation rushed to the surface afresh, and I was sure every one of my ginger freckles had been consumed by pink.

"And Jacob, how are you these days? Any big plans?" she asked.

Jacob smiled kindly despite what I knew was churning in his belly. He was the one who had rescued me from Halvor's advances. The one who found me in what anyone else would have assumed was a compromising position. But Jacob knew me. And he knew Halvor. He knew immediately who had forced the compromising, and his knuckles bore the marks of his knowledge for weeks afterwards. I could only imagine how long Halvor's face had taken to rid itself of the black and blue bruises.

"It is something I'm working on," Jacob said, exchanging the loaves for the coins in her outstretched hands.

"Berit," Pappa said. "Get the door for Fru Sorenquist, please."

I plastered a smile on my face before turning to her.

"Allow me," I said, opening the front entry.

"Are you feeling alright, dear?" she said, stopping to look me over from head to toe. "I think your father may be over-working you. Don't want to push the bloom off the rose before the rose can attract a husband." Her loud remarks were directed over her shoulder to Pappa.

"Oh, no, I wouldn't do that," Pappa replied without a hint of the anger I saw in his eyes being reflected in his voice.

"Well, you take care of yourself, Berit. And I'll tell Halvor you'd love to see him," Fru Sorenquist said, going down the steps that led out onto the sidewalk.

I closed and locked the door behind her without allowing myself a response. That was not what I said and she knew it. Leaning my head against the cool glass pane, I steeled myself to resume the conversation that was so unpleasantly interrupted.

Jacob came up behind me and gently turned me around with one hand on each shoulder. The understanding I saw in his crystal blue eyes reminded me once again of why I loved this man so deeply, why he had captivated my heart.

"He cannot hurt you," Jacob whispered. "I will not let him."

Despite Pappa's presence, I allowed Jacob to pull me into an embrace.

When we separated and turned back to the counter, Pappa was staring at us with tears rolling down his cheeks. He was not a hard man. Just a man bound by the conventions of his times. Although Jacob had lived in our household since he was eight years old, and had been baptized in the Lutheran church, everyone in town knew his father was Jewish. A merchant who travelled to our seaside village in south Sweden carrying wheat from the fields of Prussia.

His name was Judah Lewinski. "A good and honest man." That's what Pappa had always said about him. His wife had died in childbirth, leaving him a son to raise on his own. Jacob Judah Lewinski. A boy who grew up on a boat, on the sea, in the open air. Educated by his father. Beloved of the deckhands. Until his father had died and left him an orphan.

"Come," Pappa said, resuming his seat behind the counter. "Let us reason this out… before I tell your mother."

"Are you saying…" I began, but Pappa stopped me.

"I am not saying anything, yet," he replied.

But something had shifted in him. Something big. I felt it deep within my soul. Jacob grabbed my hand, and we walked together back toward the man we both call Pappa.

"You know you are not allowed to marry in the eyes of the government or of the church, yes?" he asked, his hands clasped together over the ledger book.

"We know," Jacob said.

Tears washed over Pappa's eyes again, and he wiped them with the back of a hand still displaying remnants of flour in every crevice.

"Then you are planning on leaving us?" he asked.

Jacob and I looked at one another.

"If we must," I said. "We would rather stay with you. With Mama and the children. But we are not abandoning you. Peder is no longer a child. He bakes better than any of us. He will carry on your legacy. Your business."

"He was always the one who would," Jacob added, not resentfully but with certainty.

Pappa nodded, closing his eyes. Long seconds ticked by.

"First, you must tell me what happened between you and Halvor Sorenquist," he said, opening his eyes and staring at me. "I may be old but I am not blind. I have seen how he lurks around you and pesters you, Berit. Even when you give him no encouragement, he walks up to you as if…" He swallowed down something that had risen in his throat. "…as if he owns you."

Jacob squeezed my hand.

"Tell him, Berit," he said. "He needs to know now."

I swallowed down the bile of anger, disgust, and shame that threatened to close my airway and strangle my voice. I kept my eyes on the well-worn wood of the counter, away from Pappa's for I could not bear to look him full in the face. But I began. And as I did, courage rose up in me. The entire story of the assault behind the graveyard last summer came rushing out. My cheeks were aflame but I did not care. Pappa knew well what the various shades of my skin revealed. For once, I was glad of the confirmation.

When I finished, Pappa's head rested in his hands, his face averted from ours. I did not know if he was processing or praying. Probably both. Jacob and I waited for him to respond.

Without lifting his head, he began to speak.

"My cousin Bjarne is a good man, a good baker. He lives in Østerdalen by the Glomma River in eastern Norway. I have not seen him in many years," he said so quietly we took a step closer to hear him. "I will write him." Then he lifted his head. "I will ask if there is a place for my daughter and son-in-law in his business."

I nearly vaulted over the counter to hug him but he held up his hands to stop me.

"I will not tell him of your heritage, Jacob," he continued. "The laws of Norway are no different than here. Perhaps even a bit stricter. So, that secret… that burden will be yours… both of yours for the rest of your lives. Or until change comes. But that may be some time. Can you do that? I will not even inquire of Bjarne if you cannot abide by that caveat. I cannot require of his family what the Lord has required of us."

I turned to Jacob. His face was impassive but the firm set of his jaw informed me of the depth of this moment for him.

"Pappa… Sir," Jacob said. "If you entrust me with your daughter, I will endure anything. Even this. For I know God looks not on the outside but on the heart. That is what you have taught me. That is what my father taught me. I carry both of you with me wherever I go for as long as I live, even as I carry the God of Abraham, Isaac, and Jacob. I may not be able to tell of who I am, but I will never forget."

"We will never forget," I added.

A slight smile entered Pappa's eyes, though not reaching his mouth. He came around the end of the counter and stood directly in front of us.

Placing his right hand on Jacob's head and his left on mine he said. "Then I give you my blessing. Shalom, shalom, my children. May His favor go before you and behind you unto the thousandth generation."

I threw my arms around Pappa and wept, his beard resting on the crown of my head.

"And may He help us find a trustworthy man of God who will marry you," he said over me to my future husband.

FELiX

"WHAT A MORNING, EH?" I say to Max who lies curled up at my feet.

He looks up without lifting a muscle save those of his eyelids.

"Thanks for all you've done," I say, rubbing under his neck with my foot. "You've already had a full day's work. But I'd better get back to mine."

I am finishing a cup of coffee and a sandwich before resuming my back door project. Billy, his farm hands, and the fellow from the DNR are all gone. The quiet of the north woods has descended once again. I stop to bow my head and pray over all that has gone on today thus far, and I allow my mind to wander into what may yet come.

"Thank You for this time with these people… my people," I whisper to the Almighty. "Show me what my part is here in this place called Solbakken with these descendants of my descendants' descendants. I believe Tora is the key. She does not yet understand. Every time she has chosen life and goodness is no small thing in view of the future, in view of forever. But she seems to feel overlooked or passed by. Oh, Father, if only she could see what I see and know what I know of the generations who have gone before her—of the acts of service, the steps of faith, the sacrifices of love that flow through her veins. The compounded blessings she has inherited. The legacy she advances without awareness. The ripples she is sending into eternity. How can I be of assistance to what You are doing in her?"

The March wind rattles the slightly ajar back door, reminding me of one act of service I can easily fulfill. Leaving my dog to his nap, I say my "amen," clean up my dishes, and set to my task.

Hours slip by as I lose myself in the flow of work. Before too long, I can open and shut both the screen door and the wood door with satisfying confidence that they will serve their purpose. I return to the kitchen and cross off item number four from the to-do list. Scanning the remainder of the twenty-two requests, I check to see if any should clearly take precedence over any other.

5. Bathroom tiles. 6. Drip under sink. 7. Linoleum by washing machine. 8. Light fixture over front door. 9. Hole in pantry floorboards—mice? 10. Railings on front porch. 11. Window shade fixed upstairs. 12. Shed door derailed.

I scratch that one off.

13. Upstairs bedroom closet—light bulb, shelves, mice?

Retrieving a mouse trap from the St. Gerard Hardware and Bait Shop bag on the kitchen counter, I venture upstairs. Haven't spent any time up here and this is a good excuse to snoop around a bit. With all the excitement over the wolves this morning, Billy and Tora and I never did get around to scouring the house for possible evidence of who may or may not have been here recently.

There is just one bedroom upstairs. It is long and narrow with a slanted roofline that only allows me to stand fully upright if I am in the middle of the room. Two single beds are tucked under the eaves on either side of the window that looks out toward Einar's house. Faded gingham curtains are gathered to each side with matching loops of fabric. A pull-down shade hangs cockeyed half-way down the window and dead flies line the windowsill. I try to tug the shade back into place but it only pulls so far and then sluggishly retracts into the exact same position.

Peering under the curtains, I shove the entire contraption out of its brackets and rewind the plastic shade evenly before replacing it under the upper window frame. Gently, I draw the shade down until it reaches all the way to the fly-covered ledge. Then with a tug, it snaps back into place, sending a few of the dead insect carcasses skittering to the floor. I will return with a broom and dustpan but for now, I wipe my hands off with a sense of satisfaction and make a mental note to cross off number eleven.

The closet is at the other end of the room across from a set of low bookshelves and a little desk and chair. All appears to be in order although quite dingy with dust. I bend down, setting the unarmed mousetrap atop the desk and open the sole drawer. Stubby pencils and broken crayons lie next to a few rusty paperclips. Names have been scratched into the bottom panel. Janet 'hearts' Ricky has been marked over with pen but is still visible. Mary 'hearts' Ricky remains clear and unmarred. I lift up two scraps of paper. They are blank. Underneath, a peace sticker is stuck next to a yellow smiley face sticker. I set the paper back down and shut the drawer but it doesn't want to go back in. Something seems to be impeding its progress.

Kneeling on the braided rug, I stick my head under the drawer. A large manila envelope has been stuck through the bottom support bar but has slipped backwards and is crinkling up against the back desk frame. I reach under and extract it from its place, trying not to cause any more damage than I already have.

Sitting down on the rug, I smooth out the envelope and undo the metal clasp. Peering inside, I can see a laminated page like that from a scrapbook or photo album. I extract it. Under the slightly yellowed plastic overlay is a sheet of paper with the faint impression of a tree filling its entirety. Along the tree's branches are boxes of white space. Some are filled with names. Most are not.

At the bottom of the tree, in the middle of the trunk, is the name Einar Gottlieb Anderson—DOB August 20, 1913. The date of death has not been filled in. Next to it are the initials G.A.E.—DOB February 12, 1919 and DOD June 18, 1991.

Above these entries, on the first branch to the right, are more initials and a birth date.

T.E.E.—December 6, 1946.

And above him, there is quite a fully leafed out branch.

Birth dates are carefully recorded behind each set of initials.

The last one at the top reads—S.G.E.—January 16, 2013.

As I replace the page into the manila envelope, I spy a much smaller envelope tucked into the bottom. I turn the large envelope upside down to loosen it from its place. An aged, letter-sized envelope falls into my lap. Turning it over, I can see it is addressed to Einar Anderson, c/o GE Aviation, Lynn, Mass. The postmark reads December 20, 1946.

Retrieving the letter from inside, I undo the tri-folded sheet. It feels almost soft to the touch as if someone has handled it so often all the paper's irregularities have been worn smooth. The writer begins with, "Dearest Nephew, you are well? English hard for me to write. Please forgive."

The rest of the letter is all written in what I assume to be Norwegian. Not a language I am familiar with, unfortunately. It is signed at the bottom, Tante Tora. Scanning the unfamiliar words, I make out a couple of names—Grace, George, Joseph, and Thomas. And one date.

December 6th.

Standing to my feet, I set the contents of the envelope on the desk and consider the discovery I have made.

Tora will want to see this.

TORA

I AM ROUSTED FROM MY NAP by a firm rapping at the front door. Wiping the drip of drizzle from the corner of my mouth, I check my phone—two missed calls and three texts. I tuck my hair behind my ears and rub my eyes. It feels as if I have slept for days, though, in reality, it has only been an hour. But this is much longer than I usually allow myself to nap in the middle of the day lest I be up all night.

"Coming," I yell as I sit up.

A letter falls from my chest into my lap. The last line catches my eye.

Mormor Kari. Shalom. Shalom.

And I am transported back to a bakery. To a young couple. To a moment. An insight. Oh, I need to write this down.

"You awake, Tor?" Billy yells through the kitchen. "Got Sheriff Dumfrey with me and Felix too."

"Yup, yup," I yell back. "Just a second."

I whisper a prayer that the images from my dream will remain until I have time to record them.

Sliding my feet into my slippers, I carefully fold up the letter and place it atop the box of letters on the floor. I grab my lunch dishes from the footstool and hustle into the kitchen to greet whatever is about to unfold next. It is not easy to keep my mind focused on the here and now. Thoughts and images flit in and out like a movie playing overhead or a soundtrack running in the background.

Jacob. Berit. Sweden. Østerdalen. Norway.

"Sorry to barge in on you like this," Sheriff Dumfrey says. "Billy called me and told me about the findings over across the way. I was just heading back to Bemidji from Waskish. Thought I should swing by and see what's what. I did try to give you a call but I understand what with the reception being what it is out here."

"Yes, I see you tried to call. Sorry I missed you. I've, uh, been napping actually," I say.

"No need to apologize," the sheriff says. "Billy and Felix filled me in on the unfortunate events around here this morning. Understand you saw the wolves over here too?"

"About 4:30 a.m. Right outside that window," I say, pointing behind me at the dining room. "Gave me quite a start. And, well, I couldn't get back to sleep after that."

"We showed Sheriff the microwave that Felix discovered over in Janet's shed," Billy says. "And he's got some news about the lawnmower. Mind if we sit down somewhere? I'm a little bushwhacked and Felix has something to show you too."

"Oh, sure. Let's sit at the dining room table," I say, turning back into that room and sweeping stacks of paperwork to one end of the table built long ago by my great-grandfather. "Think I've got four empty chairs here. Anybody need coffee?" I ask.

"Not me," Felix says.

"I'm good," both Billy and Sheriff Dumfrey defer.

"Okay then," I say, going to the far side of the table and sitting with my back to the window. "Fill me in."

Sheriff Dumfrey sits at the head of the table, placing his wide-brimmed sheriff's hat in front of him, the gold star facing outward. Felix sets a manila envelope down before taking the chair directly across from me. Billy sits next to him.

"Before I forget," I say. "Did you tell the sheriff what Clayton said about the coins, Bill?"

"Nope. Plumb forgot," he replies.

"What did he find out?" the sheriff asks.

"Just that the coins look to be quite valuable. Some Clayton had never seen before. And with him, that's saying a lot," I reply. "Thankfully, nothing comes up as stolen or missing from any collections."

"Good news, I'd say," Sheriff Dumfrey remarks.

"Yes, it is good news. But now we need to make some decisions about what to do with them. Based on the letter from the Italian benefactress that Felix translated for me, it may be that some of the coins were meant for one of Uncle's army buddies. So, there are some things to sort through still," I say, looking at Felix. "Say, where's Max?"

"He seems to have had the same response as you to the morning's activities," Felix says. "I left him at home napping."

"You've had quite the morning out here in Solbakken," Sheriff Dumfrey says. "I've gotta tell you, Felix, you may have arrived at the busiest week in Solbakken history. At least since the last Sons of Norway lutefisk festival. When was that anyways? You recall, Billy?"

"Summer of 2019. Before all this COVID crap," my cousin replies.

"Ah, yup. That seems about right," the sheriff replies.

"I have never eaten lutefisk," Felix says. "Any chance of another festival this summer?"

"Well, now, Carin is on the committee discussing that very thing," Billy says. "They're getting more optimistic since things seem to be opening up a little bit. Nothing set in stone yet though."

"If there's anything I have learned in the past few years, it's that very few things are set in stone," I say with a sigh.

"True that," Billy concurs. "But if you've really got a hankering, Felix, my wife makes some of the best lutefisk this side of Oslo. She'd whip ya up a batch anytime you'd like. Truth is, she doesn't get too many requests for it."

"Not everyone's cup of tea," I add. "Just the smell can vanquish the faint of stomach."

"Might be how the Vikings won their wars," Billy says. "So, then now, let's get down to business. Sheriff, give Tora the lowdown, if ya don't mind."

"Alright then. We've identified Janet's grandson Mikey as the one who brought the lawnmower into the pawn shop," he says. "Got a good picture of him off the store's video security. And the clerk identified him too. Said he didn't give him a very good price. Mikey didn't seem to care. Just wanted some cash."

"Oh, boy," I say, putting my chin onto my steepled hands. "That's not great. Have you located Mikey?"

"Not yet," the sheriff continues. "We found out he's been staying at his girlfriend's apartment in Bemidji. We chatted with her, and we're pretty sure she didn't have anything to do with the break-in out here. But she said she would not be too surprised if Mikey had been involved. Seems he's been acting edgier than usual the past few weeks. Hasn't seen him since Monday night, and didn't know where he might be now but was pretty pissed off because wherever he is, he took her car and left her with his junker of a pickup."

"Does Janet know?" I ask.

Sheriff Dumfrey nods. "I have informed her. Might be that he will turn up on her front porch in Florida. So, she's got instruction of what to do if he does."

"She must be so disappointed," I say.

"We all are," Billy says. "Sheriff talked to his Auntie Mary, too, and she just broke down and cried he says."

"After all she's done for that boy, I can understand that," I say. "Did his girlfriend have any idea why he did it?"

"She thought it was some kind of revenge on his grandma for kicking him out of her house. Plus, a need for some quick cash. He hasn't had a job in a while. Guess he figured Einar might have better trappings sitting around here than what they knew was left at Janet's," Sheriff Dumfrey says.

"I can see that perhaps. But why go through all the paperwork, books and photo albums? There's plenty of fairly valuable knickknacks sitting on those shelves right behind you," I say, pointing to the glass doors of the built-in hutch.

"Well, he's just a young guy who probably doesn't know about that sort of thing or have the patience to find out," the sheriff replied. "Maybe thought Einar had cash stashed in books. Lots of older folks do, ya know."

"My ma had hundred-dollar bills stuck in her Bible," Billy says. "Only discovered that after she passed and I was looking for something to read at her funeral. Sixty-six of 'em in total. One for every book in the Good Book. Pretty much paid for all her end-of-life expenses."

"Good thing you opened up the Scriptures," Felix says.

"Oh, Ma was wily like that. Always finding ways to make following Jesus real rewarding," Billy adds. "After I made it through the whole confirmation process back in high-school, she drove into the yard the next day on a brand-new dirt bike. Stepped off it with a big grin and handed me the keys. Told me she had plans to keep it for herself if I'd have bailed out on my catechism."

"She was quite a lady," I say, remembering well Billy's spunky mother. "Generous to a fault. I will never forget the way she would fight over the after-church lunch check with my dad whenever we were up here on a weekend. My dad had to get real creative to pre-empt her penchant for paying. He'd find a way to get the check before the waitress ever got it back to the table."

"Yup, that was Ma," Billy says.

"Oh, hey, that reminds me," Sheriff Dumfrey says. "I've got something out in my rig for you. Be right back."

He dons his hat over his salt and pepper hair and heads outside.

A moment of quiet settles before Billy speaks up.

"Mikey's not a bad kid," he says. "Just really could've used a dad in his life for a few more years. Think David could have really made the difference for him but… we will never know."

"Fathers seem to be underestimated in general these days," Felix says. "At least, from what I've experienced."

"I'd say you've got a point there," Billy replies. "My dad was a quiet guy but his actions spoke volumes. I will never forget all he did for us."

"Yeah, my dad was quiet too. Unless, of course, you got him talking about the Peloponnesian War or the presidency of Teddy Roosevelt or some such subject. Then it was hard to shut him up," I add. "Oh, what I'd give to hear one of those orations again."

"How about you, Felix? What was your father like?" Billy asks.

Felix's face gets thoughtful and a bit guarded.

"He was a military man," he says. "Very authoritarian. But honorable and fair. I never saw his softer side until close to the end of his life. Then, he was, uh…"

The stomp of the sheriff's boots up the front steps and the opening of the kitchen door interrupt Felix's words. A brisk rush of cold air precedes the sheriff's return into the dining room. He enters carrying a small, carved table.

"Uncle's table!" I say, clapping my hands together.

"Thought so," the sheriff says. "Mikey's girlfriend said he'd given it to her last week as some sort of peace offering. But once she knew it might be stolen, she didn't want anything to do with it. Where would you like it, Tora?"

I point to the living room.

"Right where that footstool is by the sofa, please," I say.

Sheriff Dumfrey moves in response to my direction, shoving the footstool back to its place by the rocking chair and returning the table to its home by the sofa.

"Perfect," I say. "Oh, it's so nice to see it back in its place."

"I've got the lawnmower out in the rig too," he says. "Remind me to get that out before I leave."

He returns to his chair and again removes his hat.

"The pawnshop guy said there were a couple of other guys with Mikey when he brought in the lawnmower, but they never came into the shop so he didn't get a good look at them," the sheriff adds. "We're guessing maybe one or both of them might have been involved to some degree as well. So, we will keep investigating as we get leads. Speaking of which, Felix, you want to show Tora what you found at Janet's?"

Felix slides the large envelope across the table toward me.

"This was stuck underneath the drawer in the little desk in the upstairs bedroom. I stumbled upon it when I was doing my repairs. Think it will be of interest to you," he says. His eyes meet mine. Warm and brown and familiar. Flashes of brothers on a road. Brothers washing fish. A puppy named Maximus. My dream scrolls over his face. It is the same face. The same eyes.

"Tor, you gonna open it up?" Billy says. "Felix wouldn't let me see it until you saw it. So, come on. I'm dying of curiosity."

I draw the envelope to me and peek inside. Sticking my hand in, I pull out a laminated sheet of paper. Turning it over and around, I instantly know where it comes from.

"This is from Uncle's family history album. There's a whole stack of these sheets right over here," I say, indicating the end of the table. "I've been trying to get them back into some semblance of order before setting them back in the bindings."

I scan the imprinted tree before me. It is just like my mom and dad's. Just like Tante Tilda's and Uncle Richard's. Except the only full name written upon it is Einar Gottlieb Anderson with his date of birth and the initials G.A.E beside it with another set of dates.

G.A.E.

I suck in a breath and glance at Felix.

"Grace?" I whisper.

He nods. "That's what I was thinking."

"I believe her last name is… Everwind," I add, checking each face around the table to see how that name might land.

Billy looks perplexed.

Felix crosses his arms with a smile and simply says, "Hmm."

The Sheriff leans his forearms onto the table and asks, "As in the Redby Everwinds?"

"I believe so," I reply.

"Wait a minute," Billy says, reaching across the table. "Let me see that."

I hand it to him.

"There's a letter in there too," Felix says, indicating the manila envelope. "Looks like it's from your Tante Tora to your Uncle Einar. Mostly in Norwegian though, so I couldn't decipher the contents. But I could read the names Grace, George, Joseph, and Thomas."

"All Everwinds," Sheriff Dumfrey confirms.

I pull the letter from the envelope and open it.

"How's your Norwegian, Billy?" I ask, reaching the letter his way.

"Pretty rusty," he says, taking it from me. "But I will take a look."

I retrieve the family tree page from beside his elbow and peruse it once again. More dates. More initials. Each one astounding me more.

"I can't make head nor tails of this letter 'cept it's definitely my grandma's handwriting," Billy says, looking back at me. "You're gonna catch flies you keep that jaw dropped like that. What is this all about, Cousin?"

I clamp my gaping mouth shut and take a deep breath.

"Well, Cousin," I say. "It would appear that perhaps you and I have more cousins."

"More cousins?" Billy replies. "From where? From who?"

"From Uncle Einar," I say, turning the sheet back around for him to see. "And Grace Everwind."

Now it is Billy's turn to catch flies.

TORA

MY DINNER DISHES ARE DRIP DRYING in the dishrack, and I am sitting at the kitchen table nursing a cup of tea and writing out a grocery list for the weekend. I will need to run into town before the troops arrive. The radio on the counter is playing Babe Country 98.3FM. Not to be confused with the Sports Illustrated swimsuit kind of 'babe,' this moniker refers to Paul Bunyan's sidekick—Babe the Blue Ox. The station plays contemporary country music, which is not exactly my listening preference. I know who Blake Shelton is because I've seen him on TV, and I know who Tim McGraw is because of a movie or two. But the other Justin's, Dustin's, Luke's, Dierk's, Carly's, and Carrie's are pretty much lost on me.

Mostly I am listening because it is the station that comes in with the least amount of static, and I am hoping to get an updated weather forecast on the hour. Billy mentioned on his way out the door this afternoon that a winter storm watch has been issued for the Dakotas tonight and is probably headed our way this weekend. Not what I want to hear when I have folks on the highway tomorrow.

A ping from my phone sets me on a hunt for the latest place I have misplaced it. I have to wait for it to sound off again before I locate it under a hand towel in the bathroom. Honestly. I should keep this thing on a leash.

It is a text from my son-in-law.

"Check your email inbox," it says. "Have attached translations of the two letters. Some blank spots due to faded ink. But all in all, very interesting."

I had sent the letter from Tante Tora, as well as the one from my Great-Grandmother Kari, home with Billy. He had promised to scan and email them to Isaac as soon as he got home. I am surprised, however, to hear back so quickly. That software must be good.

"Will do," I text back. "Thx for quick service. How's Mariah?"

"Resting. Relieved to have some hours without kid or pup ahead. Thx so much."

"My absolute pleasure! Give her my love. Please make sure Hazel has full winter gear packed. Looks like snow this weekend."

"Yes. I have heard the reports. Getting everything gathered."

My heart flutters with anticipation.

She's really coming.

At last.

"Any further wolf sightings?" Isaac shoots off another text.

"No. You've chatted with Peter?"

"Yes. Disconcerting. Have not told Mariah. Hope that's okay. Don't think she could handle that right now."

I sigh.

In my lengthy discussion with my husband before dinner in my 4Runner phone booth, we had decided to leave the dispensing or withholding of the wolf attack up to Isaac. Now I wish we hadn't. As a mom, I think she has the right to know. But I understand. Mariah can get fixated on things. Part of her strength and part of her weakness. Isaac knows that better than any of us and he has to live with her.

"Totally your call," I reply.

"Thx Mom."

I read those two words over and over again. Thx Mom.

The welling tears surprise me, though, by this stage in the game, you'd think I'd expect them. I let them spill over before catching them with a napkin. At least they are happy tears.

I pick up my phone again.

"Okay if I come down and use your computer?" I text Billy.

"You bet," comes his quick reply. "Just watching the Wild game. Come on in."

Finishing up my tea and my list, I stand and reach to turn off the radio, but a baritone voice singing about the love for his dearly departed mama freezes me, reaches me, and melts me. Choked up all over again, the tune comes to an end and I turn the knob to Off, deciding that maybe later I will pull out Grandma's one and only Johnny Cash album.

"You sure I can't get you anything else?" Carin says, poking her head into their office just off the kitchen where I sit in front of their computer.

"Not unless you have some of that banana bread laying around," I reply.

"No, that's long gone thanks to you know who," she says, tipping her head toward the living room where Billy sits in his recliner yelling at the TV. "But I do have a couple of Edna's lemon bars squirreled away from ladies Bible study this morning. Want one of those?"

"Who can say no to that?" I reply.

"Ah, come on guys! Shots on goal. Shots on goal. Can't win without getting the puck in the net!" Billy's voice carries easily across the house.

"The Wild can't possibly win without him," Carin says with a sardonic grin.

"I might be guilty of some vociferous armchair coaching myself from time to time. Learned it young from my brother Andy. May be a family trait," I reply. "Is it okay if I print out what Isaac sent?"

"You betcha," Carin says. "I'm hoping I might get a peek at those letters, too, if ya don't mind. Billy came home with some wild tales after your meeting with the sheriff."

"Don't mind at all. We've come this far together. In for a penny, in for a pound, as Grandpa used to say."

"Goooooooooaaaaaal!" comes the cry from the hockey fan. "Honey, they scored!"

"Really? How would I ever have figured that out?" I hear his wife mutter on her way to the kitchen.

I grin and press 'print'. I have briefly scanned the letters as I opened up the attachments but am eager to soak in all the details. The butterflies in my gut are stirring with anticipation of what is about to be revealed.

Carin returns with the delectable goodies and two short glasses of milk on a wooden tray.

"Always find these bars go down even better with a wee shot of milk," she says, setting the tray down on the desktop and handing one of the bars to me. "These are left over from Samantha's gender reveal party a few months back." She points to the bright pink napkins that hold the yellow bars. "Take a guess what she's having."

"That's a tough one," I say, feeling my saliva glands activate at the mere sight of our second-cousin Edna's world-famous, or at least Solbakken famous, dessert.

"Our first granddaughter after four grandsons in a row. We are tickled pink," she says, sitting down next to me on a straight back chair she pulls from the side of the desk.

I wheel the office chair I'm in over to the printer and retrieve the four printed pages from the extended paper tray.

"This ought to be interesting," I say, rolling back to Carin, whose lips are covered in powdered sugar. "Which one should we start with?"

She takes a swig of milk and runs her tongue around her lips. "Let's start with the one to Uncle Einar. I'm just so curious about this whole connection with the Everwind woman."

"You girls gonna begin without me?" Billy says, filling the doorway.

"We thought you were committed to your role with the Wild," his wife replies.

"We're between periods," he says, coming into the room and plopping down on the love seat situated under the Terry Redlin painting of white-tail deer. It resides directly below a rack of antlers from the same species. "So, let's get 'er going, Tor. I've only got a few minutes."

"Okay. I guess I will read this aloud then," I say, squinting at the translated letter in my hands.

Carin tugs open a side drawer on the desk and pulls out a set of readers. She hands them to me without a word. Setting them on the end of my nose, the words come into wonderful clarity.

"Hey, where'd ya get the lemon bar from?" Billy says before I can begin.

"Mind your own business," Carin says. "You already had a Klondike bar after dinner."

"Oh, yeah, well… Didn't think you saw that," he says, sinking further into the well-worn leather cushions.

Carin sighs before saying, "Go ahead, Tora. I will defend your lemon bar."

"Dearest nephew, you are well? English hard for me to write. Please forgive," I begin to read. My hand is quivering, making the printed words shake before my eyes. Isaac has made all the translated Norwegian words bold and italicized. Any of the missing or ambiguous words he has put in brackets with several possible options.

"I hope this missive reaches you before the New Year that you may begin 1947 with good news. At least, I am confident it will be good news to you. I write in the midnight hour while John sleeps. Your news is safe with me unless or until you want me to share it."

"Oh, boy," Billy says, rubbing his hands together. "Here come the family skeletons. I never knew Grandma to keep anything from Grandpa. Must be juicy."

A crumpled pink napkin hits him in the chest.

"Just be quiet," Carin says. "We are going to give Einar all the benefit of the doubt he deserves. Now, let Tora read, please."

"Alright, alright," Billy says, clamping his arms across his chest. "Calm down. It's not every day we get this kind of reality TV drama in Solbakken. Just relishing the moment."

I hold up a hand of peace between husband and wife and resume.

"The next sentence is unclear. It may say, 'I drove to the sands' or 'I visited the shoreline,'" I start again.

"Maybe the sand dunes on Red Lake?" Billy interjects while casting a wary eye at Carin.

"Yup, that could be, although the letter was written in December," I say. "It goes on. 'I drove to the (sands/shoreline) yesterday after note left in mailbox last evening. Did not see delivery person. Told John I had a yearning for fish for lutefisk. Would visit Redby. On the way stopped by road leading to (sands/shoreline). Grace was there.'"

"The stew thickens," Billy says.

"Either keep quiet or go watch hockey," Carin says.

Billy zips his mouth with his fingers and tosses away the key.

"Go ahead, Tora," Carin says.

"Got into her car," I continue reading. "Cold day. Brisk wind. Not good for a baby to be out in. She handed me…" I stop, trying to assess the bracketed words. "She handed me a (bundle/blanketed basket). Your son. Thomas Einar. Born December 6. He is strong and handsome. Looks like his mother. Good for him. Although I see your lips and chin clearly."

"Holy mackerel," Billy whispers, unable to contain himself. "We really do got cousins on the rez."

"Oh, my goll, Bill," Carin says. "It would seem you may have Ojibwe cousins, yes. And I think it's amazing."

"I'm not saying it's not cool. I'm just… ah, you know me. Not the most politically correct guy in the crowd."

"Yes, we are aware," Carin replies. "What else did Grandma Tora write?"

I clear my throat and refocus on the page in my hand.

"Grace is giving her last name to the boy," I read. "She has not married. Does not want to but may be forced to if you do not return. Please, come home. You have a family waiting. We—I will support you. I am sure your parents will come around, too, one day if you will let them. Her father is saddened you have left his daughter in dishonor. But he has said he will welcome you with open arms should you return. Her brother George is still very angry, however. Threatened to (take/throw) baby away. But their father intervened."

I take a deep breath as I move the page to the back of the stack and resume reading on the next page.

"I know you love this woman. And I know she loves you. Do not let other people's judgments rob you of your life. You can write me via Lena Walden at the store. She is trustworthy and has said she will set any correspondence from you aside. I have not told her any details. There are many rumors as to why you left so suddenly last summer. Lena is one of the few who does not speculate. A good godly woman she is."

My eyes flash over the closing sentence and I inhale sharply.

"What is it?" Carin says, leaning toward me.

"Yeah, what is it?" Billy, too, leans forward.

I look back and forth between their two eager faces, content to keep them in suspense for a moment.

Billy makes a grab for the letter but I jerk it away.

"Oh, no you don't," I say, slapping his hand. "Your hockey game is probably back on."

"Hockey, schmockey," he says. "Just tell us what it says, already!"

I laugh before returning my eyes to the final paragraph.

"I gave Grace the pouch of coins you left with me. The ones George refused to accept on behalf of his brother Joseph." I glance up to see the impact of this news on my cousins. They are appropriately shocked. I continue. "She said George had never mentioned anything about your attempt to give them to the family. At first, she didn't want to accept them. Wanted you to keep them. But I told her you had your own share of them. These were always meant for Joseph. She cried when I told her the story of how you and Joseph came to have them by caring for the woman Isabel. If only Joseph was the brother who still lives, she said to me. Yes, if only he was. Let me know you have received this news. I pray for you daily as if you were my own. In His loving grace, Tante Tora."

The office is quiet save for the distant play by play commentary of Anthony LaPlanta and Lou Nanne from the TV in the living room.

"Well, good golly," Billy says, his hands crossed atop his head and his elbows akimbo as he drops back into the love seat. "She got the coins."

I nod and skim back over the revelatory words.

"I wonder why Einar left and didn't come back?" Carin says after finishing off her milk and removing any vestige of moostache from her upper lip.

Taking up my lemon bar, I hardly notice how scrumptious it is but am happy to have something besides words to chew on for a moment. She's right. Why didn't he come back? And why did he leave to begin with?

"My sisters always told me Einar was a CIA agent," Billy says. "Maybe he was in witness protection after getting caught on a big case or something."

Carin rolls her eyes and sighs.

"What?" her husband objects. "We just found out he's got a son we never knew about and bags of gold coins from some Italian lady that he's passed off to his Ojibwe lover. What's so far-fetched about him being a spy?"

I hand the printed pages to Carin who takes them over to Billy and squishes next to him on the love seat. They read and re-read the letter several times before making any further comments.

"You ever meet this Grace Everwind?" Billy asks me.

"No. I was about to ask you the same thing," I reply. "I was only on the reservation a few times when I actually interacted with any of the population. We did hike onto the sand dunes a time or two, but we were always the only ones there. But a couple of times when I was up here by myself in the summer, Grandpa and Grandma took me over to the 4th of July powwow."

"Yup, we went to that quite a few times too," Carin says. "I always loved the dancing and drums and the wonderful authentic costumes. I remember asking my dad if we could dance, too, but he said no, we were only there to observe and honor our neighbor's traditions."

"Well, me and my sisters danced with them," Billy says. "Nobody seemed to mind a couple of towheaded kids stomping around. In fact, I remember getting some footwork lessons from a kid just a couple of years older than me."

"Judging by the way you dance now, I'd say that perhaps you should go back and find that guy for some more lessons," Carin says.

"What are you saying? You don't like my moves?"

He jumps up and gives us a quick John Travolta disco move or two and strikes a pose—one hand up in the air, one leg bent forward, other hand on hip.

Carin and I applaud.

"8.5," I say with a laugh.

"I give you a 7," Carin adds.

"What? You blind, judge?" He bends down and tugs his wife up by her hands, sending the printed copies flying to the floor.

I quickly pick them up before Billy steps on them. He twirls Carin around and flings her into a dramatic dip, her head barely missing the edge of the desk. She comes up smiling and gives him a kiss.

"Okay, okay. I will give you a 9," she says, resuming her place on the leather couch, her cheeks flushed and her grayish-blond hair askew.

"I'll take that," he says, tugging his shirt over the exposed regions of his generous belly and flopping down beside her. "We really should go out dancing sometime again."

The TV announcers' voices in the other room ramp up to a pitch of excitement and Billy pushes himself back up and out of the low seat.

"Gotta check the score real quick. And then we'd better read that next letter," he says, bounding up the one small step out of the room.

"He moves remarkably fast for such a big guy," I remark.

"And his moves aren't all that bad either," Carin adds with a grin.

"Uh, uh, uh. Too much information," I say, holding up a finger.

I set the letter from Tante Tora on the desk beside the computer and ready myself to read the one from Mormor Kari.

"So, this is your Grandma Arnie's grandmother, right?" Carin asks.

"Yes, her maternal grandmother. That's right," I reply.

"And she lived where?"

"Born, raised and died in Norway. Think she lived in a little town in the Østerdalen valley her entire life. At least, that's what I can make out from the family records Uncle amassed."

Billy's frame fills the door and he announces, "We're up 4 to 1 with only a couple of minutes left."

"Thank goodness," his wife says. "I will sleep better tonight."

"Oh, can it and scootch over," he says as he reenters the room and slides back into place, taking up more than his fair share of the seat. Carin docsn't seem to mind. "Okay, Cousin. Let's hear the next bombshell. Even though this one is all on you, right? Not my relative."

"Yes, this one is unrelated to the Hallstrom clan except via marriage and proximity," I reply, setting the reading glasses back on my nose and focusing on the task at hand. "The letter is dated April 18, 1906. It begins, 'My dearest granddaughter, you have been gone from these hills for one full year now and my heart still aches at your absence. Your goat, Little Lena, still searches for you in the (underbrush/berries) where you hid beside the creek. We all miss you but hope you are happy in America. Please write when you have a chance. Your letters brighten these old eyes. I read them many, many times over. Your birthday has come and gone and now you are thirteen. An important year my Morfar Jacob told me. A year to enter into womanhood. How I wish you could wear the beautiful dress Mormor made for me when I turned this age. It sits wrapped in my trunk waiting. Perhaps your cousin Marit will wear it next year. She is stronger. We hope and pray she continues to get better. She sends her love.'"

An eruption from the sportscasters interrupts my recitation.

"Go turn that thing off." Carin nudges her husband up out of their cozy chair.

He wrestles himself to standing and complies.

"It's always so amazing to me how our forefathers left home and didn't look back," Carin says with a sigh. "I just don't know how both the ones who left and the ones who were left behind coped with the separation."

"Yes, I imagine it was almost as if they died," I concur. "Letters, I guess, were their way of staying connected."

"We're just so blessed nowadays that even if our kids live halfway around the world, we can still visit or see their faces and hear their voices most any time we want," Carin says.

"True, but I still hate that Brian lives so far out west and we only see one another in person a couple of times per year. At least, in normal times we could," I reply. "I would never tell him that, though. He needs to live his life. Just wish his life was a tad bit closer to ours."

Billy clomps back down the step into the room. "Game over. Wild win," he says. "Did I miss anything?"

"No, we waited for you," his wife replies.

"*Tusen takk*," he says and gives her a peck on the cheek before settling back into his spot with one armed draped over her shoulder. "Carry on, Tor."

I search for the place I left off with my finger. Finding it, I proceed.

"Our Easter celebration was in snow this year. The way to and from church was very difficult but we endured. The sun shone brightly just before dusk and cheered our spirits. Our feasts (coincided/overlapped) this year. A happy thing that fulfills the longings of my (split/diverse) heart and shows me again God's faithfulness through all generations. Your cousin Dag asked the questions and read the scriptures at our candlelight (secret/mystery) meal with our curtains drawn from any curious neighbors. I hope you will never forget the stories of the God of Abraham, Isaac, and Jacob."

I pause and look at my attentive listeners.

"She has underlined the name Jacob several times," I say.

"What's she saying?" Billy asks.

"Is she talking about observing Easter and Passover at the same time? And maybe even a Bat Mitzvah for turning thirteen?" Carin adds. "Was she Jewish?"

The dream from my nap runs across the screen of my imagination and I am reminded that I have yet to write it all down. Could it be true?

"Tor? You alright?" Billy asks.

"Uh, yes. I, uh, don't know for sure if she was Jewish. But it seems that perhaps her Grandfather Jacob was… which, of course, would mean she would also have Jewish DNA," I say, giving voice to the implications from my dream.

"Which would also, of course, mean that you have Jewish blood," Carin says, clapping her hands. "How exciting!"

"Jiminy Cricket," Billy adds. "Our family is becoming more interesting by the minute. What else does your great-grand have to say?"

I flip to the next page and read, "Now you are a woman, how can it be so soon? There are many things I would tell you. Your father wanted you to stay away from our celebrations. Only ask your mother why. You would be wise to keep this letter from your father's eyes. His heart has become hardened due to (mean/hateful) people. Perhaps one day, he will come to his senses and remember his Savior's people. But I have promised to never forget. And so, I sign this letter with the blessings of the generations. Shalom. Shalom. Mormor Kari."

My eyes remain locked on these last words.

The blessings of the generations.

Shalom. Shalom.

"I seem to remember your Grandma Arnie using those exact words," Billy says. "Whenever I'd leave her house. Shalom. Shalom. That's what she'd say. For years, I didn't know what it meant. Thought it was probably Norwegian."

"It means peace," Carin says.

"Yes, I know that now," Billy replies. "But it ain't Norwegian. It's Hebrew, I believe."

"Yup. It actually means so much more than our simple English meaning of peace. Grandma Arnie told me it was a full-blown benediction like the one the pastor always says at the end of the service," I say, setting the letter down and lifting my hands over my small congregation. "The Lord bless you and keep you. The Lord make His face shine upon you and be gracious to you. The Lord lift up His face upon you and give you peace."

Silence descends upon our small gathering.

My hands slowly descend as well and rest atop Mormor Kari's words.

The wind whistles down the chimney of the woodstove in the kitchen and rattles the windowpane behind the computer. A windchime on the front porch sounds its sonorous notes. The hoots of a barn owl join the spontaneous chorus.

Carin lets her head rest upon her husband's shoulder and closes her eyes. Billy, too, lapses into a thoughtful repose.

It's as if the ancient blessing has drifted across time and eternity to hover with its power in our midst. Three cousins in their upper-middle-prime years. In a simple den. In a log house. In Solbakken, Minnesota.

Residing in shalom.

FELIX

MAXIMUS STIRS IN HIS PLACE on the rug beside my bed. The wind is whipping up outside jiggling the back door and causing pine boughs to scratch along the house's siding.

"It's okay, buddy. Just the wind," I say in Aramaic, reaching down to pat his head.

He relaxes at the words of our native tongue and slides back into his upside-down sprawl, his front paws at the head of the bed, his rear ones stretching to the foot board. His length is quite impressive when on full display.

I set my bookmark into the pages of *The Call of the Wild* and switch off the bedside lamp. It's a book I found in the closet upstairs. Inscribed "To Janet, Christmas 1961, Love Onkel Sig and Tante Arnie," I was attracted to it both because of the storyline and because it was a gift from Tora's parents.

The midnight hour glowing from the clock on the wall tells me I have been captivated by the tale longer than I intended. This is one book Max himself would thoroughly enjoy reading. Too bad he has yet to develop this skill. But there's always time… an eternity, for that matter.

"Would you like to learn to read?" I whisper to the now snoring mass of fur on the floor.

I can detect no interest.

"Indifferent, it would seem," I reply to my own inquiry.

After reading of the exploits of the half-St. Bernard, half-sheepdog protagonist of Mr. London's novel, many memories of Max spin through my mind. He has been through at least as much turmoil and drama as the fictional dog, yet, hopefully with a more consistently kind master.

I am grateful that this massive canine companion of mine has not had to engage in warfare for many years. He is capable of the most ferocious escapades, and earned a reputation with my fellow soldiers of being worthy of all respect at all times.

"Don't underestimate the captain's dog," the seasoned recruits whispered to the new ones.

Max was the picture of decorum and obedience whenever I first introduced him to the men. But those who had been around for a skirmish or two were well aware of his strength, power, and determination.

And, of course, there were the stories of his remarkable recoveries from the most heinous wounds. Inexplicable. Miraculous, even. The legends he inspired were as many or more than the ones revolving around me. Afterall, dogs' years fly by even more quickly than men's. Only he and I, and our heavenly witness, know that every legend is firmly grounded in reality but a reality so supernatural people have to catalog the stories on the shelf of fiction in order to fathom them. Who knows? Maybe Jack London's dog was a spin-off of tales passed down through generations of my very own Max.

I smile at the thought, rubbing the surface of Mila's coin necklace that rests around my neck, as always. Over the course of the years, Trajan's features have smoothed somewhat under my fingers, but still remain recognizable. He was the only emperor under whom I served that did not scoff at my supernatural agelessness. He listened and marveled at my story the one time I was taken in for an audience with him. He even acknowledged to me privately that he believed in the possibility of the existence of a being more divine than himself. And although he never did embrace a faith in Yahweh, at least not that I ever knew of, he was a virtuous man who ruled his people well. I sigh at the remembrance of those days so long ago. My days as a soldier.

I let my other hand drift down to linger under my dog's chin. He gives one lick and returns to his dreams. I am right behind him.

"FELIX!" MY FATHER'S VOICE RINGS down the hall from his station inside the temple fortress. "Come."

It is morning, yet the sky is still so dark that the marble walls glimmer with reflections from the sconces that line the length of the passage all the way to the outer courtyard from whence myself and my two companions have just come. Soldiers and curriers are marching purposefully from place to place in the building complex, but other than the sounds of their feet, the place is eerily quiet. Even the officer who ushers me into my father's office, who is normally obnoxiously chatty, has few words this morning.

"Stay here," I instruct Titus and Fabian, pointing to an alcove just outside the large office doors.

"Max, stay," I order my dog. He freezes, but as soon as I turn my back, he follows me up to the office entry. I turn on him. "Sit!" I hiss and point. He begrudgingly obeys.

We had been summoned from our usual station only a quarter of an hour previously. The temple guard who directed us through the courtyard to this hallway did not tell us the reason behind the summons. After the upheaval of the Jewish community over the past few days, we are not surprised. Many soldiers have been required to serve extra shifts and double duties in order to keep the peace in Jerusalem. At this hour, everything seems calm but only in a calm-before-the-storm sort of way.

The entire city lays under a simmering pall after the events of the previous day. My unit had not been part of the retinue assigned to Golgotha. Thank God. But I had been assigned to the guard that helped subdue the crowds along the Via Dolorosa—the route my childhood friend Yeshua had been forced to take yesterday on his way to his own crucifixion. My mind reels at the scene I witnessed and all the incredible reports of what lead up to this most horrific outcome.

I cannot fathom it. Yeshua. The healer. Yeshua. The Rabbi. Yeshua. The miracle-worker.

Yeshua. The Messiah.

All these names and the incidences that provoked them have come to my attention through various means over the course of the past three years. Not the least of which have been letters from my mother, sisters, and Nathan who have taken to following The Teacher (as they call him) whenever and wherever they can.

Each letter more remarkable than the last. Each testimony more miraculous. Each revelation of power, wisdom, kindness, and love more filled with the thought that perhaps, finally, at last, the hope of generations has come.

And then yesterday happened.

I don't know if Mother, Martha, and Agnes looked for me in the crowds, or if I just happened to be stationed right where they had managed to find a place amongst the mourners, curiosity-seekers, and enemies of Yeshua along his death march. All I know is when I turned around to subdue a particularly vitriolic man to keep him from rushing into the road, there they were among a group of weeping women. Their anguished faces wet with tears, their eyes red and puffy. I looked around them but found no sign of Nathan.

"Felix?" Agnes cried and reached out her hand.

I dared only acknowledge her with a slight nod before turning back to my duty.

My gut wrenched at the sight of them, and despite all the hubbub surrounding me, I could still make out their quiet sobs. It was all I could do to keep my own tears in check.

"Not today. Not now," I coached myself into remaining outwardly unmoved by the day's proceedings. I would find a quiet place later and process my turmoil. But not in front of the crowds. Not in front of my fellow soldiers.

But then I saw him.

Yeshua.

Trudging, stumbling up the road, a tall sturdy man behind him, bearing the beam of the cross on which my former neighbor and friend would be crucified. His head was bent down, a crown of sorts stuck upon it. I gasped when he looked up and blood ran down his bruised face in steady streams. As he approached, I saw the crown was made from thorned branches woven together and jammed into his skull. Bile rose in my throat, but I could not tear my eyes away from him.

Was this the same boy I knew? Who had he become? What had they done to him? Maybe there had been a mistake. Maybe this was not the same Yeshua but some other man.

Then he stopped.

Right beside me, he stopped.

And he spoke to the women who were weeping.

They quieted and strained to listen to his raspy voice.

And, despite the years and changes and abuse of the hour, I knew this voice.

Older. Deeper. Weary and worn.

But Yeshua's voice still the same.

Before he was prodded along by one of my fellow temple guards, he cast one glance up at me.

With much effort in the lifting of his head, our eyes met.

My breath stopped.

The world stood still.

And then he was gone.

"**FELIX! COME!**" again my father's voice rings out.

"Sir, yes, sir. Coming!" I answer, giving Max one last stare to ensure he remains in his spot.

I shake off the memories of yesterday, stride into his office and make a smart salute before his desk. We are alone.

"At ease," Father says. "Where's Max?"

"Just outside the door, sir," I reply, letting my shoulders relax and my feet widen in their stance.

"Good," Father says. "I want him to go with you."

"Yes, sir," I reply. "Where to, sir?"

"Close the door, please," he says, and I do as directed. When it is closed and I am back in my place by the desk he says, "We are alone, son. You can go easy on the 'sirs.'"

I nod. Very rarely over the course of the decade I have served under his command has he ventured to call me son. Only when we are certain that we are alone. And that is quite a rare occurrence.

"You saw your mother yesterday?" he asks.

I am surprised that he knows. But now I understand the familiarity of his greeting.

"She sent a note," he says in way of explanation. He shakes his head and rubs his hand over his face. I see that his usually close-shaven cheeks are thick with grey stubble, and the circles under his brown eyes are darker and deeper than usual.

"Yes, I saw her and my sisters. Though we did not speak," I reply, leaving Nathan's name out of the conversation. He is, or has been, a known follower of Yeshua. "Are they in the city still? Do you know?"

"Yes. She says they are staying with some friends, though I urged her to go home. Jerusalem is a mass of unrest just waiting to erupt. I would prefer she not be in the middle of it but… she is a woman who lives her own life… especially since the death of your step-father."

"I know," I say. "And she was devoted to Yeshua."

My voice cracks and I drop my chin.

"Yes… I am, uh, sorry about what happened to him," he says, sitting back into his chair and sighing deeply. "I owe he and his family so much. They saved you and your mother. And then when he healed my servant, my friend Elihu… I only wish I could have returned the favor. I recommended clemency… but to no avail. Even Pilate himself could not sway the crowds."

When I look up, he is staring out the window toward the rooftops of the city.

"What have we done?" he whispers.

Max lets out a deep growl beyond the closed door.

"Sir, a message," a voice cries out from the hallway.

"Let him in," Father says. "Keep Max under control."

I manage to do both.

"Sir, for you," the messenger says, squeezing past me and my dog. He hands a tightly wound scroll to my father.

I keep one hand on Max's collar.

"Do they require an answer?" Father asks the messenger.

"Sir, yes, sir, they do, sir," he says crisply.

"Then wait outside until I summon you with my response," he orders, and the messenger steps past me and Max into the hallway. I close the door again behind him.

"I have an assignment for you and Max," Father says when we are alone again. "A request from the chief priests via Pilate to go and secure the tomb where they laid the body of Yeshua. They are afraid some of his followers may try to steal the body and make it appear as if he has risen from the dead on the third day."

I remember words from one of Nathan's letters.

"I believe he said such a thing would take place," I say softly.

"Whether he did or did not is not the point," my father and captain replies. "Right now, my job is to secure the tomb. Did you bring two other men?"

"Yes, sir… uh, yes. Titus and Fabian await me in the alcove," I reply.

"Are they trustworthy men?"

"The best I know."

"Good. Take them and your dog over to the Sanhedrin where some priests are waiting to go with you to see that every measure has been taken to keep the man in his grave… if such a thing is possible." He says the last so faintly I wonder if I have heard him correctly.

"Yes, sir."

He nods silently and his eyes register a vulnerability I have rarely ever seen in him.

"I will see that it's done well, sir."

He nods. "I know you will, son. I know. And…. truly, I am sorry it has come to this."

A lump lodges in my throat and the tears of the day threaten to spill out. I can manage no response.

"Dismissed," Father says before turning his attention to the message in his hand.

Max stands alert, tugging at my hold on his collar.

I pull the door open, my mind and heart spinning at this new assignment - to guard the tomb of Yeshua.

TORA

THE GARAGE DOOR SLIDES UP at the touch of the button by the back door, and snow whips into the garage on all sides. The wind is blowing directly from the northeast on this Friday morning. I dash into my vehicle, dropping my tote bag onto the passenger seat, securing my phone into its spot, and starting the ignition. My bum feels the warmth of my seat-heater almost immediately, even through the puff of my long down coat.

I tuck my chin deeper into the zipped-up collar and crank the defroster. My dashboard tells me it is five degrees above zero—and that's in the garage without a windchill factor. I shiver at the thought of it, hoping Peter might be talked into a jaunt down to Florida in the not-too-distant future. The clock turns to 9:17 a.m. as I go into reverse. My all-wheel-drive tires crunch into the accumulation of white that has piled up against the garage overnight. The weather report calls for snow showers off and on all day. Thankfully the weather system seems to be situated across the northern tier of the state so Peter won't have to drive in it until after Bemidji.

At least, I hope that is the case, I think, punching the garage door opener and watching the large, paneled door slide down into place. A five-hour drive in snow is not fun, nor recommended. But I cannot bring myself to warn him to stay home. Nor has he even hinted at the idea. Hopefully Mariah and Isaac are as resolute in their decision to send Hazel north as we are to have her come north.

"Oh, Lord, let them come safely. Let them come swiftly. Let them come," I whisper, making fresh tire tracks to the end of the long driveway.

Billy is coming down the road with his snowplow attachment on the front of his rig. He gives me a chins-up greeting under his ballcap as he turns into Janet's place and begins his self-assigned duties of snow removal. The county snowplow will eventually reach our lane, but it will be a while, or not at all if the main roads need attention throughout the day.

"Thanks again for Bill," I add an addendum to my prayer as I pass the Hallstrom home. The light in the kitchen shines brightly against the heavy gloom of the gray cloudy morning. "And for Carin, of course. And their kids and grandkids and Felix and Max and, well, for all of Solbakken, past, present, and future."

My tires slip and skid at the stop sign at the end of our road, sending my anti-lock brake system into gear with grinding efficiency. I am surprised to find the road so slippery under the dusting that has gathered on it since Billy's blade scraped it clean.

"Note to self—take it easy this morning. There's no rush."

Before getting up to full moderated speed, I hit the call button.

"Call Peter," I command, and my vehicle complies.

The phone barely has a chance to ring before I hear my husband's voice, "Hey, only have a second. What's up?"

"Just checking to see that all systems are go for today."

"Pedaling hard to wrap things up here and get over to Mariah's place as soon as possible. Am hoping to get out of The Cities before three o-clock, maybe even two if I'm lucky."

"Oh, good. Will they have Hazel ready to go by then?"

"Chatted with Isaac last night to go over everything. Think he would have been happy to hand her and the pup off to me last night, but guess his wife had promised Hazel a playdate this morning with some friend she hasn't seen in a while. So, this afternoon it is. How's the weather?"

"Honestly, not great," I admit. "The sooner you can get on the road, the better."

"Ten four," he replies. "I will shoot you a text as soon as my wheels are pointing north."

I let out an involuntary sigh.

"Don't worry, Hon, we will be just fine. Gotta go now though. Love ya. See ya soon."

"Shalom, shalom," we say in unison.

"Wait, wait," he says before I can hit the hang-up button. "I got a call yesterday from Southdale Hospital. I guess they've been trying to get a hold of you. Might want to check your voicemail and email. Anyways, they are getting ready to open up the baby-cuddler volunteer program again and wanted to get their primary volunteers back online ASAP."

"That is good news. Did you tell them I am out of town for a bit?"

"Yes, the gal said not to worry, they are just making preliminary calls to get the ball rolling again. Alright, now I really do have to go. Looking forward to seeing you."

"Me too," I reply and then he is gone.

I let this good news settle for a few minutes before making my next call. Images of all the precious little babies I have held, cuddled, and cared for over the years flood my mind and heart. For the first time in some time, I feel a smidgeon of hope that perhaps things truly are starting to edge back toward normal.

"Call Katie," I command once my mind returns to my present journey.

I marvel briefly at the wonders of modern technology as the phone rings. Surely this is a blessing that many generations would have loved to have seen, and I am grateful for every small step of mankind that has led to this simple (at least simple in application) feat of automation, telecommunication, and computerization.

"Hey, Cousin, can you hold?" Katie's voice jars me from my musing.

"Yup, can do," I reply.

I glance over at my tote bag, checking to see that I remembered to stash the pages from the family history binder into it. An inch of them sticks up reassuringly from the top of the bag. Now I am hoping I also tucked the grocery list inside. Deciding it is better to keep both hands on the wheel this morning than to rifle through the bag, I mentally run through what I can recall off the list.

"Tor? You there?" Katie saves me from a moment of panic over an emerging blankness right after eggs, grated cheese, and…

"Yes, I'm here. Just driving into town and wanted to check in with you. Got a minute or two? It won't take long."

"I am good for another half hour or so before I meet with my next client. You getting snow up there yet?"

"A few inches early in the morning and some flurries again now," I reply, getting the obligatory weather conversation accomplished. "The reason for my call in particular is, I am wondering if it would be okay if I dropped in on your mom again this morning."

"She can't stop talking about your visit the other day. You're making me feel guilty, but I just can't get away right now."

"I had a negative COVID test yesterday if that helps ease your mind," I add.

"Really? I'm not implying that you need to get one. Why did you?"

"Peter is coming up for the weekend and he's bringing Hazel with him," I say with a slight tremor in my delivery.

"Wow! That is great, Tor. So happy to hear you and Mariah are working things out. It seems like everyone is loosening up as this last wave of the damn virus—pardon my French, but it's the only adjective I find that's applicable—anyway, as the latest damn variant passes by without wreaking as much havoc as the last ones. Part of the reason I'm so slammed at the moment. Clients I haven't seen in person for a couple of years are wanting me to meet at their homes or their businesses again. And, I have to tell ya, it's pretty refreshing. I truly hope the worst is behind us," Katie says. "So, yes, please, go visit Mom."

I don't bother to fill her in on the exact reasons for Mariah's "loosening up." Not my story to tell just yet.

"Great," I reply. "I ran across more intriguing information in the midst of Uncle's family tree binder."

"Do tell."

"Well, I guess I always suspected it but my folks never talked about it," I say.

"Yes?" she urges me on.

"Last night, as I was trying to sort through the piles of genealogy information on the dining room table to make room for my company, I got sucked into pouring over it. Didn't get to bed until after 1 a.m. Anywho… on the family tree page assigned to my parents, with Andy, Clay and me and our families listed on it, I found the name of a baby. A little girl named Ann Marie," I say.

"Really? A sister or a niece or what?"

"It would appear to be a sister."

I hear Katie draw in a breath.

"Oh. Oh, my," she whispers.

"The date of birth was two years after Clay. And the date of death was only a few weeks later."

"Wow, Tor. That's, uh, that's amazing and sad all at the same time."

I hit my blinker before turning left onto the river road, thinking it has a better chance of having been cleared than my usual backroad into St. Gerard. I am relieved to find that it has been.

"I know. I remember asking my mother once when I was a teenager why there was such a big break in years between me and my brothers. She only laughed and said something about needing time off after those two. But not before I saw the look—you know, the one she got whenever a conversation was finished or a subject matter off the table?"

"I remember that look," Katie remarks. "She was not a woman to be argued with once you got that look, as I recall."

"Yeah, so, I didn't pursue it. But I have always wondered."

"Good golly," Katie remarks. "I hope maybe Mom can shed some light on that for you."

"That's what I'm hoping too."

"She and your mom were quite close, especially during those years when you guys lived in Alexandria and Mom and Dad were in Fergus Falls. Before my time, of course. But I have heard the tales and seen the pictures."

"Yes, me too. So, we shall see what blanks your mom might be able to fill in for me about this baby named Ann Marie," I say, feeling a constriction in my throat. "I am surprised at how emotional it makes me."

"I can imagine. It's so strange how things… how people can be relegated to a place of shadows and memories, isn't it? Maybe it was just how folks coped back then. Maybe not a bad idea. Nowadays, with social media, we seem to err on the side of oversharing."

"Agreed," I reply. "I will give your mom a call and let her know I'm dropping by."

"Good idea. And thanks for taking time with her. It means a lot. Let her know, I am doing my darndest to come up soon."

A beep tells me my cousin has another call coming in.

"Speaking of sisters…" Katie says.

"Deb?"

"Yeah. I'd better take this."

"Tell her hello and… let me know if there's anything I can do to be helpful," I say.

"Well, probably not, but thanks for the offer. Love ya," Katie says. "Chat soon."

"Love you too. Shalom. Shalom," I add before she hangs up.

Sisters. I have often envied friends and family who have them. Sometimes I liked being the only girl in my family. Liked the attention it brought me. But sometimes… sometimes it was lonely. An ache opens up deep within me for the sister I never knew—for Ann Marie.

TORA

Tante Tilda is standing at the front window in her fuchsia bathrobe waiting for me when I pull up to the curb. She waves and moves toward the door, opening it for me before I've even gotten myself out of my vehicle.

"Close the door, Tante. You will get a chill," I yell out my car door over the gusty wind.

She steps out onto the front stoop.

"What's that?" she hollers, strands of gray hair that have escaped the confines of her braided crown blowing wildly like the limbs of an inflatable tube men in front of a car wash.

I shake my head and grab my tote bag quickly before she decides to traverse the length of the entire snowy sidewalk.

"Coming, coming," I say, slamming my door shut and hustling up to her while trying not to slip and land on my keester. "Let's get inside."

"What are you doing out in this awful weather?" Tante says as I usher her back into the house.

"Coming to see you," I reply, shutting the door behind us and brushing snowflakes from my hair. "Remember, I called on my way in from the farm to see if you were up for a visitor?"

"Of course, I remember," she says, tightening the belt on her robe. "You think I'm daft or something? You're the daft one, out in this weather without a cap on. You will catch your death of cold leaving your head naked like that."

I laugh and assure her I have a cap, scarf, and gloves in the car should I need them.

"Alright then," she says. "Don't want your mother giving me holy heck for dragging you out in this blizzard and getting you sick. That's the last thing I need right now."

I am surprised to hear her talking about my mother as if she might walk into the room at any moment to scold her after I return home with a runny nose.

"I think Mom will be fine with me coming to visit her favorite sister-in-law," I say, shedding my sleeping-bag-like outer gear and hanging it on the coat rack in the corner.

"Her only sister-in-law," Tante remarks.

"Then clearly her favorite," I add, moving toward the kitchen with my tote bag and depositing it on a chair by the table. I am mindful of the fact that there is another woman who may also have been a sister-in-law to my mother if Einar had come back and married her. I need to explore that avenue more deeply with my auntie too. But today—today is about the mystery name next to mine on the family tree. With Tante's energy span being as diminished as it is these days, I have to choose my battles. "Mind if I make myself a cup of tea?"

"Make yourself at home," she says, shuffling behind me in her slippers.

"Do you want some too?" I ask.

"No thanks. Just finished breakfast."

"Sort of late in the morning for you to just have eaten, isn't it? Are you feeling alright?"

She eases herself down onto the floral pad of one of the four chairs around her kitchen table, and tucks the recalcitrant strands of hair back atop her head.

"Oh, I'm fine. Didn't sleep much last night is all. And couldn't seem to get warm this morning once I finally did drag these old bones up and out of bed. I'm not still in my nightgown, ya know," she says, flashing open her robe to reveal her thick, hand-knit sweater.

"I assumed as much. But some tea might do you good," I offer, holding up a mug and a tea bag.

"Oh, alright. Guess it can't hurt."

I busy myself around her familiar kitchen, noting the unwashed dishes in the sink and the drooping plants on the windowsill above them. Without comment, I take care of these small tasks while the water boils.

"You talk to Katie lately?" Tante asks.

"Spoke with her on my way into town this morning before I called you," I reply.

"You'd think owning her own business she could free up her schedule and come and see her mother sometime."

"She told me she is working on that very thing," I say, pouring the water into the readied cups and bringing them to the table. "But for today you will have to make do with a visit from me. Besides, I need to talk to you about something."

Tilda leans forward onto the table with a fresh spark of interest in her eyes.

"Is that so? Got family troubles or something?" she asks.

I smile at her sudden eagerness.

"Sugar?" I ask, taking the striped kitty sugar bowl from its spot on the counter next to its twin kitty creamer—one paw extended upward as a spout.

"Don't think I have any," she says, stirring her tea. "No creamer either."

Removing the kitty's heads, I find she is correct.

"No worries. I'll grab some for you at the store today and bring it by."

"I'd appreciate that, Tora-bird," she says, setting her spoon down. "You talk to my daughter Katie lately?"

I nod and repeat my conversation with Katie, and she reiterates her complaint. And we move on.

"Now tell me what's on your mind that an old lady might possibly help you with," she says.

I reach over to my tote bag and withdraw the laminated family tree page that is designated for my father and mother, leaving the one for Einar in its place. Setting it before her, I say, "I came across this amidst a bunch of genealogy records from your brother Einar."

She pulls it closer, squinting her eyes.

"Get my glasses, will ya?" she says, pointing to the inset in the wall where her telephone resides.

I comply and she dons them.

"Haven't seen this for quite a while," she murmurs, poring over the page. "Sigurd Alan Anderson and Louisa Mae Aronsen. Married June 15, 1944—right before he shipped off to the war. Always thought it was so convenient for your mom."

"How's that?" I say, bemused by her comment.

She peers up at me over her glasses, her blue eyes still clear inside their sagging frame of flesh.

"She never had to change her initials," she says as if this should be the obvious answer. "She went from LMA to LMA. I went from Tilda Inez Anderson to Tilda Inez Tornstrom. Always got embarrassed when I had to sign my initials to some legal form or another after Richard and I were married."

I grin at her conundrum.

She, however, does not seem amused.

"What would you rather be? A TIA or a TIT?"

"No, sorry, you're right. Part of the challenge of having a vowel for a middle initial," I say, trying to ease the sting from the subject matter.

She returns to her perusal.

"So, what's this got to do with your family troubles?" she asks.

"Auntie, I don't have any family troubles… well, none to speak of," I reply. "I came to ask you about this name right here." I reach across the table to point at the leaf designated for my older sister.

"What's that say?" she says, leaning forward until her nose almost touches the page. "Ann Marie," she reads. Her head lifts up sharply.

"What do you know about her?" I ask.

She sighs and returns her gaze to the family tree. Lifting her hand, she places a gnarled finger gently over the name of the baby girl. When she looks back up at me, tears are running down her cheeks.

"Oh, Tante," I say, pulling a packet of tissues from my tote bag, extracting one and pressing it into her hand. "I never knew about her until I saw this last night. Can you tell me what you know?"

She dabs at her eyes and sips from her tea but does not speak.

"Please?" I plead. "Whatever pact or promise you had with my folks about this, I think we can safely say no longer applies."

A deep breath rattles her fragile shoulders, and her head nods up and down as if she is acknowledging old agreements and making new ones.

"Her little face was so pretty," she whispers without raising her chin.

I bend closer to hear every word.

Removing her glasses, she wipes her eyes and cheeks. "She looked like your mother. Deep eyes, dark hair, and the most perfect pink lips," she whispers.

I let her sit in her memories for a moment.

"What happened to her?" I prompt.

At last, she glances back up at me. The struggle to control her emotions evident in her clenched jaw and brimming eyes. I reach over and hold her hand.

"It's okay. Take your time. I'm not going anywhere."

Tilda takes some deep breaths and gathers herself.

"It was a long time ago. I haven't even spoken her name in years, God forgive me," she whispers.

"Ann Marie," I say. "It's a pretty name."

She nods.

"After your mother's auntie—the one who never had any kids. Louisa wanted to honor her but then…"

"Then what?" I urge softly.

"Then she died," Tilda replies, peering up at me.

"Who died? My great-auntie?"

She shakes her head and drops her chin. "No… no… not her. Little Ann Marie. She died right in my arms."

I gasp. "Oh, Tante," I say, squeezing her hand.

Now she is truly weeping, unchecked tears dripping onto the plastic sheathing of the family record.

"Her head… it wasn't right. Too big for her little body and… Just not right. The doctors said her brain wasn't formed. That she had water on it or in it or something." Tilda stops to blow her nose. I set the whole packet of tissues at her disposal and she grabs another.

"Was there nothing they could do?" I ask.

She shakes her head. "No. Not back then. Just told your folks to take her home and keep her comfortable for as long as… For as long as they could."

I let out an anguished sigh.

"They called it hydro… hydro-something or other. Never could remember that awful word," she says.

"Hydrocephalus?"

"That sounds about right."

I sit back in my chair and take a sip from my now tepid tea, giving my auntie and myself time to process. The rumble and scraping of a passing snowplow underscores our selah moment.

"Why the secrecy, Tante? There's no shame in having a child born with a birth defect. Why did they keep this all so hush hush? Even my brothers have never said anything to me about her. Surely Andy, at least, was old enough to remember her."

"Oh, Tora-bird. It was your mother," she says. "You know her. So strong. So capable. So physically fit. She was way ahead of this whole exercise craze you young people are so into these days. She believed she'd caused the whole thing. Heard one doctor say, 'That's what happens when women do too many sports' or something stupid like that. Sig tried and tried to convince Louisa it had nothing to do with that. 'Just look at the boys,' he'd say. 'They're as healthy as can be. That doctor is full of beans.' Course, he used a different word but you get the idea."

"Were you and Uncle Richard able to speak to her? Surely you held some influence over her in those days."

Tilda slumps back into her chair and looks out the window at the falling snow.

"Oh, we tried," she says. "But there weren't enough words in the world. And once the doctors sent little Ann home, it was as if your mother wouldn't let herself love that baby. Wouldn't nurse her cuz that wasn't easy for either one of them. Then wouldn't even hold her. She got so depressed, she couldn't take care of the boys. They got sent away… I think maybe up here to my mom and dad. Can't remember all the details. Just know they were both gone until after…"

She slips back into silence.

I wait for her as I ponder what those days must have been like for all of them.

"I stayed with her," she says, still gazing beyond the room to the clouds. "My Richard, God rest his soul, told me to just go and stay with your folks as long as they needed me. We were newlyweds but he said he'd be okay. Said he could fend for hisself. He was a kind-hearted soul underneath all his bluster, ya know."

I nod, recalling a time or two when my Uncle Richard had let his macho guard slip in front of me, and I saw the veracity of her claim.

"Two weeks. Every day. I held her and rocked her and fed her." Her voice is soft, her eyes distant as if seeing things beyond my scope of vision. "She had the sweetest face… pretty little Ann."

We pause again.

"And my dad? How was he?" I ask.

Her eyes turn back to me.

"He was broken-hearted. Did the best he could to care for your mother. Had to go back to teaching though, so mostly he was gone during the day."

"They were so blessed to have you there," I say with tears beginning to drip down my cheeks as well as I see the grief from those days wash afresh over Tante's entire frame.

She shrugs slightly and shakes her head. "No, I was the blessed one," she says. "I held an angel in my arms… For two weeks. Every day. An angel."

Pushing the page back across the table, she starts to stand.

"Take me to the couch, please," she whispers, struggling to lift herself up from the chair.

I move quickly to her side and help her upright. I stay close, one hand gripping the fuchsia belt of her robe in the back to ensure she stays that way. Her feet barely clear the lip of the low-pile carpet as we progress from the linoleum of the kitchen to the front room. She seems to have aged markedly since I first came into the house.

"Here ya go," I say as we reach the desired destination, and I help her lay down on the floral cushioned couch. "I'll get you all tucked in and you can take a little snooze. How's that?"

As I am stepping back from settling the multi-colored afghan around her, she grabs my wrist. I stop and kneel down by her side.

"What is it?"

"I'm glad you know now," she says.

"Me too," I say, brushing a tear from her cheek. "Thanks for telling me."

"Don't think less of your mom. She could handle a lot of things better than most people but this situation… just more than she could bear."

I nod, choking up at the thought of my invincible mother having met her match. And me knowing nothing about it. Until now.

Tante puts her hand on my cheek.

"I've wondered many times whether or not maybe Ann Marie was the reason God gave you a heart to take care of all those babies the way you do. Makes me so proud of you," she says as her hand slips down to her side. "Stay for a minute. Will ya?" she whispers, her eyelids drifting shut.

"Of course, Tante," I say. "Of course, I'll stay."

"Maybe we can call Katie and see when she's coming up," she mutters before surrendering to sleep.

FELIX

MAX LETS OUT A BIG WOOF and spins in circles by the front door. “What’s got you so excited?” I ask, peering out the kitchen window, my hands deep in soapy water.

I don’t see anyone or anything approaching so, I turn back to washing the dishes. But Max’s display of enthusiasm continues. As I set my coffee mug into the drying wrack, a red Dodge pickup pulls into the driveway and two men disembark from the rig. They are dressed in appropriate cold weather gear from cap to boots as if they belong in the north woods of Minnesota. But I know they are most definitely not from these parts.

“Well, will ya look at that?” I mutter to myself while stepping to the entry door. “How’d you know?”

Max’s nose is stuck like glue to the threshold as if hoping to get the first whiff of our visitors.

"You're gonna have to move back, buddy, if you want me to let them in."

He goes in reverse for two steps and plops himself down into a quivering sit.

I swing the door open and step out onto the stoop before the men have a chance to even knock.

"What wind blew you two into Solbakken?" I say, feeling a big, silly grin spreading over my face at the sight of them.

The men bound up the steps two at a time, nearly knocking each other off into the bushes as they attempt to be the first to reach me. In the end, we wind up in a ferocious group hug with Max shoving past us and leaping up and down the stairs, barking the entire time.

Titus and Fabian release me and turn their attention to their four-legged friend.

"Max, you big hunk of fur, give me a hug," Titus shouts, bracing himself for the encounter he knows is coming.

Fabian and I back up into the house as Max takes the stairs in one leap, lifts his front paws up onto Titus's thick chest, and begins to lick his face with abandon.

We all laugh at the sheer joy we feel at being together again, though Max seems to be able to express it better than we humans.

"Alright, alright," I yell at Max after what I feel is an appropriate amount of jubilant canine harassment. "Enough, boy! Down!"

Reluctantly, my dog returns to all fours.

"Come in quickly before he changes his mind," I urge Titus. "Besides, it's blasted cold out here."

"What, this?" Titus says, spreading his arms wide and lifting his face into the blustery skies. "This is a walk in the park compared to where I was on my last assignment."

"Oh, really? And where might that have been?" I ask, closing the door behind my friends and my dog.

"Iceland," Titus says with a laugh. "Can you believe it? I've got family in Iceland now. And not in Reykjavik either.

Oh, no. These folks live on the other side of that big old island in the middle of nowhere. It was quite the adventure. Was just telling Fabian all about it on our way up here."

"And where did you two meet up?" I turn to ask Fabian.

"Titus met me in Wisconsin yesterday. I had no idea he was popping in, as usual. But it was perfect timing, as usual. Just got done with my own assignment over in Milwaukie. And he came through the door saying, 'Felix needs us. Let's go!' And so, here we are. What's up?"

"Yeah, what's such a big deal that the Big Guy wants all three of us together again?" Titus echoes.

I shrug.

"I've gotta tell ya, I don't really know. I mean, we've had a little excitement up here but nothing I haven't been able to handle on my own," I say.

Max hits my hand with his head.

"Well, nothing Max and I couldn't handle together," I correct myself. "So, if there's something big involved, it has yet to happen."

Fabian wraps his arms over his chest in his thick Carhartt jacket.

"Hmm," he says, his eyebrows scrunching in thought. "Well, maybe we need to settle in and wait for a minute. What do ya say, Felix? Got room for a couple of cloud-riders in this inn?"

MAXIMUS

It is the usual course of events.

Something in the air shifts and I know.

They are coming.

Our friends from times gone past.

Our friends in times still to come.

Our friends now and forever.

And I cannot help but bark and spin.

Joy, they call it.

Happiness like a plunge in a cool lake. Like a romp through a mound of snow. Like a nap on a fireside rug. Like a bowl of Master's leftover stew.

All thrown together.

This is joy.

They bring it with them without seeming to know how much.

There are so few friends like them.

Who know our beginnings. Who have lived them.

Who understand our losses, our loves, our lives.

I have marched with them through battles and mourned with them at graves.

I have licked the faces of children, grandchildren, great-grandchildren, and more.

Titus raised generations of my pups. Maximus the sixteenth was his last. Couldn't bear to part with another.

Fabian lets me sleep in his bed.

We do not tell Master.

Oh, it is good to have them here.

My head resting on Fabian's knee, I listen to their talk.

It flows. It ripples. It bounces and fills the house.

If I were a cat, I would purr.

But, alas, not part of my DNA.

My eyelids droop with fingers gently scratching my ears.

I wonder, though—why have they come?

There is a different scent with them this time.

Something peculiar yet familiar.

Something vaguely unsettling.

It fires something deep in my bones.

And I wonder. I wonder.

Yet I will not let it steal from the happiness of their arrival.

No, now is a moment for joy.

TORA

"TANTE, I NEED TO GET ON THE ROAD back to the farm," I say while I dry the last of the dinner dishes and stack them back into the cupboard.

"That's okay, dear," she says, attempting to snap the lid shut on a Tupperware container of leftover stew. "Darn things. Why'd they have to make it so hard to get 'em shut?"

"I'll get it." I hang my dishtowel on the handle of the stove door to dry and step over to help. "I have a hard time with these too," I say.

"Thanks," she says. "I sure have enjoyed having your company today."

I bend down and kiss her cheek, realizing how many inches lower I need to go to accomplish this feat then I did in days gone by.

“It has been my pleasure,” I say, setting the leftovers in the fridge, and checking to see that the kitchen is generally back in order after our impromptu supper date.

When Tante woke up from her nap, she asked if I could take her to the grocery store. Which I did. Then she needed something from Thompson’s Drug Store. So, we went. Then she wondered if I still remembered how to play cribbage. Which I do. So, we played a game. Then the woman who usually comes and makes a meal for her on Friday evenings called to say she was snowed in and wouldn’t be able to get into town until tomorrow, but that there was some beef stew in the freezer if I could thaw that out for Tilda. So, I did. And, of course, Tante wanted me to eat with her, which I did. But, now it is after six o’clock.

Peter texted me at 2:30 p.m. saying Hazel was in her booster seat, ShoSho was in his kennel, and they were about to leave Mariah’s. Hoped to get into Solbakken before eight, road-conditions, kid and dog permitting.

I check out the kitchen window into the backyard where a light on a telephone pole in the alley illuminates snowflakes whipping by on the wind. I can’t tell if it is still actually snowing or if these flakes have simply blown off roofs, trees, cars, or whatever surface which they have accumulated upon over the past hours.

“What’s the temp out there?” Tilda asks, peeking around my shoulder at the thermometer mounted on the window frame outside.

“Looks like it may have gone up a few degrees. Right around fifteen above,” I say.

“Well, that’s good,” she replies. “I hope I didn’t keep you too long. Thanks for everything.”

I turn and place a hand on both shoulders of her brightly striped sweater.

“Auntie, I am the one who called this meeting, remember? And I am the one who should be thanking you for all you have given me today. I don't know how I can ever repay the kindness you did for the sister I never knew, but I want you to know, I am forever grateful. And I'm sure my mom and dad are too."

Her eyes start to glitter with moisture.

"It sure was nice just to say her name again," she says.

I pull her into a hug. She does not resist but wraps her arms around me too.

"Yes, it sure was nice to say her name," I murmur into the crown of gray atop her head. We cling to each other for a lingering moment. I realize I am in the same arms that welcomed and cared for my sister until her last breath. I savor their fragile strength around me today.

We pull apart, each with our own tearful smiles.

She pats my hand. "I'm tuckered out," she says. "Think I need to turn on the TV and watch through my eyelids before I go to bed."

I get her situated in her recliner to watch *Wheel of Fortune* before wrapping up in my coat and grabbing my tote bag.

"Maybe Peter and I can bring Hazel in on Sunday afternoon before they leave," I say after giving her one more peck on the cheek.

"That would be nice," she says, her face beginning to relax with sleepiness.

When I open the door and take one last glimpse into the house, she is already oblivious to the third toss-up puzzle—*What are you doing?* Taking a nap, would be the answer.

BY THE TIME I REACH THE OUTSKIRTS OF ST. GERARD, the snow is not falling vertically but is whipping horizontally across my headlight beams. The white blur is reducing my visibility significantly. My gloved hands grip the steering wheel, and I lift and lower my shoulders to release the tension that is beginning to build into knots. I practice the breathing techniques I have learned over the course of the pandemic months to ease anxiety while remaining focused on the road. Then one thought floods my system, pushing out the cortisol and replacing it with a wash of welcome serotonin.

Tonight, I will hug my granddaughter.

The chemical reactions do more for me than all my relaxation techniques. Though, perhaps one may have given room for the other. I don't know and I don't really care.

Hazel is almost here.

I turn on my favorite Lauren Daigle album and settle in for the road ahead. The happenings of the day play through my mind. Ann Marie has moved into my heart as if I have always had a room reserved for her there. A strange combination of sadness and contentment fill this space. Sadness that I missed out on all these years of having a sister. But contentment in the knowledge that she lives on the other side of suffering. Healthy, whole, and waiting.

Perhaps my musings have lessened my vigilance, but I don't see the deer bounding up out of the ditch until we are eye-to-eye at my side window. Its panicked eyes must reflect my own, I think in one nano-moment, as I yank the steering wheel to the right to avoid a collision and hit my brakes. The deer diverts its path on a dime and somehow, we miss one another. But as I attempt to steer back into my lane, my right front tire catches on some ice, and I skid out of control. Before I know it, I am nose first in the ditch, my windshield completely filled by a wall of white.

Maybe the snow slowed me down. Maybe I hit the brakes harder than I thought. Maybe my guardian angels served as bumper pads. I don't honestly know what happened for sure, but the airbags did not deploy, I am uninjured, and my vehicle seems to be in one piece.

I lean my head onto the steering wheel, and offer up a quick prayer of thanks over the fiercely pounding rhythm of my heart.

Lauren Daigle's voice still plays over my speakers.

"Oh, I will rescue you…"

I almost smile at the timing of the lyrics, but not quite.

Sitting upright, I turn off the music to assess my situation. I need to hear myself think.

"Okay, Tora. You are okay. You can do this. Find the four-wheel drive shift lever," I coach myself.

Looking down at the center console, I push aside some of the contents of my tote bag that have spilled out during the incident. I locate the shift lever.

"Now, do I need four-high or four-low?" I run through the scenarios Peter gave me the day he brought this rig home. "I'm thinking high is for faster speeds…"

Putting the SUV into neutral, I pull back hard on the shift lever and then thrust it up and to the right. Lights appear on my dashboard indicating I have engaged the four-low system. Taking a deep breath, I congratulate myself on remembering this much under these circumstances. Then I shift into reverse and hope for the best.

The tires grip and crunch on the ice and snow, but I don't move more than a few inches. Keeping my foot on the brake so I don't slide back to where I started, I prep myself for a good hard stomp on the gas.

"Ready… and… go!"

I punch down on the gas.

I move another few inches, but the rear end begins to slide to my right, edging precariously closer to the brim of a steep embankment that falls off into the darkness. Stopping with the latest effort before I wind up rolling the whole rig over on its side, I shift back into park and turn on my hazard lights. The glowing red reflects off the drifting snow all around me, making me feel as if I am in one of Hazel's fancy glow toys. If only I was having fun.

I am most definitely not.

"Maybe I should call for help," I muse. "Not Peter. He's still too far out and I don't want to freak him out. Maybe Billy? No, he and Carin are up with the grandkids tonight…"

Then I remember I do have a AAA card. Reaching for my tote bag, I plunge my hands into the depths of it until my fingers brush upon my wallet. Retrieving it, I turn on the overhead light to find my card. I have no problem locating it, but when I look down to punch the number into my phone, I realize it has vanished somewhere under a seat or into some nook or cranny.

"No need to panic." I try to fend off the rising tide of anxiety that is threatening to shut off my mental acumen and constrict my blood flow. "Maybe I can call myself?"

Giving the voice command, I give it a try.

"Call Tora."

It works!

My phone lights up on the floor mat of the passenger seat underneath the family tree documents. Removing my seat belt, I stretch toward that far corner with no success.

"I am going to have to either climb over this seat or get out of the vehicle…"

Neither idea fills me with ecstasy. Maybe if I was five-foot-two and twenty-five years old I could wrestle my way out from behind the steering wheel, across the console, and into the other seat. But I am neither of those things.

Zipping up my coat and pulling the hood all the way up and over, I test the door. It resists due to the snow around it, but after a few good hard shoulder slams that a Viking offensive lineman would be proud of, I manage to make an opening large enough for me to slip out.

The wind grabs my hood and threatens to rip it off. I snug up the fasteners around my neck, leaving the door slightly ajar so as to keep the overhead light on, which helps me see where the heck I'm going. My boots are covered completely in a snow drift up to my mid shins. Gripping the handle of the back door, I hoist myself up toward the road using every handhold I can find until at last I stand on the shoulder.

Hoping beyond hope to see headlights coming toward me, I am disappointed to see only darkness. The snow stings my cheeks like little ice shards being flung from the wicked white witch of Narnia's scepter.

I search the horizon for yard lights or the outline of a barn or house. But I don't see anything remotely resembling those things. Though I have driven this road many times, I cannot figure out exactly where I am. My mind was so full of other things as I drove that I don't remember much of anything until the moment the deer nearly jumped into my lap.

Bolstering myself for the plunge back down into the ditch, I ease myself along the passenger side of the 4Runner. I reach the door, with much exultation, only to find it is locked.

"Oh, for corn sake!" I yell into the wind.

Tears threaten, but I refuse to give into them.

Reversing my trek, I climb once more up to the road and go back down the other side, hitting the unlock button firmly before making my return ascent. I am halfway back down toward the passenger door when headlights flash in my peripheral vision.

A car is coming!

I clamber up the incline. Falling to my knees in my haste, I crawl with the ferocity of a mountaineer about to reach the summit of Mt. Everest. From my lowered position, I begin to wave my arms wildly overhead, making the hazard lights become strobe-like in their patterns.

To my utter relief, the vehicle begins to slow.

I am almost blinded by the glare of the headlights from the pickup, which parks only a few feet from me. Realizing I am still on my knees as if in the throes of supplication, I scramble to an upright position just as the driver's side door flings open and a man emerges into the night.

"You alright there?" he yells over the wind as he advances.

"I am now," I yell back, giddy with relief.

"What happened?" he asks, coming up beside me, surveying my situation.

"A deer came out of nowhere. We managed to miss one another. It darted off the road in that direction and… well, as you can see. I wound up in the ditch."

He nods from underneath the brim of his wool cap.

"Won't come out in four-wheel drive?" he asks.

"I tried. A couple of times. But the rear end started sliding and I did not want to wind up worse than I already was," I say, pointing to the ravine on the other side of the ditch.

"Yup, yup. Probably a good decision," he says, tugging his gloves on over his bare hands. "Mind if I give it a go?"

"Not at all. Have at it. She's still running," I say, sweeping my hand in a grand gesture of assent.

"You want to get in my rig and warm up while I see what I can do?"

"That would be wonderful."

He steps back to his truck, opens the passenger door, and instructs the teenage boy who has been sitting there to get into the back of the crew cab with his sister.

"I could have gotten in the back," I say, approaching the open door.

"It's okay. It's warmer up front," he says. "Plus, my grandson is not exactly on my nice list at the moment. So, he's got no room to argue with me."

I step around the door and hoist myself up into the warmth of the pickup cab.

"Thanks for letting me have your seat." I turn to smile at the young man behind me.

"No problem," he mutters in a surprisingly deep voice, his eyes cast down away from mine.

"Hey, I know you," the young girl sitting next to him remarks.

"Oh, you do not," her brother murmurs.

"I do so. I saw her at school the other day. She's Pastor Mel's friend."

Swiveling around, I peer into the darkness of the back seat but I cannot make out the face of the one who seems to know me. The flashing red lights of my hazards offer little assistance.

"Well, yes, I do know Pastor Mel," I reply. "But, sorry, I'm afraid I don't remember you."

She flicks on the light in the middle of the cab and leans toward me.

"Oh," I gasp. "I do remember you. Sophia, isn't it?"

The girl turns triumphantly to her brother.

"See, told ya."

He plunges his chin into his jacket without gracing her words with a response.

"So, is that your grandpa in my car?" I ask, my heart once again thumping at an accelerated pace.

"Yeah, he's my gramps," Sophia replies.

"And is his last name Everwind?" I ask.

The boy's head comes up and hard dark eyes meet mine.

"How did you know that?" he asks.

"She heard my name at school, dumbo," Sophia says. "And if my name is Everwind then, duh, his name is Ever-wind."

"Not necessarily," her brother replies. "Could have been Grandpa Bourdain, dumbo."

Sophia sits back and crosses her arms.

"Yeah, well, it's not," she says.

The roar of my 4Runner's engine grabs all of our attention, and we watch as their grandpa, who I am guessing is my cousin, attempts to free my rig from its snowy confines. But alas, to no avail. The rear end only slips even closer to the lip of the embankment. My Good Samaritan quickly shuts down the attempt, exits the vehicle, and comes back to the truck. He motions for me to roll down my window.

"We're gonna have to give it a tug with my chains," he says. "Tommy, get your gloves on and come out and help me."

Before I can say anything else, he is heading to the cano-pied bed of his truck to pull out whatever gear he needs to drag my SUV up and out of the ditch. His grandson is not far behind him.

Sophia and I sit in silence, watching the two men attaching the chains under my bumper and then back to the truck. I can feel her eyes assessing me though.

"So, do you know Gramps or something?" she finally asks.

"Would your grandpa's name be Thomas Everwind?"

She hesitates.

"Yeah…"

"Well, then, I sort of know him," I reply. "More like, I know of him."

Tommy climbs into the driver's seat of the truck and rolls down his window while his Grandpa Thomas stays outside.

"Put her in reverse," the older man hollers. "Okay, slow but steady now."

Tommy's face is a study in confident concentration. I can tell he is not put off by this situation in the least but has probably done something like it on numerous occasions.

"Give it some gas," Thomas yells when the chain stretches taut. "Not too much, though. Easy now, easy. That's it!"

My vehicle slowly begins to straighten itself and emerge from the ditch. Thomas waves his arms with directions and then holds up a closed fist when, at last, the 4Runner is back on solid ground. Tommy puts the truck into park and gets out to undo the towing mechanisms with his grandpa.

The whole time this feat of rescue is unfolding, I am pondering what to say to Thomas when he returns to the truck.

"Hey, fancy running into you out here, Cousin."

Or, "Wow, who'd have believed this is how we'd finally meet?"

Or, "Ever heard of a guy named Einar Anderson?"

In the end, all I can think of to say is, "Thank you so much. I don't know what I would have done if you wouldn't have come along just now. Can I pay for your services?"

"Nope, wouldn't think of it," Thomas says, settling back behind his steering wheel and brushing the snow from his eyebrows and eyelashes. "Just doing what's right. That's what we do, isn't it, kids?"

Sophia nods eagerly but Tommy, back in his corner of the crew cab, acts as if he hasn't heard.

"Isn't that right, Tommy? We do the right thing even when it's inconvenient and costs us something. Yeah?" Thomas says, leveling a steady gaze at his grandson via the rearview mirror.

"I guess," Tommy replies.

"You guess? Or you know?" Thomas continues.

Tommy lets out a deep sigh.

"I know," he mutters.

"Tommy's in trouble cuz he broke into somebody's house and took some stuff," Sophia declares.

"Soph, that's enough," her grandfather quickly shuts her down. "That's none of this lady's business. You want me telling her about the trouble you got into at school the other day?"

Sophia's chin drops. "Doesn't matter," she says defiantly. "She already knows."

Thomas turns to me with a quizzical look.

"You've met my granddaughter before?" he asks.

I smile and nod.

"We are slightly acquainted," I admit.

"Oh, yeah. How's that?" he asks.

"She knows your name, Grandpa," Sophia pipes up.

"Excuse me?" Thomas looks from his granddaughter in the mirror back to me. "Is that right? Well, now I think of it, you've got one over on me. I don't know yours."

I take a deep breath and unsnap the top fastener under my chin. Suddenly I am very warm.

FELIX

"NO, I'M SERIOUS," Fabian insists. "Milwaukee, Wisconsin, calls itself the Beer Capital of the World."

Titus and I look at one another over our second bottle of Blatz and laugh.

"They have clearly never filled a stein in Munich!" Titus remarks.

"Or tipped a pint in Dublin," I add, taking a swig.

"Ah, you two miss the point. I'm just saying if you want to truly call yourself a connoisseur of brewed beverages, you'll have to make a trip to Milwaukee sometime. Not everybody gets a chance to test the drink from all over the world, let alone from pretty much every epoch of time since the resurrection of Christ. We three may have taste tested more beers and ales than anyone who's ever existed save God Himself… If He, in fact, imbibes," Fabian says.

Titus lifts his glass.

"To Milwaukee, then," he says. "May their vats brim over and our assignments lead us to their taphouses."

We clink our bottles together.

"Here, here," I say after emptying the last dregs in one gulp.

"Here, here," Fabian adds, wiping a drip of foam from his lips. "Anyone need another?"

I hold my hands up in front of me. "Nope. Two is my limit," I say.

Titus shakes his head. "Somethings never change," he says.

"Same old Felix," Fabian agrees.

I smile at their gibes, but I know the truth. And so do they.

"Never the same old Felix," I say softly.

My friends turn to me with sober faces and nod.

"True, my friend," Titus says. "None of us have ever been the same since…"

My dog suddenly lurches up from his spot underneath the table, nearly upending the entire apparatus. We three grab our drinks as best we can while Max wrestles his way out between chair legs and human legs. He plants himself by the front door and growls.

"What's up with him?" Fabian asks.

"Not sure," I say, getting up from my spot and meeting Max at the door. "Easy now, pal. Sit," I command, and he obeys. I flip on the front porch light at the same moment someone knocks on the door.

Max quivers in his effort to stay seated but the rumble in this throat persists.

"Stay," I command, moving past him to open the door. "Make sure he doesn't attack someone, will you?" I say over my shoulder to Titus, who jumps up and scuttles close to Max's side, slipping one hand around his collar. Of all the men I have known, Titus may be the only one big enough and strong enough to handle my dog with sheer force.

I open the door a crack to see a man I've never met before standing on the stoop. In his arms with her stocking-cap-covered head drooping on his shoulder is a little girl who looks to be about three or four-years-old.

"Can I help you?" I say, opening the door wider, allowing icy crystals to fly into the house on a cold gust of wind.

"We're looking for Tora Dahlgard," the man says. "She's been staying over there." He points to Einar's place.

"Ah, you must be Peter. Come on in out of the weather," I say, welcoming them into the house. "I'm Felix, by the way."

The man and girl come in and Max's growl turns to a wiggling excitement.

"Pleased to meet you," the man says, extending a hand to mine and then returning it to its place on the little girl's back. "This is Hazel, my granddaughter."

"Oh, how wonderful to meet you," I say. "Your grandma has told me all about you, and she's been beside herself with excitement to have you both here."

"Well, that's what I thought too. But we got to the house and it's all locked up and completely dark. I tried to call her but no answer," he says. "Frankly, I'm a little concerned."

This last part he adds in a whisper so as not to disturb Hazel, who appears to be in a bit of a sleepy fog.

Closing the door behind him, I offer him a seat but he declines.

"These are my buddies from my days in the army. Titus and Fabian," I say by way of introduction. "They just arrived this morning and surprised me. So, I have been a bit preoccupied today and haven't spoken to Tora at all since yesterday. Although I do recall seeing her rig leaving the house this morning."

"Yes, I talked with her when she was on her way into St. Gerard to see her auntie. And I texted her when we left the Cities. She replied right away that she was still in town. But that was hours ago," Peter says.

"We could go looking for her," Fabian offers as he stands.

Peter surveys the empty bottles on the table.

"Uh, thanks for the offer, but I think I'll drive down to Billy's. Looks like you guys should maybe not be on the roads. No offense," he says.

Fabian sits back down with a chagrined smirk.

"It looks worse than it is," he says. "But you're probably right."

"We have handled things under worse circumstances," Titus says, turning to argue with his pal.

As he does, Max jerks free from the grip he has had on his collar and lunges toward Peter. Before I can stop him, he is licking Hazel's boots as if they were covered in liver pâté. I stare at Titus, who mouths, "Sorry."

"Whoa, there, big fella," Peter says, backing up a few steps.

Hazel stares down at Max with no sign whatsoever of alarm.

"He's a big doggie, Papa," she says, reaching a hand down to pet him.

Max lifts his snout and slurps his tongue over her small fingers.

I go to yank him back, but Peter stops me.

Hazel is giggling.

"His tongue is so big," she says. "He could give ShoSho a bath with one lick."

Peter is smiling now despite the circumstances. It's clear that whatever enthralls Hazel, enthralls him as well.

"Yes, he probably could," he says.

"Your grandma told me you were bringing your puppy with you. Max loves to play with other dogs. And, believe it or not, he's very gentle with puppies," I say to Hazel.

Max sits placidly by Peter's leg and allows Hazel to ruffle his ears.

"Where is my grammy?" Hazel asks.

Peter and I return our attention to the puzzle before us.

"Do you want me to try and call her?" Fabian offers. "I know Felix says the cell reception is lousy out here, but I've got a satellite phone."

"That would be great," Peter says, reaching into his coat pocket for his phone. "I'll have to look up her number. I'm so used to just saying her name that I haven't had to use the actual number in years."

As he scrolls through his phone list, I peer out the window toward Einar's place. It is, indeed, dark. I can see why Peter might be anxious.

"Okay, here it is," Peter says and reads off the digits to Fabian.

We all wait and listen to the sound of the call connecting and ringing.

Finally…

"This is Tora, leave a number after the beep and I will get back to you. Thanks, and have a great day."

Peter waves off Fabian's questioning look as to if he should leave a message or not.

"I've already left her about ten messages," he says with a sigh. "I guess we will head over to Billy and Carin's. I know they have a key to the house in the very least. And maybe they have heard from my wife."

Just then, through the kitchen window, I catch the sweeping arc of headlights turning into Einar's driveway. In fact, I see two sets of headlights one after the other.

"Peter, I think you can save that trip down the road. Looks like Tora just pulled in and someone else too. Maybe she's got Billy and Carin with her," I say.

Relief washes over Peter's face, and Hazel squeezes his neck.

"I want to see Grammy," she whispers loud enough that my friends and I can hear.

"And she wants to see you, too, kiddo," Peter says. "Thanks for the offer to help guys. Tora has nothing but good things to say about you, Felix. I feel as if I already know you, but maybe we'll get a chance to visit more over the weekend."

"I sure hope so," I concur, tugging the door open for their exit.

"Shalom," Fabian and Titus say in unison.

Peter stops in his tracks and stares at them before replying, "Shalom, shalom."

TORA

SEEING PETER'S CAR IN THE DRIVEWAY as we pull in lifts my spirits and suddenly, I realize in all the excitement of the past hour, that I have not returned his messages. I turn toward Thomas, who has driven with me back to the house so that we could continue the conversation that was started along the side of the road. Tommy and Sophia are in the truck behind us. In an even stranger twist than what has already been twisted, I have come to find out that Thomas was actually on his way out to Solbakken to see me when our paths crossed, as it were, prematurely along the side of the road.

The house is dark and empty and so is my husband's BMW.

"Oh my gosh," I say. "I've locked them out. I can't believe I forgot to leave a key or leave a message. There are very few things in this world that could have distracted me today from the arrival of my husband and granddaughter."

Thomas smiles.

"I guess I should be flattered, then," he says.

"You most definitely should be," I reply, scanning the stoop and front porch hoping to see some sign of movement as my headlights illuminate the front of the house. "But where are they?"

"The house across the way has lights on," Thomas offers. "Maybe they went to look for you there."

"Maybe," I say, hitting the garage door opener. "Tommy can pull up right next to my husband's car. That is, if you can spare a few more minutes. I would dearly love for you to meet my… uh, your family."

"We can spare the time," he says. "Besides, Tommy still has some property he needs to return to this house."

"Oh, yes. I'd forgotten about that too," I say as we enter the confines of the garage. "What a day it's been, and it's not over yet."

I fumble with the gear shift and ignition as if seeing them for the first time. My mind has been scattered into so many different avenues; it is hard to focus on the immediate tasks at hand.

"Turn to your left," Thomas says, indicating that direction with a tip of his thick black head of hair.

I gasp when I find Hazel's face pressed to my window with both hands on either side.

"Grammy! I'm here!" she yells.

Tears spring up and over and I cannot figure out why I am unable to get out of my seat once I've opened the door.

"Your seatbelt, Tora," Thomas says with a grin as he unlocks the mechanism that constricts me.

I put my hands over my dripping cheeks. "Argh… I'm just a mess," I laugh.

Finally free from my restraints, I leap out of the SUV and allow Peter to dump Hazel into my outstretched arms. The grip of her small arms around my neck, the feel of her breath on my cheeks, the smell of French fries, all threaten to overwhelm me with delirious joy. I close my eyes and drink in every sensation of her. When I open them, I see Peter staring at us with a tear-filled, goofy look that I am sure mimics my own.

"We made it," he whispers, rubbing a hand over Hazel's bright pink coat. "We made it."

I nod and allow myself to absorb that thought.

We made it.

Without us hearing them, Tommy and Sophia have come into the garage and stand beside their grandpa.

"Uh, what's going on here, Tor?" Peter asks, casting a glance in the direction of the Everwinds.

"Oh, gosh, there's so much to tell. And I need you to meet these folks. This is Thomas Everwind and his grandchildren, Tommy and Sophia," I say, grinning at my long-lost cousins. "Let's go inside and we will sort it all out."

"Don't forget ShoSho," Hazel says, looking with concern at Peter.

"I'll get him out of his kennel and let him go potty before we come in," he replies. "You guys get inside. I will be right behind you."

He steps up to the back door and opens it wide for me, Hazel, and our parade of visitors. Once inside, I switch on all the lights, turn the heat up a notch, and usher everyone in and around the dining room table. Hazel refuses to be put down though, so I sit with her on my lap and begin to help her off with her coat and boots.

"You know what? I don't have anything to offer you until I get the groceries in from my rig. Would you mind terribly, Tommy, if I asked you to bring them in?" I ask.

The look between grandfather and grandson leaves no room for argument.

"There is no need to feed us anything but I am sure Tommy would be happy to help bring in the groceries,"

Thomas speaks on Tommy's behalf. "And Sophia can help too."

Sophia gives her grandpa a look as she passes him but doesn't protest with words. I hand the car keys to Tommy, indicating the button that will open the back of the 4Runner.

"Thanks so much. You can just set them on the table in the kitchen when you get in," I say.

Hazel watches their every move and then whispers into my ear.

"We'll have to ask her when she comes back in," I reply. "Hazel is wondering if Sophia likes to play with puppies."

"Oh, I'm sure that would be something she would like very much," Thomas says with a warm smile at my granddaughter, who gives him a quick glance and then snuggles back into my shoulder.

I soak in the reality of Hazel in my lap and Thomas Everwind at my table. Actually, at our great-grandfather's table.

"What an amazing thing it was for you to drive up right when I needed you," I say to him.

"Our paths wind where they are meant to wind, my mother used to tell me," Thomas replies.

"Yes, I believe they do."

He surveys the room. "Mind if I get a closer look?" he asks, pointing to a family photograph of my grandparents' fiftieth wedding anniversary that has been blown up and made into a poster. It hangs on the door between the kitchen and dining room.

"Not at all," I reply. "Be my guest. They are as much your family as they are mine."

He acknowledges this with a nod. "A fact I am still getting used to."

I have just disengaged Hazel from my lap and am taking off my coat when he says over his shoulder, "Is this Einar?"

I turn to see who he is pointing at and nod.

"Hmm." He stares at the man who is his father. "Tommy is right."

"How's that?"

"I have seen this man before. He used to come to the boy's baseball games. Tommy told me he saw the picture of that man when he was here. I just thought he was… I don't know, a baseball fan."

I'm not sure what to say, but Thomas saves me from throwing out some hollow platitude when he speaks again.

"I have been in this house once before."

"Really? When was that?"

"I was only a kid. Probably about the same age as your Hazel," he says, turning slightly back toward us.

"You were a kid like me?" Hazel asks.

"I was," Thomas replies, turning and crouching down so as to meet her eye to eye. "And when I was a kid like you, my Grandpa Thomas brought me here to meet some people."

Hazel tilts her head and says, "Isn't your name Thomas?"

He smiles and nods. "It is. I am named after my grandfather and Tommy is named after me."

"I think I have my own name," Hazel states but looks up at me for confirmation.

"You do. But your middle name, Mae, is the same as your Grandmother Louisa Mae," I say.

"Was she a kid like me once too?" Hazel asks.

"Believe it or not, we all were," I reply. Turning back to Thomas I ask, "Why were you here?"

He stands up and points to the couple at the middle of the large picture. Both Hazel and I step closer.

"My grandparents, Axel and Arnhild," I say. "Who would also be your grandparents."

Thomas stares at the picture.

"I was not told that at the time. My grandfather came to bring them some fish. At least, that's what he told me. I do remember they paid quite close attention to me. And, I think I remember there being some tears shed too. Grandpa Thomas told me they'd just had some very happy news, which can sometimes make people cry just like sad news."

"Like Grammy and Papa when they saw me today," Hazel remarks.

"Yes, a lot like that," Thomas says.

Tommy and Sophia arrive laden with grocery bags and I escort them to the kitchen.

WHEN THE GROCERIES ARE PUT AWAY, the dog pottied, and the girls situated in the living-room with ShoSho romping gleefully between them, Peter, Thomas, Tommy, and I settle into our chairs around the dining-room table.

After an explanation about how I came to run into Thomas and his grandkids this evening alongside the road between here and St. Gerard, Peter is effusive with his thanks to the Everwinds and relieved that both his wife and her new vehicle are unharmed.

"Okay, well, that solves one level of this mysterious encounter, but I am guessing there are more levels of mystery yet to be explained. Am I right?" Peter asks.

Thomas nods.

Tommy remains completely still with his eyes downcast across the table from Peter and I.

"Let me start," I say, looking around for my tote bag. "Thomas, did you happen to see the tote bag I had in my car that was down by your feet?"

He points to the rocking chair behind me.

"Ah, thanks," I say, getting up to retrieve it. "This will make things easier to understand, I think."

Pulling the family tree document out and laying it in front of my husband I say, "For your viewing, I give you Exhibit A."

"Are you reporting me to the cops?" Tommy suddenly speaks up, his eyes taking in the document and then gazing at me. There is a healthy dose of fear in them.

"I'm sorry, Tommy. That's not what I meant to imply. Peter is an attorney and I was just speaking in a language he understands."

Tommy's shoulders relax slightly, but Peter is studying him now more than the document.

"Is there some reason you might be concerned about criminal charges?" he asks the teenage boy.

Tommy glances at his grandfather, who remains stoic in his chair, his arms crossed over his chest. Tommy lowers his eyes and says, "I didn't mean for it to happen. I only wanted to find something… Something about him."

"Him being…?" Peter asks, peering up at me.

I take my seat next to him and point to the name on the family tree.

"Uncle Einar," I say, allowing my finger to flow to the initials alongside Einar's at the bottom of the tree. "And this is Grace Everwind," I say, stopping at Thomas's mother's initials.

"What was her middle name?" I ask my newfound cousin.

"Anang," he replies. "It means 'star.'"

"Grace Anang," I repeat. "Very pretty. She died fairly young. Do you mind if I ask of what?"

"It was a heart-attack," Thomas says. "But I have wondered at times if it was more of a heart break than an attack. She was a very kind woman but she battled with what we called back then 'the blues.'"

"Oh, I'm sorry to hear that," I reply, realizing as I see the date of Grace's death that it was shortly after my Grandpa Axel's death. And shortly before Einar returned to live in this house.

I sigh and bring myself back to Exhibit A.

"T.E.E., December 6, 1946," I read aloud.

"Yes?" Peter says.

"This is T.E.E.," I say, indicating Thomas. "Thomas Einar Everwind."

Thomas nods. "Yes. Only recently did I find that the middle name comes from my father."

Peter sits fully upright and leans back into his chair. "Holy mackerel…"

Thomas smiles. "Walleye, bass, northern pike, and perch, more likely," he says.

Peter shakes his head in bemusement.

"The Everwinds are in the fishing industry in Red Lake," I explain. "And it was through a fishing-like incidence that our families first crossed paths many years ago."

"Alright, well, that's about as clear as mud," he mutters.

"Don't worry, I will catch you up on all the family lore later tonight," I say before turning back to my cousin. "So, this is your wife?" I point to the initials M.J.E. beside his initials.

He nods. "Margaret Joy Everwind. She died in 2012. Mouth cancer."

"Oh, I'm so sorry," I say, noting that the date of death has indeed been filled out.

"Thank-you," Thomas replies. "But now, I think, we need to get to the reason I brought my grandson here to begin with."

All at once, ShoSho comes scampering out of the living room and bolts under the table away from Sophia who is close on his heels.

"ShoSho," Hazel yells, bringing up the rear. "Bad boy. You come here!"

The puppy hunkers down, his tail swinging ecstatically.

Sophia gets down on all fours. "Here, puppy," she says, reaching out a hand.

ShoSho retreats further away and yips with delight at the chase.

Suddenly his yips cease as in one swoop, Thomas lifts him up by the scruff, and presents him to his granddaughter. "Keep him occupied, please," he says.

"We're trying but he's very fast," Sophia says as ShoSho squiggles in her arms.

"Let's go," Hazel says, tugging on her new-found cousin friend.

The girls retreat to the other room, which is only separated from us by the placement of a couch and a desk. Their interruption briefly dispelled the tension that had begun to mount around the dining-room table. But as soon as they are gone, it settles back into place.

Thomas sets his hand on Tommy's shoulder. The boy looks at him, takes a deep breath, and begins to talk.

"I had a project for social studies class. Everyone had to make a family tree," he says, clearing his throat and taking a quick peek over at Peter and me.

I try to give an encouraging look.

"My mom's side of the family was easy. She's got records going back a long way to places like Montreal, Canada, and even France. I thought that was cool. So, I started digging into dad's family… But, uh, I got as far as Gramps and all I could find was information about his mom, Grace. Nothing about his dad."

The noise from the other room has gone suspiciously quiet.

I turn to investigate and find Sophia peering over the back of the couch, a sleeping dog in her arms. Hazel's hair falls over a pillow on the arm of the couch. I suspect she has fallen asleep as well. I smile at Sophia, seeing that she is eager to hear all that is being shared among the adults. She is directly behind her grandfather, and I quickly turn my attention from her, fearing that he might shoo her away. Maybe it's not my decision to make, but I think she's old enough to hear what's unfolding. It is her family tree, too, after all.

"Go on," Thomas prompts.

"So, I sent some DNA into one of those websites without my parents knowing it. You can do that when you're eighteen, ya know," Tommy continues. "And when I got it back, like, right after Christmas, I was super excited to check it out. But there wasn't much new information specifically except that I had a pretty high percentage of DNA from places like Norway and Sweden and some other places like Germany, Italy, Eastern Europe, and even a little bit of Jewish. I finally told my folks about what I'd done. And I asked them if they knew about anybody from that part of the world in the family line. Neither one of them had a clue one way or another. They thought maybe the DNA place had made a mistake. And then, when I asked Gramps about it, he was pretty tight lipped about the whole thing. I mean, the records I got from the company suggested a few second or third cousin kind of things that did not make much sense to me. But then, a couple of weeks ago, I got this email notification. A clue, or whatever they call it, had popped up. At first, I ignored it, but then I saw it was a clue about a possible first cousin match for my grandpa."

"Oh, my gosh," I say.

"Which reminds me," Peter says to me. "I've got the whole DNA profile thingy the genealogy company made for us saved on my computer. We can look at it sometime this weekend."

"So, you're saying, when I sent in my DNA right after Christmas, that your profile connected us?" I ask Tommy.

He nods. "Yup, I guess so."

"Isn't that something?" Peter says, tapping his hand over Uncle Einar's tree document.

"I mean, it took some investigating still, but eventually, I worked it out that my great-grandpa was either Sigard Anderson or Einar Anderson. And I sort of, well, I sort of stalked you and your family on social media… Sorry," he says, lifting his eyes without lifting his head.

"Understandable," I reply.

"And I figured out that Einar lived somewhere up here before he died. But I didn't know where until one night I was partying with my buddy Mikey."

"Mikey Bjorklund? Janet's grandson?" I interject.

"Yeah, that's the guy. And he was telling me how his grandma had kicked him out of her house out here in Solbakken. And he was kinda drunk, I guess, cuz he started spouting off about all kind of people from out here. Like Billy somebody and Ole somebody. And then he said Einar somebody used to live right across the road. But that he was dead and nobody even lived in his house anymore."

He pauses for a breath and readjusts his thick dark hair across his forehead.

"So, I talked him into bringing me out here sometime to check out the abandoned house. And I swear, when we first came out here, it was just me and Mikey and all we did was look through junk. He didn't know why I was really here and I didn't tell him. But we didn't ransack anything! You gotta believe me."

"Okay, okay," Peter says calmly. "Just tell us what happened then."

Tommy wipes his palms along his jeans and takes a quick peek at his grandpa, who has not changed positions throughout his confession. But now, he gives his grandson a small nod of encouragement.

"Well, Mikey was upstairs looking around and I found that cupboard over there," Tommy says, pointing to the cupboard doors at the bottom of the stairway. "I couldn't believe all the genealogy crap that was in there. Mikey got way into going through some old baseball cards or something upstairs, so I dug through as much as I could. And that's when I found that." He thrusts his chin out toward Exhibit A.

"And what else?" Thomas breaks his silence.

Tommy reaches into an inner pocket of his coat and pulls out another piece of paper. He unfolds it and stops to look at it.

"Mikey and I went over to his grandma's when we left here. He took some baseball cards and stashed them somewhere, and I put that family tree paper and a letter I found with it into an envelope and hid it under the desk drawer upstairs. I didn't want to bring it home and have Mom ask questions. I was gonna come back for it later, but then I came out here and some guy was living in Mikey's grandma's house. So, I left it. But this…" He pauses and looks at the paper in his hand once more before sliding it over to Peter and I. "I don't know why I held onto it. Guess it just felt like something really important that sort of filled in a bunch of holes for me. I didn't even show it to anyone until yesterday when I finally got up the guts to show Gramps."

Peter draws the document toward us until it rests right between us on the table.

"Thomas Einar Everwind," I read the name at the top left box. "Date of birth December 6, 1946. Place of birth, Bethany Hospital, Thief River Falls, MN. Weight, six pounds, thirteen ounces. Length, twenty inches. Mother, Grace Anang Everwind. Father, Einar Gottlieb Anderson."

I read the last two names slowly. Almost reverentially. For it feels like a sacred moment. I look over at my cousin Thomas, who remains in his same position, but I see the hint of emotion that slashes through his eyes.

We are all quiet. Even the sound of snow pellets hitting the window has ceased and a bright full moon is rising on the horizon over the treetops outside.

Peter sets the birth certificate atop Exhibit A, crosses his hands on them, and looks back at Tommy.

"So, you maintain that you had nothing to do with the ransacking of this house, but I am assuming you know who did. Is that correct?" he says with hints of attorney in his words.

Tommy nods. "I didn't do it but… I think maybe I'm sort of responsible for it," he admits.

"And how's that?" Peter continues.

Tommy lets out a deep sigh, blowing his bangs up and out with the exhale.

"I didn't think they'd come back here looking for them," he says.

"Looking for what, Tommy?" I ask.

He glances at his grandpa, then at me, then at Peter and even at Sophia before answering.

"I know we're supposed to keep it in the family and everything but I guess… I guess I'd read… I mean… I took a picture of the letter from the other lady named Tora. And when I ran it through a translation app, it said something about Einar having them, too, and I guess I'd had a few beers and they were all telling tall tales about stupid stuff they've done, or stupid stuff they're gonna buy some day, and it just sort of came out…"

Dots connect in my mind.

"You told them about the coins?" I ask.

He looks at me and for the first time, tears and repentance are evident in his stare.

"I didn't think they'd believe me. I'd have never said anything if I thought for one second they'd come here and loot the place looking for them. I just never thought… I mean… I mean… I'm really sorry," he finally admits in a near whisper.

Thomas uncrosses his arms and sets one hand on his grandson's shoulder. "And?" he prompts.

Tommy looks at him sideways and drops his chin.

"Look them in the eye, son," Thomas coaches.

Tommy raises his eyes to ours.

"I am truly sorry for taking what didn't belong to me and for leading those guys to do what they did and… if you can… would you… will you please forgive me?"

Peter takes my hand and looks into my eyes. I know he is saying that I am the one who needs to answer this question. I nod, knowing this to be true.

"Tommy, I very much appreciate those words and your honesty. I can imagine how difficult it has been to come here and do what you've done tonight. That takes some courage." I give a smile to Thomas. "And an honorable grandfather at your side."

Thomas gives me a nod.

"Yes, of course, we forgive you," I say. "And I can understand how precious these pieces of paper must seem to you. So, if you don't mind waiting a day or two, I'd like to make some copies of them for our family records and then, I'd like you to keep the originals."

For the first time since I've met him, Tommy's face relaxes into something resembling a smile.

"But before you go," Peter adds. "It would be really helpful if you could give us the names of the guys who did the damage around here. I'm sure Sheriff Dumfrey would see your cooperation as going a long way toward distancing you from any mark on your record."

"Wow," Sophia says, and her grandpa swivels to find her fully engaged in what has transpired. "He's just like those lawyers on TV."

TORA

HAZEL SNORES IN LITTLE WHIFFLES from her place on the floor beside our bed. ShoSho is in his kennel in the kitchen only a few feet from the threshold to the bedroom. We negotiated even that distance with our granddaughter, who insisted that her puppy always sleeps with her. Isaac had warned us she might try to convince us that this was the case—it is not. We had, however, relented on allowing Hazel to stay in our room and not in the bedroom upstairs. It was hard to find fault with her argument that it was too far away. Besides, neither Peter nor myself can bear to have her out of our sight.

So, we wrestled the mattress out of the hide-a-bed couch in the living room and arranged it on the carpet by our bed. This satisfied her little heart, and she fell asleep in mid-sentence as she said her bedtime prayers.

Then, in the stillness that has engulfed the house once the winter storm passed, my husband and I catch up in whispers about various things large and small that have passed our way since we last held one another. He tells me of meeting Felix and his buddies Titus and Fabian right before I arrived back at the house.

"Buddies?" I say. "Really? When did they get here?"

"Just this morning, from what I gathered. Felix said they were friends from his days in the army. Just showed up unexpectedly and surprised him."

"Hmm, that's interesting. Hope I get to meet them. Did you meet Maximus?"

"Oh, yes. He made quite an impression on you-know-who."

I smile into the darkness, imagining Max and Hazel together. "I can see how they might take to one another," I remark.

But my remark is met with no answer save a decidedly more baritone snore than the ones coming from the floor. I slip out from under my husband's arm, and he rolls over onto his side.

"Shalom," I whisper.

"Shalom," he whispers back before drifting into a deep slumber.

Ah, to sleep like a man. Or like a child. Or like a puppy, for that matter. I lay on my back and let the events of the day wash over me. How sweet was my time with Tante Tilda and her stories of little Ann Marie? What are the odds of everything happening the way it did with Thomas, Tommy and Sophia? And can it be that Hazel is really here? I insert prayers of gratitude in the midst of my musings. The final picture that fills my mind once my eyelids are finally heavy with sleep, is the image of Max and Hazel looking into each other's eyes.

A BABY IS CRYING SOMEWHERE. Not a lusty, strong cry but a soft whimpering.

I open my eyes and check on Hazel. She still sleeps. Tossing onto my side and rearranging the blankets, I fall quickly and deeply back to sleep.

And the crying begins again.

I follow it to the canopied space under the large, brilliant oak tree. Taking a seat on the bench, I wait for someone to meet me but no one does. Yet the whimpering continues. I stand and am about to circle around the huge base of the tree when a woman takes me by the hand and pulls me into an ornately furnished bedroom.

"You must take her," the woman whispers in my ear. "Harold will not abide a child with… with these issues."

I struggle to make out the face behind the voice. The room is dark. A solitary candle flickers in a far corner but, the woman has her back to that faint light, and her face dwells in the shadows. In the grand four-poster bed near the candle, a figure lies under a thin shroud. It is very still.

"But where?" I hear myself ask. "And to whom? Who would take her?"

I feel the woman press the whimpering bundle into my arms. It is so light that if I had not heard the noise, I would not have known a child lay amongst the soft linen blankets. They are of a fine quality, and I know in a moment that in this house, money is not an issue.

But something else is.

Something else is definitely wrong.

The woman hustles toward the bed, crossing herself as she nears the shrouded figure and kneels by a desk under a curtained window. I hear keys jingling as she retrieves them from a pocket and inserts one into a drawer. I walk closer to her and peer over her shoulder toward the figure on the bed. I am confused and disoriented. Yet suddenly I know, in a way beyond common knowledge, that the person lying so still is my sister. The revelation stirs no sadness. My sister lies dead on the bed, but my eyes are dry.

I struggle to remember why my emotions toward her are so flat. It is as if I am trying to remember somebody else's life. Somebody else's family. Somebody else's feelings. The infant in my arms seems more real to me than the body on the bed. I gaze at the tiny face but cannot see the deformity the woman speaks of. The eyes that stare back at me are deep—so deep that no light seems to emit from their depths. And the mouth, though perfect in shape, struggles to send out the cries of distress with any amount of gusto. Swaying back and forth while I watch the older woman, the motion has the desired effect, and the infant soon quiets. Her eyelids flutter and then shut in rest.

Footsteps sound in the hall outside the closed bedroom door.

The woman desists in what she is doing.

I hold my breath.

Whoever is outside stops at the door as if waiting to hear a sound.

The woman stands and quietly closes the desk drawer while slipping something into the voluminous folds of her skirt. She sets a finger to her lips. We wait.

The footsteps move on down the corridor, echoing on the marble floor and walls.

"We must hurry," the woman whispers. "He will not stay away much longer."

"Does he know she did not survive?" I whisper, eyeing the bed. "Does he know about the baby?"

The woman stops and eyes me strangely.

"You ask me, Arabella?" she says, and the light flashes over her weary wrinkled face. "You delivered the child with me. You are the one he sent to find the physician. Don't you remember running for him?"

I stare at her. I have no memories whatsoever of what she speaks. And I don't know why she calls me Arabella.

She places a kind hand on my shoulder.

"It has been a difficult night," she says. "Everything that could be done for Susanna was done and yet… "

"And yet she is dead," I reply, turning to stare at the still body. "Why… Why am I not sad?"

"Shh now, Arabella. Shh. No one can blame you. She was a hard woman. She gave you a place to live, but not much more. We all understand how you feel," she says, looking deeply into my eyes. Her face is weathered and old but kind. It seems as if I should know her, but I do not. "So, both for you and for the baby, this will be good."

She pulls me toward the flickering candle and withdraws what she has taken from the desk. A small leather pouch drawn shut by some sort of animal sinew. It is weathered and worn unlike anything else that surrounds us in this ornate room. The woman stretches open the sack, and I hear the metallic clinking of coins. She carefully sets the pouch down and takes out a necklace. Holding the chain up to the candlelight, the fine silver sparkles as brightly as the lone gold coin that hangs from it.

"Wear this. It belonged to your grandmother—the one who bore your name," she says, securing the necklace around my neck. She reaches back for the pouch. "And take these coins. They should be more than enough to get you and the child all you need on the journey."

"The journey? To where?" I ask.

I am baffled by the weight of the pouch in my hand. What sort of trek could possibly require that kind of money?

"Won't they miss it?" I ask.

The old woman steps to the bed and tugs the shroud over the bare toes of the woman she calls Susanna. The woman she says is my sister.

"Susanna could be difficult, but she was not always so," she says with a sigh. "She traded her heart for security. For a man who could meet all her needs save one. The need to be loved." She turns back to me. "She would want you to do this. This treasure comes not from Harold's coffers but from your own mother, God rest her gentle soul. Susanna told me it was her safety net should her husband tire of her."

"Then why did I not know of it?" I ask, still trying desperately to piece together what is happening.

"We do not have time to discuss your entire family history. Suffice it to know that tonight, when you and the child need a safety net more than ever, tonight the treasure has come to you. And by the time anyone knows it is gone—if they ever do—you will be far from this place. Far from this tragic night. And I will take any blame that must be taken. I shall say we did all we could for the child but that she passed just like her mother. That we knew the despair of the father, and to save him from any further grief or shame, you and I made all the arrangements for the tiny body to be laid to rest."

She reaches out and folds my fingers securely over the pouch.

"Do not lose them," she admonishes. "They and the necklace will be the only proof you have."

She walks away to the window. Pulling back the curtains, she looks up and down the street outside, which is several stories beneath us.

"Proof of what?" I ask, coming up behind her.

She turns back to me and stares into my eyes before answering.

"That the child belongs to his family," she whispers at last.

I wait for her to expand upon this statement but she does not.

"To whose family?" I say, growing more agitated by the minute.

A small smile floats over her face, and her eyes take on a distant look.

"He would be your great-great-grandfather or something like that," she says.

I gasp. "The ever-living one?"

She nods.

"I met him only once when I was newly employed, as a girl even younger than you," she says. "It was right before he left."

"But, but, uh, isn't it forbidden?"

I have some vague uneasiness about this far off relative.

"Yes, he made a vow to never again live with family," she admits.

"But why?"

The footsteps are coming back down the hallway.

"You must go," she says. "He lives on the outer reaches of the empire. In the land of Britain by the wall of Hadrian."

"But how do you know that?" I ask.

"Rumors, gossip, and stories never cease where he is concerned. And my sister's neighbor's nephew is stationed in his legion, so, I know things," she replies. "My boy Damon will go with you as far as the sea. He awaits you even now. He has food and milk for you both along with an extra cloak. Go."

She is pushing me toward the far door that leads down the back stairs to the street. The child in my arms stirs and mews like a tiny kitten.

"But what if she doesn't survive?" I ask, feeling the fragileness of the newborn I carry.

"Then we have done all we could do, and you must take the coins and build a life for yourself," she says, giving me a quick kiss on the cheek. "You can do this, Arabella. You have been given this task. Perhaps, my pet, you have come to this household, this family, for just such a time as this."

"But she does not even have a name," I stammer, taking the first steps down into the dark corridor. "What shall we call her?"

The woman is about to close the door but stops and whispers, "Your sister gave her a name with her last breath. Her name is Mila."

FELIX

BEAMS FROM THE MOON GLISTEN through the bedroom window onto the empty rug beside my bed. Max is upstairs with Fabian. Probably together with him on the bed per usual. I smile into the darkness at the thought of the two of them scrunched together onto the single bed. Good luck, my friend. Maximus may be my closest companion on my earthly adventures but sleeping next to him? That only happens if we are in some sort of outdoor setting where the temperatures necessitate the extra body heat. Never indoors. Never in my bed. That's just the way I like it, and Max has learned to accept it. Honestly, I would never know he even wants to sleep in a bed again except for the times our paths have crossed with Fabian and I find the two together drooling onto the same pillow. They think I don't know. I let them enjoy their little secret.

Titus lies in the room across the hall from me, snoring rhythmically and loudly. He loves my dog but has no illusions of making him a snuggle-buddy. Besides, Titus is so statuesque that finding him a bed that he can fit in all by himself is challenging enough. As it is, I'm sure his feet are extended at least a foot beyond the end of the bed he lies in now. It is one of the few times I do not envy him his impressive stature.

No, I am quite content tonight.

With myself. My friends. My dog. And my extended family in Solbakken.

It has been a good day with good surprises.

My mind drifts to the moments when my friends showed up in their big red truck. And the moment when Peter and Hazel came through the door.

She is a lovely, bright little girl. That is easy to discern. I can see why her grandparents are so smitten with her. I wonder what the reunion was like with Tora. I wonder who was in the other car that pulled into the driveway. I am wondering still when sleep finally finds me and invites me into another place and time with another granddaughter… Or two.

"SIR, THERE'S SOMEONE HERE who says she has important business with you," the centurion assigned as my current assistant says upon entering my stone office quarters atop the expansive wall.

I shift back in my chair and set down my writing quill.

"Is it someone from the village?" I ask, unable to think of any other female who might need to speak to me.

"No, sir, I would say not, sir," he replies.

"And where would you say she is from, Anthimus? Have you asked her?" I try to not become aggravated by this unexpected intrusion into an already very busy day.

"I did, sir. But all she says is she's come a long distance and judging by her clothes and, well, her smell, sir, I'd say she's been on the road for quite some time."

I rub my hands over the stubble on my chin, reminding myself to make time with the barber to have a close shave again soon.

"And did you inquire as to what is the nature of her business?" I ask.

This centurion is not as efficient or intuitively helpful as the last one I had. I remind myself that it took many years to achieve the sort of working relationship we had. Many years, many experiences, and much effort. I sigh deeply, wondering if I have it in me to train yet another young man in the way he should go.

"Sir, I did as you instructed, sir. I asked the nature of her business, sir, and she said it was personal, sir. For your ears only, sir."

I hold up a hand and say, "Only one 'sir' is necessary, please."

He clicks his heels together and says, "Sir, yes, sir."

I sigh.

"Alright. Send her in," I instruct.

Anthimus nods and exits back into the hallway.

Looking out the window to my left, I can see the verdant rolling hills of Britain and the undulating stone structure that divides the island in half from east to west fading out of sight under grey skies. There are days when I long for the brilliant, piercing sun of Palestine, Egypt or Italy. The warmth that suffuses my skin and thaws my bones. And yet, I have come to appreciate the mystical greenness of this island nation. It seems to never fade but only deepen from season to season. But perhaps… perhaps my next station will be less foggy and wet. A man can hope.

"Sir, your visitor, sir… I mean… uh, just your visitor," Anthimus says, stepping aside to allow the woman entrance.

I stand as she comes over the threshold and soon understand what the centurion was trying to say. Her aroma precedes her and fills the room.

"Thank you, Anthimus. You may go but, uh, leave the door open, will you?"

Anthimus gives me a knowing smile behind the visitor's back and exits.

Assessing the dirty garments, skin, and hair of this recent arrival, I am hard pressed to guess how old she might be. There is something vaguely familiar about her but in a far off, distant sort of way I cannot place. She has a bundle in her arms that she clings to with a quiet intensity. Her blue eyes stare out at me from under thick lashes as if she is seeing the emperor himself. There is something akin to terror in their depths.

"Come in," I say with a warmth to my words that I hope eases her distress. I have no time in my schedule to try to pry information from a mute, fear-filled woman. "Please, take a seat." I indicate one of the two chairs that sit by the desk across from mine.

She edges slowly toward the chairs but does not sit.

I, however, do. If she chooses to stand, that is up to her.

"Now, how may I help you?" I ask.

Her eyes have not left my face for even a moment.

This intense gaze might be disconcerting to someone else, but I have grown accustomed to it. It is the same one I have seen many times on the faces of those who have heard the stories about me and have come seeking a glimpse of the legend call The Ever-Living One. But it has been quite some time since I have experienced this level of agonized wonder.

I clear my throat and try again. "I hear you have traveled a great distance to see me. There must be some reason behind this venture."

The bundle in her arm stirs, and a small hand reaches up toward the woman's face. She finally tears her gaze away from me to look at the infant in her arms. Her face softens as the tiny fingers reach her chin and stay there for a moment. It is as if the touch breaks off her starstruck terror and infuses her with courage, for when she looks back at me, I see determination piercing through her eyes.

She opens her mouth to speak but nothing comes out.

The baby's hand descends back into the folds of the blankets.

"Is this your child?" I ask.

She shakes her head.

"But you have come about something regarding this child?"

She nods.

I am hoping I won't have to ask a hundred questions in order to unravel the mystery, but even as I think that, she speaks.

"Her name is Mila," the woman says.

"A lovely name." I nod and smile encouragingly.

A long silence follows, and I search for yet another question to lead her forward.

But as I do, the woman tugs down the scarf that enfolds her neck and carefully extracts something from around her neck. Her fingers grip what seems to be the pendant of a necklace as she stares at me again. Taking a deep breath, she unwraps her fingers one by one, steps closer to the desk, and displays the pendant for me to see.

A sudden shaft of light breaks through the window and reflects off what lies in her hand. I lean forward.

My heart stops.

It is not a pendant.

It is a coin.

A gold coin with the image of the emperor Trajan clearly visible.

"Where did you get this?" I ask, standing to get a closer look.

She backs away, but I reach out a hand to stop her.

"Please, may I see it?" I ask, my hand on hers. "You don't have to take it off. Just come around the desk and let me get a closer look."

The girl sucks in a ragged breath and nods.

I release her hand, allowing her to come of her own accord to where I stand.

The pungency of her person nearly gags me. I wonder if perhaps the baby has soiled her clothes recently.

The woman seems to recognize my concerns.

"She needs a bath," the woman says by way of apology. "And so do I."

Her cheeks redden, and I can see that I am not dealing with a woman at all but a girl of perhaps fifteen years or so. Why does she look so familiar?

"We can arrange all of that," I say as she nears, holding up the coin necklace for me to inspect. "How did you get here? Where did you come from? Surely, you did not travel all by yourself?"

"No, sir. Damon came all the way from Paris with me," she replies.

I bend toward her.

And I know by the fine silver chain and the tell-tale nick on the coin's edge; it is the necklace I gave to my great-granddaughter Arabella so long ago.

A lump constricts my throat and tears sting my eyes.

She was my favorite. Not that I would have admitted that to any of her siblings or cousins or aunties or uncles. I couldn't even explain exactly why. She simply was. Not the prettiest or brightest or smartest. Arabella was, well, she was Arabella. And that was enough.

"Do you know it, sir?" the girl asks.

I nod and wipe the drip from the end of my nose.

"How did you come by it?" I ask.

The girl steps back and drops her chin to look at the child.

"On the night Mila was born," she begins. "Her mother, my sister, died in childbirth. Her husband, Harold, is not a kind man. A rich one but not a nice one. I was instructed to take the baby for he would not abide her. Take her and bring her to you."

I seat myself on the edge of the desk in order to see the girl eye to eye.

"And why would he not abide the child? Because he was so grieved at the loss of his wife?"

She shakes her head, and a slight tremor ripples over her frame.

Slowly, she unwinds the bundling from around Mila's body. The infant is awake with eyes staring at the ceiling but she is quiet. Her hands shoot out as they are freed from their bonds and grasp at the air around her. I see matted dark curls capping her skull and the most darling of rosebud lips puckering and unpuckering as if looking for sustenance.

"She grows hungry, sir," the girl says, checking back at how I am responding to the unveiling.

"We will get her fed once we have surmised what is to be done," I say, wondering why she hesitates.

The last unfolding reveals the mystery.

Where Mila's legs should be, only two short stumps exist. They kick up and down with abbreviated flutters. I try not to turn away.

"Sir," the girl commands my attention away from the malformation. "I think that perhaps she is also blind. And maybe… maybe deaf too."

Her last words are quiet and slow.

She rearranges the blankets back over Mila's limbs, tucking her flailing hands back into a swaddle.

I wave my hands close to the baby's face and click my fingers near her ears.

There is no response.

I take in a deep breath and sigh.

It is hard not to recoil from this needy, grimy pair.

The girl again senses my reticence.

She digs into a pocket in her cloak and pulls out a pouch.

"I had to use some to get here, but there's still plenty left," she says, handing me the pouch. "She can pay her own way. At least for a while."

I recognize it immediately and accept it with a hand that trembles.

The coins inside clink together, and I have no need to check them. I know where they come from. I know they too were a gift to Arabella. I am nearly overcome by waves of emotions over my darling lost girl. Her passing was the last straw. The final deciding factor that I could not handle one more loss. And I had simply walked away from the family with strict instructions to let me go and never follow.

The singular ray from the sun lands directly on Mila's face, drawing my attention back into the present. She does not blink. Only stares upward. A sadness enters my heart. One I have not allowed to enter for many years. It is a sadness I attach to another vulnerable feeling—love. Mila's skin is perfectly clean and smooth as if the girl who carries her has taken special pains to present at least this much in the best of lights. I feel my forehead wrinkling in a frown.

There is no way I can help with this child. I do not have the time, the skill, the energy, or the heart.

And then it happens.

Mila smiles.

A smile that seems to illuminate the entire room.

I cannot peel my eyes away from her.

"She's beautiful, isn't she?" the girl whispers, staring along with me at the radiant baby.

I nod.

And I know.

Despite all my reservations.

Somehow this child is mine.

Standing to my feet, I return to my place behind the desk, giving myself a few moments to think. The girl remains where she is. Fearful but expectant.

"One condition," I say slowly, reluctantly, hardly believing what I am about to say. "I will only take her if you will stay and care for her."

Tears stream from the girl's face and drip onto Mila's face. The infant blinks at the sudden stimulation, and her little tongue reaches out for more.

The girl nods.

"Can Damon stay too?" she asks.

"Is he a friend?"

She nods.

"Is he reliable and not lazy?" I ask.

"He got us here, didn't he?" she says with the first of what sounds like spunk in her voice.

"Then, yes, he may stay too."

"Okay. Then we will help," she says.

I sit up straight and assess this young woman who is about to become part of what? I know not.

"Excuse me, miss," I say. "If we are to become… well, family of sorts, it would be good if I knew your name."

"They call me Arabella, sir," she says. "Named after my grandmother I am told."

I gulp. Could it be that she truly is family?

Her face relaxes completely for the first time since she has entered my office and she smiles at me. The smile changes her entire countenance and recognition floods my mind.

She is younger by many years.

She is completely out of context.

She is soiled and worn but I know her.

"Tora?"

Her smile broadens.

"Hello, Felix."

TORA

"CAN YOU BUILD A SNOW CASTLE for me and ShoSho today, Papa?"

"Sure thing, baby girl. Looks like a perfect day for it."

"Yippee! Did ya hear that, ShoSho? You're gonna get an ice castle."

"Hey, let's keep it down. Grammy is still sleeping, remember?"

The chatter from the kitchen quiets some, but I can still hear Hazel's loud whispers through the closed door. I stretch my arms overhead and soak in the noise. What a lovely wake up call. I lay under the cozy covers a few more minutes and enjoy a sense of deep contentment I have not felt since… well, since I don't remember when.

The clock over the dresser says it is after nine o'clock. I can't believe I've slept so long, especially knowing I have a day ahead with Hazel. But for some reason, I feel as if I have been busy all night with some kind of important matters.

"Probably just a hangover from family revelations," I tell myself. I wonder how Tante is doing this morning? I wonder how Thomas, Tommy, and Sophia are doing? I wonder if the whole Everwind family knows about the Anderson Solbakken connection by now? I wonder if they're okay with it?

The aroma of fresh brewed coffee and toast seep under the door, enticing me. I am about to sweep back the quilt and grab my bathrobe when a name flashes across my mind.

Mila.

Her name is Mila.

I sink back into the pillow and place my hands over my face.

A vivid rolling scenario plays on the back of my eyelids like a movie on the screen of an IMAX theater. A death. A birth. A baby. A journey. And a man.

Not just any man.

Felix.

My hands drop and my eyes pop open as the bedroom door creaks.

"Grammy," a little voice whispers. "Are you gonna get up sometime today and play with Papa and me and ShoSho?"

Hazel's head is sticking through the door with hair disheveled and raspberry jam on her cheek. Her eyes glitter with anticipation.

The movie dream recedes into the background at the sight of her. I make a mental note to get back to it later and write it all down. But in this moment, I have more pressing matters to attend to.

I whip back the covers and pat the mattress next to me.

My granddaughter bounds across the room and leaps up next to me, her puppy close behind. I quickly envelop her in my cozy cocoon while ShoSho scrambles atop us seeking a face to lick. We giggle and cuddle as he yips and spins between us.

"Hey, what's going on in here?" Peter says, coming in from the kitchen.

I pull back the covers on the other side of me and invite him in.

He quickly takes me up on the offer, grabbing the blur of black fur and subduing him by his side. We spend half an hour together listening to Hazel's non-stop chatter, enjoying every second of it.

Finally, a knock on the front door disturbs our bliss.

"Tor? Peter? You guys decent?" Billy hollers as he comes through the porch and into the kitchen.

"What does 'decent' mean?" Hazel asks.

Peter and I smile at one another. I'll let him field this one.

"It means 'ready for visitors,'" he replies.

That is why he is the lawyer.

"Yup, we're decent," Hazel hollers back and begins to wriggle free from under my arm. "Come on, ShoSho," she says. "We have got visitors."

The puppy leaps off the bed and sprints into the kitchen.

"Well, hello there, Hazel. And hello there, little fella," we hear Billy greeting the dynamic duo.

"His name is ShoSho," Hazel says, stepping through the door.

We hear the two exchange further information about the dog while we extract ourselves from under the covers. I don my bathrobe over my pj's in order to make myself truly decent.

"Hey, guys," Billy says as Peter and I enter the kitchen. "Sleep well?"

"Slept like a baby," Peter replies, putting an arm around my shoulder.

"Good deal," Billy says, not waiting for my response, which may have been slightly different. "So, Pete, I've got my snowmobiles up and running if ya wanna take a run with me out to the saw mill? Got some new machines in place since ya saw it last fall."

"Tempting, but I'm going to have to pass," Peter replies. "I have already promised Hazel that we are going to build a snow fort today."

"A castle, Papa," Hazel says. "Not a fort."

Billy smiles and holds up his hands in surrender.

"I can see you've got your agenda set for the day," he says. "Sounds like a great plan. Think the snow will be perfect. Gonna be sunny and up in the mid-twenties today."

"Thanks for checking in with us," I say, moving to the coffee pot. "Got time for a cup before you go?"

"Nope. Already fully caffeinated for the morning, thanks," he says, turning to head back outside.

"Hey, Bill," I call after him. "Can we get a Zoom call set up at your place for tomorrow morning around eleven or whenever you guys get back from church?"

He stops with his handle on the porch door and turns back.

"You bet," he says. "I'll get Carin to send out the invites. Who all you want on it?"

"Well, my brothers for sure, and I think I'd like to include Katie," I say, pouring some creamer into my cup. "Oh, and I've got one more person."

I hustle into the dining room looking for a scrap of paper I think I left on the table. Finding it, I smile at the name and email address written there as I take it to Billy.

He reads it and scratches his chin.

"So, now, I'm guessing you've had a conversation with our new-found cousin, then?" he asks.

"We sure have," Peter adds, coming up behind me. "Quite a guy, Mr. Thomas Everwind. Think you'll like him."

"Wait, you've met him too?" Billy says, tucking the slip of paper into the front pocket of his coveralls. "Yeesh, Tor, I can't keep up with you these days. Every time I turn around, you're bumping into more folks and digging up more facts than most Minneapolis police detectives."

I shrug and sip my coffee.

"Why do you think I'm always minding my P's and Q's?" Peter says, following my cousin to the front steps.

Billy laughs over his shoulder. "Yeah, I know what you mean. Tora and Carin should set up a private investigation firm, if you ask me. See ya all later," he adds, getting in his truck and slamming the door.

ShoSho slips outside between our legs and romps over the snow-covered yard, heading straight for a bush.

Hazel pushes her way between us and is about to step outside in her stocking covered feet when Peter halts her progress.

"Easy there, baby girl. You've got to get your snow gear on before you venture out there," he says.

"But ShoSho," Hazel protests. "Daddy told me we can't let him run outside all by himself up here. That it's not like living in the city where everyone has fences."

Peter and I exchange a look.

"Your daddy is right," I say, grabbing her hand. "Papa will watch ShoSho while you and I get dressed for action."

Peter steps out onto the front stoop in his slippers and whistles sharply with his fingers in his mouth.

I watch the puppy who stops, perks up his ears, and then promptly runs the opposite direction toward the shed.

"Papa, no," Hazel admonishes, yanking away from me and running out onto the icy steps beside him. "Not so loud. That hurts his ears. Do it like this."

She puckers up her lips. The sweetest, gentlest whistle escapes and floats over the yard.

ShoSho abruptly halts in his tracks, turns around, and flops onto his belly.

"Okay, Papa," Hazel says. "Now he'll wait for you, but put your boots on first. It's icy out here, ya know."

FELIX

"HEY, TAKE IT EASY, MAX," I say, yanking on his collar to get him to sit down. "We'll get there. We'll get there. Just let me get my boots on first."

My dog obeys, but his trembling whimper tells me he is barely hanging on to self-restraint. I can't tell what it is that has him so excited to go outside. He had been in the yard not long ago with Fabian and Titus as they donned their helmets and gloves for a ride through the woods with Billy on his snowmobiles. Maybe he was upset that we were left behind. But there really was no room for us on the small, sporty vehicles. Fabian hopped on one behind Billy and Titus took up practically the entire seat of the other machine all by himself.

"Let's go for a nice, long walk, buddy," I say. "Looks like a beautiful day outside. It will do us both good."

Max's whine only intensifies, and he spins in a circle before plopping himself right beside the front entry.

"There's no way you'd even fit on one of those snow machines," I say, shaking my head at his anxiety. "Even if you did, there's no way you could stay on it, especially with Titus's driving."

My remonstrances don't seem to be having any demonstrable affect.

"Alright, alright," I say, standing from the stool and tugging my stocking cap over my ears. "Let's go."

The front door is barely open when Max bolts forward, leaps off the stairs, and gallops down the driveway.

"Uh, okay. Don't worry about me. I'll catch up," I laugh, latching the door behind us.

Max does not stop at the road but continues straight ahead down the approach to Tora's place. Peter's car sits directly outside the garage door behind which, I am guessing, Tora's rig resides. They must be home.

"Max," I yell. "Come!"

My dog honors me with a slight turn of his head and a small de-escalation, but not a full obedience.

"Max!" I holler again, and my voice echoes back to me from the woods on the far side of Tora's snowy yard.

Funny, I think to myself, how I have come to think of the place as hers and not Einar's after only a few days. She seems to inhabit it so naturally.

Max finally stops right at the base of the stairs leading up to the porch. I tromp toward him, hoping he is not disturbing my neighbors with his enthusiastic arrival. As I am about halfway down their driveway, the porch door flings open, and I see Hazel trundling out covered from head to toe in a brilliant pink snow suit.

"Max!" I hear her exclaim as she sits on her bottom and bounces down the steps one at a time until she is face to face with my dog, who promptly licks her face from chin to forehead.

Oh, boy. I pick up my pace and jog toward the house, hoping to rescue the girl from any more enthusiastic slobbery kisses. But as I come within ten feet of them, I pull to a stop.

Hazel has her arms wrapped around my dog's neck and is giggling enthusiastically. He turns his big, soulful eyes to me, and I know that it was not the snowmobile ride that had him so excited to get outside this morning. It was the girl next door.

The front door swings open and Tora appears with Peter close behind. They are also dressed in full snow regalia. He is holding a puppy in his arms that is squirming with all his might to be let down.

"Don't worry," I say, coming up to the steps. "You can let the pup down. Max is quite gentle with small dogs."

Peter bends down and the little black puppy charges down the stairs, runs behind Max, charges back up the stairs, circles around Peter and Tora, then charges back down the stairs again. He stops in a playful wide stance and barks with all his might up at his much larger, much older canine neighbor.

Hazel releases Max and says to him, "That means he wants to play."

Max turns and lopes away from the house, turning to see if the pup has followed. He has. And so has Hazel.

"Good morning, neighbors," I say to Tora and Peter, who are watching the dogs and their granddaughter frolic through the snow with grins as wide as a country mile stretched over their faces.

"Good morning, Felix," Tora says, descending the stairs to greet me. "Peter tells me you have guests. How nice. Hope I get to meet them."

"Yup, a couple of old friends from my days in the army. Just stopped by unannounced," I reply.

"Well, I guess when you don't have a phone, it can make it hard for people to get a hold of you," Tora says as we watch Peter join the jovial fracas.

"Oh, it's fine," I say. "It's how we've always rolled. But you will have to wait to meet them until later. They went off on a snowmobiling expedition with Billy a few minutes ago. He wanted to show them his sawmill and a few other notable attractions of the Solbakken area."

I find that Tora is eyeing me with a scrupulous gaze, making me a bit uncomfortable.

"Did I miss some crumbs or something from breakfast?" I say, brushing my hand over my face.

Tora turns away and laughs nervously.

"Oh, no. It's just that… no, it's nothing," she says, waving off whatever notion had entered her thoughts.

"If we've interrupted your family morning, just say so and we will take off. No worries at all," I say, taking a long look at her as well.

In all my comings and goings through time and eternity, I have never revisited that moment when Mila was delivered to my office, until last night. It was so long ago. Maybe my memories of Arabella and Tora have become intertwined somehow. I stare at her a moment longer. It is undeniably the same face I saw last night. But maybe… I don't know… maybe it's just a strong family resemblance from across the generations. But she responded when I called her Tora, didn't she? And she said, "Hello, Felix," as if she knew me.

"Did you sleep well last night?" Tora says, turning slightly, she peers at my neck.

My hand goes up to make sure the necklace is tucked safely in place. It is.

"Grammy, come and build the castle with us!" Hazel yells from beside Peter, who is on his hands and knees busily compacting snow into walls and turrets.

"I'm coming, sweetie," Tora yells back. "Can you keep an eye on ShoSho for us? I know Max will be fine with him, but I just don't want them wandering too far afield because, well…" She lowers her voice. "Because of the big bad you know who."

"No problem. ShoSho? That's the pup's name?"

"Yes. I believe it's short for 'Shalom, Shalom.' Which is a family sign-off from my Grandma Arnie and perhaps… Perhaps from a few generations before that," she says, leaving my side to go assist with the building project.

If she only knew.

I smile thinking of my own mother's words of blessing and wander over to the shed where Max and ShoSho are engrossed in an excavating project of their own.

"Hey, what are you two digging for? China?" I say as I approach.

Both their crystal covered snouts turn up to me in unison and then return to their efforts.

"Max, leave it," I command, but he persists. "Max!" I raise my voice but to no avail. I am about to yank on his collar when a pure melodic whistle drifts from the workers at the snow castle.

Max and ShoSho stand to attention, immediately leave their dig, and romp toward the builders.

"Incoming!" I yell as the two hounds crash straight through the structure.

MAXIMUS

She knows the whistle!

It is not sharp, piercing, or shrill. But bright, gentle, soft.
Almost creamy, I'd say.
Like a drink of milk straight from the cow.
Warm, smooth, and satisfying.
It's been so long since I have heard one like it.
This pup is one lucky fellow to have her.
He does not know it yet.
Just like I did not know it then.
It is a rare thing to walk with one who knows the whistle.
It is not so much the notes or the tone.
Nor is it the force behind its delivery.
The thing that makes it special is the heart of the whistler.
You can tell a lot about a person by their whistle.
Some folk's whistles are demanding and sharp.
Some melodic and meandering.
Some folks never whistle at all.
I'm a bit suspicious about them.
Hard to know what might be inside.
But this little girl must have a heart of creamy goodness.
I will bet she could sooth even the wildest of beasts with that trill.
For who can resist such a perfect whistle?

TORA

"SO, THE FOLKS WHO RESCUED YOU from the side of the road just happened to be Thomas Everwind and his grandkids? Imagine that," Felix says, taking a stack of dishes to the sink from the kitchen table where Peter, Hazel, Felix, and I have just finished eating lunch.

"Yes. Can you believe it?" I reply, joining him at the sink.

I start the water and pump in some dish soap.

"Hazel, do you want to help Grammy wash the dishes?" I ask.

She tilts her head to the side and scrunches her nose.

"Do I have to?"

"No, you don't have to," I reply. "I just thought you might like to splash in the soapy bubbles."

"Grammy," she says, slipping off her chair and coming to wrap her arms around my waist. "Bubbles are for babies. And I'm not a baby anymore. I think I need to color for a while."

My heart gives a little twist. She's right. We have missed so many months of interacting with her in person that I feel as though we are playing catch up, and I have not quite caught up. She gives me a quick squeeze and skips off to the living room where the bin of art supplies I brought with me resides.

"There's no crayons," I yell after her. "Only colored pencils and paints. Grammy or Papa needs to help you if you are going to paint."

"Pencils are great," she hollers back.

If I had dared to dream that she might possibly be joining us up north, I would have packed my art bin differently. As it was, I only put in the items I thought I might use as an art therapy break for myself if the opportunity or need arose. Of course, the week has been so full, I haven't had time to even crack open a sketch book or wet a brush. But that's okay. The week's happenings have created an artistic tapestry all their own. Though I do believe there are still a few threads that need to be woven in to hold the piece together. What they are, I'm not quite sure. But there is one thread I definitely would like to pull to see where it leads.

"Hon, can you go supervise out there please?" I say to Peter, who is stashing leftovers in the fridge.

"You betcha," he says. "From architect to artist. Her wish is my command."

He disappears into the living room, leaving Felix and me alone in the kitchen. Well, almost alone. Max and ShoSho are piled up together on the rug by the door in a contented sleep. Seeming to read my thoughts, Felix says, "Those two sure had a good time out there."

I nod and busy myself with the dishes. Felix takes up a towel and begins to dry. For the first time since we've become acquainted, I am uncomfortable in his presence. That's not completely true. I do recall thinking he may be an axe murderer the first time we met. What I am feeling now is not that level of discomfort, but something similar in that I feel like behind his accessible, congenially exterior there lies a much deeper and more complex identity that he carefully conceals.

"Did Tommy give up the names of the other accomplices to the looting?" Felix asks.

I reply with a recounting of as many of the details as I can recall from Tommy's confession.

"And did Thomas have any clue as to why Einar took off and never came back?" Felix asks, seeming to want to prolong the conversation we have already had over lunch regarding the meeting with the Everwinds from the previous night. "I mean, maybe Grace told him a thing or two about his dad?"

I shake my head. "No, he seemed to be totally unaware that Einar even was his father until quite recently."

"That's got to be quite a shock," Felix replies, setting a dish onto a stack in the cupboard.

I let Felix chatter a bit about his two army buddies Fabian and Titus. They sound interesting too. But when I ask about pertinent details like wives or children, or where they live, or how they all met, I get much the same nebulous responses as Felix has given me about his own life. He tells me things without really telling me anything.

As I rinse off the last handful of utensils and begin to drain the sink, I screw up enough courage to ask a pointed question.

Swishing a rag around the edges of the sink to wipe away all the bubbles, I blurt out, "Felix, do you have a granddaughter named Mila?"

The glass in his hand that he is about to set into the cupboard slips and crashes to the floor.

"Everyone okay in there?" Peter yells from the other side of the house.

"We're okay. No blood," I holler back. "Just a broken glass."

"I'm so sorry," Felix apologizes. "Is there a broom I could use to sweep this up?"

I point to the pantry door, and he goes there without ever meeting my eyes.

I stand with my back leaning against the counter, wiping my hands on a clean towel and watching my neighbor clean up the shattered glass. He is doing a very thorough job.

"Why do you ask?" he says, dumping the tinkling fragments into the garbage can.

"You've met my granddaughter Hazel now. And my husband. And you've heard all about my kids, my cousins, and even my aunts, uncles, and grandparents. But I know next to nothing about your family," I reply.

He nods slowly.

"Fair enough," he says, sitting on a padded kitchen chair. He scoots the placemats back into perfect symmetry on the table's wood surface before looking up at me. "But it strikes me as odd that you would ask about such a specific relation. Where did you come up with that name?"

I come and join him at the table.

"So, there really was… or is… a little girl named Mila?" I ask.

Max suddenly stirs and sits up as if the name Mila has jolted him awake. He has dumped ShoSho onto his back. The puppy looks around, startled and disoriented, spies his kennel in the corner, and pads over to the open door to find a more secure place to nap.

Felix reaches out to pet his dog's head. Max moves to his master's side and sits facing me with questioning eyes.

They both sigh deeply and in unison.

I wait.

"Many, many years ago…" Felix begins. "I was stationed at a post far removed from any family… not a punishment at all. Actually, a request I made to the higher ups myself."

Max steps even closer and lays his head in his owner's lap.

I am touched by the dog's empathy, yet anxious to hear where his owner's confession is leading. For if it goes where I think it will go, what does that mean about who Felix really is? Or his dog? Or me, for that matter?

My neighbor is staring out the window into the sunny March day toward Janet's place.

"She was so fragile… and yet, so strong," he says barely above a whisper.

Just then, the roar of snowmobiles in the driveway cuts through the quiet and both dogs transform into barking watchdogs, bouncing up from their restful reposes to full alert. Peter and Hazel appear in the doorway.

"Who's here, Grammy?" Hazel asks, her fists full of colored pencils.

"I'm guessing it must be Billy and Mr. Felix's friends," I say, watching a wave of relief wash over Felix's face.

He stands and gives me a terse smile before letting the dogs out through the porch. "Uh, we'll chat more later?"

I nod slowly, and he exits to meet his friends.

"Papa, can we go on the snowmachines?" Hazel asks.

I shake my head without her seeing me.

"Uh, we can go sit on one," he says by way of compromise. "Let's get your coat on first."

The house empties out, and I am left to ponder the knowledge I have of the existence of a little girl named Mila.

"Why do I know these things? How do I know these things?" I whisper into the air.

The only answer is the echo of the voices of men and dogs punctuated by an occasional girlish squeal.

"Oh, sweet Jesus," I think to myself. "Who is this man named Felix? And, while I'm asking, who am I?"

LATER THAT EVENING, Peter and I are huddled together on the bed scrolling through documents on his laptop. The room is dark save for the light emitting from the screen. We are both reading through the information and trying to keep our exclamations, questions, and observations as quiet as possible. Hazel is asleep on her mattress on the floor, but she is restless. Even though she played hard all day without a nap, she fought the whole 'going-to-bed' routine, wanting instead to climb up with us and read one more story.

"Just one more, Papa," she had whined, holding out the Madeline book that I had sat on the bedside table after reading it myself the other night.

Papa had, of course, complied as any good Papa would, until Hazel nodded off between us and we carefully picked her up and deposited her in her own bed.

"I can hardly believe the percentages from the southern parts of Europe like Italy and France. And then there's this from Germany and Eastern Europe," I say, pointing to the pie chart that contains my DNA results. "And here I've been claiming to be pure Norwegian for all these years."

"Right? Surprised me too," Peter whispers. "And then this little piece here." He points to a narrow slice of the pie.

"I know," I say shaking my head. "If I'm not mistaken, I think the Jewish blood comes from my grandmother's mother's side of the family."

"Really?" Peter says. "First I have heard of that in forty years. When did you find that out?"

"Oh, that would be from a letter I found that was written to Grandma Arnie from her Grandmother Kari. It was all in Norwegian. So, I sent it to Isaac for translation. Didn't I tell you all this already?"

He shakes his head.

I explain the contents of the letter to him and he listens intently.

"That's interesting. Would explain the 'Shalom, shalom' thing," he comments.

I sigh and sit back against the pillow plumped up on the headboard.

"Is there something else, Tor?" Peter asks, sitting back too.

My husband is a perceptive man. It's part of his job to read people's attitudes, words, and body language. But it is also simply part of who he is, on the job and off. I have learned that it is futile to try to hide information from him. He has a way of getting to the bottom of most anything.

"Since I have been up here," I begin. "I have been having dreams again."

"Like the ones you used to have when you were a kid?"

I nod in the dimming light from the computer.

"I wrote some of them down because they were so vivid and real," I say, reaching for my journal and handing it to him. "They're in here. You can read them in the morning."

"Okay," he says, flipping through the pages before setting it aside. "What are they about, Tor? These dreams of yours."

I drop my head back onto the pillow and stare up at the ceiling. Clouds have covered the moon tonight so, as the computer screen goes black, the darkness around us is profound. As is the stillness.

"Mostly, they're about family," I say. "One was about Grandpa Axel and the day he met Thomas Everwind Sr. A story I've heard before, of course, but with all kinds of details I've never known before."

"Hmm, interesting."

"Another was all about Uncle Einar and Joseph Everwind when they were over in Italy during the war. I saw the woman named Isabel. The one who gave them the coins."

A coyote yips outside the window causing us both to turn that direction, as if we could see anything. Peter grabs my hand and soothingly massages my fingers.

"What else?" he says, seeming to know I have barely scratched the surface.

"It's just that, I dream these things that I know nothing about. Then like a day later, I find a letter or hear something from Tante Tilda or run into someone along the side of the road, and everything I've learned in the dreams is verified. Down to the craziest little details."

"Hmm. Well, that's, uh, intriguing." The massage stops.

"I know. It's sort of freaking me out. I mean, yes, we had the letter translated from Great-great-grandmother Kari but I already knew. I had a dream about my Jewish ancestor before I even knew he existed."

I sit up straighter, dropping his hand and tugging my knees into my chest.

Peter sets the computer onto his bedside table and rolls onto his side to face me.

"Yup, that's a little freaky alright," he whispers.

My heart is thumping and I feel myself beginning to tremble. I am thankful for the darkness that hides the alarm I can imagine filling my husband's features.

"Is there something you're not telling me?" Peter continues his cross-examination.

I take a deep breath and blow it out.

"I've had dreams about Felix," I confess, turning and sinking down until we are on the same level. "Not weird, romantic dreams at all. But dreams about him living in, like, the Middle East during the times of Christ. And dreams about a little baby girl named Mila that I delivered to him somewhere up by Scotland where he was stationed as a Roman soldier. I had been told he was the baby's grandfather or great-grandfather, or something like that. Except I wasn't really me in that dream but some girl named Arabella. Who, I guess, was also a granddaughter of sorts. But when I handed Felix the baby, he looked at me and said, 'Tora?' like he knew it was really me and not this other girl."

"Whoa, whoa, whoa. Slow down a little bit. Let me catch up with you here."

I pause, allowing for assimilation of my strange story.

"What do you suppose it's all about?" he asks, at last.

"I don't know, babe," I whisper. "It has my head spinning. But today…" I hesitate. "Today… when you were in the other room coloring with Hazel, I asked Felix point blank. Do you have a granddaughter named Mila?"

"And?"

"And, that's when he dropped the glass."

"Oh."

"Yeah, oh. And he was about to tell me something more, I know he was. But then the guys showed up on the snowmobiles and, well, and then he left."

We both fall silent.

It is so dark that though our faces are only a foot apart, I cannot see the expression on his face. But I can feel him thinking.

"Am I crazy?" I whisper.

He reaches an arm out and pulls me close. I hide my face in his chest and breathe in his freshly showered and shaved scent.

He does not answer.

One of his rules.

If you don't know what to say, stay quiet and let the other guy dig himself a deeper hole. I refuse to play the game. He needs some space to process what I've thrown into his court. He will have an answer for me in the morning.

"Grammy?" a little voice pierces the silence, startling us both.

I roll over toward the side of the bed where Hazel stands. I cannot see her, but I can hear her breathing. Scooting away from Peter, I reach out into the dark until I can feel her flannel jammies. Grabbing her by the hand, I guide her into the bed beside me.

"It's okay, sweetie," I croon. "Grammy and Papa are right here. Don't be afraid."

TORA

"It's okay, Tora," a familiar but distant female voice whispers.

I try to wrestle away but am held in place by something soft and heavy in my arms.

"I'll get her, Tor," Peter says. I feel him disentangling Hazel from the blankets. She moans but does not resist. "She'll sleep better and so will you."

I nod sleepily and rearrange the disheveled sheets around me. Before my husband has even gotten back into bed, I have drifted off.

"She will be okay," another familiar voice whispers. This one is male.

"But do you think she really needs to know?" the female voice asks.

"You know how it goes," he replies. "We come to the tree because a time is full and a person is ready."

"Yes, yes, I know," she responds. "But this was told to us in complete confidence. If he wanted her to know, wouldn't he be the one here telling her?"

I rub my eyes and squint up into the brilliance of the dazzling leaves. I am seated on the tree-bench between two people. It is cozy and warm. I turn first to my left and peer into the eyes of the woman.

"Mom?" I gasp.

"Hello, Tor," she says, placing both hands along either side of my face, and bending to kiss me on the forehead.

I am nearly overwhelmed with emotions. I want to weep but somehow the tears won't come.

"Hey, there," the male voice says from my other side. "What about me?"

I turn and gasp again. "Dad?"

His face lights with a radiant smile.

"You still recognize your old man, eh?" he laughs, and I fling my arms around his neck.

I wish I could stay right here forever.

But Mother taps me on the shoulder.

"We only have a moment, darling," she says, and I settle back between them, gripping each of them by a hand.

My words are stuck. My heart is bursting. But I nod in acknowledgement of what she says. I am here for a reason. I should know that by now.

"Do you have the book?" Mother asks Dad.

"Right here," he says, holding up a leaf that transforms before our eyes into a pocket-sized, leather-bound notebook. It is frayed and tattered with muddy smears all over the cover.

"What is it about?" I ask, finally finding my voice.

My parents look over my head at one another, for I am small and young in their presence. Their smiles waver.

"You can tell me," I say, sensing their hesitation. "I've been to this tree many times already and I've heard many stories."

"Yes, we are aware of your comings and goings," Dad says.

"We think, perhaps, you might have visited sooner if we'd believed you when you told us about your dreams," Mother adds. "Sometimes it is hard to understand the ways of this realm when we live in the other."

"But it has been given to you to know the mysteries of the kingdom of heaven, Tora-bird," Dad says. "And we couldn't be happier to be able to share them with you now."

Tears again threaten but don't appear.

"I don't understand," I whisper. "Why me?"

They share another knowing look but don't reply.

Dad opens the little book gently, setting fraying edges back into place.

"Tonight, you will hear a tragic tale filled with what the earthly realm calls heroes and villains. But in this realm, we simply call them humans caught in the whirlwinds of life."

I nod solemnly. "What's it called?"

"*I'm Half Dead Already*," Dad says.

The title makes me shudder. I hunker deeper down between them.

"Don't be afraid," Mom assures me. "We're right here."

"THE WAR HAD BEEN OVER IN ITALY for months already," Einar said to Grace as they sat on a wood log before the fire, snuggled up under a blanket. "To say we were relieved is an understatement of the highest order."

He sighed and stared into the leaping flames.

"It's okay," Grace whispered. "There's no one else here. Just you and me."

A loon's haunting cry echoed over the waters of Red Lake. Waves lapped gently on the sandy shore only yards from where the pair sat atop a sand dune. Einar removed his arm from around her shoulder and hunched forward.

"A group of guys with enough points were scheduled to ship out stateside the next morning," he began. "Buck, uh, Joseph had more points than most anybody still standing in Redbull. He deserved to be on the first boat home."

Grace hunched over next to Einar, who had halted his narration. She waited.

He took a deep breath and continued. "We were in Naples at a bar. It was packed with guys… Everyone was celebrating. Even those of us that had gotten orders to go elsewhere. We all knew it was just a matter of time before it would all end… I just never thought it would end the way it did."

Grace tugged the blanket up and over Einar's exposed shoulder where it had fallen off, revealing the plaster cast on his right forearm. The October evening was crisp with hints of frost in the star-filled sky.

"Buck and I had had a few beers. More than usual. You know how he wasn't much of a drinker… So, we headed back to quarters before most everyone else. Just Cooter and Johnnie came with us. The guys from over by Thief River Falls. They were both supposed to ship out with Buck in the morning. It was less than a mile back to our beds… but it was so dark."

Einar lifted his head and stared out into the expanse of the lake. Moonlight rippled over the surface with startling brilliance.

"Cooter was stumbling drunk. Joseph and I were practically carrying him up the hill," he said, shaking his head. "And the guy wouldn't shut up. He was singing his head off with Johnnie croaking out the words right along with him. You could've heard us coming all the way in Berlin."

He inhaled deeply with a shudder.

"But we didn't think it mattered… We just didn't think…"

Long moments passed in silence. Another call from the loon went unacknowledged by the lovers, fading away on a breeze.

"Johnnie had to take a leak," Einar continued. "Couldn't hold it one more minute, he said. So, we dipped into a little side alley and waited while he found a place to relieve himself. And Cooter kept singing. Buck had him leaning up against a wall of a house, catching his breath, when all of a sudden Johnnie was cussing and running back toward us, trying to zip up his fly as he yelled, 'She's got a gun!' We took a second to figure out what the heck he was talking about. But then, there she was, this little signora in a white nightgown, her black hair flying out behind her back like a plume of smoke after a bomb. And, sure enough, she had a gun."

Grace leaned her elbows onto her knees and rested her head in her hands. Einar turned slightly to check on her.

"She never said a word to us. We thought she might even be sleep walking or something. Finally, Cooter shut up when Buck put his hand over his mouth and tried to get him to move away from this crazed woman back out of the alley. Johnnie was long past us halfway back to camp. I was backing up with my hands over my head… and she just kept coming… and we kept retreating. Your brother was using every Italian word he knew. Crooning softly to her and telling me to get outta there. 'I'll get Cooter. Just go, Gin. Go!' I told him, no way. We'd made it this far together; I wasn't going to bail on him then. But he hissed at me, 'If anything happens to you, Grace will never forgive me.' And I said, 'Ditto'… I said, 'Ditto, she will never forgive me'…"

"Oh, Einar," Grace whispered, slipping an arm through his and stroking his hand. "It wasn't your fault."

Einar shook his head as a tear slipped down his cheek.

"If I hadn't fallen and broken this," he said, lifting his right arm. "I screamed when I heard it crack and Buck dropped Cooter on his ass to come and help me… and… and… I don't know what happened, but she must've thought we were messing with her or we scared her… I don't know… but next thing I know, the gun goes off and Buck is laying on top of me… and… and… it should have been me. Not Buck …not Buck."

Einar's chin dropped to his chest which heaved with restrained sobs.

"That is the biggest crock of lies I ever heard," a man's voice boomed from the woods behind them.

Einar leapt to his feet, casting the blanket off behind him and searching for a weapon that was not there. Grace screamed and fell backward into the sand. As Einar reached down to lift her up with his good arm, a figure appeared from behind the trees, casting a shadow over the moonlit white sand.

"George?" Grace cried out from within the safety of Einar's one-armed embrace.

"I talked with Johnnie Boudreaux tonight over at The Big Dipper," George said with slurred speech as he approached the pair. "He says you ran like a baby and left my brother alone to face that woman with your drunk friend, what's his name. He says it should have been you who got shot, not Joe. That he was covering your butt like he always did. Says you'd have been dead the first day you joined Redbull if it weren't for my brother."

"George, don't," Grace cried, holding out her hands to keep him from stepping right up into Einar's face. "You're drunk. Go home."

George swayed and leaned into her, causing her to avert her face from his alcohol infused breath.

"Nope. I'm staying right here til this *angogos* gets off our land," George said, spreading his feet wide and placing his hand on his right hip where a holstered gun resided.

"George!" Grace gasped. "Don't do this."

Einar pulled her behind his back and positioned himself toe to toe with her older brother, who stood a full three inches taller than himself.

"Listen, George, Johnnie wasn't even there when it happened. He's the one who took off running," Einar said evenly, reasonably.

"Oh sure, he said you'd say that," George retorted, spitting down into his face. "You're a liar, Einar Anderson. A liar and a coward. Got yourself shipped home ahead of the crowd with your little broken pinkie."

George attempted to grab Einar's cast, but Grace slapped his hand away, causing her brother to break out into maniacal laughter.

"See, now you got an Ojibwe woman fighting your battles," he spouted. "A woman you don't deserve. A woman who should have two brothers guarding her back from the likes of you. But she's only got one. And I aim to do my duty to God, country, Joseph and this whole god-damned family."

He reached for the pistol and shoved it up under Einar's chin. Grace screamed and tried to intervene, but George shoved her to the ground.

Crying, she stood and yelled, "Stop this, George! Stop now before you do something stupid."

But her brother did not back down.

The two men stood immovable, breathing heavily.

"If you ever come near my sister again, I swear, I'll give you the same treatment my brother got," George growled.

The sound of the trigger cocking resonated in the night silence.

"Go, ahead. Do it now," Einar whispered. "I'm half dead already."

FELIX

TITUS AND FABIAN ARE STONE-COLD SOBER. And so am I. Our dinner plates still lie on the table, shoved to one side. And our beer bottles are opened but nearly untouched. I have just told them about my strange encounter with Tora in times gone by.

"So, you're telling us that Tora, the same Tora that is sleeping in the house across the road, but in a much younger version of herself, this Tora showed up carrying Mila to your post in Britain?" Fabian repeats slowly.

I nod.

"And you say she recognized you?" Titus asks, sitting back in his chair with his hands locked atop his head.

I nod again.

My two buddies look at one another.

"You gonna tell him?" Titus asks Fabian.

"No, you go. Your story's way better," Fabian replies.

"What are you guys hiding from me?" I ask.

Titus tips his chair back onto two legs and scans the ceiling before rocking forward and leaning onto the table.

"Okay, so I told you I was over in Iceland, right?" he begins.

"Yeah, and that you met up with Fabian in Wisconsin. I've got that part," I say.

"And you know how when you hung out with the Romans all those years back, but I left the army entirely and followed the Apostle Thomas into India?"

"Yeah, I remember you telling me about it, but what does that have to do with Iceland?"

"Hold your horses. He's getting there," Fabian says.

"Well, I was hanging out on this goat farm on the far-side-of-nowhere-Iceland with this old guy named Gunnar. Not another soul around for miles, and I'm wondering what I'm doing there, as per usual. Because this guy is not exactly what you'd call social. He talked more to his goats than to me."

"What was your cover story?" I ask.

"Oh, he thought I was a tourist from Italy looking for an authentic Icelandic experience," Titus says with a laugh.

"But why would he open up his home for that if he's such a recluse?"

"My thoughts exactly," Titus replies. "Turns out it was his daughter's idea. She doesn't live with him anymore and is concerned that he's lonely and broke. I booked the stay with her, and she warned me her father was a little odd but a good guy at heart with a lot to offer. Maybe so. But after his time with me, I'm doubting he's gonna want to offer any experiences for any other tourists."

"Why? What happened?"

Fabian is starting to chuckle.

"Go ahead and laugh," Titus says. "I've heard some of your stories and they're not much better."

Fabian waves a hand and tries to halt his laughter. "I know but it's just so… it's just so funny." He doubles over, hiding his face in his hands.

"Now you've got me intrigued for sure," I say, shoving my cuffed flannel shirt sleeves up on my forearms and setting them on the table.

Titus takes a quick draw from his Leinenkugel and wipes the suds from his lips.

"So, Gunnar, like I said, has barely spoken two full sentences to me in, like, three days. He makes me herd goats and milk goats and feed goats. All communication done with just hand gestures. Even when I spoke in perfect Icelandic, which did get him to raise his eyebrows, he only replied with shrugs and grunts. But then on the fourth night, I'm sleeping in the loft out in the tiny guest hut and I feel myself being called back into time. Not up into the heavenlies but back somewhere I used to live, you know?"

"Yup. I know how that goes," I acknowledge.

"And I find myself back in India on the day of my wedding to Saanvi." Titus's voice quiets. "Oh, what a woman. Beautiful inside and out."

Fabian and I shake our heads. We have met Saanvi in the other realm. She is everything he describes, and he is still thoroughly smitten with her.

"Yeah, yeah, we know all about your Indian princess," Fabian cajoles our friend. "Get on with the story."

"Alright, alright," Titus says, returning his focus to the current situation. "So, you know, Saanvi and her family are among some of the first converts to Christianity, and there is much upheaval in their village because of this. So, the family is trying to put on a wedding that honors both their culture and their newfound faith. And I, of course, am clueless about all of it. Thomas, himself, is performing the ceremony. And he is coaching me about what might be appropriate to bring to the table as the new son-in-law. He suggests maybe a new pair of goats. That will be an ongoing gift to my new family."

Max begins to harrumph and snort in his place on the rug.

We all turn to check on him, but he doesn't stir. His eyes are shut, but his paws are pedaling as if he is trying to run.

"Must be dreaming," I say.

"Probably," my buddies agree.

"Okay, so you went out to buy some goats? On the same day you're getting married?" I ask, bringing Titus back to the story.

"Yup, Thomas goes with me early that morning out to some farm in the countryside where he says he knows a guy with goats. I'm just following him, sweating like crazy in the heat and because I'm nervous as can be about getting married. We get to this ramshackle looking place, and Thomas goes in before me to talk with the guy. He comes back out to me with a man who looks like he's as old as the hills—no teeth, no shoes, no hair, and no language I can understand. But he's got goats. One under each arm. I dig out my money to give to him, and I swear to God—I'm not lying—he looks up at me and says, "Hello, Titus." And it's him—it's Gunnar. The goat farmer from Iceland! I'm so shocked, I drop the coins on the floor and run out the door."

Fabian is still chuckling.

"Wow, that's pretty weird," I say. "But it's not that funny."

"Just wait," Fabian says. "He's not done."

"Yes, well, it turns out that meanwhile back in Iceland," Titus continues, "I wake up to find Gunnar standing in my little hut in his red long johns with two goats under his arms. He is staring at me like he's seen a ghost, and he says, 'You can have the goats. But you cannot marry my daughter.' And he drops the goats on top of me. 'And you go, now!', he yells. So, I put my backpack on, still in my own pair of long johns, mind you, tuck the goats under my arms, and walk out into the night."

"And he shows up on my doorstep in Milwaukie just like that," Fabian interjects. "Long johns, goats, and all. You should have seen the looks on my neighbors' faces." He breaks out into full guffaws.

And I join in the laughter.

"What did you do with the goats?" I ask between chortles.

"Fabian and I took them with us when we left the city. Swapped them with a farm kid working at a feed store just outside Chippewa Falls, Wisconsin," Titus says.

"Oh, yeah," I say. "What did you swap for?"

"Two cases of Leinenkugel," Fabian replies.

I hoist my beer and my friends follow suit.

"To swaps well made," I say.

"Here, here," they reply.

And we drink.

We all settle back into our chairs and listen for a moment to Max's contented snores.

"Have you had that happen before?" I ask Titus. "Someone from time present showing up in time past and recognizing you?"

"Can't say that I have," he replies. "But Fabian tells me it's happened to him a couple of times in his past few assignments."

"Really?" I say, swiveling to stare at Fabian.

He nods.

"Yup. Had me pretty shook," he says. "Didn't know what to make of it. Same as you guys."

"So, what do you think it means?" I ask.

Titus shrugs. "Ask him. He's made some inquiries," he says, pointing to Fabian with his Leinenkugel.

"Who did you ask?" I say to Fabian.

"I found a couple of other cloud-riders gathered together inside the main portal last time I was there. They were clustered together having an intense conversation, so I meandered over and stuck my nose into the group."

"What were they discussing?" I ask.

"This same phenomenon. People who are in the present generation, who haven't been called to be cloud-riders like us, but who are moving back and forth in the realms. Even back and forth in time like we do, but in a totally different way."

"Huh," I say, sitting back and rubbing a hand over my chin. "What do you suppose it's all about?"

"Elijah and Enoch think it's about times and seasons," Fabian replies.

"Yeah, well, they always say that," Titus says.

"And they're always right," I add.

"True," Titus concedes. "But what sort of time or season is it? Did they say?"

"They said it was a season to intertwine seasons and a time to entangle times," Fabian replies.

We three slip into quiet contemplation.

I stare out the window at the porch light shining over at my neighbor's house and wonder.

"They have a name for them," Fabian adds. "They call them wind-walkers."

TORA

"YOU'RE SURE MARIAH IS OKAY WITH THIS?" Peter asks me again.

"I'm sure," I reply as I apply a coat of mascara to my lashes. It is the first stroke of makeup I've put on since coming north. Not sure why I feel the need to look good for a Zoom call, but with all the important things to discuss, it seems like a momentous occasion that requires I look presentable. "She said as long as we keep Hazel socially distant from the group, she would be okay with having her over at Billy and Carin's."

"And what about her playing with Sophia? Is she okay with that too?" Peter asks, leaning on the door frame with his coffee in hand and keeping his voice low so as not to alert our granddaughter that anything might be amiss. "I mean, we didn't even ask her about the other night when we first got here, but that wasn't something we exactly planned. This is."

"She is fully informed about Sophia," I say. "I told her that her father is a pharmacist and her mother a dentist. So, they are probably some of the most careful and well-informed residents of St. Gerard that she could hope to find."

"Okay, as long as everything's out in the open. I don't want our first visit with Hazel after all this time to go pear shaped, as the Brits say."

I smile, lifting my cheeks high to wipe a dab of blush on the sweet spots.

"It's all going to be fine, babe," I say.

"And do Billy and Carin know that Thomas is coming in person?"

"They do now. Just sent them a text a few minutes ago."

"And?"

"And they said, 'The more the merrier.' Why are you so nervous?"

He shakes his head and sips from his coffee cup.

"Not sure. Just have a sense something might go… I don't know. Not exactly as we planned. That's all," he says.

"Grammy, when am I going to see Sophia?" Hazel pushes past Peter into the small bathroom with ShoSho right at her heels.

"I'll go start the car," Peter says, backing out of the suddenly crowded space.

"As soon as you get your boots and coat on. And as soon as Grammy runs a brush through her hair so she can look pretty for the meeting," I answer.

"What about my hair?" she says, stepping on her tiptoes to get a glimpse of herself in the mirror.

I do a quick adjustment to her already brushed and braided tresses and say, "There. You are pretty as a picture."

She hugs me around my waist and says, "Ditto," before rushing out to find her outdoor gear.

I shake my head and smile. Where does she get these words?

Ditto.

Suddenly, my dream about Einar, Grace, and George comes flooding into my memory. I lean with both hands onto the vanity as the scene on the sand dunes plays out.

"Ditto, she will never forgive me if…"

"Oh, my stars," I whisper to myself. "What am I supposed to do with this?"

I am saved from further reflection by Hazel's appearance at the door.

"I'm ready, Grammy," she announces.

Her boots are on the wrong feet and her coat is on inside out, but, oh well. She has done what I asked her to do, and I am not about to correct her efforts.

"Good job," I say, setting the brush down and switching off the light. "Let me get my coat and we'll go find Papa. Maybe you should have him take ShoSho out to go potty before we leave."

"Okay," she says, skipping toward the back door to the garage.

As I don my coat and grab my tote bag with the things I want to share on the call, I am nearly overwhelmed with sadness for Uncle Einar. It seems to me that far more than the intimidation meted out by George, it is the guilt over the death of Joseph that kept him away and robbed him, as well as Grace, from living a life filled with love and family. Wouldn't he be thrilled to know his great-granddaughter and my granddaughter are becoming friends?

"Tor, you coming?" Peter's voice reaches me from the garage door.

"Yup, I'm coming," I yell back.

Passing the large fiftieth wedding anniversary picture of the entire family, I stop to search for Einar's face in the crowd. He is in the back on the end of a row, looking as if he wants to hide or step out of the frame of the camera's view altogether.

But standing beside him is my dad. He has one arm around my mom and the other stretching out to restrain his older brother from exiting. Though I've looked at this picture many times over the course of the years, I have never noticed this before. I wonder what other things I have seen in my family my whole life but never noticed.

"SO, LET ME GET THIS STRAIGHT," my brother Clayton says from his library in London where books, documents, and artifacts fill every nook and cranny behind him. "Thomas, you have a small group of elders…"

"A council," Thomas corrects. We have seated him between Billy and I at the dining room table of the Hallstrom home. Peter and Carin have stools situated behind and between we three, so as to get a glimpse of the computer screen in front of us, though Carin flits in and out according to the need of the moment.

"You have a council who oversees the incoming needs and the outgoing distribution of funds generated from the capital investment made with the coins. And these investments continue to yield profitable margins for you?" Clay finishes his summation.

"Yes, that is the way we have found best for our people. We are a closed reservation, so the needs are encapsulated by a small nation," Thomas adds adjusting the knot of his tie. He has come to the table dressed for business.

"But still," my brother Andy jumps in from his sun-filled home office in Arizona. "That was very generous of your mother to include the entire tribe in the benefits."

"My Uncle George was not happy about it," Thomas concedes. "But my grandparents encouraged her inclination. They were very pleased she was thinking that way, for it is the Ojibwe way."

Carin pops her head into the dining room from the kitchen with a coffee carafe held high. "Any one need a refresher?"

I notice she has also spiffed up her face and hair for the call. Placing my hand over my cup, I shake my head and so does Thomas. But Billy and Peter lift theirs up for a refill.

We have been on our call for over an hour already. It took some time to actually get around to the business of the coins since we had a lot of excitement and back story to fill in with the appearance of our newly found cousin. It is not often that I can dumbfound both my brothers into silence, but today I did it.

Of course, that only lasted so long before their usual articulate selves returned.

Vera was on with us for about forty-five minutes, but has left to go lay down somewhere. Andy says she tires quickly these days.

"Do you think we should create our own council for the Anderson family?" my cousin Katie chimes in from her studio in Minneapolis. She has been quiet for most of the discussion about the coins. Distracted, even. But clearly, she has absorbed at least some of the information.

"I think that's a great idea," Billy says.

"How about a show of hands?" Peter suggests.

Everyone raises their hands high.

Everyone except Thomas.

"Don't you think that's a good idea?" I ask.

He turns to me with a blank stare.

"I did not think I was part of the Anderson family," he says.

We all take a collective breath.

"Thomas, you are as much a part of this family as any one of us on this call," Billy says. "So, you get a vote same as all the rest of us."

Thomas smiles at him and slowly raises his hand.

We break out into applause.

"It looks like that's unanimous," Clay says. "Now all we've got to decide is who is on the council."

Again, the crowd goes quiet.

"If I may," Thomas starts.

"Sure," Andy says.

"Go for it," adds Billy.

"Be our guest," says Katie.

"By all means," chimes in Clayton.

I smile at Thomas. "I guess that means we want to hear what you have to say."

"For as long as my mother lived, she was the head of the council because she was the one to whom the coins were given. And she appointed her other advisors. As the first generation on the council slowly left us, they each appointed their replacement from a younger generation. And so, it goes to this day. My son, Patrick, is in training to take my place."

The heads nod up and down in the small boxes on the screen like a bunch of bobbleheads.

"Okay, so, maybe we start like they started," Peter suggests. "The coins were given to Einar. And the most direct descendant of Einar in this room is Thomas. Would you be willing to be our council director?"

Thomas does not answer right away.

The sound of Sophia, Hazel, and ShoSho playing in the enclosed, heated porch bounce around us, reminding us of our obligations to generations that follow us.

"I am honored by your nomination," Thomas says. "But I am already the director of the Everwind Fund. So, while I am willing to be on your council, I think it would be best for another to be at the head. And since the coins were most recently discovered by Tora, I nominate her as the director of the Anderson fund."

My jaw drops, and I don't know what to say.

"I second that nomination," Katie pipes up.

"I third it," Billy adds.

"Me too," say my brothers in unison.

Peter pats my hand and says, "I think that's a great idea."

"You guys… I don't know if I'm the right one for this job. You're all way more business-minded than me. And way more accomplished in your careers. And way savvier about finances. This is outside of my comfort zone, big time," I protest.

"Tora, you need to stop underestimating yourself," Carin says from her place standing behind me. "All those things you said may be true to some extent, but you are the one who is most connected to the needs of this family. And I think having the heart of the people at the forefront is the most necessary qualification for the job."

"Here, here," says Billy.

"Agreed," adds Katie.

And the others also contribute their assent.

I am both flattered and stunned. This is not how I envisioned this conversation going.

"Who do you want as advisors?" Thomas asks.

I spread my arms out to include the entire gathering.

"All of you," I say. "I need every one of your gifts and thoughts, please."

They each agree one by one to be founding members of the Anderson Fund council.

"What's our first order of business, Sis?" Clayton asks.

I shrug. "How should I know?"

Peter whispers in my ear.

"Okay. I think my husband is right. We need to form an agreement about how to invest our funds. Maybe, Thomas, you have some suggestions for us?"

"Yes, I can gather the most recent financials from the Everwind Fund—provided our council agrees to the disclosure, which I am sure they will," Thomas says.

"Great," I say with relief.

Then an idea comes to me.

"Once we do that, I already have a couple of family needs that I would like to put up for consideration to the council," I say, slowly warming to my role as director.

"Oh, yeah?" Billy says. "What might those be?"

"Well, I'm just going to throw these out there, and if any of you don't want them on the table, then you have the right to shelve them. Okay?" I begin.

Everyone agrees.

"First, I think we need to invest in whatever daily help Tante Tilda needs in order to stay in her home as long as possible."

"Hey," Katie jumps in. "We're doing okay with that."

"I know you are… now," I reply. "But her needs are only going to get greater, and I want to be able to help. Is that okay?"

Katie wipes a tear from her eyes and nods.

"Okay, good," I say, taking a deep breath. "I'm not going to get into details right now about the second need because, well, frankly, I don't know all the details, but I would also like for this family to lend a hand to Katie in regards to getting whatever help is needed to assist Debbie, whenever she is ready to be assisted."

Katie suddenly slumps forward with both hands over her face.

We all wait for her to gather herself.

She comes up for air and blows her nose into a tissue.

"I, uh, I don't know what to say," she chokes out. "I have just been texting with her all morning because she says she's ready to go into the rehab place I've been wanting her to go to for ages. But she's afraid of how much it will cost…"

She breaks into sobs. We wait again.

"Well, that would appear to be the place we should begin," Andy says.

Again, the group comes into total agreement.

"Okay," I say. "One more thing. Andy, you mentioned that Vera is going in for some experimental treatment sometime next month. Is that something that is covered by your insurance or could you use a little help?"

Andy drops his chin as Vera's face comes back onto the screen. "I have been resting on the couch," she says. "And I heard your proposal. I am… we are very humbled by your offer." Her voice breaks, and my brother kisses her hand.

"I have been telling her that she didn't need to worry about the cost. That it would all work out. Haven't I, my love?" he says to his wife of over fifty years.

She nods and manages a shaky smile.

"See what I told you?" Carin breaks the emotional quiet of the room. "She's got her ear to the family-need grapevine."

Peter puts his hands on my shoulders and gives me a squeeze. Relief and excitement fill my heart in a wonderful mixture. It feels as though I might possibly have found a place and a purpose for this season of my life. But my thoughts are quickly shattered when Sophia comes bursting into the room and runs for her grandfather. Her face is full of fear, and she cannot speak.

"What is it?" Thomas says, taking her by the hand.

"They're gone," Sophia whispers. "I just came in to use the bathroom and… and…"

"Who's gone?" Peter says, rising to his feet.

Sophia swings a terrified look at Peter and then at me.

"Hazel!" I say, jumping up and racing after my husband out to the porch.

55

FELIX

“I’M TELLING YOU WHAT,” Fabian says from behind the wheel of his truck. “That woman can preach!”

“By golly,” Titus says, “that is the best sermon I have heard in, well… I listened to Wesley not too long ago, and then there was Spurgeon and Aimee Semple McPherson, not to mention Peter and Paul…”

“Yeah, alright,” I interrupt from the back seat. “We get the point.”

“Just saying, Pastor Mel Strickland can stand toe to toe with the best of them,” Titus concludes.

“And you’d have thought she was listening in on our conversation last night with the way she was talking about dreamers and visionaries. And, how the heavenly portals seem to be opening up in new and expansive ways in these days across the generations," Fabian adds.

"Just wish Tora could have heard it," I say.

"Half expected to see them at church this morning," Titus adds.

"They have some restrictions I believe with their granddaughter being here. But you're right. She would have really enjoyed that teaching," I reply. "Maybe I will mention it to her later. She can always go back and watch the recorded version."

The day is bright, and I am enjoying the ride back from St. Gerard to Solbakken. The area has grown on me. Yes, it's snowy and cold, but the people are warm. And the winter landscape holds its own sort of allure with the dazzling snow reflecting up onto the pines and barren trees.

"You got any idea of how long you might be up in this neck of the woods?" Fabian asks, peering at me in the rearview mirror.

I shrug.

"Until the assignment is completed," I reply.

My fellow cloud-riders nod their heads.

We ride in companionable silence for several minutes before making the final turn toward home. Passing the Hallstrom home, I see Tora's vehicle and one other parked by the house along with Billy's pickup and another smaller SUV.

"Looks like somebody's got company," Titus remarks.

"Yes, guess I will have to catch Tora later in the day," I say.

As we approach Janet's house, I see a dark sedan parked behind my truck. For some reason I do not fully understand but have come to trust, my senses go on alert.

"Fabian," I say, tapping him on the shoulder. "Drive past the house and turn down that other road. But go slow. I want to see who's here."

Fabian nods and slows down.

Titus and I roll down our tinted windows to get a better view.

"You leave that back shed door open, Felix?" Titus asks.

"Nope," I reply.

As we pass the end of the driveway, we can hear Maximus barking inside the house. We three look at each other. We know that bark.

"Billy's not the only one with company it would appear," Fabian says. "How do you want to approach this, Felix?"

"Turn left and pull over," I say, keeping my eyes on the house.

"Hey, hey!" Titus yells out his window at a figure that is leaving the shed.

I whip my door open and leap out before the truck is stopped. So does Titus.

The man in the shadows of the shed has stepped into the sunlight. He tucks something into his coat and runs toward his car. But, seeing Titus and I charging down the driveway, he changes direction, sprinting toward the woods.

Billy's cows in the field behind the house raise their heads in unison and watch the interloper running toward the tree line.

I give Titus signals to head straight after the man while I let Max out. Fabian has already turned the truck around and is looking to me for directions. I give him the sign to head toward where we have just come from and scout the road. He quickly obeys.

TORA

"PETER," I YELL. "DO YOU SEE HER ANYWHERE?"

He has run toward the barn and come out already while I have made a complete circle around the house.

"No, not yet," he yells back.

Billy and Thomas are scouring the yard for prints. I rush up to them, hoping they have some clue as to which direction Hazel and her puppy have disappeared. Sophia is standing in the doorway crying. I feel badly for her, but I don't have time to console her. My mind is fixated on one thing—finding my granddaughter.

"It looks like they have gone this way," Thomas says to Billy as he loosens his tie and unbuttons his collar.

"Yes, I think so," Billy concurs. He kneels down and comes back upright with concern in his eyes

"What is it?" I say.

He looks to Thomas, who has the same concerned eyes.

"Could be Max?" Billy asks.

"Could be," Thomas replies.

"What?" I insist.

"Just some tracks that are bigger than what ShoSho could have made. Maybe Max," Billy says.

My hands go over my mouth as Peter's cries for Hazel ring out over the yard behind us.

"It's not… do you think…" I cannot get the words out of my suddenly dry-as-a-bone mouth.

Billy shakes his head. "Probably not."

"They have gone toward those woods," Thomas says, pointing down the driveway to a stand of pines across the road.

"Looks that way alright," Billy nods. "Think I'll get my ATV out. You want to head that way on foot?"

Thomas nods and takes off jogging.

"What about me?" I yell after Billy.

"Keep looking with Peter," he yells over his shoulder as he too breaks into a jog. I don't remember the last time I ever saw him move so fast. Well, actually I do, and the thought makes me tremble.

Peter exits the shop, shaking his head and holding up his hands.

"Not in here," he yells, striding toward me. "Where are they headed?"

I run to him. "They think Hazel has gone over the road and into the woods," I say as I reach him with tears spilling down my cheeks in rivers. I was not even aware they had begun to flow, but my nose is dripping profusely. Peter hands me a handkerchief from his pocket and pulls me into a hug. "And they found other prints. Big animal prints." I choke out a sob into his chest.

"We will find them. They can't be far," he says. "Now let's go help." He grabs my hand, and we head back toward the house where Carin is coming toward us with our coats.

"Put these on," she says, meeting us in the middle of the yard and helping me on with my coat. "Any sign of them?"

Billy comes roaring out of the barn on his ATV and shoots past us down the driveway.

"They think over there is the best bet," Peter says, pointing to where Thomas is entering into the grove of pines on the other side of the ditch.

"Okay," Carin says. "I will stay at the house with Sophia, and we'll keep an eye out for them here. Do you have your phones on you in case they show up here?"

Peter checks his pocket and nods.

"Text me," he says. "That's more reliable."

Carin agrees and heads back up the stairs to put her arms around Sophia who stands nearly as tall as her. She is speaking softly to the girl and ushering her into the house when my husband and I start jogging toward the woods. I let go of his hand.

"Just go," I urge him. "I'll catch up."

He gives me a kiss on the cheek and takes off running in earnest to where Thomas has disappeared into the trees.

I follow behind the tracks Billy has made on his ATV down a path running back toward Janet's place. My mind flashes back to the day I ran into these same woods after Felix and Billy. The day of the wolf attack. I force those images out of my mind. They are too terrifying to entertain. I can hear the roar of the engine ahead of me going away from me and then back as if Billy is systematically searching his property in a grid.

"Dear Lord," I whisper a prayer as I trot. "Please don't let anything happen to her." I wipe the continuing flow from my face and nearly double over when I think of Mariah. "If anything happens to her," I think to myself. "She will never forgive me."

I am just entering the tree line when a red pickup truck goes past slowly on the road behind me. A man is sticking his head out the window and staring at me. I don't recognize him but he waves. Suddenly, I hear Max barking furiously from down the road. It sounds as if he is headed in my direction, but I can't be sure. Maybe they really were his tracks on the driveway, I console my wildly anxious soul. Maybe Hazel and Sho-Sho followed him into the woods. I take a deep breath and will myself to believe this scenario as I plunge forward, pressing on after Billy. My pace is slowed by the wet and heavy snow.

"Felix, over here!" someone is yelling to my left.

"On it," I hear Felix reply. "Follow Max!"

How on earth do they know about this already? Maybe Carin has phoned them? But Felix has no phone.

I am trying to process this new variable when a tremendous bark and growl explode somewhere deep in the woods.

"Hazel!" the scream erupts from deep in my belly, and I burst into a frantic run.

Billy's ATV comes to a halt and a shot rings out.

My heart stops. I hear male voices calling to one another from all around me as if I am surrounded by an army. And then all of the sudden, in the midst of the turmoil a pure, clarion child's voice yells, "No! Stop!"

I nearly stumble to my knees in relief. She's alive!

"Don't," Hazel yells again.

The only thing I hear is my own labored breathing and the sound of men crashing through the woods. Then everything goes still.

FELIX

WHEN I BREAK THROUGH THE BRUSH into the small clearing, I pull to an immediate halt beside Titus. What lies in front of us is something I have never encountered in all my years—and that is saying a lot.

Max is laying on his belly next to Hazel, who is kneeling in the snow.

He is panting and still with his eyes fixed straight ahead. Red is seeping from underneath him, turning the snow pink and then crimson.

"He's hurt," Titus whispers.

I nod.

"Do something," the young man we have been pursuing pleads. He is standing frozen by a tree behind Hazel. "This kid is crazy."

Hazel has one arm wrapped around her puppy and the other around Max's neck.

"No," she insists. "He didn't mean to hurt him. Max just scared him."

Titus shakes his head and says under his breath, "What the heck is going on?"

Peter and Thomas are only a few feet behind the young man. They, too, are frozen in their tracks.

Billy sits astride his ATV with a rifle trained on his shoulder, aiming at the spot about three yards in front of where Hazel is kneeling. For on this spot lies the center of all the frenzied attention—a large, black wolf who, like Max, is laying on his belly with specks of red sprayed out around him.

"Oh, my…" Tora gasps as she enters the scene directly behind Hazel near the young man. She stops with her eyes agog and her hands at her throat.

"Mikey," Billy says evenly and firmly to the young man. "Just stay put. We will sort this thing out if everybody stays calm."

No one moves.

Then, from across the opening, I hear a soothing male voice begin to chant. It is in a language I do not understand but I feel the peace and power in the song's frequency.

The wolf tips its head slightly, and his ears twist toward the music.

Thomas takes one step forward and continues to sing.

Max lowers his head onto the snow, and his eyes begin to droop.

"Is he okay?" Titus whispers, tipping his chin toward my dog.

I shrug.

I don't know if he is relaxing or losing consciousness, but I don't dare move toward him until the wolf is taken care of.

ShoSho begins to squirm in Hazel's arms, and we all hold our breaths.

She tightens her grip on her pet, looks at Thomas, and begins to whistle along with him.

The wolf lowers its head.

Thomas moves his right hand slowly as if urging us to join the song.

I start to hum the simple melody, and as I do, the others join suit.

It is the most amazing thing.

Here we are. A group of people standing in the woods, serenading a voracious wolf that has just tangled with my dog and left him bleeding in the snow.

And, wonder of wonders, the wolf seems to be listening.

Slowly, the wild animal stands to its feet, as if knowing any sudden movement would probably cost him his life. Billy's hands tighten on his firearm, and his voice drops out from the chorus, as does mine and everyone else's, one by one until only Thomas is left chanting.

"It's okay," Hazel says, ceasing her whistling. "He won't hurt us, and he promises not to hurt anyone ever again."

Out of the corner of my eye, I catch movement. It is Fabian, advancing with his signature stealth mode behind Tora. I signal him to stop, and he does.

The wolf looks down at Max, who appears to have fallen asleep, and then up at Hazel. His head bobs up and down once, then he turns away and vanishes into the underbrush.

Titus leaps ahead of me over to Max.

Tora rushes forward to scoop up Hazel with Peter right behind her.

Billy follows the wolf with his rifle.

Thomas ceases his song.

And Fabian wraps his arms around Mikey, who is attempting his own vanishing act.

MAXIMUS

IT WAS INSTINCTIVE.
My urge to save her.
To fling myself in harm's way on her behalf.
And I did.
And he fought back.
He hurt me.
Deeply.
As severe as any wound I have ever sustained.
This long-distant relative of mine—this enemy.
The wolf.
But now I wonder.
Is he really?
She has made me see him with new eyes.
Maybe my approach was not the best.
Hers seemed so risky though.
So fraught with possible disaster.
I doubted her.
But then the man began to sing and she began to whistle.
I do not know this man, but I know his song.
It is peace.
It is power.
It is love.
I have heard it before but only from a few.

The man in the meadow with the birds.
He sang it.
The woman in the stone house.
She sang it.
Maybe I should learn this song—if only I could sing.
My thoughts grow fuzzy.
My head is heavy.
I will rest in this song.

TORA

"THAT IS THE CRAZIEST THING I HAVE EVER HEARD," my brother Andy says.

Clayton can't stop shaking his head, and Katie is sitting in stunned silence. They are all still in their places on the Zoom call, which Carin kept updated with whatever she could. Each of them had refused to leave until they knew what had happened.

"Why did Hazel go into the woods in the first place?" Clay asks.

"She said ShoSho had to go potty. So, she let him outside. But as soon as he hit the ground, he took off down the driveway and into the field," Peter says. "She chased after him because 'He's my responsibility, Papa.' That's what she told me."

Our granddaughter sits in my lap sound asleep, and my husband is next to us, his hand on her knee with ShoSho curled up at our feet. None of us, including the pup apparently, are willing to let her out of our sight even to lay her down for a nap. Yet she, unlike all the rest of us, seemed completely unfazed by the entire episode. Her only concern being if Max was okay.

That is a question I cannot answer.

As soon as the wolf left, Titus scooped up the enormous animal as if it were a little lamb. The pool of blood that was underneath him was shockingly large, and Peter wisely shielded Hazel's eyes from it as we left the scene. Felix and his friends quickly got the dog out to the red truck on the road and sped away while Billy and Thomas secured Mikey.

"I know it's Sunday and all, so I appreciate you coming out here, Sheriff," Billy's voice reaches us from the kitchen. "We'll make sure he sticks around. Got him locked up in the pantry with water and a sandwich for now."

The screen is quiet as we all seem to want to eavesdrop on Billy's conversation with Sheriff Dumfrey.

"No need to worry. The place is as big as our kitchen and Carin has made it so cozy, I might move in once we hand Mikey over to ya," Billy says with a laugh.

"Hey! Billy," a muffled voice yells through the pantry door. "I gotta use the can!"

"Speak of the devil," Billy says. "The prisoner needs to use the facilities. So, we will see ya in a few then. Yup. Okay. Thanks again."

We hear Billy unlocking the pantry door and Mikey's protestations over the inhumane treatment.

"Dude, you have more food in your 'cell' than some third world countries. You got nothing to complain about. So, get moving before I change my mind," Billy directs the proceedings.

"Yikes, remind me not to get Billy mad," Katie remarks. "Why do you think Mikey came back?"

"He said he needed cash and that he knew the baseball cards were valuable," Peter replies. "Guess he had stashed them in a tub out in the shed. Had the place under surveillance and waited until Felix and his buddies were gone to move in. Think he also had some things in the house he was thinking of retrieving but Max's presence deterred him from going in."

"Sure hope the dog is okay," Clayton says.

We all nod.

"What about Sophia?" Andy asks.

"Thomas took her home," I say over Hazel's head. "She was still pretty upset even though we assured her it was not her fault. And that everyone was okay. But she's old enough to know that, well, that it could have gone…" I can't seem to finish the thought.

"Pear shaped?" Clayton says.

"Exactly," Peter replies.

A quiet descends in our midst as we all seem to have slipped into the fearful place of contemplation called The Land of What-If's.

"Do you want to stay for dinner?" Carin asks, coming up behind me and placing a gentle hand on my shoulder.

I look to Peter. He shrugs.

"I think we'd better go home," I reply, and Peter nods. "Not quite sure what we're going to tell Mariah and Isaac."

"Yes, well, we will be praying for you on that account," Carin says.

"Thanks," Peter replies. "We're gonna need it."

"What are you going to tell them?" Clay asks. "That their daughter is a wolf-whisperer?"

Billy enters the room and pokes his head down into the camera frame.

"Thomas thinks she has a gift," he says to the group. "Says he's only ever seen it a couple of times and never with an animal as…" he looks at my sleeping granddaughter and lowers his voice, "as dangerous as this wolf."

Andy is shaking his head and smiling.

"What is it, Andy?" Katie asks.

"Well, I just had this memory from when I was a kid up at the farm," he begins. "I must have been only about Hazel's age because I don't think you were even born yet, Clay. Or if you were, you were only a baby. Anyway, I was out in the barn with Grandpa, and he was showing me how to milk the cow. She was a gentle old thing named Lulla. But I was a city kid from Alexandria, and she scared the heck out of me."

"I remember that cow," Clayton pipes up. "Grandpa put me on her back once, which she did not take too kindly to. Made Grandpa laugh but cured me from every riding another cow."

"Yup, that's the one. So, as I'm leaning in under Lulla, she gets all fidgety and starts stamping her hooves. Which, of course, scares me. So, Grandpa is trying to calm both me and her when he gets real still all of a sudden and puts his hand over my mouth. I go quiet and look where he's looking. A coyote is standing across the barn from us, staring right at us. I was so scared I, uh… well, I peed my pants at that point. But Grandpa, he looks right at that critter and starts talking. All soft and soothing and calm. Lulla starts to relax, and then the coyote gives Grandpa a little nod and trots out of the barn without looking back. Just like that. And we finish milking the cow."

"I've never heard that story before," I say.

"I was always a little embarrassed by it," Andy admits. "And Grandpa told me, after we went inside and got my pants changed, that we'd keep it just between us 'men.' I don't think he ever even told Mom and Dad. I know I never did."

"Hmm, that is so interesting," Peter remarks.

"Uh, gee, thanks, I guess," Andy replies.

"No, not your pants problem, Bro," Peter continues. "The animal whisperer thingy. Maybe it's in the family genes. I mean, today, Hazel was beyond amazing for sure, but I'm telling you, if Thomas hadn't started up his singing or chanting or whatever it was, I'm not sure what would have happened."

A shudder runs through my body, and Hazel stirs in my arms.

We take a collective beat like a moment of silence at a professional sporting event to commemorate some sort of tragic happening.

"Well, folks, this has been one heck of a call," Katie breaks the moment. "I'm glad everything worked out for the good. Very relieved about that. But I need to go. Want to get a call into my sister about what we discussed today. Let me know how you want to work the finances and when something might be available."

"We will need to work out all those details," Peter says. "I'll set up a time to go over the financial documents with Thomas as soon as possible and get whatever legal status in place for the Anderson Fund that is required."

"Let me know if I can help on that," Andy says.

"And I will get onto appraising the coins. Maybe see what the market is looking for these days," Clay adds. "Sure appreciate you taking the lead on the legal front, Peter."

"Only doing my part to serve the family council," my husband replies. "But right now, I think my part is to get the director and the heir back to the house for some R&R."

The call winds up, and Peter takes Hazel from my arms to carry her out to the 4Runner. Carin gives me a long, tight hug, which threatens to get my waterworks starting all over again, but I appreciate the strength and love she is infusing in her embrace. We separate and sigh.

"I cannot thank you enough for everything," I say to her and to Billy, who is leaning on the counter behind her back munching on an enormous chocolate chip cookie.

"Just taking care of family, Cuz," he says between bites.

Carin turns to look at him and her smile turns into a scowl. "William Arthur Hallstrom!"

"What?" Billy replies, wiping crumbs from either side of his mouth. "It's been a day, alright. Can't a man reward himself for a job well done?"

"As if you were the one who resolved it all," Carin says, snatching the cookie from his hands. "You'd have shot that wolf where he stood if you'd have had your way."

He looks at the retreating sweet woefully.

"I only shot into the air," he pleads. "Too many people in the woods to risk shooting at the animal."

Carin sighs and advances toward him.

"Oh, alright," she says, handing the cookie back. "You need some milk to wash that down?"

TORA

PETER HAS DECIDED TO SPEND another night at the farm and drive south in the morning. I am relieved. After an in-depth conversation with our daughter and son-in-law, all still while in the 4Runner with Hazel and ShoSho sawing logs in the seat behind us, we are exhausted. Thankfully, they have conceded to our request for one more night. I would not have been surprised if they had not. My only conclusion is that Mariah is struggling more than she cares to admit.

I think it's time for me to return south, too, so as to be available to serve them however I can, however they will allow. We will caravan back to The Cities tomorrow after a quick stop in St. Gerard to say good-bye to Tante.

The farmhouse is probably cleaner than it has been in quite some time. I have accomplished what I set out to do—and a whole lot more.

What a week.

Now, sitting in the living room on the couch, with the Beatles playing on the stereo and Hazel contentedly coloring in the dining room, I try to shake the anxious energy of the day.

"Do you think Mariah and Isaac will ever let us do this again?" I whisper to my husband.

"Would you?" he replies.

I sigh.

"Probably not," I admit, snuggling closer under his arm.

"Yesterday, all my troubles seemed so far away…"

The familiar refrain fills the house, and Hazel begins to sing along.

I turn in surprise.

"How do you know this song?" I ask.

"Daddy sings it," she replies without looking up. "He says it's from The Beat Ups."

I smile despite the fact that our chance of ever taking care of this precious child by ourselves again has diminished significantly today.

"It's The Beatles," Peter corrects over his shoulder.

"Oh, Papa, don't be silly. That is a bug not a band," she remarks and sings on.

If only I could be as carefree. Oh, to be a child again.

After supper, we spend a quiet evening playing cards with Hazel. She is competitive and focused just like her mother. But she isn't sophisticated enough yet to realize that Peter and I have thrown every game to allow her to win. She is gracious in triumph, however.

"You just need to be patient and learn, Papa and Grammy," she asserts after brushing her teeth and getting into her pajamas. "You can try to beat me tomorrow."

We smile and nod, allowing her to fall asleep on our bed.

We even let the dog up there with her. Her parents can fight that battle. For tonight, we are done fighting battles, and all we want to do is please her.

Peter steps outside before we get ready for bed to see if any lights are on over at Janet's place or if the red pickup truck is back. They are not.

"Things must be pretty serious," I say upon hearing his report.

"Must be," he concedes. "But I'm banking on the Good Lord hearing Hazel's prayers for Max. I know I couldn't resist answering those requests and I'm just… well, at least I hope I'm a good grandpa."

I pull his face into my hands and give him a good long kiss.

"You are a very good grandpa," I say at the conclusion.

"I hope so," he replies.

"I know so."

When it is time for us to go to bed, I crawl in next to Hazel and wrap her in my arms. Peter spoons in behind me and does the same to me, shoving ShoSho further toward the end of the bed with his feet. I sigh and let the pillowcase absorb my tears.

"Sweet, Jesus," Peter whispers in my ear. "Help them forgive us."

"Amen," I whisper. "And please, heal Max."

"Amen," a sleepy agreement comes from the angel in my arms.

WHEN THE LARGE, DAZZLING OAK TREE appears in front of me, I am not surprised. But when a little voice beside me asks, "Grammy, what kind of tree is that?" I am taken aback. Looking down, I see that walking by my side with her hand in mine is Hazel.

How did she get here?

I struggle to remember where I am.

The farm.

Peter.

Hazel.

A tug on my hand brings me back to the tree.

"Grammy, did you hear me?"

I smile down at this darling girl.

Her hair is tousled and her cheeks pink as if she has just been awakened from a deep sleep. Still in her pajamas, she bends down to pick up a leaf that has floated down in front of us.

"This is our family tree," I say as we approach the bench carved into the side.

"Ooh," she says, staring up into the sparkling leaves. "It's very big!"

"Yes, indeed. It is," I say, looking around to see who might be meeting me tonight. The bench is empty.

"Let's sit here," Hazel says, climbing up onto the weathered seat I have come to love in recent days.

It is odd to see her sitting where my ancestors have sat, and yet, is it?

I ease down next to her still hoping, still waiting for the next storyteller to appear.

"Grammy, look!" Hazel exclaims. "It's turning into a book."

She holds out the leaf she picked up, and we watch it transform into a thick tome resplendent with gold-edged pages.

"It's heavy. You take it," she says, placing the book in my lap.

It is indeed heavy. Much thicker than any book I have seen in this place. I open it and find pages densely packed with sentences. The writing is strange. The letters unfamiliar.

Hazel scoots closer and peers at the pages.

"Can you read it, Grammy?" she asks.

I am about to say, "No," when suddenly I find that the words are making sense to me. I test myself before saying, "You know what? I think I can."

Hazel claps her hands then winds an arm through mine.

"What's the book called?" she asks.

I close the pages, turning to the spine. The foreign words morph into a title I can now read.

"It is called, A *New Day Dawns,"* I reply.

"What does it say?" she whispers.

I open to the first page.

"The sun is not yet up in the garden, and the guards are still on duty," I begin to read.

"What are they guarding?"

"I don't know. Let's read and find out."

FELIX

"ARE THEY SENDING ANY REPLACEMENTS this morning?" Fabian asked.

"I don't know," I replied as I walked past him, starting on one more circle around the garden grounds with Max. "Titus should be rested, though. You can take a break if you want. Max and I are good to go."

"No, I'm okay," he replied, stomping his feet in place where he stood in front of the large rock that has been sealed in the opening to the stone tomb.

The night had been chilly and ominous feeling: the stars and moon covered by a dense layer of clouds. It was the same layer that had blown in the day before around three in the afternoon—so thick, even the rays of the sun could not penetrate it. Never seen anything like it.

My heart was heavy as I did my duty. I could not comprehend that my childhood friend's battered and bruised body lay in the tomb I was guarding.

"How did it come to this?" I muttered as we patrolled the grounds once again.

I sent prayers heavenward for my mother, sisters, and brother, though my belief in the goodness or existence of Yahweh had diminished over the course of the years to the point that I wondered if prayers were even worthwhile. And the brutal crucifixion of Yeshua had not helped my wavering faith. How could a good, heavenly Father allow such an unjust thing to happen to such a good man? I sighed, shuddered, and continued to pray. I did not know what else to do.

Coming around the far side of the large stone, which encapsulated the tomb, I saw Titus standing and stretching under a tree. I steered my dog toward him, keeping my eyes scanning the horizon as I had been trained.

"Rested?" I asked Titus.

He nodded.

"Fabian need a break?" he asked.

"Go ask him," I replied. "He's out front. I'm going to continue our circuit."

Max and I ducked under a low hanging branch of an olive tree. We marched to the far end of the garden, turned left, and began to circle back. All of a sudden, a deep growl reverberated in my dog's belly.

We stopped.

I searched the area but saw nothing.

"What is it?" I whispered.

Max was stopped dead in his tracks with his paws out wide and his chest uplifted. The growl persisted as he sniffed the air. I still couldn't see anything, but I did hear something. It sounded as if someone was whistling back by the tomb, but it was not the whistle of my fellow guards. These I knew. This was strange and out of place on such a morning. It was pure, rich, and unfathomably melodic. Max quieted, and his ears twitched, as if trying to absorb every note on the air.

Suddenly, the hair on my arms stood upright as if lightning was about to strike the ground beside us. And then, the earth began to shake beneath our feet.

"Fabian, Titus, something's up!" I yelled as Max took off in a sprint, barking loudly.

I ran behind him, my hand unsheathing my dagger as I went.

I heard strange cries up ahead.

"You guys okay?" I hollered.

No answer.

Max's bark went silent.

I slowed my stride and dipped behind an olive tree.

Peeking out from around the thick, gnarled trunk, my eyes were blinded by a brilliant light streaming from the rock or what appeared to be the rock. I didn't know for sure. I couldn't see my friends or my dog. Shielding my eyes and going down into a low crouch, I suddenly detected three figures lying sprawled face first on the ground.

"Oh, no…"

I was paralyzed.

I did not know how to proceed.

Were they dead? What was this light? Where was it coming from? What was I up against?

"Felix."

A voice came to me from out of the middle of the light.

I blinked and shaded my eyes.

The voice did not sound like Titus or Fabian. But it was familiar.

"Felix, come quickly," the voice continued.

I slowly stood to my feet. My dagger dropped from my fingers into the dirt as I stumbled forward. It was as if all strength had left my limbs and something more powerful than any force I had ever encountered was drawing me forward.

Two large figures in gleaming white light appeared. One stood beside the opened door of the tomb and the other sat atop the stone that had been used to seal off the opening. They were silent. They were massive. They were… I didn't know what.

"Felix," once more the voice pleaded.

To my far right, off in the distance, I heard the sound of somber women's voices. They were advancing in this direction.

"Come, before they arrive," the voice directed my steps.

And then, without me knowing how, I was standing face to face with Yeshua.

A risen, very much alive and well, Yeshua.

His eyes pierced my heart, and I fell to my knees trembling.

"How? What?" I asked before covering my eyes with my hands against the brilliant light. But they offered no shelter, for I could see right through them. My bones were visible, but all flesh was as transparent as glass.

A hand touched my shoulder, and I looked up.

"I am The Resurrection and The Life, my friend," Yeshua said. "And now, because you are witness to this moment of death's defeat, now you will live as I live. Do not fear. I will be with you."

I collapsed onto my face, weeping and rejoicing at the same time. Then his presence was gone. I felt him leave.

I could not move.

I did not know what to think. It was as if my mind had been scrambled and my heart burst by a million shooting stars.

What had just happened?

I didn't know for sure.

But I knew something supernatural had taken place. Something that had changed my life forever.

It was as if an entirely new day had dawned.

TORA

"OKAY, I WILL MEET YOU AT BILLY'S," Peter says, leaning into the window of my rig. "And then we'll go see Tilda. But we can't stay a long time, ya know."

"I know. But I promised we'd stop by," I reply.

Hazel, ShoSho, and I are all packed up and ready to hit the road heading south. But there is one more stop I need to make before we leave Solbakken.

"Tell Billy I'm going to try to come back up sometime in the spring when the snow is gone and the roads passable," I say. "And before the bugs invade."

"Will do. Don't take too long over at Felix's," he says, giving me a peck on the cheek.

"Don't forget Hackensack!" Hazel pipes up from the back seat.

"It's on the schedule," Peter assures.

We have promised a stop by the lake to chat with Paul Bunyan's sweetheart even if the temps have dropped again and the wind is coming in from the north. It is her one request for the journey besides the Dairy Queen in Walker, which is a given.

And today, there is not a request we can deny her.

If she only knew—up to half our kingdom.

Peter gets into his vehicle and pulls out of the drive ahead of us. I take one last glance at the house, checking to see all doors are shut, curtains drawn, and lights out, save the lone lamp in the yard. All appears to be in order.

"Let's go, Grammy. I wanna see Max," my backseat driver urges.

I want to see Max too, but I'm not sure what state we may find him in.

"Remember, we need to ask Mr. Felix if it's okay first," I say.

"Oh, Grammy, he's going to be fine," Hazel says, and ShoSho yips an amen.

I grin at their optimism.

"Well, I hope so," I say. "But we will honor whatever Mr. Felix says, right?"

I look into the rearview mirror. Hazel is staring at my reflection.

"But, Grammy, Jesus said he would live like He lives," she states as if I have forgotten the simplest of truths.

I am stunned.

"Where did you hear that, sweetie?"

She smiles and looks out the window.

"When we were walking on the wind last night," she replies.

"Walking on the wind?"

"Yeah, with Felix and Max and those guys. You know. The story by the big tree," she says, sticking her fingers through ShoSho's kennel without the least sense that she is saying anything unusual. Then her legs begin to kick the back of my seat. "Come on, Grammy. Times a wastin'."

"Where did you…?" I shake my head equally befuddled, amazed, and amused. This child. How does she know these things? Was she really with me at the tree?

My phone pings. A text message from Brian.

"Who is it?" Hazel asks.

"Uncle Brian wants to hear how the week went," I reply as I type my response to my son. "We will give him a call when we get on the road."

"Can I tell Uncle Bly about the wolf?"

"Um, we shall see," I reply, setting the phone back into its holder and putting the rig into drive, still pondering the ramifications of Hazel's observations. Just as I thought this week couldn't get any more strange or complex. Now she's walking on the wind?!

We pull up beside Felix's truck outside Janet's house. The red pickup is nowhere in sight. I get out to undo Hazel's car seat buckle as the front door of the house opens and Felix appears on the steps.

"Hello, neighbors," he says with a wave. "Was afraid you might leave without saying goodbye."

"Where's Max?" Hazel yells, bounding ahead of me.

"He's inside," Felix replies.

"Hazel, just wait for me, please," I instruct, and she obediently halts but with an impatient sigh.

"Did your friends leave already?" I ask, stepping up toward the house.

"Bright and early this morning," Felix replies. "Had to get back for some new assignments."

"Oh, I'm sorry I never got to meet them properly. Wanted to tell them thanks for all their help yesterday with… well, with the whole situation," my voice lowers at the tail of the sentence.

"They know," Felix assures me. "Billy stopped by early to thank us. And he filled us in on all the details with Mikey and the sheriff and everything. Looks like you finally got the culprit behind the looting."

"Looks like it," I agree. "I hope they go easy on him, though. It isn't as if he stole anything very valuable and, frankly, the mess he made helped me get quite a few things done that have needed tending to for some time."

"That is gracious of you," Felix says, opening the door wider. "Come on in."

Hazel rushes in to where Max lays on a thick mound of blankets. His head is up and his eyes bright, but he does not move. She kneels before him, and he buries his head in her lap. Tears spring up once again, but I am in good company, for Felix's eyes are bright with fluid, too, when we glance at one another.

"How's he doing?" I ask.

"He will be fine," Felix replies. "Had quite a gash on his belly, but we got him to the doc in time. Could have been much worse."

"Mr. Felix," Hazel says, turning her face upward. "Max says he wants a treat. Can I give him one?"

"Oh, really?" Felix says with a grin. "Sure. Let me see what we've got."

He heads to the counter in the kitchen, and I crouch down by Hazel to stroke Max's head. "You sure are some kind of hero, buddy," I croon, and he leans into my caresses.

"Here ya go," Felix says, leaning over and handing Hazel a treat.

I look up to say "Thanks," but the word catches on my lips.

Falling out of the collar of Felix's T-shirt is a silver chain with a gold medallion. A coin with the face of an emperor upon it. He does not notice my stare for a moment, so engrossed is he with Hazel and her ministrations to his dog.

He glances at me and our eyes meet. He sees what I am staring at and his face softens. He nods as if acknowledging that what I'm seeing is what I'm seeing. Then he carefully tucks the necklace back into his shirt.

ShoSho's yips carry from the driveway into the house, interrupting my moment of stunned revelation.

"Uh, sweetie," I say. "We need to say goodbye to Mr. Felix and Max. ShoSho wants to go, and Papa will be waiting for us."

I stand and tuck the strands of grey hair behind my ears, eager to do something besides look at this man standing beside me. At least, I think he's a man. But maybe he's... What? An angel? A spirit? A... I don't know what.

"Very much a human," Felix whispers as if reading my every thought. "Just one with a special identity. I'm called a cloud-rider."

Hazel pops up and grabs my hand.

"Ooh, that sounds fun," she chirps. "Grammy and I are wind-walkers."

Felix's head snaps back, and now his stare is as bemused as I'm sure mine is.

"Well, then this is surely not goodbye, is it?" he says as a big smile fills his face.

"No, I suppose it isn't," I reply as Hazel tugs me out the door.

"See ya, Max," Hazel hollers. "Here, there, or in the air!"

She skips down the stairs, opens the car door, and climbs inside all by herself.

"That is quite the young lady you have got there," Felix remarks as the two of us stand at the door and watch her go. "Very, uh, intuitive."

"Yes, yes, she is," I reply, letting puzzle pieces snap into place in my mind and heart. "And, from what I've, uh, gathered in the past few days, I'd say she comes by it quite honestly."

"Yup, I'd say that's true."

We stand together shoulder to shoulder and both take deep breaths.

"Einar's place all back in order?" he asks.

"Pretty much," I reply. "How long are you sticking around these parts before your next, uh, what do you call it?"

He looks down at his slippers.

"We call them assignments. I have almost got all of Janet's to-do items checked off. And Max needs a little recuperating time, and then we will see where we're called next."

I nod and turn to face him.

"So, your army buddies? Cloud-riders, too?"

He nods.

"Okay," I say, trying to weave more loose strands into the tapestry of this most remarkable time. "And, was I, uh, your assignment this week?"

"Part of it," he replies. "Although, I'd include Hazel, the Hallstrom's, and the Everwind's… Well, Solbakken. I think the greater Anderson family of Solbakken was my assignment."

We both gaze at Einar's house, as well as the fields and woods before us. It is a brisk but sparkling winter day. The type that keeps us Minnesotans convinced that ours is the fairest of lands despite the sometimes-challenging weather. But even these, we embrace with a sense of pride at our own fortitude. As my father would say, "It keeps out the riffraff."

"This place gets under your skin, doesn't it?" I whisper.

He nods. "Yup, it sure does."

I let the quiet seep deeply into my bones knowing I am about to step back into the noise, hustle, and bustle of the city.

At least, I am hoping the city is returning to its normal people-filled business

"Well, I guess we will be seeing you," I say, turning back to face him. "In the clouds?"

He smiles. "Or on the air."

"Or in my dreams," I add.

"Oh, that reminds me. Yesterday at church Pastor Mel had a teaching all about dreams and visions and such. I think you'd find it most revealing," he says, seeming to sense my overwhelmed state and wanting to give me a path back to the moment.

"Wonderful, maybe I can find it online and listen on the way home."

"Grammy!" Hazel's cry reaches us, and we see her waving her arms like a cowboy trying to get his cattle moving.

"Time to go," I say.

Felix holds out a hand to shake mine.

I look at it and push it aside.

"I think, after all we've been through this week, you deserve a hug," I say.

"I think you're right," he agrees, and we embrace.

Stepping back, I peer into his eyes for a brief second and he into mine. It is as if we are seeing each other for the first time.

"Best be on your way," he says, patting my arm just like my dad used to do when he was sending me off to college, or off on my honeymoon, or back to The Cities after a holiday. And although he is at least twenty years my junior, suddenly I feel as if I am the child and he my elder. I peer at his handsome face. It is the same as the first day I met him, but now I see in his countenance and stature something deeper and more profound.

In Felix Benedizione, I see a father of many generations.

I kiss him on the cheek and walk down the stairs.

He stays in place, leaning on the now sturdily fixed railing as I situate myself into my rig and roll down the window.

"Me too, Grammy," Hazel pleads, and I roll her window down as well.

"Shalom, shalom," she and I cry out in unison with corresponding waves.

Felix raises his hands and responds.

"Shalom, shalom."

Acknowledgements

Yeshua—now and forever, all my gratitude and worship are Yours.

Mom and Dad—for the foundation you laid and lives you have lived; I am truly grateful. Your examples of faith, hope, and love are precious beyond words.

Grandparents, Great-grandparents, and generations beyond—your sacrifices, adventures, sorrows, and triumphs are hidden from me by the years but still flow through my veins. My thanks for things I do not even know to thank you for.

Tante Tuppe and Tante Maria—for dolls sewn, stories written, crafts taught, holidays spent, treats baked, family gathered, and hearts shared, my soul abounds with appreciation. Everybody needs aunties like you.

People of Solbakken past and present—your stoutness of heart, loyalty of spirit, expansiveness of soul, and humbleness of service have marked me for life. I am blessed to be a leaf on your tree. *Mange tusen takk.*

Anton Treuer, author of *Warrior Nation: A History of the Red Lake Ojibwe*—your immensely readable book is now a treasured part of my library. I appreciate the education you offer.

2nd Cousin Janeen Krogseng McNiff —your collection of family lore and facts in *Krogseng: Remembering the Places and Faces* gave much fodder for my imagination and tidbits of truth for flavor in this tale. The family owes you for your generous work.

Team at Square Tree Publishing—Sherry Ward, Melodie Fox, Angela Hughes, Sophia Hanna, Stephanie Cotta, and Sharon Marta—your strengths in my areas of weakness of editing, marketing, and design make this author stand and applaud. You make me look good. Many, many thanks.

Beta readers—Cheri Perez, Wendy Boukhalil, Chloe and Amanda Wengerd —again, your first eyes on my stories are gentle but true. Thanks friends.

Husband and children—Phil Sr., Phil Jr., Delaney, and Livia—your support and cheers mean more than you know and more than I can express. My heart is yours. Shalom, shalom.

ABOUT THE BOOK

This book was birthed out of two long-term contemplations as well as the current circumstances of my world. The first contemplation began several years ago around the season of Easter. I was meditating on the wonder of the resurrection, and I felt led to imagine myself inside the tomb with the body of Jesus, awaiting the moment when He was restored to life. I got some amazing revelations about the miraculous power of the resurrection in these ponderings.

But one question I kept asking was, "Why was there no one around to witness this most pivotal moment in all of human history?" The women came to the tomb after He was risen. The disciples came to see Him in His resurrected form hours and days later. But as I read the account of the resurrection in the book of Matthew, I realized there were people present at the very moment when death was overcome by life. The Roman guards were there.

Of course, that lead me to an entirely different set of observations and questions. And I began to put myself in their shoes outside the tomb with no paradigm for what was about to happen; no concept of the promises of Scripture, no understanding of the words of Jesus. Just doing my job. Guarding the tomb of a dead guy. Then the ground shook. Two men in brilliant garments appeared. The stone was rolled away. Did Jesus Himself step out into view?

Something wild and crazy must have happened because it says that these brave soldiers shook for fear and became like dead men. Scripture goes on to tell us that these guards were bribed with large sums of money by the chief priests to say that Jesus's disciples came and stole the body during the night while they slept. But what happened to these guys after that? Were they changed by this experience spiritually, mentally, and/or even physically?

In my ongoing meditation, I chose to look at the resurrection like some sort of atomic explosion of life. Knowing what horrific things an atomic death bomb can do to the human body, I began to wonder how much more an atomic blast of life might accomplish. Thus, the characters of Felix and his buddies Fabian and Titus were given life in my imagination.

The second contemplation is entangled with my current season in life. My parents, who have always been a source of life, stability, and wisdom for me, are slowly disappearing into dementia, aphasia, and general fragility of body and mind. In a very real sense, my brothers and I and our spouses have now become their guardians. It is a painful role reversal. Not new to the human experience, for sure, but new to my human experience.

On the other side of the generational coin, my children have all left the nest and are living their own lives. All good and in its proper order but still difficult in its own way. So, I am left standing between two generations. One whose fingers are slowly being extricated from their grip on life, and another whose grip is becoming more and more sure and impactful.

One of the ways the Lord has led me to contemplate the interconnectivity of the generations is through a particular song— "The Blessing" by Kari Jobe and Codi Carnes of Elevation Worship. I know many of you are familiar with it. If you are not, I would urge you to give it a listen, or two, or a hundred.

When I engaged with it over the past many months, I began a practice of imagining the generations who have gone before me singing it over me. I pictured those I knew or had heard of like my parents, grandparents, and great-grandparents who were people of faith, and allowed them to put their hands on my cheeks, or on my head in the Spirit, and bless me. Some mornings I replaced those individuals with my predecessors in the faith from the family tree I have been grafted into in Christ. Sometimes that was biblical heroes and sometimes historical heroes.

Then, after I soaked in the blessings of many generations who have gone before me, I turned around, stretched out my hands, and blessed the generations coming up behind me—both those who are currently here and those who have yet to arrive. As I practiced this form of meditation, I began to experience a wonderful flow of the blessings of the generations.

I know that many of us have had to deal with generational curses, or ongoing familial destructive patterns, through counseling or prayer. And I understand how this can be a necessary thing to free us up. I do not mean in any way to lessen the importance that may have for us. The Scripture does tell us in Deuteronomy 5:9 that God visits the iniquities of the fathers upon the children to the third and fourth generations of those who hate Him. But in the very next verse He says that He shows mercy, favor, or blessing to a thousand generations to those who love Him. Wow! If the sins impact three or four generations, how much more must be the repercussions of the blessings on a thousand generations?

Selah.

On a different note, in setting this story in current day, I was forced to include some of the stresses and strains between the generations regarding COVID. While the plot is intentionally not about the pandemic, it would not have been a true representation of our times without including some of the ramifications from it.

I have tried not to make anyone out as being totally right in their opinions or totally wrong. As has been my experience during this stressful time, none of us have had a corner on the market regarding the complete truth of this strange phenomenon called a pandemic. What I have disliked the most during this time, besides the obvious tragedy of loss of life, is the division and rancor that erupted in the middle of families. No one that I know of escaped these challenges or the myriad of other difficulties caused by COVID, not to mention the political and cultural battles.

To be certain, we live in difficult times, but if we stop to look around for a few minutes, we also live in a time of immense blessing. Whenever I sit in the window seat of an airplane and watch the earth and the clouds grow small beneath me, I think of how many generations of people never got to experience this amazing view. That is just one example. There are so many more from medicines to cosmic telescopes to environmental breakthroughs to education, housing, transportation, and communication. I am in awe of the extraordinary people who through ingenuity, perseverance, and audacity have contributed such remarkable accomplishments to humanity.

But in writing this book, I didn't want to spend a lot of time singing the praises of the extraordinary people. I wanted to celebrate everyday people making everyday choices that send ripples large and small across the generations. Because, I am one of those people.

Like Tora, I often stare into the darkness at night, with my head on the pillow, and wonder if my life has made a difference to anyone in particular, let alone to the world at large.

I long to grab time by the neck and force it to stop until I can make sure that I have left my own set of footprints somewhere in the march of history. But inevitably, it slips through my grasp like water, and I am left to simply pray that each day I make the most of what I've been blessed to receive from previous generations, being cognizant of how my daily choices may affect my children and my children's children.

I hope that in living in this mindset, I am honoring my ancestors while serving as a conduit of the blessings to my descendants.

Beyond that, I hope that I am giving glory to the Father of us all. His truth endures to all generations, and His mercies are new every morning.

In writing this book, I have tried to acknowledge the complexities of familial relationships and the mysteries of life that get woven into our DNA. I understand that I have not included all the great challenges or possibilities in human existence, and readily admit to being ignorant of perhaps the worst that the planet has to offer.

But it is my hope that somewhere in these pages and the things I have included in the storyline, each reader may find something familiar or hopeful to hold onto for their own situations and circumstances.

It is my sincere desire that this book be a blessing to you and yours, as well as generations yet to come.

ABOUT THE SETTING

The house in which this story unfolds is an actual house. The people who built it are my grandparents—Einar and Johanna. Each was born in Norway to families who lived in the Østerdalen Valley, north and east of Christiania, which is present day Oslo; Johanna in 1893 and Einar in 1885. She came to America with her parents and siblings when she was seven years old, and they settled in the north woods of Minnesota. The first home that was built by my great-grandfather was named Solbakken, which means 'sun hill' in Norwegian. I have borrowed this name for my fictional community.

Einar showed up several years later. He came by himself, leaving his parents and brother behind in Norway but connecting to families who hailed from his home area. He worked in the lumber camps alongside some of Johanna's family members. Seeing as he was one of their Østerdalen neighbors, he was included in her family as one of their own. Eight years older than Johanna, he fell in love with her gentle, winning ways, as well as her beauty. They were married at Solbakken in June of 1917.

The home Einar built for his bride was down the road a piece from the original homestead. Unfortunately, my grandfather died long before I was born. Grandma Johanna, however, was an integral part of my youth, as was the small community in which she lived.

Her daughter, who we called Tante Tuppe, was a schoolteacher who never married. She invested a great deal of time during her holidays and summer breaks in caring for her mother, as well as all of the rest of us who visited that house. My family spent many summer days, holidays, birthdays, and weekends there.

My brothers and I played in the barn with the cats who prowled the acreage but belonged to nobody in particular. We ate Grandma's homemade bread with chokecherry jelly canned from the berry shrubs that grew on her property, and played dress-up with the clothes stashed in trunks that made the journey from the old country. We listened to Tante's albums on the stereo that ranged from the Concordia Choir, to Egil Storbekken, to the Medical Mission Sisters, to the Beatles.

The house was a safe and welcoming home where relatives and friends came and went in a constant stream that only those who live in that type of close-knit extended family community can truly understand. I didn't always remember how the latest visitor was related, though the family lineage was often repeated and explained, I simply accepted that somehow, they were.

Coffee and cookies, bars and flatbread, lefse and krumkake appeared miraculously on the most charming little plates and saucers whenever 'company' showed up. It was never anything very fancy, but it was always lovely. In the summer, dainty bouquets of wildflowers picked along the ditches, adorned windowsills and tabletops. In the winter, tatted table-runners were home to little carved figures or bowls garnished by rosemaling.

Northern Minnesota can be a very harsh environment with long and sometimes brutal winters. Neighbors helping neighbors is more than just a kind sentiment, it is a necessity. Plowing driveways, clearing steps, picking up mail, delivering meals, etc. All are done without fanfare and reciprocated without compulsion. I didn't know as a child the lessons I was learning as I observed this community of Lutheran Norwegians live out their lives. But now, I am profoundly thankful for them.

Some of the details included in the story are autobiographical, like the fact that our grandparents' home was broken into and ransacked. My brothers and I traveled from our various locations to clean up the mess and set the house back in order for our tante who still owns it. It was quite a task, but it was the least we could do for her and our grandmother who had so lovingly and freely shared the home with us over the decades.

Another story based in historical fact is the crossing of Red Lake on a boat loaded with the family belongings. No one actually fell into the lake on that crossing that I know of, but the paddle-wheeler boat was built by my great-grandfather, and it was named the Dan Patch after the famous race horse.

I have tried to carefully honor the Ojibwe people who lived on this land around Upper and Lower Red Lake long before my forefathers arrived. When I was growing up, we knew them as Chippewa, but we had very little interaction with them. A few times, we went to the 4th of July powwows that they opened up to the surrounding communities, and my brothers and I danced to the beat of their drums. We also hiked onto the reservation to swim in Lower Red Lake at the beautiful sand dunes.

These dunes were a magical place for me as a kid. The water was so refreshing and clear. You could swim out many yards from the shore, stopping at one sandy ridge after another. But there was something more to the place that I could never quite describe with words.

It was not until a few years ago when I read Anton Treuer's book entitled *Warrior Nation: A History of the Red Lake Ojibwe* that I discovered that this particular area on the shore of Lower Red Lake was considered sacred ground to the Ojibwe people.

They called it Chi-waasadaawangideg or the White Sand Dunes. Prior to the inhabitation of the Ojibwe, the Dakota used this ground as burial grounds. The Ojibwe did not follow this practice but did utilize the dunes as a place for ceremonies, prayers, and fasting for personal dreams and visions.

I was unaware of this when I waded in those waters with my grandma, but I felt it. So, to include this special shore in my story is a privilege I do not take lightly and sincerely hope does not offend those to whom it still holds sacred meaning.

Beyond these few particulars, the vast majority of this book is culled from my imagination. A few of the characters are loosely based upon real life characters from my childhood. The rest are entirely fictional save for the obvious exceptions of Francis of Assisi and Yeshua of Nazareth.

The people of this tiny Norwegian community, as well as the setting itself, are forever embedded in my heart. I hope that in sharing snippets of it with you through this narrative, you have gained a bit of appreciation for the setting.

Like Tora says, “This place gets under your skin, doesn’t it?”

GRANDMA JOHANNA'S BEST RAISIN-FILLED COOKIES RECIPE

Mix together and chill in refrigerator for 1 hour:

- 1 cup shortening
- 1 cup butter
- 1 cup sugar
- 1 cup brown sugar
- 1 cup sour cream
- 1 tsp vanilla
- 3 cups flour
- 2 cups oatmeal
- 1 tsp salt
- 1 tsp baking soda

Make the filling in a heavy saucepan

- 2 cups raisins
- 1 cup sugar
- 2 Tbsp cornstarch
- 1 cup water
- 1 Tbsp lemon juice (or vinegar)

Boil slowly 10-15 minutes

Roll out a portion of the dough.
Cut into circles.
Fill with raisin mixture
Fold and seal with fork tines
Bake until light brown at 350 degrees 8-10 minutes

This is a large recipe that can be cut in half.
But I like to make a large batch.
Just in case company drops in.

ABOUT THE AUTHOR

Born and raised in a family of educators in Minnesota, Wendy Jo traveled to the University of Washington in Seattle to complete her bachelor's degree in Theatre Arts. In 1986, she married her college sweetheart. They settled in Bellevue, WA, to run their contracting business and raise their three children.

In 2009, she received a master's degree in Psychology, which she has used to educate and counsel people in a variety of settings. In writing her first novel, *The Baby-Catcher Gate*, she found a way to combine her love of the arts and education with her passion for healing the brokenhearted. She followed up this work with her second novel, *The Agreements*, in 2020, and her third, *Solbakken: A Tale of Generations,* in 2022.

Her acting training has propelled her into narrating the audiobook versions of her books as well. And, having versed herself in the audio-recording world, she began her own podcast, *So, God Told You to Write a Book, Now What?* in May of 2022.

Started in the midst of writing *Solbakken,* the podcast is a talking journal of the process of getting a book from the earliest conception stage, across the finish line to publishing as an indie author. You can subscribe to the podcast at Wendy Jo's website or most any platform where podcasts are hosted.

Follow her on social media:

Instagram.com/wendyjocerna

Facebook.com/wendyjocerna

Website – www.wendyjocerna.com

CPSIA information can be obtained
at www.ICGtesting.com
Printed in the USA
LVHW040742200523
747580LV00019B/309

9 781957 293165